FALCON RISING

C. H. COBB

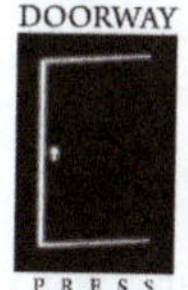

Published by Doorway Press,
Greenville, OH, USA
doorwaypress.com

Signed copies are available by ordering from
chcobb.com.
Print version is also available on Amazon.com.
An E-version is available from Amazon for the Kindle.
Other E-versions may be obtained from the author.

ISBN: 0-9848875-3-9
ISBN-13: 978-0-9848875-3-8
Library of Congress Control Number: 2013954574
First Edition, 2013

Cover design by Dani Snell,
www.refractedlightreviews.com.
Cover photo © Kris Klop / clearskyphotography.com,
used by permission.

Acknowledgments

I love this story. I've been living with it and dreaming about it in one form or another for over ten years. Consequently, so has my wife! Her participation has gone way beyond toleration and patience—she has actively encouraged me to write. Authors are like fanatics—no, scratch that. Authors *are* fanatics, and those of us who have a real job and write on the side are even worse. We have a much more compressed time frame in which to dream up the disaster, doom, and mayhem to which our characters are subjected. All of which means that on our days off, or the evenings on which we don't have appointments, our minds are haunting the fantasy world of our current tall tale. The spouse of an author pays a hefty price. Thanks, Doris, for your love and support! You're the love of my life!

My editor has paid a price of a different nature. As she's been patiently correcting my tidal flood of commas, my superfluous uses of the word "that," and my numerous other syntactical errors, she's been wrestling with a severe case of Lyme disease. At times the side effects of her medication have rivaled the disease in its ability to make her feel miserable. Yet she has soldiered on, not only correcting my errors but explaining the fine points of the English language as she does. And she's done it with patience and good humor. Every time I write a book, I receive from her the equivalent of a college course in grammar and composition. Elizabeth, you're the greatest—thank you! My writing is much improved because of your good work!

And thank you to my readers. Nothing so motivates an author as knowing that you missed your bedtime because you were in the grip of the tale and just couldn't put it down. Thank you for letting me know that you can't wait to find out what happens next to Jake Kelly. I would warn you, however: there's at least one more book in the series! Enough said.

Any errors of fact or grammar that remain are mine.
Soli Deo Gloria!

Dedication

Odd as it may seem, *Falcon Rising* is actually the first book I ever wrote, even though it is my third published novel. It's a long story, and somewhat complicated. I won't get into it. But being my first, it is very special to see it in print. And frankly, it's because of my big brother.

There is significant disagreement in my household regarding when I began writing this story. I thought it was in 2002, my wife says it actually began earlier. But really, it began with a cell phone message from Louie.

We were driving north on Interstate 65 through Kentucky, having reached the end of a vacation. We had started with a fun family reunion in Virginia, then visited the Biltmore in North Carolina, then on to Gatlinburg and Mammoth Cave. At the reunion I had given my brother the first couple chapters of this tale and asked if he would read it and tell me what he thought. I felt kind of silly—didn't think of myself as a writer. Tried writing some poetry in high school, but it was pretty awful.

And then Lou left a message on my cell phone and that changed everything. He was beyond complimentary; he was enthused, effusive, wanted to read more. And it dawned on me that perhaps I could write stories others would enjoy. From that time to the present Lou has been quick with praise, wise and honest with critique, and generally helpful in every way.

Louie—this is for you. If I could somehow custom design a perfect big brother, when I was all done he would look just like you. Thanks, bro.

Cast of Characters

Al Mercer- NSA satellite surveillance technician

Anatoly Geredin- Member of the Soviet Politburo, head of the KGB

Clifton (CE) Edwards- NSA cryptologist

Dan Daniels- Captain, USN, CO of Adak NAS

Ed Devlin- Special Investigator in the Alaska Bureau of Investigators (ABI)

Evelyn Stinson- NSA translator

Fred Banks (aka George Thompson)- Professional assassin, owns small engine repair shop in Anchorage

Galina Toporova- Former co-director of Sidima Timber Co-operative, and in love with Jacob Kelly

Georgi Suhkarov- Smuggler, former member of Soviet military

Jacob (Jake) Kelly (aka Falcon, John Meeker)- Major, USAF, assigned to Project *Hydra*, and shot down by Soviets in 1986 over the Bering Sea

James Franks- General, USAF, Project Director of Project *Hydra* (wife is Shandra)

Jason Devoe (aka Ralph Goodwin, Carl Stafford)- Professional assassin, works for Fred Banks

Jesse Pierce- Lieutenant Commander USN, intelligence officer at Adak NAS

Jim Stewart- Special Agent in the Seattle Office of the FBI, Foreign Counterintelligence Division

John Bridger- Rear Admiral, USN, CO of Navy Special Warfare Group One

Karl Randolph- NSA satellite surveillance technician

Ned Bascomb- Smuggler, former Navy SEAL Commander, USN (ret)

Nikolai Pavlovich Chernikov- Major General GRU, Commandant Prison 87, director of Project *Krasnyy Voskhod*

Roger Bates- Captain, USN (wife is Susan)

Roscoe Raines- Captain, USN, commands the USS *Honolulu*, SSN 718

Sam Bergman- CIA counterintelligence analyst

Stephen Carrock, MD- Administrator, Kotzebue Hospital

Tim Treadwell- Special Agent in the Alaska Troopers Bureau of Investigation

Valeriy Patrikeyev- Lieutenant General, Soviet Army GRU, head of the GRU Ninth Directorate

William (Bill) Jensen- Family friend of the Kellys, full professor of Political Science at Georgetown University

William (Bill) Ott- Major, USAF, chief of intelligence, 6985th Electronic Security Squadron, Eielson AFB

Chapter 1

His running lights were extinguished. There was no moon. There were no stars either, only an inky overcast that absorbed light like some great black hole. The boat rocked slowly, rhythmically, locked in a gentle waltz with the swells coming off the Bering Strait. The smuggler kept an eye on the dim glows of his binnacle, depth finder, and chronometer. It was about all he *could* see. When the water depth was on the shallow side of twenty feet, he would turn west. This was not something you did if there was a sea running. They met at this dangerous spot on Gambell Shoal because they knew that no one else would be within miles. And in this business, encountering other boats by chance was not good for remaining in business.

The Russian would be on time—he always was. Ned Bascomb had never worked with a better partner. He was solid, dependable, honest so far as smugglers go, and he kept his mouth shut. Georgi and Ned had long since stopped trying to cheat each other out of a fast buck. After the first dozen or so trades, they had discovered that it was more profitable to dispense with the haggling, make fast honest swaps, and build a clientèle based on each other's goods. Georgi was good for vodka, caviar, and various other "duty-free" delicacies. In return he would take electronics, clothing (L.L. Bean was best), and pharmaceuticals.

Three years ago they were manually hoisting one hundred-pound, sealed cargo barrels over the gunnels. On a good night they were able to transfer about one ton of cargo from each small vessel to the other. Then Georgi hit on the idea of outfitting the boats with a good electric winch mounted on a small rotating boom with a counterweight and traveling block. For stability they tied up to each other with fenders between the hulls, running at three knots with the sea. They met only at high slack tide, and only if the sea state was less than four. Under those conditions they could transfer six tons of goods in half an hour, in specially designed, sealed containers holding five hundred pounds each.

Georgi had designed the system and the containers and Ned had everything fabricated in a small shipyard in Nome. Ever since installing it their business had increased sixfold. Each boat was crewed by four tough, tight-lipped, and increasingly wealthy seamen. They never dealt in illicit drugs, firearms, or human cargo. The profit would have been several orders of magnitude greater but neither Georgi nor Ned cared to transact business with the dangerous port scum such cargo would have required.

The infrared (IR) detector mounted on his bridge beeped. Georgi must be within a half-mile. With sophisticated listening posts sprinkled all over either side of the Strait, they did not want to be discovered by some curious sea captain, so they avoided radio communications and used IR.

Twenty minutes later the transfer was underway and the lanky six-footer crossed over to Georgi's boat. Like the rest of his crew, Ned was wearing a bright yellow immersion suit and a black Navy watch cap. "I have something special for you, my friend—actually it's for Irina." As their trading and mutual trust had grown they had become close friends.

"You're trying to steal my wife with gifts?" Georgi chuckled.

"Well, Georgi, the thought had occurred to me. But no, this is from my wife. She made it for Irina. It was supposed to be for her birthday last month, but since the seas did not co-operate it is late."

The Russian examined the sealed package. Through the tough plastic he could see an afghan done in Irina's favorite colors. He grinned at his friend. "Karen thinks Irina is cold without me and this will keep her warm? Where is mine?" he laughed.

Georgi checked the boat's chronometer. Because of the direction of the wind and seas that night they could remain tied up for forty-five minutes on this heading. Plenty of time.

"Ned, I've got something for you, too—information—and it's not good news. Very bad, in fact. My neighbor's cousin Vasili is home on leave. He's in the Soviet Air Force—a fighter pilot. Two days ago he was drunk, and he told me a strange story about a night mission he was ordered out on. He claims he shot down an American fighter."

"What? You're kidding, right?"

"Afraid not. Happened a little over a year ago. His controller vectored him to an F-16 flying very slowly, very low over the Bering Sea, about three hundred kilometers southwest of Providenija. He was ordered to shoot it down."

"Are you sure that wasn't just a vodka story?"

"Positive. Vasili is not given to tales, even when he's wasted. The controller gave him strict instructions not to paint the aircraft with radar. He was to take it down with a heat-seeker. So his missile locked on target and he fired. The instant he fired all of his comm radios were jammed with a powerful, broad-spectrum signal. Vasili said the jamming signal was Russian, not US."

"Wow! Sounds like somebody wanted to wax an F-16 without starting World War III. Was there a parachute?"

"Yes, and that is the strangest part of the tale. He orbited the site briefly and the jamming signal stopped within seconds of splashing the Falcon. There he was, three hundred klicks from land, and a Kamov KA-27 shows up within a minute or two. It was as though it had been waiting. Just before Vasili was ordered to return to base, he saw the helicopter snag the pilot's chute with a grappling hook. Plucked him right out of the air."

Ned ran his fingers over his stubbly chin and looked steadily at his friend. For a moment neither spoke. Georgi turned away and watched the cargo transfer briefly before he turned back to Ned and continued.

"Ned, Vasili thinks they were after the pilot. It all seemed like too much of a setup: the Kamov, the jamming, the fact that the controller had Vasili on station right on the Falcon's flight path."

"Georgi, when did this happen?"

"July, '86. Vasili said that when he landed he was met by a general. He was congratulated for a great victory for Mother Russia. He was also told that if he ever talked about the mission to anyone his wife and children would be shot."

"Why did he tell you?"

"He was drunk. He said it has bothered him ever since. 'Combat is one thing,' said Vasili, 'but this was criminal.'"

****

Ned and his friend had never spoken to each other of their lives prior to becoming freelancers in the "import-export" business. They knew of each other's families and aspirations for the future, but the past never came up. Though neither realized it, it was not coincidental. Ned had been a Navy SEAL commander prior to resigning his commission eight years ago. Georgi, the older of the two, was a retired Soviet Air Force major. Each had learned to be quite tight-lipped.

Despite their dubious way of earning a living they were both loyal to their countries and each considered himself a patriot and warrior. But they were not at war with each other, and Georgi was concerned that a rogue operation was at work that could change that peacetime status. He had long been wary of party hacks and true believers in the Soviet system. Sooner or later some yahoo was going to do something really stupid and plunge the world into a conflagration from which no winners would emerge. The smuggler was not a doctrinaire Communist Party member: he simply loved the *rodina*, Mother Russia. Always had.

As Georgi motored back to Providenija, he was unable to put his finger on exactly why he had chosen to share this information with Ned. But he was confident that Ned would not jeopardize Vasili's family. And he had a vague foreboding that somewhere in the Soviet Air Force, GRU, or KGB was a gunslinger feeling his oats—someone who needed to be reined in. Ambushing and shooting down a military aircraft in international waters was an act of war. And what nobody needed right now was war.

****

Each June when the ice broke up and Gambell's small harbor was again accessible, Ned resumed weekly trading trips to the villages of Gambell and Savoona on Saint Lawrence Island. His little business brought new meaning to the term "Merchant Marine." It was the maritime equivalent of a small-town general store. Medicine, staples, canned goods, clothing, sewing supplies, traps, rifles, ammunition, foul-weather gear, candy and a small selection of toys—all from the mainland—lined the shelves in the old World War II-era Quonset hut that Ned used for his store.

Saint Lawrence Island was home to the Yup'ik Eskimos. For the last two thousand years, both Siberian and Alaskan Yup'iks had lived there, whaling, fishing, and hunting walrus and seal. Few families were living much above subsistence levels, but maintaining their way of life was more important to them than wealth. Ned allowed the residents to purchase from his store on credit and if any family seemed to be having a really tough time, Ned would "lose" his records or claim they had already paid. Each year when he made his last trip before the ice returned, usually in late October, he would hand over the keys of his store to the village elders. Whatever stock was left on the shelves would be purchased on credit throughout the winter with one of the elders keeping track of the accounts. In five years Ned had never been cheated.

The store ran at a loss but it made a perfect cover for his smuggling operation. He made the 120-mile crossing from Nome weekly, weather permitting. A year-round general store in Nome (this one was profitable) rounded out Ned's holdings and gave him something to do in the winters. But his first love was the sea and he lived for his trips to Saint Lawrence Island and Gambell Shoal.

****

"Karen, Georgi wants to know when you are going to make something for him. He said Irina will love the afghan."

"You tell that old scoundrel that he'll have to wait his turn. I am working on a couple of pillows for Irina's new grand-baby, and I have promised Makill in Savoona a quilt for her daughter's marriage."

Laughing, Ned turned from Karen, pulled off his anorak, and began peeling off layers of clothing. Part of his mind was on the light banter with his wife, but another part was chewing on Georgi's strange news. Ned was sorely tempted to simply forget what he had heard. As most of his business was on the wrong side of the law, he could not afford to stir up attention. It wouldn't do to be the subject of even a friendly interrogation. He was not about to put his family livelihood at risk.

But there was another part of his heart that held long years of SEAL training and black ops. One of the functions of the SEALs was extraction: covertly rescuing downed airmen, hostages, or intelligence operatives from enemy territory. It simply went against his grain to leave "one of ours" behind.

After two days of rationalizing and arguing with himself the SEAL side won, and Ned began thinking about how to get the intelligence where it would do some good, with as little damage as possible to his own family. Who to call? What to say? If he did not start with the right guy the information would languish on some bureaucrat's desk, or worse, he might call down some gung-ho FBI type who would notice that his reported income didn't add up to his lifestyle. *Got to move carefully here*, the smuggler thought.

Ned was in agreement with Georgi's analysis: the shoot-down was transparently an attempt to nab the pilot. *Was the pilot defecting?* Ned discarded that possibility immediately. If the stick jockey was attempting to defect, he would have simply turned the Falcon over to the Soviets and there would have been no shootdown. No, the officer must have been a high-priority intelligence target. There would be no other reason to take such a huge risk.

He chewed on that for awhile. *What secrets would an Air Force pilot know that would be worth the risk of an international incident?* The smuggler rolled it over in his mind but got nowhere. And something else was troubling Ned, too. He felt as if he had enough information to make some other necessary conclusions, but he could not make the leap from the sparse data. Ever since Georgi had spilled the tale four days ago, the former SEAL had known that something was not right, something was dreadfully wrong, but it hovered just outside the grasp of his consciousness, eluding analysis. It was like the vanishing act of a dim star when you looked straight at it.

No matter. Tomorrow morning he was going to call someone. Then it would become their problem.

****

Five black-clad figures glided silently toward the darkened house. Each was wearing military-style night-vision goggles (NVGs). In the backyard a swing set and toy wagon glowed in unearthly green through the NVGs. One man cut the phone line and disabled the alarm system, then silently gave a thumbs-up gesture to the squad leader. The leader positioned one man in the front yard to provide covering fire for the inside team in case something went wrong. He silently signaled two others to cover the back yard and the rear exits. The dark forms merged into the shadows around the house and disappeared.

Ned sensed Karen roll over, and then he drifted back to sleep. He did not hear the silent, invisible figure open the door to his children's room, nor the *pfffft!* of the silenced weapons as his children were murdered in their beds. Not so much as a whimper escaped little lips before the steady breathing stopped.

It was the squeaky board in the hall that brought Ned to full consciousness. He didn't know what awoke him, but a sixth sense honed by years of living on the edge of death in the SEALs told him that he'd just heard a night sound that didn't belong. His level of alert heightened and his senses reached out, straining to identify the danger in the darkness. He raised his head in time to see the muzzle flash of the silenced MP5 as a three-shot burst killed his wife. Too late, he threw himself off the bed. Another burst from the MP5, and his own life was pulsing out in red all over the floor. "You knew too much," snarled the dark phantom at his door in perfect, unaccented English.

****

Trembling and drenched in sweat, Ned awoke with a start. He gingerly raised his hands to his chest to see how bad the wounds were. *I should be dead! No wounds at all? What?* Confused, he realized he was still in bed. Karen rolled over again and he then understood that he had been dreaming. *What a nightmare!* Weeping with relief, he padded to his children's room. They were sleeping in complete peace. Careful not to step on the squeaky board, Ned went to the kitchen and checked the clock. It was 5:05 AM. Since his alarm was going to ring in ten minutes anyway, the former SEAL commander started a pot of coffee, sat down at the table and tried to stop shaking. The nightmare had been as real as any he'd ever had. The accusation of the assassin sounded again in his mind, "You knew too much!" *Too much what?*

The dream clearly had something to do with Georgi's unsettling story. Slowly the data points of the shootdown assembled themselves in his mind until they all pointed to one thing, and then it dawned on him. *Inside information!* That was the missing puzzle piece! Somehow the Soviets knew the pilot was going to be where he was, flying low and slow—which probably meant it was some sort of test or training flight. And there was only one way to know that: they would have to possess inside information! *Somewhere at some level there is a spy in the operations section of one of the armed services, probably the Air Force, and probably here in Alaska!*

Fortified by a swig of hot, black coffee Ned Bascomb stared at the ceiling and mulled over this latest revelation. It was one thing to learn that an aircraft was going to be on a specific flight path at a certain time: it was something entirely different to ensure that a specific officer would be the pilot assigned to the mission. *Somebody had to make sure their designated target was at the controls of that Falcon when it went down*, he thought. If this guy had been a high-value intelligence target, then he was probably not the average jet jockey. And that implied that someone at the Pentagon was involved, or more likely, Langley. All of this added up to the very strong possibility that one of the services had been compromised in one—possibly two—places: operations and maybe personnel placement.

And now he understood his dream. He, Ned, was probably the only American who knew what really happened to that pilot. If he simply called someone at a local air base and made his report, what if that someone was the spy? Or what if the spy at Langley, for instance, had access to the intelligence network? Certainly they would be watching for any hint of breaking information on the incident. If that information could lead them back to Ned, his life and that of his family would be forfeit. And since the spy—or spies—were obviously in cahoots with the Soviets, Vasili and his family would be toast, too.

This wasn't going to be as simple as making a phone call to the military. He had to protect Vasili's identity and he also had to ensure that his own family would be safe. Not for the last time he wished that Georgi had kept his info to himself.

Chapter 2

**Tuesday, September 8, 1987: 1030 local time
Nome, Alaska**

"Admiral Bridger, if you wanted to share some sensitive, possibly explosive, information on the Soviets, who would you talk to? Who would you talk to if you were afraid of some of our guys getting the information, because it is possible that some of our guys are not really working for us? And if you were afraid that your life or the lives of your family would be in jeopardy if you were somehow connected with the inform-ation?"

"You are joking, right, Ned?"

"No, sir, I am dead serious, and I am afraid for my family and I am afraid for the confidentiality of my contact, because he will surely die and his family with him, if this information is mishandled."

"Ned, this line is not secure—do not say anything more! Are you still in the same place you were when you called last Christmas? Don't name it!"

"Yes."

"Don't make any further attempt to contact anyone! Do not speak with anyone claiming to represent me. I will contact you. I will contact you in person. Is that clear?"

"Aye-aye, sir."

****

Ned replaced the receiver on the hook and wiped his sweaty palms on his pants. He'd driven down to the airport in Nome to make the call from a pay phone in the passenger area. At least he didn't have to worry that the call would be traced back to his house. Neither he nor the admiral had used anything but his first name.

Ned Bascomb was not a man given to fear, but the dream he had two weeks ago wouldn't leave him. It had recurred four or five times since and always ended the same way. This was really getting old. He had to act, now!

Since the dreams began—four days after the night when Georgi had brought him into his confidence—Ned had begun to carry his old 13-round Browning Hi-Power in a shoulder holster under his coat. He didn't advertise the fact he was carrying again, but Karen had noticed. He'd told her nothing about Georgi's explosive news: he didn't want to worry her. Nonetheless, she had noticed his much more cautious behavior. Her days as a Navy SEAL wife had taught her that he would talk when he was ready, so she didn't question him now. She'd wondered if Ned was still occasionally involved somehow in Navy operations. He wasn't, but since she'd never been a full party to his naval career in the past—because of security concerns—she had no way of knowing for sure now.

It had taken Bascomb several weeks to decide whom he could safely share his news with. The civilian intelligence community was out, at least for now. He was concerned that the spooks would want to look too closely at his own life and business. They would probably object to the fact he had a Russian trading partner, or perhaps they would try to co-opt Georgi. In any case, Ned had a military man's basic distrust of civilian intelligence agencies; talking to anyone from Langley was pretty far down the contingency list. But because he figured the military had been penetrated by Soviet agents, neither could he call Naval or Air Force Intelligence. He had no idea who was trustworthy and who was not.

The strength of a good military outfit is certainly affected by training and equipment. Discipline is essential to morale. Drill and rote enable men to do under a hail of bullets what has become second nature during times of peace. While these things are important, what ultimately transforms a good combat team into a great one is relationships: trusting and loving the men you work with, fight alongside of, and maybe die for.

It was his personal relationship with the man who led Navy Special Warfare Group One, Rear Admiral John Bridger, that resulted in Ned's decision to call him. The first year Ned had been assigned to SEAL Team 5, based out of Coronado, California, then-Captain Bridger was his commanding officer. Between the security clearance that Bridger carried and the caliber of his leadership and personal integrity, Ned knew he could trust the admiral.

****

"Georgi, I'm going to talk to a friend about the information you shared with me several weeks back. A military friend. I trust him." Georgi said nothing but to Ned's eyes it appeared that his shoulders sagged a little.

The Russian watched his crew run the traveling block and counterweight up snug to the opposite sides of the mast of his small cargo boom. They were securing the equipment after a transfer of cargo on a pleasant sea. It was a stunningly beautiful night. Other than the quiet sounds of the two crews as they efficiently stowed equipment and cargo, there was nothing to hear but the creaking of the fenders between the hulls, and the soft *whoosh* of water from a bilge pump.

"He will be careful, Georgi. Neither you nor Vasili need fear. It will not be traced back to you."

Georgi turned and faced him. "Ned, I told you then because I trusted you and because I knew that you would get the information where it needed to go. I trust you now. I am not worried about you, my friend. What worries me is that some cossack in Moscow evidently feels at liberty to perpetrate an act of war against another sovereign state. If these renegades get used to doing this sort of thing, sooner or later it will erupt into a conflagration that no one can control. If by telling you I can get the information into calm hands, perhaps a diplomatic warning will be all that is needed to return us to sanity. Perhaps my children and grandchildren will die of old age after all." He stood silent for a moment watching the stars, and then continued softly, "I have no intention of betraying my country, not even for friendship, but I will not hesitate to betray those who have already compromised the *rodina* by their foolish arrogance. Perhaps, after all, this is the price of peace."

A seaman approached the American and reported, "Ned, the cargo is stowed and the transfer booms are secure. Shall we cast off?"

"Yeah, Harry. Let's head for Gambell. We need to stock up the store there while the weather holds. Georgi, *do svidaniya,* you old pirate!"

The Russian laughed and embraced his good friend, then became serious once again. "Ned, do not misunderstand me: I will not betray my homeland. But if I hear anything else that might help you track this incident down I will find a way to get the information to you. But I will meet with no one but you and I will talk with no one but you, understand? Please— do not even ask otherwise. *Do svidaniya.*"

With that he stepped over the gunwale and motioned to two waiting seamen, who then cast off the lines from Ned's boat. As the two smugglers smiled at each other across the frigid black waters, Georgi brought his hand up to a salute. Without thinking, Ned snapped a crisp one back. Georgi slowly nodded and grinned again. The Russian brought his craft around and pointed the bow into the west. The twin marine diesels throbbed, and the boat slowly disappeared into the inky blackness.

Ned stood there, savoring the moment. He chuckled to himself at his reflexive return of the salute. *He knows,* Ned thought to himself, *Georgi now knows I've been in the military. And I know that he has served, too. Somehow, in the back of my mind, I think I realized it a long time ago. But I should have saluted him first: he probably outranks me!*

The smuggler turned from his thoughts to see Harry grinning at him in the dark. "You don't hide it as well as you think, Ned. Oh, don't be so surprised! It was obvious what was going through your mind. We all know you've been in the service. That much is obvious. The guys have a bet going on which branch, and what your rank was when you got out."

Ned grinned back. "My secret. Take us to Gambell, will you, Harry? I'm going down to the galley. Want a cup of coffee?"

****

Wearing a black watch cap, a black wool shirt, jeans, and rubber boots the admiral looked like the waterman that he was. His face was perpetually sunburned, his hands were rough, and he had the relaxed gait of a man more comfortable on a pitching deck than on a sidewalk. No watching eye would have guessed that he was the commanding officer of a Navy Special Warfare Group. He looked more like a local crabber.

Ned slid into the booth, and Bridger took the opposite side. The admiral was a cool operator, just blathering away about the local fishing until after the waitress had brought their order. They had picked a booth in an empty section, but this was a popular watering hole with the boys from the harbor so the place would be filling with rough men and lots of noise before long.

"Okay, Commander, this had better be good. You know how much I hate having a plate of seafood in this dive." Bridger looked around approvingly. This was his kind of restaurant. He'd eaten here with Ned once several years back when he'd had business at Adak NAS. Best salmon he had ever tasted. The truth of it was that he'd been trying to think of a way to get back here at the Navy's expense ever since.

"Well, sir, if you'd really rather, there *is* a hamburger joint just down—"

"Perish the thought," Bridger cut him off, "this will just have to do!" With that he busied himself with a mouthwatering plate of fresh salmon and a side of clams. "Business first, pleasure later," he declared out of the side of his mouth, around a big tasty chunk of salmon.

The two men settled into their meals, and neither spoke for the next ten or fifteen minutes. Admiral Bridger had been like an older brother to Ned. Too close in age to be a father figure, too distant to be overly familiar, he'd treated Ned with respect when Ned had moved into his group as a newly minted lieutenant commander. John Bridger knew competence and leadership when he saw it, and Ned had a double dose of both. The admiral had carefully mentored the younger man, letting him make his big mistakes and then carefully debriefing him when the stuff hit the fan. From Ned's perspective, Bridger had taught him about tough-minded leadership, about taking responsibility, and about navigating safely through the built-up reefs of the officer-bureaucrats, lifers who wore the braids but had no heart for the mission. Bridger had helped him see that the Navy was defined not by the paper-shufflers, but by the sailors and officers who manned the ships and flew the aircraft. Ned had learned from the admiral not to allow the rear-echelon types to spoil the experience.

A deep sense of mutual trust and respect had slowly developed, and Bridger had felt as if he'd lost a family member when Ned resigned. When the former SEAL commander telephoned for help, the admiral knew immediately to take him at his word and to handle his information seriously.

"Ned, lay it on me. I've been watching for a tail ever since I left Adak, and I'm confident that I'm not under surveillance. I think you are safe spilling the beans. I can see you're wearing a hogleg there inside your coat, so whatever 'it' is must be serious.

"You've really got to get a smaller piece, you know? I think a blind man would notice that bulge under your arm. The local gendarme could not pick you up on a concealed-carry violation because that thing is so obvious. Why don't you just get a bazooka and be done with it?"

"Hey, lay off it, sailor! You guys took all the really neat toys from me when I resigned. Good grief, you would think after all those years sweating my butt off in unnamed corners of the world trying to make you look good to the brass, you could have at least given me a gold-plated pop-gun rather than that watch!"

"Hmm. I suppose. I'll take it under advisement. You did make me look pretty good, by the way, when I wasn't having to rescue you from the paper clips or the shore patrol."

Ned smiled. Bridger had not changed a bit.

"Okay, Ned, what's going down? What has got you so spooked that you'd embarrass yourself in public with that ancient pistol?"

"Here's the deal, John. I have some information that I believe is vital to national security. But you can't ask too many questions—at least not on the record—and I can't give you my source. Not unless you swear that his name goes no farther than your memory. No notes, no computer records, no nothing."

The admiral looked at him closely for a few seconds before responding, "What are you into, Ned? What are you doing that is so secret?" Seeing Ned's glare he added, "Off the record, of course! Off the record, what are you doing?"

"What about my source?"

"His name goes in my brain only and will not pass from my lips to another's ears. Look, Ned, let's just do it this way. The entire conversation is off the record. When you are done sharing your information, then you can tell me what part I can repeat. I will not compromise you, I promise."

"Okay, here goes then. Admiral, I am a smuggler." At that, the admiral's eyebrows went up and his eyes narrowed. Ned quickly added, "Nothing illegal. No drugs or people. Just medicine and consumer goods. The only thing I am avoiding is the hassle and expense of Customs. Oh, yeah, and taxes, too."

"Who is the buyer?"

"I have a Russian friend and he trades Russian goods for American. Over the years he has become a very good friend and I would never, ever allow him or his family to be harmed."

"Okay, I don't approve of going around the law, but as long as you are sticking it to the IRS, stick 'em good for me, too! But so far nothing you told me is of national significance. I have to assume that your Russian friend is well connected and he let something slip. Am I right?"

"Well, not really. I don't know about Georgi's life prior to our business relationship, although I can guess he has had military service. But he's not well connected in the sense that he has an ear in Moscow or anything like that. Let me just cut to the chase, John, and you'll have an idea why I called you. Several weeks ago Georgi related to me a story that one of his friends told him. The man—I'll call him Ivan—"

"Very original," the admiral interjected dryly.

"Thank you. Anyway, Ivan is a pilot in the Soviet Air Force. In July of '86 he was vectored over a specific spot in the Bering Sea, three hundred klicks southwest of Providenija. He was flying under EMCON standards, only listening with his radio, no radar, etc. Along comes an F-16 flying low and slow, and the controller tells him to shoot it down with a heat-seeker. The controller is very emphatic—he is not to use any radar or anything that would reveal his presence.

"So Ivan fires on this F-16 and no sooner than his missiles are away he detects a jamming signal jamming the comm frequencies. A *Soviet* jamming signal, Admiral."

Bridger scratched the stubble on his chin and observed, "So they didn't want the F-16 pilot to get off a distress call."

"Correct. But that's not all. Ivan sees the American jet jockey bail out, sees his chute open, and poof! A Kamov KA-27 helo is there on the spot to recover up the pilot."

"Okay, Commander, analyze what we've got and give me the summary."

"Admiral, we have an intentional shootdown of an American fighter, for the express purpose of nabbing the pilot. It is a hi-tech military kidnapping with no witnesses. Or, almost no witnesses. We also have a spy in the operations section—and maybe the personnel section—of whatever branch of the service was flying that F-16, because the Soviets knew the time the aircraft would be there, its flight path, and the pilot's identity. Somebody had to pass along that intelligence.."

Suddenly Admiral Bridger wasn't hungry anymore. Ned had pieced together the story and nailed it. With growing conviction, Bridger softly asked, "And motive, Ned, what was the motive? Why did they do this?"

"The only thing I can figure is that this pilot had some sort of value to the Sovs, probably information. If he's not dead yet he's probably in some compound in the USSR right now, being pumped dry for everything he knows about something. What, I don't know."

Bridger sighed. "I think I do. The F-16 has been going through some top secret development at Edwards, I'm not at liberty to say anything more. But Eielson AFB here in Alaska was being used to put the new stuff through its paces though I don't know why they needed to fly tests up here. I'll bet my bottom dollar that the Sovs nabbed one of the chief development test pilots."

"That would make plenty of sense," Ned agreed. "That guy could do more than simply tell them what our Falcons can do. He could probably go a long way in telling them how to make their aircraft do the same thing."

"Uh-huh, I think so. Especially with the help of a little sodium thiopental." Bridger pushed his plate back, finished with the meal. "Ned, what part of this conversation can I repeat and what part do you want permanently off the record?"

"Permanently off the record is my smuggling business, my friend, and his friend. What you're going to have to do is research this and 'accidentally' correlate some data that will lead you to at least a theory about the loss of a Falcon in the Bering Sea last July. If you even breathe a word of what I have said, that Russian pilot will die along with his family. The trail will lead to Georgi, and he will die along with his family, and that trail leads to me. I will die and my family with me. The Soviets cannot afford to have any witnesses, Admiral, who could demonstrate that they perpetrated an act of war against the USA."

Chapter 3

Major Jacob Kelly looked out on a tiny anchorage protected by a rocky breakwater. He could hear waves crashing on the shore beyond the anchorage. The salty, stiff breeze in his face carried moisture and the stars to the north were blotted out by oncoming clouds—a storm was blowing in from the Chukchi Sea. He paused and examined the southern sky, looking for Orion. The Hunter had not yet risen and he turned back to the sea, disappointed. *But I am thinking of you, Galya. I will return.*

Jake was thirty-two years old, unmarried, the American son of an Irishman and a Russian—Clancy and Galina Kelly. His maternal grandparents had escaped Stalin's Soviet Union, and from them Kelly had gained a mastery of the Russian language. His grandparents and parents had since passed away and he now possessed no other family—none but the Air Force, anyway. An accomplished fighter pilot, he'd earned the nickname *Falcon* from his buddies in the 34th Fighter Squadron because he'd practically memorized the technical manuals for the advanced, multirole fighter. Then, in 1984, he had been selected as chief test pilot for a secret development project for the F-16, and was transferred to Edwards AFB.

At the moment, however, Falcon was on the wrong side of the Bering Strait and he planned to rectify the situation tonight. He walked down onto the gravelly beach. Six kayaks were lying upside down in a row well above the high tide mark.

"What do you do here?"

Kelly whirled about, drawing his pistol. Standing in front of him in the faint light was a man of squat, powerful build.

He was unable to make out facial features in the gloom, but realized the man must be a Chukchi, one of the indigenous Siberians he'd been told about. It was not likely the fellow had any love for the Soviets. Jake decided to lay out his cards and see what happened. He was, after all, the one with the gun.

"I only wish to leave," he responded. The man did not appear to be holding a weapon.

"To where?"

"Across the sea. I want to go home."

"Alaska?"

"America."

"The Sovs look for you." It was a statement, not a question.

"Yes, they do. I do not wish them to find me. I was brought to this country against my will. I escaped from them and I want to go home."

"Not many escape from this place."

"But I will."

Ignoring Jake's pistol, the man walked past him down to the row of kayaks. "You were going to steal a kayak?"

"Yes. I'm sorry. I have no choice."

The man paused, as though thinking. Then he looked up. "Come. You must eat first. You have far to travel and a storm is rising. I have a thick stew I will share with you. And then I will give you a kayak."

"I thank you, but there is no time. The soldiers are searching for me. I must leave now!"

"There is time. The Sovs went the wrong way. They are checking out a village east of here. It will take them an hour or so. My son will watch for them, and warn us before they come close." The man began walking up the beach toward a cluster of homes. Falcon shrugged his shoulders, then followed.

****

Jacob Kelly was a man on the run. It wasn't a lifestyle he had chosen. About fourteen months prior on a beautiful moon-drenched night, he'd been piloting an F-16 over the Bering Sea on a test flight. Without warning his aircraft had been rocked by an explosion and transformed from a sleek, aerodynamic fighter into a hunk of shredded metal with the flight characteristics of a cinder block. He'd pulled the ejection handle and the next thing he knew he was riding atop a Roman candle euphemistically called the ACES II Ejection System. Kelly later learned that the explosion had actually been a Soviet air-to-air missile—he'd been jumped by a MiG and shot down.

That was just the beginning of his troubles. A Soviet helicopter had snagged his parachute out of the air and reeled him in. He was shackled, drugged, and deposited in a secret GRU interrogation facility deep within Siberia, imaginatively labeled *Prison 87*. There he discovered an audacious program of espionage. Apparently somebody way up in the Soviet ranks had decided that if you can't beat 'em, kidnap 'em. The facility was holding eight scientists, all specialists in various areas of weapons development, plus Kelly and one other military man. Each had been kidnapped and was being interrogated for the top secret information they possessed in their area of specialty.

But Kelly was not just your run-of-the-mill fighter pilot. As the chief test pilot for Project *Hydra*, he was closely involved with a top secret development effort aimed at creating the electronics for a new strike package for the Fighting Falcon. The new weapon system leveraged the currently existing technology of the Precision Avionics Vectoring Equipment (PAVE) into an intelligent target assignment network for target-rich battlespace environments. Up to thirty-two PAVE-equipped, armor-penetrating bombs could be simultaneously released by multiple fighters, and the weapons would establish a short-lived radio network during their descent, selecting and assigning multiple illuminated targets based on individual trajectories. Just four F-16s could eliminate three entire companies of Soviet T-80 main battle tanks. *Hydra* would tip the balance of power in European ground forces back to NATO by neutralizing the Warsaw Pact's advantage in armor. It was a conventional weapon system with strategic implications.

In order to increase his effectiveness as part of the *Hydra* development team, Kelly had trained with special forces as an Air Force Combat Control Team operator. The goal had been to give him hands-on experience with the PAVE targeting lasers so that he'd understand the difficulties and limitations of field operations. He'd gone downrange on multiple combat missions as a CCT leader and was an experienced and successful operator.

To protect *Hydra* as a black-development project, Kelly had been given a secret identity as Major John Smith for his CCT training and missions. Not more than half a dozen people knew Kelly in both capacities. No Air Force records anywhere, paper or computer, linked Jacob Kelly and John Smith. As a consequence, the Soviets had no clue as to what sort of bronco they'd saddled when they grabbed Kelly. He escaped less than one month after being captured, leaving much of Prison 87 in flames.

Using his fluency in the Russian language and marshalling all his skills as a pilot and special forces operator, Kelly had fled east across Siberia by train, truck, car, helicopter, airplane, and sometimes on foot. Carried with him were the names of the other nine hostages in Prison 87; by hook or by crook Jake was planning on freeing them. Also carried in his heart was the love of a woman by the name of Galina Toporova, whom he'd met above a little Siberian town named Sidima. He had wintered as a laborer in the timber collective she and her brother managed. A quasi-black market operation, it had been the perfect place to hide out during the brutal Siberian winter. Bearing the same name as his mother, Galina had ignited in him a passion to settle down and begin a family. Jake had made a commitment to come back for her, take her to America, and make her his wife.

But the pursuing troops had finally found him in the spring, and he'd fled northeast up the Chukchi Peninsula. And now, standing on the shore of the Chukchi Sea not a mile north of the Arctic Circle, Kelly realized that American soil— Alaska—was a scant one hundred miles away. It would be hard; but if he could make his final escape and if he was exceedingly lucky, a kayak could take him there. It was so close. And after so many months on the run, Jake was ready to go home.

****

An hour later Kelly was back on the beach. He retrieved everything from his backpack that he wished to save, and then filled the pack with rocks and zipped up the pockets. He stepped into the kayak and balanced the knapsack in front of him. After drawing the skirt tight, he paddled out to the breakwater and sank the pack.

It was hard to let his gear go. He'd paid a pretty penny for it. During the prior winter he'd befriended one of the founders of the timber cooperative, an older man named Sevastyan. He'd been a corpsman in the Soviet Navy until he retired. When Kelly met him he was functioning as the cooperative's doctor. Sevastyan was one of the few in the camp aware of Jake's true identity. Knowing the American would be on the run again as soon as the winter turned to spring, Sevastyan had helped Jake secure the black market Soviet military survival gear that he would need to cross the taiga. It was expensive but it could be had if you knew the right people, and Sevastyan was well connected. One of the most useful pieces of gear was a dry suit, and Falcon was wearing it now.

According to his maps, he was on the northern side of the Chukchi Peninsula just above the Arctic Circle. He figured that the anchorage was about one hundred miles from the rugged coast of Alaska. At this latitude he could expect roughly twelve hours of daylight. He could also expect a heightened amount of surveillance and not simply because the Soviets were pursuing him. With freedom so temptingly close, the Soviets would be keeping an alert eye on the Strait. It would not do to have the vaunted New Soviet Man running off to pursue the American Dream.

A kayak would not show up on radar. It was possible that once he got into the ocean swells, he would be virtually undetectable by ship, unless an alert lookout happened to be staring in the right direction at precisely the right time. Of course, from the air he was easily detectable—if there was a moon. The ripples caused by the tiny wake of his kayak would interfere with the normal glimmer of a moon-washed ocean. An attentive pilot would spot him immediately. But with the storm approaching Major Kelly knew that he'd not have any problems from an air search, at least not until daylight tomorrow.

****

A cold wind was freshening out of the northwest, off the Arctic ice pack. Strands of cold mist ghosted past him, and a low fog began to develop on the water. Straight above him he could see stars peeking here and there through the scudding clouds, but across the water he could not see but thirty, maybe fifty meters. Occasionally an opening in the mist would occur, but mostly the fog settled around him. Soon the overcast from the oncoming storm would make the sky solid with clouds and Jake would have to rely on his compass—if he could see its face in the dark. Otherwise he'd have to rely on the wind and the set of the waves, and those could change as the low pressure system shifted.

During the long months of his flight across the taiga, Falcon had given much thought to an escape route once he had attained the sea. The Big and Little Diomede Islands in the Strait had to be avoided at all costs: the former because it belonged to the USSR, and the latter because as US soil it would be closely monitored by the Soviets. If he passed anywhere near the Diomedes both sides would have on their screens his course, speed, direction, height, weight, favorite color, and— for all he knew—his dental records and college GPA before he'd paddled another kilometer. Nuts, they would probably be able to take his x-rays from four klicks. *Have to stay away from there.* Besides, once the Soviets realized that he had secured a kayak they would be expecting him to make directly for Little Diomede, as it was the closest American soil. So Jake decided that he would absolutely *not* do that.

Since his escape Falcon had perfected the art of the unexpected, and he employed that artistry in his planning now. He intended to paddle northeast for about eight hours, putting himself about forty kilometers above where they would expect to find him. He knew that he was not in danger of encountering the ice pack, not this time of year, but it would be a cold and unforgiving Chukchi Sea surrounding him. Hypothermia would be a problem, even with the dry suit. Even if he stayed completely dry—which wouldn't happen—the icy sea on the other side of the thin skin of the kayak would still leach the heat out of his body. Only the effort of paddling would generate the heat required to keep him alive. But the paddling and the cold would consume his energy reserves rapidly. He hoped the packet of blubber and smoked fish his host had given him would keep his metabolism operating until he could collapse on American soil. The whole venture was dicey at best, if it was even possible at all.

Once he had traveled far enough northeast, he would angle back southeast. If his navigation was good, he would make landfall somewhere on the tiny barrier islands lining the north side of the Seward Peninsula of Alaska, between Cape Prince of Wales on the south and Cape Espenberg on the north. If things went well he *might* make it alive. If they didn't he would make landfall, certainly, but as a lifeless corpse in a boat. With the route he was planning the entire trip covered around 160 miles. The only advantage he would have was that the currents, wind, and wave action would be with him once he started southeast.

He looked back. The shore was no longer visible nor could he hear the crashing of waves. Falcon settled into a steady cadence of paddling. He had good balance and the well made kayak rode easily on the ocean swells.

****

With a start, Jake came back to a state of alertness. He'd been paddling for hours, dimly aware of his watery environment and dully fixed on keeping the wind on his left shoulder, but otherwise unthinking. His fingers were permanently contoured to the curve of the shank of the paddle. He had little feeling left in his hands and yet plenty of strength remained. He just couldn't open his fingers; and if he got them open, he wasn't convinced that he could hang on to the paddle. His legs felt like leaden blocks of ice, stiff and immovable. It suddenly occurred to him that even if he attained his destination he would be completely unable to disembark. But that was a problem for later, and he was not going to worry about it now.

His watch told him that he'd been in the kayak for about four hours. The wind had continued to freshen, but in the open Chukchi Sea its effect had not yet been too dramatic on the sea state. The rhythmic ocean swells were larger and there was moisture on the wind, but he felt well able to handle the weather thus far. It seemed counterintuitive, but a tiny kayak handled better in this sort of water than a larger vessel. It was small and light enough to ride on top of the water, much the way a fishing bobber might. Jake found that he was able to handle the boat rather easily. There wasn't much danger of broaching in these conditions; so as long as he stayed awake and did nothing stupid he would be fine.

The problems that didn't exist in deep water at the moment *would* become a factor if the wind rose sufficiently to form the waves and cause them to begin breaking, or if the water became shallow, or if he encountered rough tide lines. Once the water roughened considerably it would demand all his strength and concentration to stay out of trouble. If he spilled the kayak in these temperatures he would die.

Jake did not fear death. He was a fatalist. When his time came he would die. Until his time came he would remain alive. It was that simple and that ironclad. Nothing he could do would prevent the hour of his demise. According to his philosophy he was a cog in an unfeeling machine. If there was a god, he sure didn't seem to be hanging around this particular corner of the solar system; he seemed fully disconnected from the tragedies and trials that comprised daily life.

It had never occurred to Kelly to think deeply about his

personal beliefs. Everything seemed so obvious and so inevitable. He'd never stopped to consider that the powerful, driving will that had kept him alive in his escape from Prison 87 could not be explained by fatalism. He didn't realize that the self-sacrifice called forth by love, the joy that arose from watching a glorious sunset, or even the ability to distinguish between the beautiful and the ugly or between justice and injustice was inexplicable by the cosmic machine. He'd never allowed himself to consider the intrinsic inconsistencies in the way he viewed the world. What he did know at the moment, however, is that while he didn't fear death he *did* want to live.

As Kelly considered the very real possibility of his own death his main concern centered around Galina Toporova. He'd made a promise to her, one that he would keep as long as blood flowed in his veins. He wanted to survive because he wanted to free that lovely woman from the continent-sized prison in which she lived. In addition, locked in his mind were the names of the innocent inmates of Prison 87, incarcerated there by the Soviet GRU at the command of Major General Nikolai Pavlovich Chernikov. *I want to live, because I want to kill that lunatic Chernikov!*

****

With no small satisfaction he realized his physical condition was not worsening. Another two hours of paddling had given him that confidence. Apparently he'd reached a quiescent state, an equilibrium in which his body heat was being produced by metabolic activity at the same rate at which the icy water of the Chukchi Sea was leaching it away. Now the only question was whether the energy supplies of his body could continue to fuel the production of heat and propulsion long enough for him to reach the American shore.

The weather conditions had worsened considerably. The wind had risen and squalls of icy rain were racing across the black seascape before him. Bits of foam were being driven by the wind. Jake's military-issue parka was holding up well and shedding water better than he had hoped, but it was gradually becoming heavy with moisture. Still, except for his hands and face he was warm enough from the waist up. Underneath the coat his dry suit was covered by several layers of wool, compliments of the Soviet Army.

His lips curled in a feral smile as he paddled. He was, after all, an officer in the United States Air Force, a skilled pilot who could fly just about anything fixed wing or rotary. He was highly decorated and outwardly cultured, an officer and a gentleman who'd been a guest in demand on the base cocktail circuit. He'd contributed to the design aspects of the *Hydra* weapons package. But underneath the fighter-pilot exterior Jake was a special forces warrior who'd escaped from Prison 87 and his Spetsnaz keepers with his bare hands. He'd destroyed enough of their equipment and killed enough of their best to outfit an air cavalry company. He'd just escaped from the largest police state on the planet despite their best efforts to recapture him. He'd done well, and he was just thirty-six hours or so from home.

A black mass loomed in the darkness some two hundred meters off his starboard bow. He had seen it out of the corner of his eye, though he could not locate it when looking straight at it. He'd heard nothing. Whatever it was, it was running without lights. And it wasn't clear whether it was coming or going. Jake stopped paddling, and sat completely still.

****

Ilya Gregov was miserable. He was seasick, he was cold, he was wet, and he was tired of this duty. He stayed passably awake and alert, reasonably completing his assigned tasks, not because he loved the Navy but because he feared the punishment reserved for careless or unfaithful seamen. He came from a little village in southwestern Siberia of no particular importance to the Party; his father had no position or influence and was a subsistence farmer on the giant *kolkhoz* there. The only reason Ilya joined the Navy was to avoid starvation: at least you were fed when aboard ship.

The blow on the Chukchi Sea was pitching the patrol boat

about like a cork in a cataract. The *Smernov* had been sent to live out its remaining days patrolling Soviet waters between Cape Dezhneva and Cape Onman. This was a ridiculously large area for one ancient patrol craft, but a combination of shore and air patrols supplemented the coverage. And besides, what with the brewing economic crisis in the *rodina* there was simply no money to send ships to this frigid backwater of a patrol zone, even if it was less than two hundred kilometers from American soil.

The old *Osa-1* class, of which the aging *Smernov* was an early edition, was one of those ideas that was great on paper —but only on paper. It was a small, cheaply produced floating weapons platform. According to its design it packed a wallop, carrying two rails of SS-N-2 Styx anti-ship missiles and one rail of SA-N-5 Grail anti-aircraft missiles. The Israelis and the Pakistanis had learned from experience that the Styx could live up to its name. However the armament took such a pounding from rough coastal seas when mounted on a tiny platform like an *Osa-1* class vessel that its almost permanent operational status was "down for maintenance." In an actual conflict, the four 30mm machine guns would have been more useful than anything else on the tub.

Four bells sounded on the midnight watch. *Two more hours to go*, Ilya thought dejectedly. He hated midnight watch duty! Then again, he hated the Navy! His ambition was to farm potatoes; he hated the sea. In eighteen months he could return to his village and all the girls would think him a man now, a Navy man! He would enjoy a few weeks of prestige and then it was back to scratching out a living in the dirt. *But at least the dirt doesn't pitch you out of your bunk.*

Ilya was looking but not seeing, outwardly alert but inwardly lost in his thoughts. It really didn't matter. On a night like tonight the kayak was all but invisible several hundred meters off the port bow. The *Smernov*'s three twelve-thousand horsepower diesel engines, laboring against an opposing sea, powered the vessel past Jake's tiny craft. It would be midday— another ten hours or so—before the *Smernov* would return on its boring, predictable patrol.

****

Floating across the misty dark from the ghostly ship came the sound of four bells. *Oh-two-hundred*, thought Jake. He remained still, knowing that movement attracted the eyes. If he remained immobile a lookout could be staring straight at him and never see him.

The small ship passed him, headed west. He could make out no visual details, but he could hear the throbbing of diesel engines. Since it was running without lights he concluded that it was either a smuggler or a patrol. Whoever it was, he had no desire to find out.

****

The repetitious motion of paddling had become mind-numbing, a trance-inducing pattern lulling him into a stupor. He was feeling like the sleepy driver who comes to consciousness with no recollection of how he has arrived at his destination.

Jake stirred and tried to engage with his surroundings. One false move in the rising seas and he would die a cold and lonely death in the Chukchi Sea. To stay alert, he reviewed his steps over the last fifteen months. He thought about his friends at the Sidima Timber Cooperative. His true story was known by only three: Sevastyan, Galina, and her brother Boris. The others knew Jake as Sergei Primakov, a runaway from a *kolkhoz* who'd gotten tired of farming—or so his cover story claimed. They had fed him and sheltered him, and in return he'd worked as hard as any man, cutting timber and joining in the various duties of a busy sawmill operation. Boris had died during the winter, victim of a freak accident. Galina and Sevastyan had kept the operation going even while they kept Falcon's secret at the risk of their own lives. They were not disloyal to their country, rather, they were battling what they saw as a rogue injustice contrary to the interests of the USSR.

As he turned these thoughts over in his mind, his attention

kept being drawn back to Galina Toporova. She was a beautiful woman, yes, but she was a lot more than that. She was made of steel, able to hold her own with rough-hewn loggers without sacrificing her own femininity. Galina was intelligent, perceptive, hard-nosed when she needed to be but compassionate in the face of suffering—she was a remarkable woman. Jake was head over heels for her.

Her parents had died when she was young and she'd been raised by her older brother Boris. While he'd worked in various factory jobs, she'd gone to the university and earned a degree in mathematics. For a number of years she'd taught school, and then the brother and sister had moved to Khabarovsk. There they'd met Sevastyan, and together they'd begun the timber cooperative. Living halfway in the official world of permits and quotas, and three-quarters of the way in the black market, it had become a very profitable venture.

Over the years they had cultivated some contacts where it counted, including in the KGB office in Khabarovsk as well as in the office of the local head of the Communist Party. A discreet bribe here, a gift there, *a few extra rubles for you, my comrade,* and before long they had assembled a local network of informants who would warn them of inspections, raids, and other official actions that might jeopardize their operation. So it was that Galina had received a call from an informant warning them that their cooperative was the next target in the village-to-village search for Jacob Kelly. Galina, Sevastyan, and he had fled with mere minutes to spare.

There were many unsolved puzzles about the beautiful young woman he'd fallen in love with, but one stood out in his mind. She'd once mentioned wondering whether someone high up in the Soviet hierarchy was looking out for her and her brother. The permits and permissions came too easily. The travel requests were approved too readily. There was too little interference by the State in their operation. It was as if they had an anonymous patron in a position to protect them. But she was unable to account for why or how they should have such a benefactor, and no one had ever tried to contact them. Kelly wondered if there was something in her family history that explained the mystery, something of which Galina might be unaware.

It started to sleet, making a soft drumming sound on the skin of the kayak and pulling the flier from his thoughts. Jake paused paddling for a moment as he checked the direction of the wind and the waves. Satisfied, he dug the dripping paddle into the water again. In another hour or two, he would turn what he hoped would be southeast. He wished he could see his compass but it was too dark and his hands were too numb and clumsy, no longer able to handle small items.

****

When Jake made his turn to the southeast the storm had risen to such an intensity that he was forced to concentrate on his handling of the small boat. Straight-line winds came out of the northwest, blowing off the ice pack. Spray was now curling off of the tips of the waves, and sea foam was blowing in the gale. The temperature had dropped dramatically. The only good news was that he was now paddling with, instead of against, the waves and wind. Jake discovered that, without too much effort, he could surf the larger waves. His increased forward speed rapidly ate away the distance separating him from the Alaskan coast.

Chapter 4

Friday, September 25, 1987: 1515 local time
60 miles north of Cape Prince of Wales, Alaska

The Ilyushin Il-38 aircraft, NATO code name *May*, entered another lumbering circle as its curious occupants wondered at the sight below. The day had dawned in the fury of an early fall Arctic storm, but by noon the sky was clear and the seas virtually bathtub calm. Another approaching low pressure system was scooping relatively warm air off the Bering Sea and producing a clear, unusually warm day for late September on the Arctic Circle.

The crew of the surveillance aircraft examined the bobbing kayak on the water far below. Binoculars revealed a listless occupant, slumped over and unmoving. Captain Petrov Shevchik keyed the intercom to his navigator: "Edor, what is our current position?"

"Captain, when we began to orbit the target we were at sixty-six degrees, thirty minutes north, and one hundred sixty-eight degrees, thirty minutes, seven seconds west."

"Roger that. Mikhail, contact Provideniya, provide them with our position, and tell them that we have a visual contact, designate Victor-one. Tell them that it appears to be a tiny vessel drifting toward the east, one soul aboard, possibly dead. Ask for instructions."

****

In the game of cat-and-mouse that was played every day in the Bering Strait, each cat was also a mouse. The hunters were themselves hunted by other hunters. Over the years unwritten rules kept the forces of the United States and Soviet Union at arm's length. Except in times of great tension each navy tended to stay well clear of the other's territorial waters and opposing aircraft maintained respectful and non-threatening distances. Although the use of air and surface search radar was common, it was rare that targeting radar was ever employed. For all the hot rhetoric of their political masters, the men who crewed the armed forces concentrated in the small space in and around the Bering Strait knew that safety lay in benign and clearly telegraphed patrols and movements. Neither side had any interest in an international incident: both militaries were concerned for the safety of their men. While they engaged in covert operations elsewhere, mixing it up in the Strait was something no one on either side wanted to do.

All of which meant that the American aircraft, an Orion EP-3 orbiting fifteen miles north of the Soviet Il-38 surveillance aircraft, was making no attempt to hide itself or its intentions. Nor was it getting too close. At least, not yet. All of the spy plane's electronic ears were turned on and tuned in. Its communications officer spoke Russian as well as he did English (better, according to his wife). As border patrol communications on the Soviet side were not commonly encrypted, the Orion's communications intercept officer amused himself during slow moments by eavesdropping on the USSR border patrol chatter. Typically worthless from an intelligence standpoint, it was at least something to do on a long hop. But something he was hearing now made him sit up and listen closely.

"Commander, we've got something going down on the Russky spectrum."

"Go ahead, Ears, what's up?"

"About five minutes ago those guys on the May just ahead of us called in a visual contact. Some poor stiff in a small boat, possibly dead."

"Too bad for him. Are you asking permission to call it in to the Coast Guard?"

"Actually, Commander, that might not be a good idea. It's about to get rather crowded out here. I love the CG and all, but they're not really equipped to mix it up with the big boys."

"Talk to me, Chief. I don't want to play 'thirty questions.'"

"Sir, we have one *Nanuchka* class corvette, two *Osa-1* class missile patrol boats, and two MiG-23 Floggers headed our way. Whatever or whoever is in that little boat, they want pretty badly."

****

The May was orbiting at just over one thousand feet, so Commander John Erskin brought the Orion in underneath at a wave-clipping one hundred feet. The roar of the four Allison turboprop engines reflected off the water and back to the airship, raising the noise level on the flight deck. Erskin was concentrating on his flying but all other available eyes were at every window and porthole with binoculars.

"Nuts, John, why don't you just put the wheels down and bring it in," groused his executive officer. Lieutenant Commander Bill Johnson was not worried, he was just living up to his nickname, "Grumpy."

"Well, Grumpy, I would but I haven't qualified for water landings in the Orion yet," Erskin chuckled.

"I've got it!" shouted the flight engineer. "It's about a half-mile ahead, maybe three hundred yards to the right of our flight path. Some sort of small boat."

"It's getting a little crowded in here, boys." Now it was Erskin's turn to complain. Several crew members were gathering in the cockpit, trying to spot the target through the windshield.

"Sorry, John, but thirty million dollars' worth of the finest SIGINT hardware is not going to identify that contact. We've got to look out the windows, and in the Navy's perverse wisdom it decided the pilots should have the best view on this bucket—Okay . . . our, our contact is a kayak, one occupant, and he appears to be slouched as far as possible into the boat's skirt. Not moving. Hey, boys, that kayak is the real deal—definitely not fiberglass—looks like it's made out of skins. Better not let PETA find out," quipped Wally Samuel. Samuel was the flight engineer and had the sharpest eyes of the bunch. He provided a running commentary as the EP-3 roared past the kayak.

"Commander?"

"Go ahead, Chief, what do you have?"

"The Sov is advising that he has the situation under control. He says that the contact is a Siberian native fisherman who got swept off by the storm last night. Claims that Soviet rescue vessels are on the way. He has thanked us for our assistance, but insists that it is not needed. He's asking us to leave the area immediately."

"Roger that." Commander Erskin thought about it as he pulled into a climbing left turn. He intended to go into a racetrack holding pattern at two thousand feet while he decided what to do.

"John," his XO said quietly, "you don't send those kinds of assets out here to retrieve a fisherman who appears to be dead. The Russsky wants that kayak—badly—and whatever or whomever it contains. And if *they* want it that much, it probably means *we* want it more."

"Sammy, how far inside international waters are we?" Erskin asked, speaking to his navigator.

"'Pends on who you ask, Commander. But right now we are in the dead center of this part of the Strait, over forty miles from the Soviet coast and about the same from the Alaskan coast. Out here, sir, that's as good as a hundred."

Erskin knew his navigator was right about that. In narrow spaces like the Bering Strait even short distances took on great importance. The crews of vessels were typically jealous to guard their rights and would assert "international waters" if they could verify they were as much as two hundred yards or so in the clear. Which meant that the first guy to pick up this kayak would win. If the Americans retrieved the kayak first and it did turn out to be Soviet, the little boat would be returned (after a thorough search) but its occupant might not be. With the sort of assets the Russians were throwing at this recovery the occupant could be someone important attempting to defect.

"What should I tell him, Commander?"

Erskin sucked on his cold coffee and thought for a minute. "Thank him, Chief, and tell him that we will remain on station until the fisherman has been rescued, just in case additional assistance is needed."

A palpable silence greeted Erskin on the intercom. It was finally broken by the navigator: "Are we just going to let 'em have him then, Commander?" Erskin turned in his seat and saw that everyone still on the flight deck was staring at him with disappointment written on their faces.

"Of course not, Sammy! But we're not going to tell *them* that, now, are we?" He addressed the petty officer on the communications panel, "Get me a secure connection to the watch officer at Adak. We're going to have to move real fast on this! Chuck," he said to the weapons officer, "be ready to bring the Sidewinders online, but with full safeties. Make sure that countermeasures are ready if we need them. Manually designate the kayak as Sierra-1, and enter its position on the threat board; designate the May as Alpha-1. Make the kayak a friendly. Chief Bowles," he said to his radar officer, "light up both our air and surface search radar—I don't want any surprises sneaking up on us. I'm climbing to eight angels so we can see a little farther.

"Okay, ladies, time to earn your paychecks! Oh, and Grumpy? Take over, will ya? I'm due a *hot* cup of coffee."

****

The watch officer at Adak also found it strange that Ivan would be so adamant about rescuing a "Siberian fisherman" in a kayak. Besides, today's watch duty had been particularly boring up until now and a little action would spice things up a bit; it was not too difficult for Erskin to convince the watch officer that something important was unfolding.

"Ensign," he called to the communications operator on duty, "see if you can stir up the OIC in the Intelligence Section. I may have something of interest. And make it quick!"

****

Lieutenant Commander Jesse Pierce was having one of those *aha!* moments. Every several days for the last two months the stocky intelligence officer been getting intelligence updates on unusual air and land activity in the far eastern Soviet Union, movements that had slowly crawled their way northeast up the Chukchi Peninsula. The speculation in the US intelligence community was that a search was on for a moving target of some sort, a target that had proven to be remarkably elusive. There was an informal office pool run by one of the CIA spooks at Langley taking bets as to what all the activity was about. The Air Force boys had their money on a defector. The Navy swabs were guessing it was a politician or high-ranking military officer who had pushed a little game of bribery, or perhaps blackmail, too far with someone in the Politburo and had failed to read the signs indicating enough was enough.

Whatever. What was clear to Pierce after talking to Commander Erskin was that a possible high-value target was now bobbing in a boat on the Bering Strait, ready for the plucking. The intelligence officer was betting the person in the kayak was the object of that intensive search. And now, if Pierce played his cards right, he was going to get there before the Sovs did.

He ran his hand through his red hair, and considered his options. The first thing he had to do was convince his superior, the CO of Adak NAS, that it was worth pursuing. If the US was going to get in the game it would require an assist from the Air Force, and only his CO had enough clout to make that happen.

****

Captain Dan Daniels listened as his intelligence officer related the unusual Soviet search activity, the intercepted conversation between the Illyushin Il-38 and its control, and the rather extravagant hardware the Russians were throwing at an ostensible rescue operation.

"How soon are the bad guys going to show up, Jesse? How much time do we have, if we are going to do anything?"

"Based on the latest estimates, sir, the corvette was about seventy nautical miles south-southeast of the Ilyushin's position. If they run flat out, which is unlikely, it could be on location in two hours. One of the *Osa-1*s is coming out of Uelen, but it was on patrol about eighty miles southwest when the orders went through. The other *Osa-1* is only about forty miles due west, and can be on the scene in about ninety minutes. To summarize, sir, in likely order of appearance, I am guessing that the Floggers will be there in about an hour, followed by one of the missile boats, and then everyone else will show up over the next two-and-a-half hours. I'd say that the party starts around 1630 hours, sir."

"What about the May? How long will it be able to remain on station?"

"For the duration, sir, according to an estimate from our boys in the Orion. They've tracked it all the way from its point of origin and believe it has sufficient fuel to remain on station as long as necessary."

Daniels rubbed his chin wearily, "So stuff begins happening in an hour? That gives us very little time. Give me a rundown on what we have available, Jesse."

"Well, sir, we have the *Navajo*, a *Powhatan*-class tug up at the Alaska Maritime Naval Weapons Range, but it's above and east of Cape Lisburne right now, so it's effectively out of play. There is an *Edenton*-class patrol boat off Gambel, another in the eastern part of Norton Sound and another off Port Lay, all too far. The *Ute*—another *Edenton*—is within range off Diomede but is reporting engine problems and is barely able to make steerage way. Commander Watkins in Operations is dispatching the *Navajo* to tow her in to Anchorage for repairs. Other than that, we have a pair of F-14s about to touch down at Galena AFB on a refresher flight but they aren't carrying ordnance. That's about it, Captain."

"Jesse, looks to me like we're out of luck on this one. I'm

sorry, but we don't have any assets we can bring to the table."

"Danny, I want this guy and his kayak. I know there's something important at work here. You know Ivan is not going to commit assets like this to pull a dead Siberian fisherman out of the drink! Something big is going down."

"Jesse, it's an interesting story and you are probably right, but we don't have any hardware close enough to beat Ivan to the punch." Captain Daniels spread his hands in frustration, "Look, Jesse, we cannot rescue a boater in trouble using fixed-wing aircraft! We can't recover the kayak. Nuts, we can't even put a man in the water! Eielson is two hours away at the cruise speed of an F-16, and we cannot do the job with Falcons! What do you want me to do, *sink* them if they try to rescue this guy?"

Pierce glared at his CO from behind a mug of steaming coffee. Daniels was a solid officer, a wise leader, a friend and mentor to boot, but definitely not a guy to put anything at risk. Pierce smiled ruefully to himself: lieutenant commanders can afford a little recklessness: captains cannot.

Dan Daniels pretended to ignore his subordinate's irritated glare and rummaged around in his desk drawer looking for the last piece of Werthers hard candy that he'd seen in there just last night. It was a stalling tactic. He knew his junior officer had good intelligence instincts, great ones even, but in this case the Navy was too far away with too little hardware. It was sheer luck that the EP-3 had been paying attention to a routine Soviet border patrol, and even luckier that they'd heard the transmission from Provideniya.

The captain located the Werthers under a stack of requisition slips (triplicate requisition slips, of course). He grunted: it was an old one and the wrapper was stuck to the candy. Holding it at arm's length so he could see it clearly, he began to disengage the wrapper from the sticky candy. Out of the corner of his eye he saw his subordinate's impatience mount. Daniels deliberately ignored the storm warnings and concentrated on his candy. It would be a good exercise for his young intelligence officer to be forced to think outside the box. The fact that Jesse had entered his office having already done his homework on available Navy assets was the sign of a good officer.

Furthermore, the fact that Lieutenant Commander Pierce knew what he wanted and was now fighting for it was not an irritation to Captain Daniels; it was a delight. Daniels encouraged his junior officers to make decisions quickly, and to fight passionately for them. A man wasn't worth much as a leader of warriors if he could not formulate a course of action quickly and then pursue it aggressively. Daniels' own personal passion in life was to develop good naval officers. Over the years the men who had served under him had climbed high in the ranks and distinguished themselves. None were washouts. Daniels had a personal rule: if a commissioned officer was not competent to wear his stripes, his posting under Daniels' command would be his last posting in operations.

What Pierce did not understand—what he, in fact, misunderstood—was that Daniels still wore the braids of a captain and not an admiral precisely because he *was* an unorthodox risk-taker. Daniels was willing to go beyond the book to get a difficult job done. He frankly made admirals a little nervous, though they readily acknowledged his command had a way of producing great officers.

Finally freeing the precious hard candy from its foil, the captain popped it into his mouth. The rising storm in his intelligence officer's face had subsided and Pierce was staring at the floor with a sense of resignation. Daniels decided to prod him a little.

"Jesse, if you could have any piece of equipment on site to grab this guy, what would it be?"

Without hesitating, Pierce responded, "A helicopter—probably a Seahawk."

"And the Navy does not have one close enough?"

"No, sir, and neither does the Coast Guard. I already checked."

Daniels allowed the silence to grow for a moment before he continued, "Well, who else uses helicopters out here in Alaska?"

"Just about everybo—wait a minute! Could we do this?

Could we use civilian or commercial assets?"

"Jesse, this is a rescue operation, a *rescue*! Not a Navy intelligence operation. Right?"

The glimmer of a smile passed over the intelligence officer's face as he replied, "Of course it is. A rescue. Yes, sir, that's exactly what it is—exactly! It's a rescue operation! And I know just who to call." Maybe he was wrong about Daniels after all. He jumped out of his chair.

"Oh, and Commander Pierce," Daniels called as the newly energized lieutenant commander raced out of his office, "As a forward operating base for Elmendorf, Galena has an ordnance dump. We have an informal agreement with 'em for fueling and ordnance, so their boys have been cross-trained to arm both F-15s and F-14s. I'll call the base CO, and ask if his ordnance guys could slap some Sidewinders on those Tomcats, and fuel 'em up. If they expedite matters, those boys can be on location in an hour and provide air cover for the whirlybird. I'll also call Eielson AFB and have them scramble their Falcons. That will give us a credible surface threat if the Russians decide to play chicken. The Falcons won't be there until 1730 or so, but if the situation develops slowly we might be glad to have them."

****

The *Smernov* throttled up to its cruise speed of twenty-five knots and made a slight course adjustment to the northeast. During the night a radio message had been received warning of a possible escape attempt by an English-speaking Siberian fisherman. All border patrol units were to maintain the highest vigilance to ensure that this dangerous enemy of the People did not escape to the Capitalist Pigs. Captain Gerchenko had thought the message sounded implausible—silly even —just the sort of pap the Communist hierarchy would say with a straight face and expect the average uneducated peasant to believe. The captain had the good sense, however, to keep his thoughts to himself. They could shoot you for what you had the foolishness to say, but they were not yet able to shoot you for what you were thinking, as long as you kept your mouth shut.

Such a message probably meant that somehow an American had been trapped spying in-country and was trying to return home any way he could. More than likely some high-ranking official in the Party or the military had botched his capture and was now trying to save his own skin. The second receipt of orders from Provideniya had confirmed his suspicions and had also been the cause of his change of course. An American spy was attempting to escape across the Bering Strait in a kayak and had been spotted in international waters, apparently dead or unconscious. An Il-38 was keeping an eye on the kayak.

The call had come to the *Smernov*: he was to make best speed and take the foreign agent into custody immediately. The Americans were liable to interfere but under no circumstances were they to be allowed to retrieve their spy. If the man could not be captured he was to be killed if possible. Gerchenko was given permission to do anything short of firing the first shot, including gaining target lock on American units with his fire control radar, but he was not to fire unless fired upon.

This is lunacy, Gerchenko mused to himself. Acquiring target lock with a fire-control system would certainly invite the Americans to fire in self-defense. Even if no one had intended to shoot first, painting a target was virtually the same thing, and a messed-up spy operation could rapidly become an international conflagration in the confined Bering Strait.

The captain wondered what American units he might encounter. As of the last message, the only units reported in the vicinity of the kayak were the May and the Orion. He knew that another *Osa-1* had been dispatched, as well as a *Nanuchka* and a pair of Floggers. Enough hardware to start a small war. And little wars had the unfortunate tendency to grow into big ones. Gerchenko sighed.

He rang the ship's steward and asked for coffee. Rising from the captain's chair on the *Smernov*'s small bridge, he looked out on the rapidly improving sea conditions. It was a beautiful day, virtually no wind, with a chill autumn snap in the air. The swells and the chop from last night's storm had virtually disappeared. A seaman appeared soundlessly at his elbow bringing his coffee. He thanked the man and continued pacing the small bridge.

How far up the chain of command would such reckless orders come from? It was a puzzle. Probably not very far, Gerchenko finally decided; it was most likely a local operation and someone was trying to cover their backside on a botched arrest. In fact, it was likely that no one in Moscow had approved these orders. All of which meant, Gerchenko realized, that his career was on the line. The only possible outcome that would be good for him would be recovering the spy without incident. If he failed to recover the spy and the Americans retrieved him instead, he would be accused of dereliction of duty and perhaps even cowardice by the local chain of command. If on the other hand he caused an international incident by triggering a deadly confrontation with US military units, Moscow would have his head whether or not he retrieved the spy.

There was, then, only one path to success. *I've got to get there first. Might as well use this calm sea while we have it,* he thought. Picking up the bridge telephone, the captain rang the *Smernov's* engineering officer.

"Vladimir, what would be the impact on our engines if we ran at flank speed for an hour or so? Are they able to take it?"

"Captain, our engine maintenance has been good, and the diesels are in great shape. Whatever else is falling apart on the *Smernov,* it's not the powerplant. I think I can get that speed for you if you require it, sir, for perhaps an hour, maybe two."

"Excellent, Lieutenant. Thank you." Gerchenko replaced the telephone and ordered the helmsman to increase to flank speed. Everyone aboard the small vessel felt and heard the increase in power. The *Smernov's* ETA had just shortened from ninety minutes to little over an hour.

****

The Global Petroleum Exploration Group (GPEG) owned a drilling rig about seventy-five miles south-southwest of Point Hope in the Chukchi Sea. Seismic readings and core samples held out the hope of a rich oilfield seven thousand feet under the sea floor. On this particular day, a Bell UH-1 helicopter sat on the helo pad of the GPEG North Field Rig 17. George MacDonald, known by some as Mac, had just finished fueling the Huey when the GPEG rig foreman called him into the radio shack. The foreman wordlessly handed him the radio telephone and Mac had found himself talking to Connor Lincoln, the GPEG Vice President of Alaskan Operations.

"Mac, this is Lincoln in Nome. The Navy has requested our assistance with a maritime rescue and recovery operation. A civilian in a light watercraft has somehow drifted out into the Strait and was spotted by a naval patrol aircraft. It seems that there are no rescue-capable Coast Guard or naval assets close enough to help. That's why they called us.

"The patrol aircraft orbiting the site is indicating that the individual may be unconscious, and will not be able to assist in his own recovery, so you'll need a pair of divers. The position of the watercraft is sixty-six degrees, thirty minutes north, and one hundred sixty-eight degrees, thirty minutes, seven seconds west. Mac, do you have divers and equipment available for a small-scale marine rescue?"

"Yes, Mr. Lincoln, we can be in the air in fifteen minutes. I just now finished refueling the chopper. I'd say we could be on site in about forty-five minutes."

"Excellent! I really appreciate it. I'll call them back and let them know. By the way, Mac, they will have backup on hand, just in case you need any help."

"Backup, sir?"

"That's right."

"Sir, if they have rescue-capable backup units, why don't they just do the job themselves? I'm supposed to be shore-bound to pick up some geologists coming out to the rig. What kind of backup units will be there?"

"A pair of Tomcats and four F-16s."

"Uh-huh." Mac rolled his eyes, shaking his head slowly. "Um, sir, would you mind explaining why I need fighter cover as backup for a rescue operation?"

"Listen, Mac, there's more to this thing than meets the eye, but you've gotta treat it as a simple rescue mission. The naval officer who called me is the intelligence officer at Adak NAS. He's a family friend, his dad was under my command back when I was in the service. The problem is this: the Soviets are also trying to mount a rescue operation with some cock and bull story about a Siberian fisherman swept out to sea, only they are running their operation with a couple of gunboats and a pair of fighters. Navy thinks it may be an attempted defection. Apparently the Russians want this person very, very badly."

"I suppose so," Mac replied dryly.

"We have to get there first, and you are all we've got. We're not expecting any shooting, mind you, but you'll have air cover just in case. What do you say?"

Mac stared at the ceiling of the flight shack, saying nothing. *Not again.* He didn't want to fly into a combat situation again. And this time he would not even have weapons. He noticed the curious face of the rig foreman; the man was staring at him, apparently dying to know why a GPEG veep would personally call a lowly chopper pilot. *You don't want to know, buddy,* Mac thought silently.

"Mac, I've checked your file. I know you flew extraction missions in 'Nam. I have seen your commendations," Lincoln said, speaking into the obvious, prolonged silence. "The choice is yours. The company won't ask you to do this unless you're willing. There is some degree of danger. It's your call."

"Mr. Lincoln," Mac said slowly, reluctantly, "as far as I'm concerned, I was under the command of idiots in Vietnam. I am unconvinced that those idiots have moved on; I think they're still running the armed forces. But if my crew will go, I will go—but not for love of country or the Navy, but only because some poor sucker out there is liable to die if somebody doesn't pull him out of the water. I'll tell my crew the whole story—if they're willing, we will do it."

****

It's easier to ask forgiveness than it is permission. But it's much better for your Air Force career if you get permission. *The Air Force doesn't do the forgiveness thing*, Major Clark reflected. His flight group had been in the hot seat during this watch, the pilots in the ready room and the aircraft on the tarmac loaded out with a mix of air-to-air and air-to-surface ordnance. They didn't run a CAP at Eielson in peacetime without good reason but they did keep a flight of Falcons ready to go on a moment's notice: and that's all they had this time. When the call had come through they'd been scrambled immediately, with details to follow. He toggled his mike as he taxied his F-16 into position for takeoff.

"Control, this is Batman One. Please verify rules of engagement for this mission."

"Batman One, this is control. You are at weapons hold, repeat, weapons hold. You may take defensive action only, unless otherwise directed."

"Roger that, Control. We are at weapons hold, defensive action only."

Within two minutes his flight of four F-16s was streaking westward, leaving Eielson Air Force Base far behind them. Their mission was to provide an immediate and intimidating show of force to the Soviet military units in the area, and provide support for the US rescue mission. The controller briefed the flight on what to expect: a pair of Floggers, a pair of missile patrol boats, and a highly capable corvette.

"Control, this is Batman One. I am picking up emissions from two air contacts. One of them looks like our EP-3: it's responding to IFF as a friendly. He's running both air and surface search radar. The other contact must be the Ilyushin."

"Roger that, Batman One, two radar contacts, a friendly and a neutral."

"Okay, Bat Flight, this is Batman One. Time to go active on air search. We're supposed to be obvious and intimidating. Double-check your IFF transponder, and then light up the sky!"

Clark thumbed the APG-66 target detection radar to Up-look mode with his throttle switch. They were still much too far away for their own radar to reveal the positions of the May and the Orion, but that wasn't the point. He wanted the Russkies to know he was coming. The Ilyushin would pick up his flight's radar emissions immediately.

"Batman One, this is Batman Four. Why are we being so obvious? What's the game?"

"Well, Bat Four, let's just say we're sending Ivan a message in the diplomatic pouch. A contested rescue operation is underway and the goal is to let them know that we've got a horse in this race. Some naval intel genius down at Adak figured maybe they would fold their tent and move on if they saw the cavalry coming."

****

The inbound flight of Falcons was picked up immediately upon going active with their target detection radar. Both the May and the Orion registered the emissions simultaneously. The second thing that registered simultaneously with both air crews was that the US had dealt itself into the game and was raising the bid. Both surveillance aircraft loitered over the kayak and its motionless occupant like two great buzzards competing for road kill. What was still unclear to the respective crews of both the May and the Orion was how the US planned to get into the water. So far as anyone on the scene could tell, no American military hardware capable of actually mounting a sea rescue was in range to do so. To Captain Petrov Shevchik in the Ilyushin, therefore, that could only mean one thing—the Americans intended to mount a spoiling operation to prevent the Soviet recovery effort. And that meant somebody could get nervous and make a mistake. And mistakes could, with little encouragement, become disasters. He sighed and rubbed his temples—it was going to be a long afternoon.

Shevchik instructed his radioman to patch him directly to the radio operator on the *Smernov*. "This is Coastal Patrol

Flight 5 to *Smernov*, CP5 to *Smernov*, what is your status?"

"*Smernov* to CP5, we are fifteen kilometers southwest of your position, ETA twenty minutes. We have you on radar, as well as a second contact identified as an American Orion, plus we've picked up over-the-horizon military radar emissions from bearing one-one-zero true. We have no other contacts. We've been instructed that operational authority has been given to Captain Shevchik. We are inbound and awaiting further instructions."

"This is Captain Shevchik. Let me speak directly to the CO of the *Smernov*."

A brief silence, then a voice obviously accustomed to command came over the radio, "This is Captain Gerchenko of the Soviet ship *Smernov*. Captain Shevchik, what are your instructions?"

"Proceed to our position with all speed and be prepared to launch a boat immediately to recover the— the— ah, fisherman. There are American aircraft in the area. The contacts your RO has reported at bearing one-one-zero are a flight of four USAF F-16s. You are authorized to defend yourself if fired upon. This will be a contested rescue operation, Captain. We need to demonstrate our seriousness about recovering the fisherman without provoking a conflict. I recommend that you move to General Quarters, illuminate your fire control radar, but do not paint individual targets."

"Very good, Captain, I will comply immediately. Do you have further instructions?"

"Comrade Gerchenko, you had best consider that the inbound F-16s are surface-capable. We have also identified three additional contacts. There is a helicopter coming in at low altitude from the north-northeast, bearing two-one degrees, range about sixty kilometers. It appears to be a commercial aircraft, but it is on a course that will place it on site in about twenty-five minutes. We are also getting a pair of intermittent, undefined passive contacts coming from the south, bearing one-seven-zero degrees, at just above wave-height, range uncertain."

"Understood. *Smernov* out."

****

History often turns on providential events, things unforeseen by the most careful planners and the most brilliant strategists. So it was with D-Day in World War II, when Eisenhower got his thirty-six hour break in the weather on the very night the German command was in Calais, wargaming. So it was at Pearl Harbor, when the American flattops were not at home for the Japanese raid. And so it was with the ill-fated *Smernov.*

The *Osa-1* class vessel has three high-performance marine diesels, each one capable of producing twelve thousand horsepower. The high output of the engine is accomplished by a much higher-than-normal compression in each cylinder. Each cylinder head, therefore, undergoes a rigorous quality control process that includes examination by x-ray in an attempt to eliminate defective parts. As it happened, all twelve cylinder heads in the starboard engine of the *Smernov* were produced on the same night in the same factory in Leningrad. Problems in the forge that night caused premature and uneven cooling of the cylinder heads, producing microscopic cracks. The factory began to slip from its centrally mandated production quota, so the factory manager pulled the quality control tech off the line long enough for the last twenty-three heads —needed for quota—to pass by the x-ray station unchecked. Unknown to anyone, fifteen of those twenty-three heads were defective. Eight of the defective ones were presently installed in the *Smernov*'s starboard engine. Five kilometers shy of the goal, providence intruded on the little vessel.

****

First Engineer Lieutenant Vladimir Sibotin was confident of his men and his equipment. He was a rarity in the Soviet Navy. He actually loved his job, was a stickler for quality, and he managed to inspire the same devotion to excellence in his subordinates. His men knew him as a tough but fair leader and a world-class mechanic. His maintenance logs were accurate and invariably truthful (also a rarity in the Soviet Navy). He didn't give a bucket of warm spit for quotas or goals, or Communist propaganda nonsense. He was good at what he did and he knew it, and that was enough for him. Captain Gerchenko had complete faith in his first engineer and often wondered why the man had not been promoted to larger ships. The truth was that Sibotin's refusal to sign off on shoddy work had earned him enemies in the Soviet naval bureaucracy.

On this day, however, Sibotin would become the innocent victim of a system that valued quota over quality. The trouble began with the number four cylinder. Running at flank for sixty minutes was weakening the cracks in the defective cylinder head. It finally shattered, spraying parts all over the crankcase inside the engine. The loss of the head placed an unbalanced load on the crankshaft, and four more heads blew apart in succession. By this time the crankcase had filled with a finely misted diesel fume from the five now-open cylinders. The simultaneous failure of the last three defective heads, in various stages of their downstroke, raised the compression in the crankcase just sufficiently to support detonation of the diesel fumes. All of this took place in less than one second. With a kind of violent burp the engine blew its seals, throwing parts and shrapnel across the engineering compartment, and spraying diesel fuel on the surfaces.

Sibotin was caught in the back of the head with a four-kilogram shard of aluminum engine casing, and went down first, unconscious and bloody. One of the three remaining ratings in the engine compartment ran for the emergency fuel shut-off for the number three engine, but skated off the catwalk because of the slippery diesel mist spraying from the ruined engine. Falling onto the number two engine, he was badly burned before he managed to roll off into the bilge. The second crewman dropped and begin stanching the flow of blood from Sibotin's head. He screamed to his remaining companion to kill the fuel to the number three engine. Reacting rather than thinking, the third seaman missed the number three emergency fuel shutoff and hit the master shutoff instead, instantly killing all three engines.

In a big ship the sudden loss of engine power would be compensated by the inertia of the heavy mass of the vessel. As it lost way you might have to steady yourself but you wouldn't be thrown off your feet. Not so, however, in a fast, lighter craft. At one instant, thirty-six thousand horsepower was driving *Smernov* through the waves at flank speed; at the next instant all power was lost. The effect was devastating, all the more so because it was so completely unexpected. The sudden and complete loss of propulsion caused crew members to lose their footing and be thrown into forward bulkheads or onto the deck. The radio operator, standing at the time, pitched headfirst into a bulkhead, snapping his neck and instantly killing him. Two of the three members of the deck crew preparing to launch a boat for the recovery effort, were thrown overboard by the sudden and unexpected loss of momentum. In the engine compartment all three ratings and the officer were down with serious injuries.

Chaos reigned as the crew of the *Smernov*, now dead in the water, tried to comprehend what had happened. Gerchenko, getting back to his feet on the *Smernov's* tiny bridge, blood streaming from his face, called for damage reports and rallied his men sufficiently to begin recovering the sailors who had been thrown overboard. For now at least, the *Smernov* was out of the race for the kayak.

****

Screaming in at low altitude, the two Mig-23s pulled up and climbed vertically past the nose of the EP-3, passing within two hundred yards. Even though he had been informed of their presence, Grumpy still lost hold of his coffee cup when the two Floggers roared by his front windshield. Both pilot and copilot had a few choice words at the flyby.

"I suppose that would be a Soviet Air Force courtesy call," growled Grumpy, furious at himself for spilling his coffee. "They certainly want us to know they have joined the party.

Nuts, I just poured myself that coffee."

Commander Erskin keyed his intercom to the weapons officer, "Chuck, make sure those Sidewinders are ready to jump off the rails if we need them. These boys mean business. Chief Bowles," Erskin continued, speaking to his radar officer, "where in the world are the good guys?"

"The F-16s are about twenty minutes out, sir, bearing one-one-five, and the Tomcats are invisible, I can't pick them out of the surface clutter and they've maintained radio silence since leaving Galena. I have no idea where they are."

"Good. If we can't see them, I expect Ivan can't either. I just wish they would hurry up!"

"Agreed, sir. By the way, the incoming *Osa-1*, contact Sierra-2, is now dead in the water about five klicks out to the southwest, and appears to be drifting without steerage way. I have no idea why. Also, sir, the rescue chopper is arriving on station and it's squawking a civilian code. It's a Huey, contact designation Alpha-4, sir."

"Civilian?"

"Yes, sir. Civilian."

****

The Bell UH-1H clattered onto the scene and hovered about twenty feet over the gentle swells, close enough for the propwash to raise a patterned mist off the water. The surface wind speed was close to zero, so MacDonald had no difficulty holding position. The loadmaster slid open the door and pitched out an inflatable raft. Two divers in dry suits stepped out, jumping feet first into the frigid water one after another. The loadmaster turned his attention to the winch, rigging a rescue harness onto the cable.

The old Hueys didn't have legs long enough to operate for any duration this far from the drilling platform. The Vietnam-era chopper had a range of only about 270 miles in its military-surplus configuration. But when the Global Petroleum Exploration Group had purchased a dozen of the birds in 1978 they configured them with spare fuel tanks that provided the chopper with double the range, at the expense of cargo capacity. It was not fuel that was on Mac's mind right now. He flicked his radio to the maritime rescue frequency.

"US Naval Aircraft, US Naval Aircraft, this is Bell Chopper Golf Papa Echo Seven on a rescue and recovery. We have divers in the water, repeat, we have divers in the water. Please advise foreign units that we are a civilian aircraft conducting rescue operations, and request they stand off."

"Roger, Bell Chopper, this is US Naval Aircraft, we will deliver your message. Good luck!"

Mac didn't hold out much hope that the Soviets would turn around and go home, he was just following standard procedures. He turned his attention back to his instruments.

****

Captain Shevchik ignored the American message and instructed the MiGs to make the helicopter pilot uncomfortable. The Flogger pilots nosed over at ten thousand feet and began an intimidation run at the Huey. The chopper pilot was maintaining station just north of the kayak, about fifty feet above the surface. The MiGs dropped like rocks to the deck and then from a mile out made a near wave-height pass at the helicopter, straddling it, and then climbing up and around for another run. For the return trip, their target detection radar flickered on.

The targeting radar ploy didn't succeed in intimidating Mac because of the simple fact that the avionics necessary to warn him that he was being targeted had been removed from the chopper before Global Petroleum had ever bought it from the Navy. It did, however, succeed in turning what little hair remained on Chief Bowles' bald head pure white.

****

"Commander, the MiGs are making another pass at the Huey with their targeting radars on!" Chief Bowle's voice was calm and under control, but it had a hard edge to it.

Erskin addressed his weapons officer, "Chuck, if those boys light one off, you are authorized immediately to launch your Sidewinders, targeting both Floggers, do you copy?"

"Yes, sir, I copy. I am approved to fire if they take hostile action. They won't get a second chance, sir. But you've got to line me up to take the shot, sir, otherwise the seeker heads won't acquire the target."

"I know what I've got to do, Chuck," muttered Erskin, watching the developing scene below.

"Commander," his radar officer piped up, "we might splash the Floggers, but if we wait to shoot until they do, that won't help the chopper. He's a sitting duck."

Erskin sighed, "I know, Chief, I know, but I've not been authorized to initiate action. Until the cavalry gets here I am afraid the Indians are going to have their way with us. We need to sit tight." Erskin watched in frustration as the pair of gleaming Soviet aircraft buzzed the stationary chopper again and again, coming closer each time.

****

"There's no sign of trauma and every sign of hypothermia! We've got to get him out of this kayak and into the chopper now, or he'll die. I barely have a heartbeat! We don't have time to do this by the book!"

"Roger that, Tommy. Get him into the sling, and we'll bring him aboard," replied Mac.

The divers quickly slipped a chest harness onto the frigid, seemingly lifeless form, and signaled the loadmaster to lower the cable. After snapping the locking carabiner on the end of the winch cable to the ring on the rescue harness, the divers quickly loosened the skirt of the kayak. The winch began slowly taking up the slack, until Jake was pulled right out of the kayak. While the loadmaster and another crew member secured the unconscious man to a stretcher, and wrapped him in wool blankets, the divers rigged a sling around the kayak. Soon that too was hoisted into the helicopter.

Mac's radio startled him as he carefully nursed the collective and hovered over the rescue site.

"Bell Chopper, this is US Naval Aircraft. The bad guys are starting to get a little aggressive. Those Floggers are taking a bead on your butt with targeting radar. What is your status?"

"This is Bell Chopper. I have recovered the boater, but still have divers in the water. I was told I would have some air cover, Navy. Where the devil is it? Somebody screw up, or what?"

"This channel is not secure, Bell Chopper!"

"I don't give a rip, Navy! I'm doing a maritime rescue here, I don't care who is listening in! Part of my team is still in the water and I'm not leaving until I recover them! Just keep those hotdogs off my six, do you copy?" Mac's voice rose until he was shouting into the microphone.

Suddenly Mac's headphones were filled with a blood-curdling cry that he immediately recognized as a rebel yell, and two F-14 Tomcats screamed past the chopper, quickly overtaking the Floggers. The sleek jets had come in at barely wave height on afterburners, and hadn't been detected by either surveillance craft or the Floggers. As soon as they gained the advantage on the MiGs, they illuminated the hostiles with targeting radar and stayed right on their tails. Dropping all thoughts of harassing the Huey, the MiGs instantly began climbing and jinking, taking evasive action. Within seconds, all four jets were just silver dots up in the sky far over the rescue site, weaving, twisting, and engaging in every part of a dogfight short of pulling the trigger.

"Um, is that satisfactory, Bell Chopper?" a chastened voice asked over the rescue channel.

"Not bad, Navy, a little dicey with your timing, but not bad at all! Always good to see a friendly F-14 in the neighborhood."

"You're telling me! This is US Navy Aircraft, out." The relief in the voice was palpable.

Mac would never admit it to anyone, but his hands were a little sweaty, too.

****

Moments later the flight of Falcons arrived and Commander Erskin directed them to the approaching Soviet ships. The balance of power had shifted decisively to the Americans. When the Soviets saw their prize was gone they stood down and returned to patrol. What had appeared to have the makings of a ruinous conflagration in the Bering Strait was suddenly over, now nothing more than a matter for after-action reports and bragging rights in the Officers' Club. The only casualties—besides a few careers—were aboard the ill-fated *Smernov*. She limped into port on two of her three engines, bearing both dead and injured.

As soon as George MacDonald recovered his divers he headed directly to the small hospital at Kotzebue. At long last, Major Jacob Kelly had returned to the United States.

Chapter 5

Saturday, September 26, 1987: 0945 local time
Moscow, USSR

Major General Nikolai Pavlovich Chernikov shivered in his great coat as he strode into GRU headquarters in Moscow. This was not a meeting he was looking forward to; in fact, it was a meeting he had been telling himself would never be necessary. Major Nikitin, his loyal and highly competent staff officer, would deploy the lavish resources seconded to him, run the American to ground and bring him back to the Prison 87 compound in shackles and that would be that. There would be no investigation, no recriminations, no embarrassment. Major Jacob Kelly's interrogation would continue, and when he had been drained dry of useful information his body would be placed in an unmarked grave and Chernikov would move on to other conquests. It would be just one more achievement in the pattern of unbroken successes he'd enjoyed since being commissioned as an officer.

But that was not how the drama of Major Kelly's escape had played out. The American had broken out of Prison 87 by pretending to be a coward; Chernikov's troops lost their respect for the prisoner and therefore their caution. Kelly had played them all for fools. He had baited two guards into his cell, killed them, and then escaped from the compound in one of their uniforms. Things had gone downhill from there. No matter how close Chernikov's troops came to Kelly he had always managed to elude them or to escape shortly after capture, usually killing men and destroying valuable military equipment in the process. The American's methods had been so audacious Chernikov would not have believed the reports if he'd not had personal knowledge of their truthfulness. Twice the man had stolen helicopters. He'd hijacked a truck at gunpoint. He'd hopped a freight train at least once. After burning down a hangar and killing half a dozen soldiers, he'd stolen a biplane. The vast distances of Siberia, a feature Chernikov had counted upon for Kelly's eventual recapture, had proven inconsequential against the man's bold, unorthodox initiatives. The further east the American ventured, the lower sank Chernikov's star. And at the last he'd gotten clean away. Their final attempt to grab him in the Strait had failed.

Kelly had turned the tables on Chernikov. Now it was the general who was in deep trouble. Not an hour ago a curt summons had come, bidding him to report to the Aquarium—GRU headquarters. Retaining his life would be a small miracle; keeping his command was out of the question.

Since Chernikov was in Moscow on other business it was but a short drive to Khodynka Airfield. Surrounded by a cluster of high-tech Soviet military research facilities, the Main Intelligence Directorate headquarters was located in a glass-clad, nine-story tower at the airport. The directorates comprising the sum of the GRU's activities were based there. General Chernikov's superior, Lieutenant General Valeriy Patrikeyev, was the head of the ninth directorate, responsible for acquisition and protection of military technology.

Chernikov ran his badge through the scanner, and the door to Patrikeyev's section buzzed open. He stepped into a large reception area with halls going in several directions. Another sixty steps, and he was opening the door to Patrikeyev's personal domain. His mouth was dry, his heart was racing, his gut was rumbling, and his palms were sweaty.

Patrikeyev's personal secretary was a businesslike platinum blond. The woman had always been brusque. Now she seemed positively frosty. With cold civility she informed Chernikov that her boss had left the premises for a meeting several hours ago, leaving instructions that Chernikov was to wait for his return. Would he like a cup of tea?

Chernikov nodded and sat down heavily. The tea settled his stomach, but nothing could eliminate the sense of impending doom. As he sat drinking his tea, he reflected on the distinct possibility that—in a matter of hours—he might be leaving the building in a pine box.

The door opened and General Patrikeyev strode in. Chernikov jumped to his feet and opened his mouth to greet his boss, but was silenced with an upraised hand.

"I'll see you in a moment, General Chernikov. Please, be seated." He closed the door to his inner office, disappearing from Chernikov's view.

After another ten minutes of nerve-wracking dread, he was admitted to the inner office. He stood at attention before Patrikeyev, feeling like a condemned man before a firing squad.

"General Chernikov, I've called you here to review your management of *Krasnyy Voskhod*, and Prison 87. I have been going back through your reports and find a disgraceful level of recklessness, irresponsibility, and disregard for authority! Furthermore, your attitude towards your comrades in the KGB is unacceptable!"

For the next twenty minutes Patrikeyev did a painstaking critical analysis of every portion of Chernikov's command. None of his successes were noted, his failures were blown out of proportion, and his attitude toward the KGB, which Chernikov knew was but a model of Patrikeyev's own opinion, was soundly rebuked. He was accused of putting the USSR in danger of international humiliation, now that Major Kelly had escaped. His boss raised his voice, shouting with anger several times.

Finally, Chernikov sensed the tirade winding down. He chose his moment carefully. "General, am I to be given an opportunity to defend myself?"

"Defend yourself? Why? Nearly everything I have said has come from your own written reports! You've condemned yourself in your own handwriting, General. You have witnessed against yourself! What defense could you possibly mount?" At that moment there was a knock at the door.

"Enter!" Patrikeyev barked.

It was his secretary. "General, the diplomatic flight for Berlin leaves in thirty minutes. You asked me to remind you."

"Yes. Call for my driver now, please. I've got to run to my

flat and pick up my travel bag. I forgot it this morning."

"Sir, shall I have your driver get your bag?"

"No—I'll do it. I need to get out of here for a while," he said, glaring at Chernikov. "You," he barked, stabbing his finger in his subordinate's direction, "will come with me! I'm not finished with you yet."

The two men left the building in silence. Chernikov was stung. Never in his career had he been so dressed down, and treated so unfairly. He had thought that his relationship with Patrikeyev was more like a patron to a favorite artist, than superior to subordinate.

When they entered the Zil and the driver had pulled away, Patrikeyev produced a bottle of vodka and two shot glasses. "I figured you'd need a good stiff drink after my little performance, Niko. Here—bottoms up."

"What?" Chernikov asked, struggling to keep up with Patrikeyev's mercurial changes of temperament.

"Nikolai, my office is bugged. My secretary is a KGB plant. I've spent the morning in informal meetings with the Politburo trying to save both you and *Krasnyy Voskhod*. My systematic destruction of all you've done since coming forth from your mother's womb will be duly noted and duly reported. It will restore my credibility with the doubters. Saving me allows me to save you, eh? You know how it works."

"But what about the car? How do you know—"

"The car is swept for bugs and searched by hand every morning. My bodyguards are enlisted men whom I brought with me from the 106th—Spetsnaz. They work for me and me alone. There is always one of them with this car, twenty-four hours a day, no matter where I am. Even when it goes in for repairs. This car is the only place in Moscow where what I say is not recorded and reported to someone."

"But how are you assured of their loyalty? How do you know they have not been turned by the KGB?"

"You've got to trust someone, Niko. These men would die for me, and I for them. It's an interesting story going back to our days in Afghanistan. All six of them were on a patrol that was ambushed and trapped in a shallow declivity in the

Panjshir Valley in '84. The mujaheddin held the high points all around them, and were picking them off, one by one. The area was one we'd been trying to pacify by working with local leaders. The only way we could relieve the patrol was to drive our armor through a village where the regional headman lived, and he was not letting us through. I was ordered to sacrifice the patrol in the interest of preserving our relationship with the headman."

"What did you do?"

"I disobeyed my orders, exterminated the village and the headman, and rescued the patrol. I'd had intelligence telling me he was playing both sides of the fence. So I took him out."

"What happened?"

"I was court-martialed. Bumped down a couple of grades. Several months later we captured one of the caves being used as a regional HQ for the insurrection. Among the treasure trove recovered was hard evidence that I'd been right all along about the headman. Consequently, my superior officer was reassigned to a desk in Moscow and I was restored to my rank. Several months later I was promoted and took his place commanding the 106th.

"When I was tapped for this position with the GRU, I took the surviving members of that patrol with me. They knew the whole story, because they'd heard the orders to abandon them over their squad radio. They knew my insubordination cost me my command. They are loyal to me because I was loyal to them. Just as I'm loyal to you, Nikolai.

"Now, I've got ten minutes to bring you up to date before I catch my flight. First, I was late this morning because I've been trying to keep your neck out of the noose. If the head of the KGB, Anatoly Geredin, had won the day you'd be standing in front of a firing squad right now, and that was his most humane choice of doing away with you. He'd argued for several, ah, less pleasant ways to execute you.

"I had to remind the Politburo of your successes, especially those in the last ten days. I assured them that this was just the beginning, and I trotted out several of our own scientists to speak in your favor. It took an hour of argument, but they finally decided to leave your head attached to the rest of your body.

"Next I had to persuade them to allow Project *Krasnyy Voskhod* to continue, and to leave you in charge of it. That took another ninety minutes. But I was successful. You, however, are on a very short leash and the tongue-lashing I gave you this morning was part of the price I had to pay to get my way."

Chernikov felt the strength draining from his body and was glad he was already sitting down. He'd expected to lose his career if not his life, and was unprepared for Patrikeyev's reassurance.

"General, I never expected to lose this man. We have had several thousand troops looking for him under the direction of my best officers. At every turn and every twist, Major Kelly outthought us, outfoxed us, outran us. Nothing in our intelligence brief on the man prepared us for him. We now believe that he's had special forces training, though we don't know when, how, or why. There's no reference to it in his service records.

"We had over three dozen casualties, good men all, because of him! Our tracking teams became so spooked and began moving so slowly he could have outdistanced them if he were in a wheelchair. When I got news an hour ago that the Americans had recovered him from the Bering Strait, followed by the summons to come here—well, frankly sir, I began to put my affairs and effects in order."

"Nikolai, you have made enemies over the years. But you also have friends, and your 'intelligence gathering' activities," Patrikeyev paused at this phrase with a slight smile, "have yielded such excellent information that it was ultimately decided the project should continue with you in command. But there is a detail that must be taken care of. Major Kelly must be eliminated before he is able to tell the Americans what we are doing.

"I've made a few contacts with an organization that handles this sort of messy business, Nikolai, and they assure me they will take care of it."

****

Friday, September 25, 1987: 2155 local time
Kotzebue, Alaska
(Saturday, September 26, 1987: 9:55 AM Moscow time)

It was a strange rocking motion. No matter how he finessed the collective he could not dampen or stop the rhythmic rocking motion of the helicopter. It felt like being in a small boat on a gentle sea. He looked over at his copilot and realized with a shock that the face didn't look even vaguely familiar. Not only that, but rather than wearing a flight suit the copilot was wearing some sort of diving gear.

"It's a good thing we got to him before the Russians," said the unfamiliar face.

Jake stared at him, not comprehending. And then a voice that seemed to come from his own lips but did not, responded, "Yeah, it was pretty dicey after those Floggers showed up!" But he knew it was not his voice.

Who is this guy, and what is he talking about, wondered Jake, *and why is this cockpit so cold?* He turned to ask his copilot to turn up the cabin heat but found he was now alone in the cockpit of an F-16. He was flying with the canopy open, which explained the freezing cockpit temperature. The roar of the rushing wind was incredibly loud and he was so cold. His hands and feet were like blocks of ice, but burning with painful intensity. He couldn't sort out the contradictory sensations —he just knew that his extremities hurt like crazy! He tried to shut the canopy but his hands refused to respond.

The gentle rocking sensation continued, but he figured he was just battling a touch of vertigo. The horizon, after all, was rock solid. *Trust your instruments*, he told himself.

A skirmish line of Soviet soldiers appeared from the distant tree line, headed his way. Soon they would overtake him. He clambered out of the cockpit and jumped down to the ground, although he had no recollection of landing. The snow-covered field he jumped into became waist-deep water. It was freezing and chilled him to the bone. *Wait a minute! Stop! None of this makes sense*, he thought. He ceased trying to run and turned and looked back at the approaching infantry. One of the soldiers lifted his weapon and fired a burst; Jake could hear the angry buzz of the bullets as they whipped by. *Okay, run now, figure it out later!*

No matter how hard he tried, he could not flee from the ever-nearing skirmish line. Every time he tried to thrust off with his foot, he floated up. He could get no traction, and the troops were coming closer. *How odd*, he thought to himself: the soldiers were walking on top of the water and having no difficulty at all! He knew he had to get away but he simply could not keep his eyes open. He was so cold! He drifted off to sleep, still rocking gently, rhythmically, constantly.

He awoke in the kayak, bobbing in a gentle ocean swell. It was exceedingly hot. He began to remove his coat but found with surprise that he was wearing only a flimsy blue gown. The sun was so bright! It hurt his eyes and made it hard to get his bearings. Trying to shift his weight, he put both hands down on the side of the kayak in order to lift himself. *Strange*, he thought: the sides of the boat felt like smooth metal rails, cool to the touch. He sank back down into the bed. Nothing seemed real. The gentle rocking sensation put him to sleep again. This time he slept for hours.

****

Saturday, September 26, 1987, 0950 local time
Kotzebue, Alaska

Kelly heard the low buzz of voices as he clawed his way back to consciousness. His sensations were the first thing to register with any clarity. The rocking motion had stopped and he felt warm and dry. But months of being on the run for his life had made him very cautious and Jake decided to feign unconsciousness until he'd fully appraised his situation. The voices faded and he heard the click of a closing door. The first order of business was to ascertain where he was, and the second was to escape.

****

"Grab the gear, we've got a job." His tone didn't encourage questions or disagreement. Neither—for that matter—did his build. Standing at five feet eleven inches he weighed a solid one hundred eighty pounds and nothing about Fred Banks was soft. He walked with the grace of an athlete, and kept in tone by constant use of the neighborhood gym and fitness center. Banks' temper matched his aggressiveness, and only the fact that he was a professional kept it in check. Most of the time, anyway.

His companion had a face that must have been in mind when the word "weasel" was defined. If Fred was physically intimidating, Jason DeVoe had the appearance of someone who would knife his own mother. Not as physically capable, Devoe made up in brains and deviousness what he lacked in physique.

Fred owned a snowmobile and small-engine repair shop in Anchorage. Jason was one of his two employees. The third guy knew just enough to not ask questions when Fred and Jason would disappear for three or four days, as they did periodically. He never saw anything, he never heard anything, he never suspected anything, and he *especially* never showed any interest when the strange phone calls would come. He didn't want to know. He figured it was safer that way. He was right.

Jason and Fred were mercenaries, professional assassins for hire. They were very good at what they did. They never knew where the calls came from or who their employers were or why the marks were selected for death or intimidation. But they appreciated the fat envelopes of cash that appeared on the front seat of their cars after a successful job. As far as they were concerned the cash covered the details—whatever the details involved. Needless to say, the extra income wasn't reported on a Schedule C.

Jason crossed the shop to a large, reinforced locker. He

glanced at the other employee busy overhauling the carburetor of a snowmobile, who was studiously ignoring him. Jason said, "Bo, take a couple hours off. You don't need to punch out, but don't come back until this afternoon, okay?"

"Sure, Jason. I needed to pick up a parts shipment at the air freight office anyway. I'll just do that now."

Jason waited until Bo drove out of the parking lot and then unlocked and opened the steel-reinforced locker. He retrieved two gym bags—each containing clothing for three days—and then selected an assortment of smaller bags containing various weapons and tools of the trade. The smaller bags he put into a large duffel and then loaded the luggage into the back of Fred's jeep. Jason slipped behind the wheel as his partner locked up the shop.

"Where to, Fred? What's the job?"

"Drive to the airport—civil aviation side. We've been given a target in the hospital at Kotzebue. Some Siberian fisherman was hauled out of the drink yesterday, and needs to be scratched. It's an ASAP job. Needs to appear as though he died of complications from exposure and hypothermia. The bad news is that he might have a military guard. The good news is that our employers are paying us double for this job, triple if we can wax him before midnight."

"Midnight today? For crying out loud, it's 850 air miles to Kotzebue!"

"Shut up and drive! I know how far it is! Our mysterious paymasters have arranged a Learjet to shuttle us to Kotzebue, flight time around two hours. We'll be there in plenty of time and we're going in style for once."

****

Everywhere he could see any lettering or printing, such as the labels on his intravenous drip bag or the charts on the wall, it was all in English. *I must be somewhere on American soil.* The door opened, and Jake quickly shut his eyes, pretending to be asleep. He sensed—rather than saw—the nurse hovering about, checking the IV drip rate and making notations on a chart.

There was a sound of footsteps in the hall and then a male voice spoke, "Ma'am, I'm just checking in. We're changing shifts out here, didn't want you to be surprised. I'll be sitting out here in the hall, ma'am, if you need anything."

"No problem. I just came on the shift myself. Do you mind me asking why this 'Siberian fisherman' requires a guard? Are you protecting us from him, or him from us?"

"Uh, ma'am, I'm told it is standard procedure for a foreign national being held—I mean, treated—in a stateside medical facility. That's what they told us when we were dispatched, anyway. Seemed rather odd, especially when our, uh, supervisor was in such a big hurry to get us here. We were told to report back as soon as the patient regains consciousness. Has he woken up yet?"

"No, he hasn't. It could be several more hours since his core temperature was so dangerously low when the rescuers brought him in. Perhaps we can release him tomorrow, but it will take him several days to regain his strength. Thankfully he didn't suffer frostbite and he is not going to lose any limbs, but he is going to have a good deal of pain once he starts moving around. I don't think you'll have any trouble chasing him down the hall for the next day or two."

"No, ma'am, I don't reckon he'll be much trouble. Besides, he'll be transferred to, uh, a different hospital tomorrow anyway."

"That's strange. Is that standard operating procedure too, for a non-US citizen? He must be a real mystery man."

Kelly heard footsteps retreating down the hall, and the creak of a chair as the guard settled into his seat. The sound of the door closing let him know he was alone in the room.

He considered what he'd just learned: other than being physically drained, his body was undamaged. And he was under guard, though he didn't know why. It was a safe bet the hospital was located somewhere in northwestern Alaska, though the nurse had an unmistakable Texas accent.

The clumsy cover story he'd overheard from the guard made him wonder if the hospital staff was being kept in the dark for some reason.

Why are they calling me a Siberian fisherman? Is that what they think I am? Jake pondered this for a moment. *If so, then why am I under guard? And why would they transfer me to a another hospital? Certainly, my condition does not demand it.* They couldn't possibly know who he was, he thought, for he carried nothing that could identify him.

But what if they have somehow learned my identity? Fingerprints, maybe? If so, Jake knew he could expect to be detained by the Air Force and interrogated as to his whereabouts for the last eighteen months. But with a mole in place somewhere within the service, that would create a potentially dangerous situation for him. He could not afford contact with the US military, not yet anyway. He needed to escape and stay free long enough to research his own disappearance, and to have a talk with someone in military intelligence. If the Air Force got to him first, they might jump to the conclusion that he had defected to the Soviets and was now trying to resume his military service as a double agent. He'd have absolutely no credibility and no believable explanation for his disappearance.

As Falcon considered the situation, he realized that there was another distinct possibility. Perhaps they really didn't know who he was but were guarding him to protect him from the Soviets. He struggled to remember the events of the last twenty-four hours. Perhaps they held some clue.

He remembered that he had been paddling the kayak for what seemed an eternity. His energy level exhausted, he had gone past the point of being cold. There was a dim recollection of hunkering down in the little craft and pulling the skirt as high as he could. He'd planned to rest until daybreak, hoping the sun would provide him with the energy to continue his journey across the Strait. That was the last thing he remembered with any clarity.

But traces of strange dreams lingered in his mind like an elusive scent on a windy day. He remembered dreaming that he was in a helicopter, then back in an F-16. The dream had made no sense. As he tugged gently at the wisps of memory an image slowly emerged: a diver, an unfamiliar face saying,

"It's a good thing we got to him before the Russians."

There was something else, too. What was it? Ah! Someone responded! Someone had said something about the situation turning dangerous when . . . *when the Floggers showed up!* That was it! Apparently his rescue had been contested! Which meant that by now General Chernikov knew that he had been retrieved by the Americans.

What an irony! The Soviets knew whom the Americans had rescued, but the Americans did not! As far as Kelly was concerned, it was important that the situation remain that way for a little longer.

****

"George Thompson?" the man in sunglasses asked as Banks and Devoe got out of their jeep with their bags. "George Thompson" was the alias Banks was using for this hit.

"That's right. You must be with Alaskan Wilderness Charter."

"Yes; I'll be your pilot today."

"What is our ETA to Kotzebue?" Banks asked.

"Your charter contract was secured just thirty minutes ago, and our mechanics were already in the middle of a maintenance job on the Lear 35. They've got to finish that first. After that, we have to gas up and do the pre-flight. It's going to be an hour and a half at least before we can take off. I can give you a more accurate ETA once the cabin door is closed, but I'll be surprised if you're not having dinner with your client in Kotzebue by 7:00 p.m."

"I have a vital meeting in Kotzebue this evening which involves a very large petroleum contract. You had better hope I make that meeting on time!" Banks said, his face turning red. Devoe fervently hoped his choleric partner would keep his cool. If Banks were not veering toward an angry outburst, Devoe would smile at his choice of words. Contract indeed. It was a "contract" all right, it just had nothing to do with oil!

The pilot paused to allow the roar of a departing 727 diminish before he promised, "We'll do everything we can, Mr Thompson, to get you there safely, comfortably, and on time." Banks nodded without replying.

"Well, George, let's grab a quick bite to eat as long as we have to wait," suggested Devoe. Jason knew the best way to keep a lid on his partner's temper was to keep him busy. They put the bags back in the jeep and pulled out of the AWC parking lot to find a late lunch.

****

Jake lay in the bed and considered his precarious situation. He'd realized during his long trek across Siberia that he couldn't simply show up at the front gate of a military installation upon his return to the States. For one thing, every time he reviewed the details of his fateful last flight from Eielson AFB he came to the same conclusion: someone involved in USAF operations had leaked the details of the flight to the Soviets. Ivan had been waiting to jump him. If the spy was still in place—and there was no reason to believe otherwise— Kelly was confident that within hours of showing up at a military base he would be marked for death. Chernikov would be informed of his location and soon thereafter an attempt would be made on his life.

Depending on the depth of Soviet penetration, they might even tinker with his service record to make him look like a defector. That thought brought forward a third possibility: even apart from any disinformation the Soviets might spread, US military intelligence might suspect that Jake had been compromised, or brainwashed. They might even land on the defection theory without help. Worse, they could suspect that he'd been turned and was now a Soviet plant!

Falcon was flooded with despair. His entire purpose for the last fourteen months had been to get back to the States. But being here was almost worse than being over there! He seemed to have nowhere to turn, no one to trust. He would have to come in from the cold under his own terms and place himself in the hands of someone he could trust with his life.

Shaking off the gloom, the major took inventory of what he needed for the next leg of his saga. He needed money for clothes, food, and shelter, and he needed to escape from the hospital. The guard outside his door would present a problem. Jake was not going to start killing Americans—in the USSR he'd been dealing with the enemy. All's fair in love and war. But that option was off the table in the States. Lethal force was not something he could use: he would have to finesse each situation.

Somehow he had to fly below the radar. He needed a place to hide, somewhere they would not be looking for him. He also needed the ability to communicate—access to a phone at least. *But how can I accomplish all this in my weakened condition, especially while wearing nothing but this stupid, flimsy blue gown?*

Chapter 6

Pressing the throttles to the firewall, the pilot smiled as the twin Garret TFE731 turbojet engines spun up. He'd been flying the Gates Learjet 35A for seven years and had never been able to wipe the silly grin off his face that appeared every time he roared down the runway and rotated the nose. There was just something special about being pressed back into your seat as though a great hand was shoving you against the cushions. Each engine produced thirty-five hundred pounds of thrust, and the jet always seemed as if it wished to leap into the air. It was a real kick in the pants.

The business jet rose easily off Runway 32 of the Anchorage International Airport, navigation lights blinking. As the pilot banked the gleaming aircraft to the right, his copilot set up the Nav instruments for the flight to Kotzebue Airport. The wheels folded and locked into their housings with a satisfying *thunk*.

Unfortunately, his departure time was later than intended and his passengers were not happy campers. While doing their maintenance, the aircraft mechanics had discovered that the backup hydraulic pump had a seal leak. Replacing it set departure back by an hour. The bigger of the two passengers, who was beginning to resemble a gorilla in the pilot's mind, was breathing out all manner of fire and threats. When asked, however, whether he would choose to fly in an aircraft that would reach its destination safely, or in one that might not, gorilla man had grudgingly conceded that perhaps fixing a broken hydraulic system was a good idea.

Once his flight plan had been entered into the autopilot the pilot engaged it and leaned back with his hands behind his head, still smiling. After fifteen years as a commercial pilot, he still could not believe he got *paid* for flying! What a job!

****

Captain Dan Daniels stopped by his young intelligence officer's desk on the way out the door. Daniels didn't normally work on Saturdays, but everyone on the base was preparing for the annual inspection by the big brass and he had too many loose ends to leave for Monday.

"Jesse, what's the story on your Siberian fisherman? I've got your report on my desk, but give me the punch line."

"Well, Captain, he's alive—which is good. The chopper pilot didn't think he'd make it. Just a few hours ago he woke up for the first time. He speaks English and claims that he was kayaking from the Alaskan mainland to Shishmaret, which is on a small barrier island halfway between Kotzebue and Little Diomede. The storm came up and blew him out to sea."

"Is he lying, or did we just spend several millions of the taxpayers' money and nearly risk an international incident over an errant boater?"

"Oh, he's lying for sure, Captain. For one thing, the wind would have blown him east—back to the Alaska mainland—not west, out to sea. The real giveaway, of course, is all the activity of the Soviets trying to snatch him. However, at the moment it serves our purposes to 'believe' his tale. It gives us political cover, especially since the Sovs have already registered a complaint at Foggy Bottom. They're angry that we grabbed their prize. For the time being we can simply tell them what he is telling us: 'it was a boating accident and prompt action by the US Navy saved the man's life.'"

"I authorized a squad of MPs, as you asked. After going to all the trouble to pick him up, we don't want this guy to get away from us. Are they keeping close tabs on him, Jesse?"

"Yes, sir. I had them in the air immediately upon your authorization, and they got to the hospital only one hour after our 'fisherman' did. In order to avoid local gossip, I told the ensign commanding the squad to relax their posture. They are going to be out of uniform, sir, and will not advertise themselves as military police. None of them, including the ensign, knows anything about the military circumstances of the rescue. All we've told the guard detail is that he is a foreign national, and since the Navy rescued him it's the Navy's job to watch him. I've got so many lies sprinkled around, sir, I hope I remember what is true and what isn't."

"That's one of the challenges of working in intelligence, son. Goes with the territory. How about local law enforcement?"

"I've managed to keep both them and the Immigration and Naturalization Service in the dark. Other than the chopper pilot and crew and the Kotzebue medical staff, no one besides the Russians is even aware there was a sea rescue. If our luck holds, we'll be able to transport him here in the morning without anyone in Kotzebue ever knowing what really happened. Hopefully Ivan won't be able to stir up any trouble before then. They can guess where we took him based on the chopper's flight path. I expect the May tracked him all the way to Kotzebue, so they've got to know where he is. I'll feel a lot better when he's safe and sound here at Adak."

"Good job, Jesse. Keep me informed. I feel as though we just hit the piñata and got showered with candy. I'll be interested to find out who this guy really is. By the way, what have we done for Global Petroleum's rescue crew? They really bailed us out on this one."

"Yes, sir, I've been thinking about that. Two days from now we will have a *Spruance*-class destroyer operating near their oil platform doing some sea trials. Is there any way you could talk the commanding officer into having his Seahawk run a case of California's best merlot over to George MacDonald, the chopper pilot?"

"Merlot? Jesse, a chopper pilot on an oil rig is probably going to prefer a keg of beer!"

"No, sir, I've done some checking. Mr. Lincoln, the GPEG veep, says that according to scuttlebutt MacDonald prefers a good wine."

"That a fact? Okay, I'll see what I can do, Jesse."

****

By five in the afternoon Jake had showered and eaten several meals. Hospital staff had given him a standard interview regarding his medical history. He passed himself off as "John Meeker," an escapee from the Silicon Valley grind. Jake spun a tale of being a recluse living on the Seward Peninsula. When the interview was done the hospital staff was completely convinced of his fabrication and informed him that he would be ready for release the following day.

In the meantime Kelly was pretending to be physically weak. When standing he clung to objects or people for support, and he made a point of shuffling gingerly and slowly when he moved. No one observing him would think him capable of vigorous action, much less escape.

Truth be told, Kelly didn't need to act. With movement had come intense burning pain in his hands and feet. The attending nurse assured him that he would suffer no long-term damage from his exposure and that the burning sensation would subside over the next several days. After he had complained loudly about the pain, lamenting that it would surely keep him awake, the doctor had provided him with a small paper cup of prescription pills to help him sleep and alleviate the painful symptoms.

As the doctor left the room, Jake smiled to himself. He didn't need the pills, but they were his ticket past the man guarding his door.

****

The pilot thumbed his communications radio to 123.6 MHz, the tower frequency of the Ralph Wien Memorial Airport, and requested landing clearance. After receiving permission from the tower, he banked gracefully onto the final approach for runway 26. It was 2030 hours, local time, and the sun was low on the horizon far to the south. There was not a hint of turbulence nor even a crosswind. It was a picture-perfect late September Alaskan dusk. The Learjet's wheels gently touched down on the runway, provoking another silly grin from the pilot and a snide remark from his copilot.

Little commercial traffic found its way to the Kotzebue Airport. It was mostly used by general aviation and air taxi service. Consequently the same structure serviced both commercial and general aviation passengers, and airport service facilities such as the tower were manned after hours only when expecting an inbound flight.

Following the tower's instructions, the pilot taxied to his assigned parking spot and unbuckled, turning shutdown procedures over to his copilot. Exiting the cockpit, he opened the hatch and put the stairs down. Devoe and Banks were waiting impatiently to leave the cabin.

"Gentlemen, welcome to Kotzebue. I trust your flight was comfortable. I hope you will be able to salvage your meeting," said the pilot.

Banks just grunted at him, Devoe said nothing, and the two passengers turned to descend the steps to the tarmac.

The pilot called after them, "Mr. Thompson, your employer has secured the aircraft through ten o'clock tomorrow morning. As I have another charter tomorrow afternoon in this aircraft, take-off time is eight o'clock. Please be here by seven thirty."

"Mr. Thompson" was already striding across the tarmac, ignoring him. Devoe ran to follow, and tossed over his shoulder, "We'll be here."

****

Banks looked disgusted. "There's no taxi, no ground transportation at all!" he complained.

They were standing at the edge of the tarmac. Nothing was there other than a parking area, a small metal building that served as the passenger facility, and the tower. The passenger building was locked, the tower lights were out, and the parking lot had only two cars in it. Disappearing into the distance were a set of taillights. Devoe guessed that they belonged to the control tower operator.

"Look, Fred," Jason said. He was pointing to a sign at the parking lot exit which displayed the international hospital symbol: a big, blue "H." Underneath was a small mileage marker: "0.6 miles" and an arrow that pointed to the right.

"Well, at least that's helpful—we can just walk. Grab the gear and let's move."

****

His hospital room was around the corner from the main hall and could not be directly observed from the nurse's station. The short stub of a hall had two more rooms on it, both empty, and the stairway door at the end of it. It could not have been better situated for Jake's plans.

Because "Mr. Meeker's" condition was rapidly improving the nurses didn't check on him frequently. As the night hour grew later they would check on him less. This, too, would be helpful. Getting out of the building was not going to be difficult, he decided.

The hard part would present itself once he had escaped the hospital. There was nowhere to hide. He could see from his second floor window that the town was small, flat, and featureless. There were no trees anywhere in sight. Once out of the hospital his every move could be observed.

Compounding this difficulty was another problem common to every small town: information traveled fast. In a town this size everyone probably knew by midmorning what everyone else had eaten for breakfast. Strangers would be noticed, remembered, and talked about. For this reason his escape would have to take place after dark: the night would help to cloak his actions.

Another great challenge had to do with travel. His intended destination was Anchorage but he had no means to get there other than walking. When he did get there money would be a problem. Once in Anchorage he would somehow ease back into the Air Force's consciousness on his own terms. He was not sure how, but he could figure that out later. *One prob-*

lem at a time.

For now, he needed to get a look at a map. He also required warm clothing, boots, and other gear. Speed was of the essence. He needed to safely establish contact with someone in the Air Force before Chernikov's clandestine operatives ruined his credibility. Otherwise, the Soviet spy who had penetrated the Air Force would ensure that it would be impossible for him to share what he knew of Chernikov's kidnapping operation.

****

"How would they know if we made the hit before midnight," Jason whined. "Couldn't we just scratch him in the morning, and tell 'em we took him out tonight?"

Fred Banks was very alert to his surroundings. Whenever he went out on a job it was as though he grew a sixth sense. As they walked along the road with a cold breeze wafting off the sea to their left, the assassin was scanning the terrain for possible hiding places and watching for other traffic, especially foot traffic. He did not care to be seen, particularly up close. This job was going to be tough: strangers stand out in a small town. Banks knew they were going to have to limit contact with the locals. That meant no meals and no staying at a local hotel, if there even was one. Jason's question stirred him out of his thoughts, and he looked hard at the weasel-faced man.

"They'll know—trust me. Jason, if you ever want to collect your Social Security don't even think about crossing our employers. They play hardball and they play for keeps. I don't know who we are working for but sometimes I get the sense they know as much or more about *our* activities as they do about our targets. If we screw up—they know it. If we lie— they know it. Gives me the creeps every time I deal with these guys. Let's just get the job done tonight."

"You realize, Fred, this town probably rolled up the carpet an hour ago," Jason persisted. "If we don't go for it now we probably won't get a meal *or* a room tonight."

"We'll just have to risk that. This job pays too well to

worry about dinner. If you need to, just take tomorrow off when we get back to Anchorage. Besides, we can't afford to be seen up close; someone could conceivably identify us later."

It was now 2045, local time. The temperature was hovering around forty degrees though it felt colder with the light breeze off the water. Following the signs to the hospital they walked down Shore Avenue and turned right onto Kodiak Airport Road. Turning left onto 5th Avenue, the two spotted the hospital several hundred yards down on the right. Dusk was slowly descending and lights were beginning to wink on around the little town.

Kotzebue is about thirty-five miles north of the Arctic Circle. It's surrounded on three sides by water with a large pond on the remaining side. No trees grow there, just shrubs and willows, with profuse wildflowers covering the terrain in summer and early fall. The town is tiny: around three thousand people call it home year-round.

Fred cursed. There was nowhere to hide, nowhere even to get out of sight. They had no place to change into different clothes, unless they somehow managed to get a room. But that would leave a trail a blind man could follow. Fred had been successful in this occupation precisely because he left behind no trace of his presence. He wasn't about to start leaving a trail now. He cursed again as he remembered that Jason had mistakenly left the disguise bag in Anchorage.

"Okay, Jason, look: we've got to find a base of operations where we'll be unobserved. We can't start anything anyway until it's good and dark. So let's split up and meet back at this intersection at 2130 hours. Look for an empty house, an old shack, even an abandoned car we could use to change clothes and get our gear together. You head north several blocks and then walk east until you hit the end of the town. I'll walk past the hospital and check out the town east of it."

****

"How long have you lived in this town, ma'am? If I was guessin', I'd say that you aren't from these parts. In fact, I'd guess you were from Texas."

The nurse was checking his vital signs and didn't respond until she had finished the blood pressure reading. "Is it that obvious?" she laughed as she folded the cuff. "I am from Dallas. I've been working in Kotzebue for about four years. I love it here."

"What keeps you here, ma'am? From this window there doesn't seem to be much to this town."

"No, there's not much here, Mr. Meeker, if you're looking for entertainment or nightlife. In fact, there's none of that here. But if you love black night skies, the Northern Lights, low-hanging fog on the water in the morning, or tundra carpeted in wildflowers, this is the place to be."

"You make it sound poetic. Is it really that pretty?"

"Oh, much more than I could describe. The Bible says, 'The heavens are telling of the glory of God; And their expanse is declaring the work of His hands.' I never really understood that verse until I moved here. This is a glorious place! The winters are very rough but they have their own beauty, too. And we all pull together. The community draws much closer in the winter and everyone helps everyone else. In four years I've made closer friends here than I ever had in my twenty years in Dallas. Sure, you miss a hot summer day from time to time, and our summers here are short. But all in all it's home to me now. I can't imagine ever leaving."

"How do folks get here? I came in a helicopter and wasn't in a condition to look out the window. Is there a major highway that comes here?"

She laughed again, and said, "The only way to Kotzebue is by water or air. In the summer, the tundra fields to our south are too boggy to travel. In the winter when things freeze over we can drive to neighboring villages, but there's no way to go far—you wouldn't have enough fuel with the great distances involved. So aircraft or boats are the only practical way of getting around if you have more than a few miles to go."

"Where is the airport?"

"About a twenty-five minute walk to our southwest."

Jake moved a hand to sweep his hair out of his eyes, and

involuntarily grimaced. Though his hands didn't sustain any permanent damage they were red and chafed, and the aftereffect of hypothermia and near-frostbite left them very painful.

The nurse saw his expression and reassured him, "That pain will begin to subside in twelve to twenty-four hours. Don't hesitate to take the pain killer the doctor prescribed, if you need it. That's what's in this small paper cup on your tray. They'll also help you sleep."

"Yes, ma'am. Can I take four of them?"

"My goodness, no! Four wouldn't harm you, but they'd knock you out good. You'd probably sleep until tomorrow afternoon. Just take one every four hours, and if it really gets bad you may have two. But no more than two."

Jake smiled to the ceiling as she left the room. Another piece of the puzzle had fallen into place: now he knew how to dose the guard without endangering him.

****

The assassination had to appear as though the patient died of the complications of extreme exposure. It would be accomplished by pricking the man lightly with a pin the tip of which was covered in a powerful neurotoxin extracted from a small squid native to Indonesian waters. The pin was concealed in a working cigarette lighter.

The victim would immediately develop a heart arrhythmia. Cardiac arrest and then death would soon follow. While the poison was traceable, most pathologists in the States had never encountered it and would miss it completely in the autopsy. The cause of death was invariably listed as a heart attack.

"Okay, Jason, here's the plan. We need to know what room he is in and you're going to do that part. When I cased the hospital earlier, I saw a small incinerator shed in back. I'll wait there. After you find out where the target is, come out and tell me. Then wait for me while I do the hit. I don't think anyone will see us coming or going from that shed this time of night."

"Got it. I'll try the stairwells first and see if I can find him without being seen. If not I'll have to dream up a story to tell the duty nurse. Wish we had that disguise bag. I really don't like the possibility that someone could identify me later!"

"Quit worrying! This job will be a piece of cake. This time tomorrow you'll be home and quite a bit wealthier. We can get this done and be back here inside of an hour. It will go fine."

****

"Officer, could you find the nurse for me? The call button doesn't seem to be working." Jake made a show of holding onto the door frame and weaving ever so slightly.

"Sure, Mr. Meeker, I'll be glad to. You get yourself back in bed, sir. Do you need some help with that?" The concern on the man's face was genuine, and Jake felt a twinge of guilt. *Sorry, buddy, but you are going to sleep really well tonight.*

"Thanks, but no. I can manage."

The policeman disappeared around the corner, and Jake slipped over to the officer's chair and dropped four of the painkillers into his coffee cup. He was lying in bed when the nurse arrived a few minutes later.

"What can I do for you, Mr. Meeker?"

"Could you bring me a pitcher of water, ma'am? I'm really thirsty, and I'd like something close by during the night."

"Certainly. You showed some signs of dehydration when they brought you in yesterday. We actually had you on an IV until midday today. Your body probably still needs extra fluids. Is there anything else I can get you?"

"No, ma'am, I think that will do."

"How's the pain in your hands and feet?"

"Like fire, ma'am, it's awful. I'm about to take one of these pills and get some sleep."

"Okay, Mr. Meeker. I'll tell the girls down at the nursing station not to wake you. You need sleep more than you need us waking you with a blood pressure reading. We'll do a quick check on you at midnight and another at four a.m., but otherwise we'll let you sleep. I'll bring your water right back."

"Thanks, ma'am."

****

Devoe was in luck: the outer stairwell was unlocked. He entered as though he belonged there and knew exactly what he was doing. If anyone walking past had seen him, he would have appeared quite unremarkable.

A quick scan of the stairwell revealed no security cameras. The place was completely unmonitored. Jason peeked through the small window in the stairwell door leading to the hall. He was disappointed to find that the hall beyond revealed only three rooms before it turned to the left. Opening the door with infinite care, Jason crept into the hall and checked the rooms. All three were empty. He peered around the corner toward where he assumed the nurse's station would be. His luck was holding out: it was there all right but darkened and unmanned. *Must not be any patients on this part of the floor*, he thought.

****

Just one floor above Devoe, Kelly heard something hit the floor outside his room. Carefully he opened the door a crack and looked out. The guard had dropped his magazine and was struggling to remain awake and seated. Falcon got to him just before he fell out of his chair. Looking around to ensure he was unobserved, Jake dragged the unconscious guard into his room and shut the door.

****

Glancing furtively about, Jason Devoe walked quickly to the nurse's station. Another stroke of luck! A clipboard containing the patient roster was lying on the desk! Scanning it quickly, he saw only one admission for the previous day, a John Meeker in Room 202. Wiping his fingerprints off the clipboard, he carefully returned it and walked stealthily back to the stairwell. With delight he noticed that Room 102 was located in the small section of the hall that led to the stairway and could not be directly observed from the nurse's station. Room 202 must be right above and probably with an identical floor plan.

After climbing the stairs to the second floor, he peered through the window. Outside of Room 202 was an empty chair and a magazine on the floor next to it. *Must have been a family member sitting here during the day*, he thought to himself. Quietly opening the stairwell door, he got close enough to verify that "Meeker, John" was the name on the door. He withdrew silently and headed for the incinerator shed to tell Fred the good news. *Fred's right! This is an easy hit!*

****

Quickly undressing the unconscious guard, Jake then clothed the limp figure in his own blue hospital gown and gently placed the sleeping man in the hospital bed. Falcon turned him on his side toward the wall, and covered him with the blanket. With luck perhaps the nurse would not look too closely and wouldn't notice that she had a different patient until the morning shift. That would give him a head start.

Next he dressed himself in the man's uniform. The guard was probably two inches shorter and thirty pounds heavier so the uniform was tight in some places and baggy in others. Thankfully the shoes were perfect. It would have to do.

****

Fred Banks looked through the second floor stairwell window. For several moments he waited, just watching. No one returned to the chair or retrieved the magazine. Jason was right—there must have been a family member here during the day. There was absolutely no activity on this short section of the second-floor hallway.

No better time than the present, he thought to himself as he slipped into the hall. He'd make the hit and get out before anyone came. Slowly, quietly, he turned the handle on Room 202.

****

Major Kelly heard the stairwell door close softly. Someone was coming! He quickly crept to the darkened bathroom and pulled the door almost shut so that he could watch without being seen. Maybe the nurse would just look in and think it was him in the bed.

The door to his room opened slowly and quietly. *It was not the nurse!* A powerful-looking man stepped in, closing the door behind him. He wasn't dressed in hospital garb, nor was he clad as a policeman. The intruder padded over to the sleeper in the bed. The stealth with which the shadowy figure moved displayed strength and great menace.

The hackles on the back of Jake's neck stood up. He now understood that Chernikov's long arm reached even to Kotzebue. The man had not crept in so furtively just to check his vital signs. Kelly knew if he didn't act immediately, an innocent man was going to die!

Chapter 7

Saturday, September 26, 1987: 2215 local time
Kotzebue, Alaska

When Kelly had dressed in the guard's uniform he'd strapped on the man's firearm. *It's just about to become handy*, he observed. Never taking his eyes off the menacing figure hunched over the bed, Falcon silently pulled the service revolver out of its holster. Grasping it by the barrel, the major slowly opened the door of the bathroom.

The assassin reached into his pocket and withdrew something. He fiddled for a moment using both hands, but since his back was to Jake, Kelly was unable to see what he was doing. The thug then reached toward the guard's neck. In his hand was an item with a metallic gleam.

Now or never, the major thought. He brought the butt of the gun down hard on the assassin's head, just behind his left ear. The man crumpled and something clattered to the floor.

That was too close for comfort, he thought. He checked to make sure the door was shut, then switched on the light. Jake searched the floor and found an old-fashioned Zippo lighter lying under the bed. The outer casing had been removed, and a sharp pin protruded from the bottom. The casing was still clutched in the assassin's other hand. *Some sort of poison must be on the pin*, Jake guessed. He placed the lighter and casing on the tray table, and looked with disgust at the unconscious figure on the floor.

"Buddy, you are a pain in the neck," Falcon grumbled. "You're messing up my plans, big time. I've half a notion to stick you with your own pin and just be done with you. Unfortunately for me and luckily for you, you probably know something useful, so I'll let you live." The unmoving figure on the floor didn't reply.

Falcon rolled the large man onto his stomach, and dragged him to the far corner of the empty bed next to the one that had been his own. Taking the guard's handcuffs, he cuffed the assassin's left arm to his right ankle, both pulled behind his back, with the cuff chain threaded through one of the bed rails.

"You might be able to move, you sorry son of a jackal, but not without making an awful racket." He searched the unconscious assassin's pockets and struck pay dirt. The man had fifteen hundred dollars in cash on him. "Obviously the wages of sin," murmured Kelly as he stuffed the cash into his own pocket. A driver's license identified the would-be killer as George Thompson of Anchorage. *Probably an alias.*

****

It was a chilly, dark midnight when Major Kelly slipped silently from the hospital and began trotting toward the airport. He'd left a note addressed to "To Whom It May Concern" under the lighter, testifying as to what he had observed and instructing the finder to turn Thompson over to the FBI for questioning, and warning them not to touch the lighter.

As he jogged gingerly on feet not quite recovered from his bout with hypothermia, he took inventory. He had clothes that didn't fit, shoes that did, a relatively warm coat, and a pocket full of cash. He was back in America and at the moment he was free. The Soviets apparently knew where he was, but he'd survived their first attempt to assassinate him. All things considered, it was going well, Falcon decided.

The Kotzebue airfield was dark and deserted when Kelly arrived. Stars glistened overhead in the black sky. The haunting cry of a loon floated over the nearby marsh. He could hear the timeless crash of the surf upon the beach, several hundred yards away. Something primal stirred in his soul. Even with all else that he had to think about, he was unable to ignore the beauty of the cold, dark landscape. *No wonder that nurse fell in love with this place*, he thought to himself, *I could, too.*

Jake prowled around in the darkness trying to locate an unlocked aircraft. He quickly realized that nearly all of the smaller ones were unlocked. Unfortunately, the sleek Lear sitting on the tarmac was locked tight.

He climbed into the cockpit of a white Mooney 20J. Rocking the master switch to the "ON" position, he was delighted to see the fuel gauges indicate full. Evidently the owner refueled whenever he landed to reduce the problem of condensation in the fuel tanks. Shutting off the master switch, he stepped back out and did a quick pre-flight around the aircraft, removing the tie-downs and the wheel chocks before reentering the cockpit.

Several minutes later he'd charted a flight to a small airfield near Anchorage. His destination was about five hundred miles away—three hours in a Mooney. With luck he'd land in the early morning gloom and leave the aircraft parked before anyone was stirring.

The four-cylinder Lycoming engine eagerly roared to life when he turned the starter switch. As he taxied out to the runway, Jake cringed at the noise of the engine. *So much for a quiet escape! Half the town must hear this racket.* Sixty seconds later he was airborne, leaving behind a handful of lights and the quiet beauty that was Kotzebue.

****

The pockets of the guard had revealed that he was with a military police detachment from Adak Naval Air Station. Jake was surprised by that. Although the man had been wearing a uniform it was not that of the military police. Kelly surmised that the MP detail was intended to look like some sort of private security. *Another puzzle.*

Falcon began assembling the pieces of data, trying to arrive at an understanding of the rescue. Apparently elements of the US Navy were involved, probably from Adak NAS. The rescue must have been contested by the Soviets. The hospital staff had no clue as to his true identity, and Kelly expected that the Navy was just as mystified. But his thin cover story as "John Meeker" couldn't last long, not now, anyway.

The attempted murder would cause the authorities to fingerprint the hospital room. As soon as some sharp detective thought to submit the prints to the military databases, rather than just the NCIC criminal database, Kelly would be identified as Jacob Kelly, a "missing and presumed dead" USAF major. Air Force intelligence would then get involved, raising the stakes for everybody. Chernikov would doubtless find out, and it would result in a new race to kill, capture, or discredit him.

With the current state of affairs, the threat axis between the Soviet general and the American major was precisely opposite from what it had been. As long as Jake had been contained within the taiga of Siberia, the long arm of General Chernikov had been a lethal threat to him. But now that he was on US soil, Jake himself—and the information he possessed regarding the GRU's scientist-kidnapping scheme—was a grave threat to not only Chernikov but the USSR itself. If Falcon could tell his story it had the potential to wreak catastrophic damage on the Soviet Union diplomatically, politically, possibly even militarily. Orchestrated by an official organ of the Soviet government, the kidnappings and subsequent interrogations could be easily construed as acts of war. Most of the targets were from NATO countries, countries whose combined military and economic strength outweighed the Warsaw Pact. Even if war was averted, the damage to Soviet prestige and diplomacy would be huge. All of which meant that Jake could expect the Soviet military and intelligence network to pull out all the stops to prevent him from telling what he knew.

Doubtless, Chernikov had expected to recapture him soon after his escape. When that didn't happen he'd deployed more and more assets until thousands of soldiers were searching for him. Failing again, he tried to recover him from the waters of the Bering Strait. Having been unsuccessful there, an assassination was attempted. Another miss. Now, Jake surmised, the Sovs would change tactics. Unable to prevent his return, they would probably seek to destroy his credibility in a delicate ballet of deception. Subtle "evidence" would be dribbled out, through channels the Americans would be sure to intercept.

The particulars weren't hard for Jake to imagine. Chernikov would plant intelligence fingering Jake as a traitor who'd delivered an F-16, complete with prototype super-secret avionics, to Mother Russia. The shootdown and his escape from Siberia would be presented as faked, a stage-managed effort of the GRU to reinsert him back into the Air Force where he could continue to feed valuable intelligence to his Russian handlers. If the Soviets' disinformation was successful, Jake's truthful tale about his kidnapping would be seen by interrogators as a lie designed to mask his defection and treachery.

Falcon cursed, and clenched his teeth. Contrived communication traffic about him was probably already floating about the Soviet intelligence network, the fabricators knowing it would be eventually intercepted by the US. No one on the planet was as skilled at disinformation campaigns as the Soviets. If they played their cards right the Air Force would think he had been a Soviet plant from the very beginning. Chernikov would also leak the fact that he was fluent in Russian, and that fact alone could condemn him.

When Jake had first applied to the Air Force Academy, he'd hidden the fact that he could speak the Russian language. The young man had heard rumors that Russian speakers were cherry-picked and placed into intelligence positions, and Jake wanted to fly fighters, not spy satellites.

His maternal grandparents had fled Stalin's Russia. As a boy Jake spent every summer with them. They'd never learned to speak English, and so between his mother and his grandparents he'd gained fluency in the language of the world's other superpower. His grandparents had died during his senior year in high school, and he'd convinced his mother to lie about his ability in the Russian language. As a consequence, when Air Force investigators were vetting his application to the academy they never found out.

While his ability to speak Russian had been one of the two factors that had enabled him to make good his escape from the Soviet Union, now it would present almost irrefutable evidence of treachery. He would be arrested and tried as a spy! *Match, set, game: score one for the Union of Soviet Socialist Re-*

publics.

Jake glumly realized that he had escaped one manhunt only to land in another. His trials had not ended—they'd only just begun. He'd be lucky if he didn't spend the rest of his life in a military prison.

"Wonderful," he grumbled, as he trimmed the Mooney for straight and level flight.

****

The partial moon hung over the horizon to the northeast on the clear, late September night, providing just enough illumination to distinguish land from sky. Directly overhead Polaris presided over the darkened landscape. Falcon made a visual check of all points of the compass and verified that, other than the receding pinpricks of light from Kotzebue, it was just the stars and him. Looking over the dark forest, watching the misting tendrils of fog that marked lakes and creeks, he felt a vast, tranquil quietness—quietness not even the roaring engine could overcome. "Magnificent desolation," he murmured, using the poetic phrase Buzz Aldrin had employed to describe the lunar landscape. It fit the scene scrolling slowly below him.

Immersed in such beauty, he wondered at the poverty of the Chernikovs of the world. Chernikov looked but did not see. He seemed to be all lust and ambition but was bereft of an appreciation for the majestic beauty of the Siberian taiga that surrounded him. For Chernikov, Jake thought, the isolated glory of the wilderness was merely useful—functional—nothing more than a remote place where he could carry out his schemes without the inconvenience of supervision.

While Falcon had a distinctly sensitive eye for the beauty of the forest, it never occurred to him to ask *why* it was beautiful, as opposed to ugly. *Why* should it be perceived as beautiful? What was there in the human creature that universally recognized such artistry? Jake feasted on the splendor of the cosmos, but it never entered his mind to be *grateful* for it. Gratefulness focuses the heart on the Giver, and for Jacob

Kelly there was no Giver.

The major finished trimming out the aircraft. He had filed no flight plan, something one generally avoided when stealing an airplane. Consequently he was flying less than five hundred feet above the dark, timbered terrain. The low altitude would keep him out of the jurisdiction of the Air Traffic Control (ATC) system and its attendant meddling. He powered down his IFF transponder, but tuned the comm radio to Anchorage Center so that he would be warned if his aircraft was spotted. Engaging the autopilot, he relaxed and weighed the positive features of his situation. His brief stay in the hospital had allowed him to catch up on much-needed sleep and to recharge his fatigued body's depleted reserves. The effects of his dangerous bout with hypothermia were beginning to diminish. He was free and not under surveillance. For the first time in a year he was able to stand down for a few minutes and not be overcome with weariness.

He considered what he had accomplished. Major Jacob Kelly, USAF, had escaped from a Soviet detention facility in the middle of Siberia. He had eluded the Soviet Army while fleeing across the thousands of kilometers that measured Siberia and the Chukchi Peninsula. Much of the distance he'd traveled by stealing or hijacking transport of one form or another. At every turn he faced disciplined Soviet troops who'd been ordered to capture him dead or alive. Some of those who had hunted him did so at the cost of their own lives. He had endured the worst of conditions and the cruel Siberian winter, surviving trials by land, sea, and air. And he had prevailed. Falcon grinned into the night—it had been a wild ride, and whatever still faced him at least he was back in the good old US of A.

Kelly checked his instruments and listened to some ATC chatter on the radio. It didn't concern him—it was directed at a Boeing 747 headed for LA. Returning to his own thoughts, he congratulated himself for safely returning to the United States. It was a remarkable feat of escape and survival. Now he faced a whole new set of challenges and dangers. There would be another manhunt and, complicating matters, he'd broken American law by stealing an aircraft. Now he had to find a place he could hide out while he figured out who he could talk to. He had to tell his story and get *someone* to believe him. *It's going to be tough, but I'll make it.*

Chapter 8

Sunday, September 27, 1987: 0345 local time
Kotzebue, Alaska

The bleary-eyed sailor of the Navy military police detail trudged slowly across the street to the hospital. He hated the 0400 watch duty—you woke from your deepest sleep to a darkened world and the most boring duty in the world, guarding some meaningless outpost from an attack that would never come. It was as though you were staying up all night to watch the hands of a clock crawl through their laborious circular paths. Tonight—or rather, this morning—it was even worse! He was baby-sitting some civilian who was sleeping sweetly in a warm bed. *There had better be coffee*, he grumbled to himself.

He reached the second floor of the Kotzebue Hospital only to find the chair outside the patient's room empty. *That's odd: where's the MP I'm supposed to relieve?* The Navy frowned on those who left their post without being relieved by a replacement. Could get a man bumped down several grades. Wondering what to do, he slipped open the door of the patient's room just enough to see a man snoring in the nearest hospital bed.

The sleepy sailor saw what he expected to. Had he looked more closely he would have also observed a motionless figure on the floor by the second bed. Fred Burn's unconscious state had ebbed into natural sleep.

Closing the door carefully, the MP decided to wait ten minutes or so: if his buddy did not show up he would have to report him absent from his post.

****

Chernikov finished throwing his clothes in his traveling bag and took one last look around the apartment. He needed to get back to Tara. Patrikeyev had turned the Kelly file over to a trustworthy friend in the GRU's fifth directorate, which dealt with military intelligence activities. Chernikov still bore responsibility for any damage done by the pilot, but now that the American major had returned to the US, he was out of Chernikov's operational purview. In a limited sense, then, he was no longer Chernikov's problem. But if GRU agents or contractors didn't manage to silence him, the consequences of the Kelly fiasco would fall upon him. It still had the potential to become a failure from which Chernikov's career would never recover. Depending on the damage wrought, it could cost him his life.

Stopping short of the door, he decided to fix one last cup of coffee before leaving. He needed to think about his next moves, and this place might be his only chance for solitude for the next thirty-six hours or so. Getting the coffee started, he set his bag and briefcase by the front door, and returned to the kitchen table to consider his situation and the changes that had become necessary due to Major Kelly's successful escape.

The memory of the smoke rising from the burnt-out generator building and the death toll among his troops caused the general's blood to boil, and he slammed his fist down on the kitchen table in renewed rage. The American had made a mockery of his whole command, escaping with little more than his wits and the help of a fellow prisoner. *Well, at least we retrieved Dr. Simmons,* he consoled himself. *And Simmons has our physicists close to a breakthrough in the field of integrated circuit miniaturization. Funny, we keep running into walls under Simmon's direction. It's almost like the scientist is toying with us. Perhaps I need to schedule him for a little more aggressive interrogation.*

The worst part was that Major Kelly had not only gotten away with an escape from Prison 87, but that he'd made good his escape entirely: he was now back in the US. At this point, his only possible revenge was to take the man's life or ruin it if murdering him proved impossible. Nikolai rebuked himself: revenge was never wise and rarely successful as motive for intelligence operations. *Nyet, but I don't have to worry about that. Somebody else is handling the hit and they won't be compromised by a lust for revenge. So I can just sit back and enjoy it.*

General Chernikov considered his latest orders. Though he remained in control of Project *Krasnyy Voskhod* he'd been directed to move the whole camp. The Politburo was taking no chances of Kelly getting someone's ear and having the NSA park a satellite over Prison 87. So now there would be a Prison 88. Whereas the former complex was located forty-seven kilometers west of Tara, the new facility would be in a very remote location thirty-two kilometers north of Magadan. The former site would be completely dismantled and reforested (with fake trees) within two weeks. The scientists would be held at a temporary camp below Yakutsk while Prison 88 was under construction. Chernikov groaned—Magadan was over forty-three hundred kilometers east of Tara. Trips to Moscow would take much longer.

After leaving his meeting with General Patrikeyev, Chernikov had requisitioned an army engineering battalion to build the facility. He'd meet with their CO as soon as he flew to Magadan. Prison 88 would have improved security, a more resilient source of backup power, and firefighting equipment —all of which had been weaknesses exposed by Kelly's escape.

****

If all was tranquil in the cockpit of the Mooney as it floated through the starry ether, bedlam was about to descend on the quiet second floor of the hospital in Kotzebue.

"Nurse, have you seen the guard outside John Meeker's room? I was supposed to relieve him fifteen minutes ago, but there is no sign of him. I even looked in the room, and he wasn't there."

"Maybe he left just before you got here," offered the nurse. She was making entries on a patient's chart, and wasn't really paying attention.

"No, ma'am, he would not do that. He was on duty and

would never leave until being relieved. We are—" The serious young man caught himself before he identified himself and his buddy as military policemen. He had just remembered a detail from his briefing: they were not to identify themselves as MPs. Which fact explained why he was now dressed, not in his regulation uniform, but in trousers, shirt, and tie that could very easily pass for an Alaska State Trooper uniform to someone who didn't look too closely. It wasn't according to regulations, but neither was the chair outside the patient's room—MPs standing guard were supposed to *stand*. In fact, nothing about this curious little mission was by the book. He wanted to give that oddity some thought, but it would have to wait. First, where was the man he was supposed to relieve?

"Yes? What were you saying? *We are* . . . what?" The nurse put her clipboard down and looked at him with a slight smile, one eyebrow raised.

"Um, ah—I mean, I am—or I *was*—supposed to relieve him at four a.m."

"Yes, you did say that."

"Uh-huh, yes, ma'am. Well, where is he?" It didn't help his increasing consternation that he'd suddenly noticed the duty nurse had the kind of matter-of-fact beautiful looks that turned men's heads and caused the occasional auto accident. She was so—intimidating.

"I believe you have already asked that, too."

How come guys never rattle beautiful women? It's just not fair, he thought.

****

Chernikov stood at the window sipping his coffee, looking down at the street below. It was a beautiful September afternoon. About to turn away, he paused as a shiny Chaika 14 sedan, one of the flagship products of GAZ (the Gorky Automotive Factory) purred up to the curb and stopped. As Chernikov watched, two muscular men—characteristic bulges under their coats, a clear indication of a shoulder holster— jumped out of the front seat. While one scanned the street about them, the other held the door open for the occupant of the back seat. A frail figure emerged in careful slow movements, obviously held captive to arthritic pain.

I would recognize that painful gait anywhere, the general mused to himself, with a sinking heart. *I'll bet he is here to talk to me. If only I had left without stopping for coffee.*

Anatoly Geredin was a member of the Politburo, and one who had gotten there by ruining other men's careers. He was the chief spymaster of the KGB, but age and arthritis would soon retire him. Geredin was a bounty hunter, a head-hunter. He knew who was sleeping with whom, who had built their *dacha* with State materials, who had feathered their nest with State funds. He was ruthless, celibate as a monk, honest to a fault, and incontrovertibly committed to the State. There was no dirt to be had on Geredin. He could not be compromised, and thus he was a terror unleashed among his peers and those who had the misfortune to be beneath him in the Soviet political pecking order. The old man was not known to lose his temper, but that simply meant he could order executions in the same soft voice he used to order tea.

All turf was his turf. Geredin respected no bureaucratic or political boundaries, no established political relationships. Though Chernikov's own patron was the powerful and respected Patrikeyev, it wouldn't save him if Geredin had determined to bring him down.

For a brief moment Chernikov considered the possibility of taking the back stairwell to avoid the confrontation, but those thoughts collided with the firm knock at the door, and so were dashed.

****

"I can see that you are at a loss for words, doubtless because of the mystery of your colleague's whereabouts. Let's just go check Mr. Meeker's room, soldier. We'll start our search there."

Recovering somewhat, the young man managed to retort, "I'm not a soldier, I am a sailor. And I already checked the room. How did you know?"

"How did I know you had checked the room? You already told me that. You seem to have a problem repeating yourself," she teased with a smile as they rounded the corner headed for Room 202.

"Yes, ma'am! No, ma'am! I mean, how did you know that I'm in the military," he managed, woefully realizing that he'd just compromised a mission that now seemed to be somewhat of a sideshow anyway. *How can I, a member of the United States Navy—on US soil, no less—compromise a mission guarding an errant US civilian boater in a public hospital?* It seemed hopelessly silly.

"Well, first, no one around here who appears to be my own age calls me *ma'am.* That sort of formality pretty much pegs you. Secondly, only the military sits and walks as though they have a steel rod surgically implanted in their spine. And seeing as how you are too young to have had multiple careers, I deduced that you must be presently in Uncle Sam's employ."

"May I buy you dinner?" It seemed to him to be the only eminently sensible thing he had said in the entire exchange.

"It's 4 a.m. and I am on duty. So are you, if I am not mistaken."

Okay, maybe not so sensible. How about this?

"May I buy you breakfast?"

****

"*Dobryy dyen'*, Comrade Geredin! Come in, come in. May I get you some coffee?" Chernikov fought to retain a friendly, open composure. Any show of fear would be like bloody meat thrown to a ravenous wolf.

"*Nyet!* This is not a social call, General. I have no time for coffee. I simply wanted to see with my own eyes the man who threatens to make Mother Russia a laughingstock before the nations."

Careful, Nikolai. Don't let him goad you. Don't show him your throat, but don't show him your teeth, either.

"Comrade Geredin, that is not an accurate assessment of the situation. Please sit down, sir, and let me tell you what is being done as we speak." Chernikov made a show of pulling out a chair from the table, and gently motioning his aging visitor into it.

"Very well, Nikolai. Tell me your best lies. Dig your own grave." Much as he tried to avoid doing so, the elderly man's face displayed relief when he sat.

His mind racing, General Chernikov decided that his only tactical option short of suicide was to tell the truth. Taking a swallow of his coffee, he began.

"Comrade Geredin, I erred in underestimating my opponent. I also erred in not having adequate intelligence as to his background. Major Kelly is not only one of the top fighter pilots in the US Air Force, he has also received training in the special forces. The best guess is that he's been trained as a Combat Control Team operator. He also speaks fluent Russian. His dossier contained neither of these two important facts. He was able to stay one step ahead of my men, and made us look ridiculous and incompetent. He outwitted us at every turn. I had my best people directing the search, or so I thought. As it turns out, my best people would have been sufficient to recapture a fighter pilot even if he had been well trained in survival techniques, but they were inadequate when it came to recapturing a man of Major Kelly's caliber."

For a long moment Geredin remained silent, studying Chernikov's face. Finally he asked softly, "And what now, Comrade, are you doing? How are you going to stop this invincible man now that he is on his home soil? How are you going to stop him before he exposes your illegal operation before the world community?"

"Da, that is the problem, Comrade Geredin. I realize that far more than my career is now at stake. We have set two separate operations in motion. One is to use disinformation to discredit Kelly by leading the American intelligence services to believe that he is a spy working for us. His claims of capture and of our kidnapping operation will be seen as lies to get himself off the hook. The other operation is to eliminate him as quickly as possible. We intend to kill him, whether or not we are able to discredit him. It will look like an accident, untraceable." For all his efforts to remain calm, Chernikov was distressingly aware of beads of perspiration forming on his brow.

"General Chernikov, I think you should know my position in this entire sorry, sordid affair. I came to this apartment prepared to leave a corpse. I wouldn't bother to make it look like an accident—it would have appeared as it was, an execution." Geredin's tone was conversational, almost gentle.

Do not react, Nikolai, your life may depend on it, do not react! Say nothing!

"There are but two things that keep me from ordering your execution even right now. First, though it pains me to say it, your past experience with this adversary probably makes you most qualified to oversee his elimination. The Soviet Union cannot afford to have someone else repeat the same mistakes you have made. We cannot afford more on-the-job training.

"Second, you have been honest with me. This is a rare quality among functionaries at your level. It may be that you can learn from your mistakes. Perhaps you will be useful to the Party after all.

"His life for yours, General, his life for yours. I am sure this will provide you with sufficient motivation to succeed. And now, Comrade General, if you will excuse me I must get back to the office. There is much work to be done." With that, Geredin stood up with great difficulty.

"Of course, Comrade Geredin. I will do my best." Chernikov rose, and opened the front door for Geredin.

The old man stopped at the door. Too stiff to turn his head, he replied over his shoulder, "Your best, Chernikov, will not save you. Only success will."

****

Rolling her eyes at the nervous MP, the pretty nurse pushed open the door to Room 202. At first, all seemed well. In Mr. Meeker's bed was Mr. Meeker. There was no sign of the guard. She too, saw what she expected to see. Then the figure on the floor began to stir, groaning itself into consciousness. The nurse let out a small involuntary scream, and the MP jumped.

"Who is that?" she asked. She flipped the light switch and the darkened room was bathed in light, revealing a handcuffed man on the floor struggling to roll over and sit up.

"OWWW! WHAT THE . . . ? Where am I? HEY! What —? Wha—? OH, my HEAD, my head! What happened?" A stream of profanities poured from the large figure on the floor. He was confused and not fully aware, but already beginning to tug at the handcuffs. In a moment he would upset the bed on top of himself.

If the MP didn't know how to handle pretty women, he was quite competent with belligerent men. In fact, the more fuss Fred Banks made the more comfortable the MP began to feel.

"Relax, buddy, cool it! I'll get you out of those cuffs just as soon as I figure out why you're in them! Ma'am, would you check on Mr. Meeker and make sure he is okay? I am going to contact the watch detail officer. Something goofy is going on here." Picking up the phone, he dialed the number of the watch officer's room across the street in the hotel.

From the nurse behind him there was a quick intake of breath. "Oh, no! He's gone!" At that moment the sleepy watch officer answered his telephone in his room across the street.

"He's *dead*?" The MP whirled around to face her in disbelief. This entire operation was unraveling so fast he could not keep pace.

"Who is dead?" the NCO barked, causing the MP to flinch. The chief was not happy to be awakened at this hour, and he really didn't care for the way the conversation had started.

"No, no, that's not what I mean! He's fine. I mean he is alive, anyway. But it's not him!" replied the nurse, calmly taking the vital signs of the person in the bed.

"Not who?" the MP asked, irritated.

"WHO'S NOT WHO?" bellowed the chief into the

phone, picking up only one side of the conversation and completely in the dark about the situation anyway.

The nurse was checking the patient's wrist for the hospital's identification band, but found nothing. "This is not Mr. Meeker! I don't know who it is! Oh! I think it's your friend, isn't it?"

"GET ME OUT OF THESE HANDCUFFS!" shouted the man on the floor, now fully conscious.

The MP raised his voice, frustrated by the chaos, "I SAID RELAX, BUDDY! I'll get to you in a minute!"

No longer shouting, but in a tone easily heard by everyone in the room, a voice coming out of the telephone handset said angrily, "Mister, I am going to bust your butt down so far you can't see the bottom unless you are looking straight up! You don't *ever* talk to me that way! Not in this Navy! Not in any navy! Do I make myself clear?"

The figure on the floor snickered quietly, "W*hoa*, son, you are in trouble!"

The MP looked at the phone as though he was not quite sure how it got into his hand, slowly put it to his ear, and said meekly, "Oh, no sir! Sir, I am so sorry, sir. I was not speaking to you. Please, chief, can you *please* come over to the hospital immediately? We have an extremely serious situation here: we have one unknown belligerent civilian in handcuffs, Seaman Jaworski is lying unconscious in the bed, and I have no idea where Mr. Meeker is!"

****

At just the time his handiwork in Room 202 was being discovered, Jake eased the Mooney onto a small gravel strip near Cottonwood Lake, about thirty miles northeast of Anchorage. It appeared to belong to a flying club of some sort, judging by the number of small planes parked in the grass along the edges. He taxied over to an empty slot and shut the aircraft systems down. After attaching the tie-downs and chocks, he grabbed a rag out of the back of the aircraft, dampened it with aviation fuel, and rubbed down every part of the aircraft he had touched, trying to obliterate finger prints.

Within ten minutes he was trotting down a gravel road headed for Anchorage. Other than one barking dog at a darkened cabin at the far end of the landing strip, it seemed no one was aware of his arrival.

Chapter 9

Monday, September 28, 1987: 1640 local time
Kotzebue, Alaska

"Dr. Carrock, I wish I could answer your questions. I understand you have a right to know what's going on in your hospital, and I know you have a genuine interest in your patients. And there are potential liability issues as well. But please, sir, try to appreciate our position also. First, *we* don't really know what is going on in this situation. For reasons I cannot get into, this has the potential to escalate into an international incident. It's also remotely possible that there are national security issues involved. I simply do not know." Agent Stewart wearily rubbed his fingers through his silver-gray hair, and sighed, "There's just too much we don't understand surrounding this entire episode. Our superiors are asking us the same questions you are, and we frankly don't know what to say them, either. Please, give us time to sort out the facts."

Because the murder attempt had happened in a civilian hospital, local, state, and federal authorities became involved, along with the Navy. Jim Stewart was a Special Agent with the FBI, working out of the Seattle office in the Foreign Counterintelligence Division. Trim, fit, and tall, he'd passed fifty three years ago. Although he'd taken practically every course offered by the FBI in field operations, intelligence, and counterintelligence, he had no desire to advance in his career beyond his present position as a senior field agent. He loved his job. Field work and analysis were his passions; administration and management were a bore to be avoided at all costs.

Lieutenant Commander Jesse Pierce watched the frustrated face of Doctor Stephen Carrock slowly relax. The slightly built administrator of the Kotzebue Hospital had initially been very angry when Pierce and Stewart stonewalled him regarding their thoughts about the elusive Mr. Meeker and the confusing series of events that had surrounded the mysterious patient.

"Of course, Agent Stewart. Forgive me. This is just all so strange and out of character for a community like Kotzebue. I imagine you're feeling as I do when family members insist on knowing whether their loved one will survive cancer. Some things only God knows." Carrock got up and shut the door of the hospital's small conference room and returned to the table. "Okay, I will cooperate in any way I can. If I get questions from the press or the staff, tell me what I can tell them. Please remember that we are a small community with an excellent grapevine. Gossip travels faster than the flu in Kotzebue."

Stewart nodded briskly and replied, "Thank you, Doctor. I greatly appreciate your cooperation and help. First of all, please lock Room 202 until further notice. No one should have access to that room except for members of the investigative team. Secondly, please instruct the hospital staff that we are being close-mouthed in order to avoid jeopardizing the legal case we are building against the would-be murderer. You may hint that it involves a personal vendetta for a financial debt. You may say that the rescue was unrelated: Mr. Meeker's kayak was blown off course, the assailant heard of his weakened condition and chose this as the best time to even the score. The guard was posted simply as a routine precaution until we had a positive ID on Meeker and had established his citizenship." Stewart looked over at Ed Devlin of the Alaska Bureau of Investigations (ABI) and asked, "Sound okay to you, Ed?"

"Yep. The talk is already going around town. I heard some of the locals discuss it over lunch. This story will drain some of the mystery out of the incident and shouldn't raise any eyebrows in press rooms around the state. Unless it's a really slow news day I doubt any media outlets will even be interested. The expense of sending a news team up here will outweigh the news value of the story." Devlin was a special investigator in the ABI and a former Marine with a graduate degree in

Business Management from Notre Dame.

For a variety of reasons, not least of which was the proximity to the USSR and the long coastline, Alaska was a prime target for infiltration by foreign intelligence operatives. Ed Devlin and Jim Stewart had worked together on several cases in which the lines between domestic criminality and foreign espionage became blurred. Out of their professional relationship a close friendship had developed. Although both were members of elite investigative units in their respective agencies, the business cards and ID badges for each man simply said, "Investigator."

Dr. Carrock stood. "Fine. I'll talk to the staff tomorrow morning. Room 202 will be sealed as part of a crime scene investigation. Now, gentlemen, if you will excuse me I have other duties to attend to. You are welcome to use this conference room today; it has not been scheduled for anything else. I'll instruct my secretary to see that you men are undisturbed."

"We are grateful, Doctor, for your help."

After Dr. Carrock had left the room the three men looked at each other, relief evident on their faces.

"Thanks for bailing me out of that one, Agent Stewart. I was afraid this whole thing was going to blow up in my face," said Pierce as he exhaled slowly.

Captain Daniels had instructed Jesse Pierce to get the FBI's Foreign Counterintelligence Division involved as soon as the MP detail had reported news of Meeker's disappearance. Pierce made an early-morning, 0600 phone call to the FBI's Seattle office, and by 0700 Stewart was on an agency Learjet bound for Kotzebue. While in the air Stewart contacted his friend, Ed Devlin of the Alaska State Troopers ABI unit. The three men landed in Kotzebue within an hour of each other.

After spending the day trying to assemble the facts, Pierce had briefed the Kotzebue Hospital administrator, Dr. Stephen Carrock. Carrock was furious when he learned that the guard detail was not a contingent of Alaska State Troopers (as Pierce had allowed him to assume) but US Naval Military Police. He had accused Pierce of recklessly placing his patients and employees in danger.

Carrock was correct. Pierce's interest and attention had been wrapped around the rescue effort. Other than providing for minimal security he had not anticipated an aggressive Soviet response on US soil after the rescue. Pierce's stumbling response to the angry administrator made it clear to Agent Stewart that the young lieutenant commander was out of his league in dealing with outraged civilians. The FBI agent's calm apology and reassurances mollified Carrock, and kept the incident from escalating out of control.

Once Carrock had left the room Stewart turned to Pierce and demanded, "Okay, swabbie, now that it's just us you can spill the beans! I don't think you've shared everything with me and I can't help you unless *I* know what's really going on. You told me enough this morning to make me skip out on a plate of the finest eggs and hash browns I've had in months, blow my agency budget on a Lear, endure a dressing down from Florence Nightingale's brother out there," Stewart gestured towards the door through which Carrock had recently departed, "and drag my buddy Ed here away from his important work counting the paper clips in his office. I pulled *your* bacon out of the fire with the good doctor, *so you owe me*, big time! What *is* going on here?"

"Agent Stewart, I appreciate you being here and all you have already done, but I'll have to check with my commanding offi—"

"Cut the crap, Pierce. Danny Daniels and I have known each other since college. I cleared the running lanes for him so he could get a big name scoring touchdowns for Georgia State. He has already spoken to me and asked me if I could babysit his favorite intelligence officer. I am specifically instructed to keep you out of trouble. For crying out loud, the Navy ought to be paying me for this!"

Ed Devlin, a smirk on his face, was enjoying watching the young officer under fire.

"I'm sorry, Agent Stewart, but I don't know you from Adam. Until I've been given the green light by my commanding officer, I'm afraid I can't tell you anything. I don't even know what kind of security clearance you have," Jesse stated firmly.

"Unless they have started giving lieutenant commanders security clearances somewhere between that of admirals and God, you don't have the clearance that both Ed and I have," Stewart responded coolly. "I may have to shoot you just for letting you see my ID badge."

"Very funny. I cannot tell you anything more until I am authorized to do so."

"Son, here is a telephone. Call your boss and ask him. Ed and I will be across the street getting supper. We'll save you a seat." With that, Stewart and Devlin left the conference room, shutting the door behind them.

****

"Sir, what can I tell Agent Stewart and his friend Ed Devlin? Devlin is with the Alaska State Troopers Bureau of Investigation. I've told them very little, and some of what I told them is not actually true."

Daniels smiled as he put his feet up on his desk. His young intelligence officer was doing well so far. "Well, Jesse, what did Stewart tell you?"

"He said you sent him to babysit me. Said that his security clearance was higher than mine. He got frustrated when I wanted to check in with you. He's an impatient guy—it was pretty intimidating."

"And what do you think, Jesse? Are you going to tell him what you know?"

"No, sir, I am not. Not unless I am assured by you that he has adequate clearance. I'm not going to take his word for it, no matter who he works for or how convincing he is."

"You'll do, Jesse. Congratulations, you passed the test."

"I beg your pardon, sir?"

"Jesse, I told Jim to try to intimidate you into telling him the story. I wanted to see how you handled the pressure. Jim told me he was going to bring Ed Devlin in on this, and I've already checked him out. They both have a Top Secret clearance from the Defense Security Service, as well as the Office of Personnel Management. Devlin's office occasionally handles attempted infiltrations and espionage by Soviet agents at Alaskan high tech operations, which is how he got a military clearance. I am officially telling you that they both have a 'need to know.' You can share any detail relating to this case with them. If you have a question regarding a particular detail in the future, check back with me for authorization to share it with them."

****

Devlin and Stewart were both snickering when Jesse slid into the booth with them. He smiled but said nothing and picked up the menu. The other two waited in silence for a minute or so, and then looked at each other and shrugged.

"Well," Stewart finally asked Pierce, "did you call him?"

"Call who?"

"Your boss, pinhead, who do you think I am talking about?"

"Sure, James Bond, I called him. He said he'd never heard of you or Devlin."

"Screw him! Look, sonny, if you want any help with this mess you're going to have to talk."

"Listen, guys," Devlin said flatly as he put down his fork, "I appreciate the friendly banter and all, but I didn't come to this little backwater for the entertainment. Pierce, I would appreciate it if you would cut to the chase. I *would* like to know what I am doing here."

Stewart cast a glance at Ed, then looked back at Jesse. "No sense of humor," he explained. "I put up with this sourpuss merely because I feel sorry for him. I'm afraid he'll die someday of a paper cut if someone is not keeping tabs on him. If I didn't let him tag around with me he'd never have any fun." Devlin looked at Stewart with an expression of disgust, shook his head, and resumed eating.

****

The mirror was fogged up, so he wiped it down with a towel. It felt good to get a hot shower, use a real toilet, and sleep in a comfortable bed. Examining his face, Kelly shaved off the beard that had grown and then trimmed his hair, trying to change his appearance so he would not be recognized. As far as he knew the hospital had not taken a photograph of him, but they would doubtless release a verbal description.

Since landing the Mooney early that morning he'd walked and hitchhiked into Anchorage, purchased needed clothes and supplies, and rented a room at a boarding house under the name "William Jones." There had been nothing on the news about him. It seemed that he had bought a little more time.

He finished dressing and sat on the bed in the small room. *What next?* he asked himself. He found his thoughts drifting back to Galina Toporova. "Someday soon I'll return for you, Galya. But I must deal with General Chernikov first. As long as he lives I will be in danger, as will anyone connected with me," Jacob spoke to the empty room. "So when all this gets straightened out I will return to the USSR, find Chernikov—and kill him."

He felt better just by speaking the words out loud. It had been so long since he had been able to have a real conversation with someone who really knew him. Though he had not been able to spend much time with Galya, he knew that she understood him and loved him. And he was in love with her; she was everything he wanted in a companion: a woman with a mind and a heart of her own who had somehow given her heart to him.

He stood up and put on his new coat and went out into the night in search of a good steak dinner and a strong cup of coffee, compliments of the hapless thug in Kotzebue. He grinned at the thought his meal was funded by Chernikov and decided to get the best steak on the menu. Finding a path through his dilemma would have to wait just a little longer, tonight he was going to relax and enjoy himself.

****

"We put enough assets on the scene to discourage them and managed to fish him out of the drink before Ivan did. But it was close. Apparently they experienced some sort of breakdown on one of their missile boats about five klicks short of the kayak. Otherwise Meeker would be enjoying the sweet comforts of Soviet hospitality tonight."

Devlin listened intently, chewing on a delicious piece of salmon, but offering no comments.

"Why do you think they wanted him?" Stewart asked. "Who is he, really?"

"No idea. But I can tell you this: for about a year our intel guys have been picking up indications of a massive manhunt that began in central Siberia, and moved slowly east and then northeast. The guys at Langley even started an office pool, betting on who or what the target was. Some of the theories are that he is a Soviet defector trying to escape to America, or perhaps an American agent who was compromised and managed to stay one step ahead of Russkies. It's a good bet as far as I'm concerned that Meeker, or whoever he really is, was their target. When I first heard of the efforts the Sovs were putting forth to recover the boater, I knew that he would be someone we would want as much—or more—than they did." Jesse Pierce attacked his salad vigorously—it had been a long day and he'd eaten nothing but a donut, and that had been at 0500 that morning.

"Exactly how many months," Stewart asked thoughtfully, "have they been searching?"

"About ten," Pierce mumbled, mouth full of tomato and lettuce.

"Then he would have had to survive in the Siberian wilderness during the winter. Either he is one heck of a survivalist, or he had help. But I seriously doubt a mere intelligence agent would survive such an ordeal. A special ops guy trained in arctic survival—maybe. A spook—no way. Some of the coldest inhabited parts of the planet are found in Siberia."

"You guys are both missing something," Devlin said mysteriously.

"Okay, genius, you've decided to abandon your private

thoughts and join the conversation? What exactly have you figured out while you were demolishing that plate of salmon?" Stewart prodded a little harder, "Do you really think a mere pencil pusher is qualified to add something to the thoughts of us real secret agent men? What exactly have we missed, Great One?"

"Stewart, you are clearly delusional," Devlin retorted, rolling his eyes. The trooper stuffed a roll into his mouth and managed to speak around it, "The kayak is what you missed."

"No, we did not miss it. In fact, pretty boy here tells us that they retrieved the kayak. So?"

"Typical FBI guy—you have all the facts but no clue as to what to do with them. You federales couldn't find the bad guys if they left a trail of shell casings to their hideout." Devlin grinned, satisfied with himself.

"Okay, Ed. I give. What are we overlooking?"

"Simply this: a trek across Siberia, ending in a kayak voyage to Alaska."

"Yes, we know all that."

"Think, dimwit! Don't you know your anthropology? Someone has reproduced an ancient, Native American migration! We are looking for an Indian. Not only an Indian, but one who knows the ways of the ancients. To survive a Siberian winter and to handle a kayak in blue water at this latitude, the man would have to be an expert. Whatever else our man *may be*, he *is* an Indian—trained in the ways of the ancients."

The two men stared at the trooper, considering his words. Pierce was the first to respond. "Okay, that makes sense. But how does it help us?"

Stewart interrupted, "Hold on a minute, Navy." He turned to Devlin and continued, "Ed, you're making a boatload of assumptions, there. For example, you're assuming that he survived the winter in the Siberian wilderness. Perhaps he actually spent it in a city. And as far as his route goes, it could be the troops searching for him were pushing him, the same way hunters will sometimes drive deer. They might have been *driving* him further north into Siberia, expecting the winter to kill him if they could not capture him. And the extreme north has no hiding places, making it much easier to corral him. It could be that the northeastern route was the only one open to him. And the kayak could have been a last resort, an act of desperation.

"He might be an Indian. But he could just as easily not be. I'll say this, you get points for trying. Keep working on it long enough, Ed, and one day you might turn out to be a decent agent." Stewart winked at Pierce.

****

Galina Toporova disembarked from United flight 1172 in San Francisco, carrying a small handbag and nothing else. The one suitcase she had checked was lost when she changed planes in Tokyo. Sooner or later it would catch up with her. She had several US dollars in her purse, a scrap of paper with an address on it, and a big grin on her face. So this was Jacob Kelly's America!

Galina had been captured by the KGB in the spring. Expecting to be tortured for everything she knew about Major Jacob Kelly, instead she had been handled with some deference. After several days of mild interrogation, she'd been released. An elderly KGB officer had escorted her to the train station in Khabarovsk. The man explained that, rather than being interrogated and executed for her collusion with Kelly, she was being sent into exile in China, as a result of his intervention. Though he never offered his own name, he did relate to the young woman that her father had saved his life years ago, and now he was returning the favor in honor of her father's memory.

Galina had gotten a job in the underground Chinese economy outside of Beijing as a translator and an English teacher. One of her pupils had been a young boy from a wealthy family who was well connected to the Chinese underground and the Chinese Presbyterian Church. The family patriarch doted on Galya, as did the rest of the family. For some reason she never could explain they seemed to delight in showering favors on her. Unknown to her, the family's second child—a girl—had been forcibly taken from their home when she was four and drowned by a zealous local official. Chinese population growth policy did not permit a second child if it was a girl. In Galya's face the family saw features of their little baby girl, especially in her eyes. All the love they had wanted to pour into their daughter now flowed to Galina Toporova. Galya's vibrancy and love of life even in the midst of her own hardships had given them a view of what their daughter might have been, had she lived.

After she had been teaching their son for three months, Chinese policy toward Soviet émigrés changed. Soviet citizens were being deported back over the border. When her benefactors learned that she would be arrested upon her return to the Soviet Union they quickly made their own plans. They drove her to an airport and handed her a suitcase, airline tickets, and a small amount of American money. A well-placed bribe enabled her to board the aircraft without a visa.

"You are our daughter, Galya," the father had said. "We will not lose you again. Go to America and make a place for us there. When we can, we will join you. Leave word here." Tearfully, he pressed a piece of paper into her hand, then turned and walked away. On the paper was the address of a Chinese Presbyterian Church in San Francisco. The man had written in English "They will help you."

She walked down the concourse to the International Arrivals Customs desk, took a deep breath, and declared what she had practiced and dreamed about for months: "I am a Soviet refugee. I fled my country under the threat of arrest. I am asking for asylum."

****

"Jesse, every investigation needs one guy at the top of it. Until it becomes clear what this is all about, I think you ought to coordinate things. That way, if things blow up in our faces Ed's and my careers will not be affected. Don't you agree, Ed?" Stewart looked over at Ed Devlin and raised his eyebrows.

"Absolutely! You be the fall guy, and we'll help. With the investigation, I mean." Devlin nodded in mock seriousness.

"Oh brother! I know I'm going to regret that I ever met you clowns. All right, then. Ed, why don't you get your ABI people to do the crime scene investigation, and handle the confinement and interrogation of the suspect who was handcuffed to the bed? Jim, you get your people to do an analysis of the lighter and every other bit of hard evidence that Ed uncovers. You can also handle the search for Meeker; I suppose he could have fled the state. I'll take care of the international intelligence side and overall coordination. Let's see, today is Monday—we'll meet again at Adak on Friday at noon. How does that sound?"

Devlin responded, "I don't mind the assignments, but flying to Adak is not in my departmental budget. We don't have any six hundred dollar toilet seats in the Alaska Bureau of Investigation, not like you Navy guys. Can't afford them. Can we meet somewhere else, maybe within walking distance?"

"Oh please! Ed, if your state would just stop building baby-changing stations for the caribou along the pipeline, you'd be awash in cash," Jim Stewart sniffed. "I'll see if I can line up the FBI office in Anchorage as a meeting place. How's that, Jesse?"

"It will work fine, Jim. I'll just fly my six hundred dollar toilet seat over on Friday. Maybe as I am riding my stretch limo from the airport, I'll give you a ride if I see you walking along the road, Ed."

Chapter 10

Tuesday, September 29, 1987: 1020 local time
Kotzebue, Alaska

"Do you have any rooms available?"

Charlie, the clerk at the imaginatively named "Kotzebue Hotel and Restaurant," looked over the counter at the stranger. His old, wrinkled face crinkled into a friendly smile. "Sure do, stranger. Got three left. We been awful busy the last three, four days. Not sure why. Huntin' season ain't for awhile yet and fishin' season's winding down. Why, if it weren't for the fact that some folks checked out early this morning, I wouldn't have any rooms available. Now, when we run outta rooms, I check 'round with the folks in the town to find out who's got a spare bed. We can't have folks left outside, too cold around these parts."

It was obvious the old-timer was just freshening to the conversation, so when he paused to take a breath, Devoe interrupted, "I'll take one for three days."

"That's fifty dollars a night, plus tax, plus phone calls. If you want a good deal, stranger, for sixty-five dollars a night you get all your meals included here at the restaurant. Choice of the menu. Now, Bonnie—she's our cook, you see—well, she makes the best baked salmon you ever did wrap your teeth around. My wife—bless her soul, she's been gone for three years now—she tried for years to wrangle that recipe—"

"I'll take it. What's the room number?" The last thing Devoe wanted was to be trapped in a one-on-one with a talkative native. He really needed to get out of sight; chatting at the front desk was not exactly what he had in mind. Jason knew as soon as he left the lobby he would be the main course of the gabby old man's gossip.

Charlie looked hurt, but being sixty-seven years old he was

by now accustomed to people cutting short his windy conversations. "Not so fast, stranger. First I need your name and home address. Most hotels want your car's license number, make, and model, but since no one drives to Kotzebue, we don't ask 'em for that. Then I'm gonna wanna see the color of your cash, 'cause credit don't go down well up here, 'less of course it's a credit card. Well, that ain't 'xactly true, because we do extend credit to local folks, but you ain't local. Never seen you before. Where you from? And where's your luggage?"

Jason removed a roll of bills from his pocket and began peeling off what he needed for the room and board. He briefly considered asking the clerk what it would cost to check in under the table without providing all the required information, but immediately discarded the thought. The attempt would cause too much suspicion, and the old coot was probably incorruptible anyway. Somehow he had to lay low and figure out how to get back to Anchorage without attracting attention.

When Fred had not returned from the hospital on Saturday night, Jason realized that something had gone wrong with the hit. He decided against catching the Lear back to Anchorage on Sunday morning by himself, because the airport would be crawling with cops. If Banks had been discovered there would be inbound flights of law enforcement officials, and Jason could not afford to cross paths with them. So he remained hidden in the back of the incinerator shed. He couldn't simply appear at the hotel later Sunday morning either, it would make it too easy to connect him with the attempted murder. So he had decided to hide out until Tuesday, when there should be enough regular traffic in and out of the airport that he'd be mistaken for someone who'd just flown in. Until all the Alaska State Troopers had left town, he would lay low at the hotel and then find a way back to Anchorage.

"I left my luggage at the airport. Wasn't sure at first if I wanted to stay here, but I've decided I do. I'm on vacation, and I hate schedules and plans, so I'm just wandering around Alaska enjoying its small towns." Devoe signed the register with the name "Ralph Goodwin" and wrote a fictitious address from Houston, Texas.

"Okay, Mr. Goodwin, you're number seven on the second floor. Just go up those stairs and all the way to the end of the hall. The restaurant is open from six in the morning until one in the afternoon. It reopens for dinner at six in the evening, closes at nine. Ain't got enough business to stay open all day."

Glad to get away from the talkative clerk, Jason took the key and went up the stairs. He was headed for the shower, the restaurant, and the bed, in that order. Planning how to get out of Dodge could wait a little longer.

****

Ed Devlin sat in the restaurant stirring his coffee and pondering the penciled notes on his legal pad. So far—other than the note left in Room 202 by the elusive John Meeker and the physical evidence they had gathered from the room—they had very little information.

The one bright spot was that the crime had been attempted in Kotzebue, and not by a resident. Since access in and out of the town was limited to boat or aircraft it should be a fairly simple matter to locate where the suspect had come from. And, in fact, the airport had a record of a Learjet landing around eight-thirty p.m. on Saturday night disembarking two passengers. The Lear had originated from Anchorage. Devlin had troopers looking into it but they had not yet reported back.

For the hundredth time he studied the text of the note found in Room 202.

> *Nurse, this room is a crime scene. Please contact the police. The man in the bed is the guard. He is okay, I just dropped a few sleeping pills in his coffee. The man on the floor was, I believe, intending to kill me. I don't know why. He was carrying $1500 in cash, small bills. I have appropriated that for my use. Make sure the Zippo is analyzed, and don't touch the sharp pin at its base. It's probably got poison on it.*

Devlin reviewed what he knew so far—which was precious little. Meeker had been picked up in the Strait out of a kayak, suffering extreme hypothermia. The Soviets had contested the rescue. There was an almost certain connection between the man in the kayak and a search in Siberia conducted by the Soviet military, which Pierce had mentioned yesterday. Devlin was personally convinced that Meeker was a Native American from one tribe or another. And finally, some time late Saturday night or early Sunday morning, Meeker vanished without a trace from the hospital leaving no clues other than the contents of Room 202. *Not much to go on*, the weary trooper acknowledged to himself.

In two hours Ed would convene the last planned meeting in Kotzebue of the ABI troopers assigned to the case. The residents had been interviewed and the entire community scoured. The basic police work was complete. If nothing else turned up his team of investigators would return to Anchorage and continue working the case from there.

****

General Chernikov sat in his office at the Prison 87 compound. It was late: other than the watch detail his staff had gone to bed. He had returned to his command in a foul mood, caused partly by the orders to move the facility and partly by the lingering memory of Geredin's threatening visit. The KGB officer's dispassionate dismissal of all he'd accomplished was both infuriating and unfair. Geredin was attempting to discredit the GRU and Chernikov was a handy foil.

Chernikov slopped another shot of vodka into his glass and stared at the clear, fiery liquid. *Careful, Niko. The answer is not in that bottle. Let it play out. You will be vindicated. Kelly was nothing more than an unfortunate anomaly.*

Escape had never been considered a genuine possibility. *It never should have been possible!* Chernikov thought bitterly. Kelly's plan had been assembled of the perfect storm of vulnerabilities. *Neither the fundamental design of the camp nor my administration was at fault.* As he replayed the event in his mind, Chernikov realized the American had instead capitalized on human nature itself: susceptibility to deception, overconfidence, the inclination to bully a person viewed as weak, a tendency to violate orders when those orders were considered trivial, the habit of making assumptions, and the confusion inherent in fast-moving events.

There was one thing that could have stopped the escape in its tracks, the general thought. *The passageway between the cellblock side of the compound and the administrative side should have been secured with a guard post. It was not thought necessary because of the machine-gun towers, and because no one considered that a prisoner might obtain a guard's uniform.* He made a note to correct that flaw in Prison 88.

****

Jake possessed the instincts of a hunted animal. He was confident that his identity and location were unknown. How long he could remain anonymous was uncertain. He figured that in less than a week the authorities would know exactly who he was, and as soon as the Mooney was discovered they would know he was in the Anchorage area. A physical description would be posted and a search would commence.

Kelly's resources would not permit much mobility, especially since he had no driver's license. It had taken an extra fifty to persuade the desk clerk to overlook that little fact. He would have to remain in Anchorage until he made the necessary contacts to reenter the military orbit. He hoped to do that before the search became uncomfortably close.

Jake re-examined his dilemma. The Air Force had been compromised in at least one place, and maybe more. If the Soviets did as he expected and mounted a disinformation campaign designed to pre-emptively discredit him, it would be aimed primarily at Air Force intelligence. So contacting the Air Force was a non-starter.

But who could he contact? It must be someone he could entrust with his life, who also had the intelligence connections to defend him against the Soviets' prevarication. It would also be useful if this person had the connections to investigate Jake's suspicions regarding a Soviet plant in the Air Force.

Every time Falcon turned these thoughts over in his mind, one name kept coming up—William Jensen. Bill had been a friend of the family since Jake's high school days. Jensen's relationship with the Kelly family had come about by chance, although Jensen himself always referred to it as "providential." The Kelly family owned a summer cabin near the Snake River. Jake and his dad had been fly-fishing on a tributary of the Snake River one beautiful August day, and had rounded a bend of the river just in time to see another fisherman slip on the rocks. The unfortunate man struck his head on a knot of granite and fell unconscious into the river. The Kellys pulled him to safety, and took him to their cabin. He stayed long enough to recover from the nasty blow on the head. From that chance—or providential—encounter a friendship developed. Within two years, the families had grown very close. Jake's dad and Jensen discovered a common love of the outdoors, books, military history, and a host of other topics. It was as though the two men had grown up as twins.

When Jacob's father had died in '83, Bill had flown back from a vacation in Australia to be at the funeral. His calm presence and unqualified assistance in every area had been a great comfort to the family. Since those days the young man had grown as close to Jensen as his dad had been, and the friendship had continued, even beyond the death of Jake's mother in '84.

Jensen was an independently wealthy academic, teaching occasionally at Georgetown University. His area of specialty was International Relations. His knowledge of countries around the Pacific Rim in particular was encyclopedic. He was a fascinating conversationalist, and had become something of a surrogate father for Jake.

Falcon had begun to suspect that Bill Jensen was perhaps a little more than he claimed to be, and when Jake noticed a pattern between political crises in the Pacific Rim nations and Jensen's "vacations," his suspicion seemed justified. Though Jensen probably would have labeled it "providential" had Jacob confronted him, the times and locations were too aligned to be coincidental. Once Jake had connected the dots with the "vacations," other points began to stand out. The Jensens were frequent guests at the Kelly home in Pennsylvania back when Clancy and Galina Kelly were still alive. As the two families had grown close, the Jensens were given the run of the house and treated as family members. On more than one occasion, Jake had awoken in the night or early morning only to hear Bill's low voice on the phone in his dad's library. Between Jensen's straight-backed military bearing, his exhaustive knowledge of military hardware, firearms, and international politics, the late-night phone calls, and the "vacations," Jacob had concluded that William Jensen was probably working in some US intelligence agency. Although he had never spoken of his suspicions, over the years they had only grown stronger.

Stepping out of his room, Jacob Kelly began walking into the city. He continued at a brisk pace for an hour and a half, and figured he would be about four miles from his hotel. Finding a pay phone, he dialed Jensen's number.

****

"Okay, what do we have?" ABI Special Investigator Ed Devlin stared sourly at his few scribbled notes, already knowing the answer to his question.

"Not much, Ed," replied agent Tim Treadwell. "We know that one aircraft—a Lear—landed the night of the incident. Based on the airport operations log, we know that an air transport company out of Anchorage operates that aircraft. An agent is working that angle. We also have the fingerprints and other bits of evidence from the hospital room. But that's about it.

"I tried to interview the suspect in custody but he refuses to talk. He's demanding a lawyer, which will have to wait until we get him back to Anchorage. We did find identification in his pockets identifying him as 'George Thompson' of Anchorage." Treadwell sat back in the booth, and shrugged his shoulders. He had hoped the suspect would talk before the legal beagles became involved, but it was not to be.

"Where is Sandy? Why isn't he here?" Devlin was irritated. He didn't want to arrive at his Friday meeting in Anchorage without having some significant information to share.

"He's on the phone with our Anchorage office to see if they have the scoop on that air transport company. He'll be here in just a minute."

"This is ridiculous!" declared Devlin, as he slapped his notepad down on the table. "We have one guy—who was *supposed* to be in a fairly weakened condition, by the way—who's completely evaporated from a town you cannot leave except by boat or plane. But he doesn't leave without first drugging a big MP and lifting him into bed, then cold-cocking Mr. Thompson, who is built like a prize-fighter. And to make matters worse, *he* leaves a note with instructions for *us*—a very considerate man, evidently," Ed said dryly, "before disappearing without a trace." Devlin played with his empty coffee cup, clenching his jaw in frustration.

"Hey, guys, listen to this!" Sandy, the youngest member of the investigative team, raced in and sat down at the table with barely contained excitement. "I've just gotten two great pieces of information that might untangle some of our riddles!"

"Well, spill the beans! Don't keep me in suspense," Ed grouched.

"I just saw Doctor Carrock. This is his day off. He keeps an aircraft down at the airstrip, and went down this morning to do a little flying. Guess what? His airplane is gone. Nowhere to be found!"

Ed sat up straight. "That is interesting, Sandy. Perhaps our Mr. Meeker knows how to handle more than kayaks. Wonder if he hot-wired the airplane?"

"No, Carrock told me he leaves the keys in the plane when it is parked at Kotzebue. He says everyone does. Nobody steals airplanes up here. Not only that, he tops off his tanks when he is done with a flight. So his aircraft would have been fully fueled, unlocked, and ready to roll."

"Well, now we have a felony theft on the part of Mr. Meeker. We probably also have a bushel of FAA regulations that have been broken. I'll get the legal team in Anchorage working on all that. What else do you have, Sandy?"

"Anchorage found the air transport company and interviewed the pilots. They gave us complete physical descriptions of two men they flew up here on short notice Saturday evening. The men, a 'George Thompson' and a 'Carl Stafford', indicated they were coming to Kotzebue to close a valuable oil contract. They were supposed to fly back from here on Sunday morning. They never showed up at the airport, and the company they were representing doesn't exist."

"*Two* men, Sandy?"

"Yep. You see, Ed, it might not be Mr. Meeker that copped the airplane. It could have been the Stafford character. What this means is that *someone is still in Kotzebue*. Unless Meeker and the other guy left together, which is doubtful. I suppose it could be some sort of major double-cross, but I doubt that, too. We probably have one guy stranded up here, trying to get home." Sandy sat back with a look of triumph on his face.

Ed grinned at him, "You know, Sandy? You actually might make an investigator yet! Okay, let's have the physical descriptions."

As Sandy went through the descriptions it was clear that one obviously matched George Thompson. The other was sufficiently detailed for a forensic artist to sketch the face.

Just then, Tim leaned in close and whispered, "Don't turn around, guys. A man just walked in and took a booth in that dark corner. He matches the other description, right down to the beady eyes and hawk nose. I think our man just delivered himself to us on a platter."

****

"Hello, this is Jensen."

The clipped, abrupt voice brought a world of memories flooding back to Jake's mind. It was the first time he had spoken to any American friend in a year and a half, and Bill Jensen was a particularly dear friend.

"Mr. Jensen, this is Jacob Kelly."

"Is this some kind of joke? Jacob Kelly went missing, presumed dead, more than a year ago. Some sort of aircraft accident." The voice on the other end of the line was wary and irritated.

"Mr. Jensen, not everything is as it seems. It is me, and I was involved in an aircraft incident, but it was an *incident* not an *accident*. And I am alive and well, but I really need your help."

"If this is really Jake Kelly, I'll do anything to help you—you know that. But I want to verify whether I'm really talking to Major Jacob Kelly. He was flying secret, experimental fighters when I last spoke him. And then he disappeared. He was formally listed as missing, presumed dead. How do I know that you are really Jake Kelly?"

"Do you remember the day you first met my father and me?"

"Of course. I'll never forget it. Your dad saved my life. But many people know about that incident. I wrote it up in an article for *Field and Stream*."

"Do you remember we took you into my dad's library once we had bandaged your head?"

"Yes, Jake, I do," replied Jensen. He thought he knew where this conversation was going.

"Do you remember the first book you pulled off his bookshelf?"

"Yes."

"It was *War and Peace* by Tolstoy. I remember because Dad and I had been discussing it just the day before. It was one of Dad's favorite books."

"So it *is* you, Jake! I just had to make sure," Jensen said gently.

"Mr. Jensen, you *should* verify my identity every time I call you. Please be sure to! Never accept the same verification twice. And if you contact me, you must verify your identity to me. Mr. Jensen, I'm over my head—way, way over my head—in something very dangerous and I need your help. I know that you have, uh, other work than teaching at Georgetown University. The people at your, uh, other business would be interested in what I have to say."

There was a brief silence on the other end of the line. "No, Jake, I am afraid you are mistaken. I'm a professor, that's all."

Kelly ignored the remark. "Listen, Mr. Jensen. I don't know how to do this. I cannot give you a phone number you can use to contact me because I don't know if your line is secure. You can't give me a phone number to call you on for exactly the same reason. But it is critical to your, uh, teaching, that I tell you what I have learned."

More silence on the other end. For a moment, Jake was afraid that the connection had been broken. Then the professor spoke up again, "Jake, are you in trouble? What sort of trouble are you in?"

"Yes and no. I have committed no crime, but something has happened to me that accounts for the aircraft incident you mentioned. In the events surrounding that incident I learned some information that is critical to, uh, well, some others, and I have to tell someone."

"Jake, why don't you call your commanding officer in the Air Force? They know you, you were well respected there." Jensen was speaking softly, calmly, as he might to an agitated child.

"Mr. Jensen, that is precisely who I *cannot* call and for reasons which are—are—much larger than myself! Sir, I *must* be able to speak with you in confidence. It is *absolutely* essential."

"Jacob, I'll have to trust you on this, although you're mistaken about whatever you think I can do for you. Let's see, how can we do this? . . . Okay, I think I know. Do you remember the trip that you, your dad, and I took when your rod tip snapped on the first day of fishing?"

"Oh, do I ever! I was heartbroken! Worst fishing trip of my life." It had been a trip to fish for brown trout in the Arkansas River during the summer of Jake's junior year of college. When he'd been breaking down his rod to put it in the jeep, the rod joint stuck. As he was trying to force it apart, it came loose suddenly and the momentum carried the rod tip into the side of the car, snapping it. For the next day all he could do was watch his dad and Bill Jensen as they pulled in trout.

"Okay, do you remember the gas station where we stopped to fix the flat on your dad's jeep on the way home?"

"Yes."

"Well, it's still there. I will leave a message there for you to-night. Call them tomorrow morning. Will you be able to find their number?"

"Yes, sir, that won't be a problem. And please, Mr. Jensen, please do not let *anyone* know that you have spoken to me, or that I am alive."

"Okay, Jake. I will be very careful. We'll talk again soon."

Bill Jensen replaced the phone in its cradle, and stared out the window for a moment. In his heart he was overjoyed that the son of his (now deceased) best friend was still alive. Jacob was as dear to him as his own son.

But what sort of difficulty had Jake been involved with, and was it related to the loss of an F-16 filled with experi-mental avionics? What had him scared and on the run—un-willing to take the chance that Jensen's own phone was being monitored? Where had he been the last fourteen months? And where had Jacob *ever* gotten the crazy notion that he, Jensen, was anything but a faculty member of Georgetown University?

Coming out of the depth of his thoughts, Jensen shook his head to clear it of all the questions. He'd have to look into this matter in the morning. He had no classes at Georgetown University tomorrow, so he'd be able to stop in at his other of-fice—the one at Langley. As the special assistant to the Deputy Director for Operations at the CIA, he should be able to get most any information he would need.

****

"Tim, I want you to walk out the front door. Be casual. Once you get on the porch, be ready to stop the suspect if he makes a run for it. I'll head for the restrooms, and seal off the back exit from the hall there. Sandy, you make the arrest. I don't expect our Mr. Stafford will give you much trouble, as the prospects for escaping from Kotzebue are approximately the same as getting off a small island without a boat."

One by one the men casually left their table without so much as a glance at the suspect. They had worked as a team before, and had confidence in one another. When the other two had taken up their positions, Sandy got up, tossed a tip of several dollars on the table, and then walked over to Stafford's table.

"Mr. Stafford? May I speak with you?"

Devoe stiffened. This was trouble. The man standing in front of his table had used the alias which he had given to the air transport company, not the alias under which he had checked into the hotel. No one in Kotzebue should know him by the name Stafford.

"Who's asking?" Devoe appraised the man in front of him with a cold stare.

"Special Agent Clark, Alaska Troopers Bureau of Investigations. I am going to have to detain you for questioning as a person of interest in an investigation into an attempted murder. Would you come with me, sir?"

"Sure, Officer. I have no idea what you're talking about, but I have nothing to hide." As Devoe slowly slid out of his booth, he furtively scanned the room. Other than an elderly couple eating breakfast and the gabby old clerk in the lobby, there was no one in sight.

Ed Devlin was peering around the corner of the darkened hallway at the rear exit. He knew that the suspect had not seen him. Unable to pick out the conversation above the clatter of dishes being washed in the kitchen, he observed as Stafford slid out of the booth. Devlin saw the man set his feet, subtly shifting his weight. Too late, Ed tried to call out a warning to Sandy.

Devoe turned toward the officer, but with his his feet spread in a fighting stance. Smiling suddenly to distract his opponent, from nowhere the heel of his right hand swept up, slamming Sandy Clark in the jaw and snapping his head back. Devoe followed up with a crashing left jab to the midsection.

Clark dropped, blood streaming from his mouth, doubled up and gasping for air.

Tim Treadwell—alerted by Devlin's shouted warning—raced through the front door, groping for his service revolver as he came. As fluidly as a dancer, Devoe pivoted on his right foot, raised his left knee, and snap-kicked Treadwell under the chin with his left foot. The agent collapsed to the floor, unconscious, his jaw broken.

In an effortless pirouette Devoe landed facing Ed Devlin. The thug assumed a relaxed but obviously lethal fighting stance. He faced an utterly calm man, pistol gripped in two hands, who had stayed out of range of his deadly hands and feet. Ed Devlin was an old professional and was not about to let this wildcat get the drop on him. For a moment no one spoke. Then the voice of the old desk clerk came from the lobby doorway, as cool as a cucumber: "I reckon, Mister Devlin, that you are in somewhat of a pickle, what with your boys there all neatly laid out on the floor. I s'pose you might appreciate a hand. Why don't I cover this young buck with my trusty old forty-five here, while you slap the cuffs on him?"

In surprise, both Devlin and Devoe turned their heads to view the old man who was standing in the doorway holding an ancient Colt .45 service pistol in a steady grip, covering Devoe. Charlie's friendly eyes had turned a glittering ice blue and he was all business.

Devlin shook his head. "Thank you, sir, but please put your gun away and let me handle this. I don't want anyone else getting hurt. Please let law enforcement handle this."

Devoe snickered, "Yeah, old man, put that thing away before you hurt yourself! I'm sure Roy Rogers here can handle me all by himself."

"Sonny, I was dispatching Germans 'afore you was born. Compared to them, you ain't nothin' more than a wannabe bad man. Sergeant Charlie Olson, 82nd Airborne, at your service. I made every combat drop during World War II that the 82nd made. I was at Salerno, Sicily, Normandy, Nijmegen, and the Ardennes. I reckon I know how to handle this here pistol safely. And right about now I'm just a little peeved at how you have treated my nice clean dining room. I wouldn't lose any sleep if I sent you on to your reward, pilgrim."

"Well, in that case, Sergeant, I'm glad you're on my side," Devlin chuckled, putting away his pistol and pulling out his handcuffs. "Why don't you keep Mr. Stafford covered while I get the cuffs on him?"

"Stafford? His name is Goodwin!"

"Actually, Charlie, I don't expect his real name is either Stafford or Goodwin. Now, I want to be able to talk to him, so, if he tries anything funny don't kill him, just shoot him right between the legs, right where it counts. That ought to get his attention. As long as he doesn't bleed to death, I should still be able to ask him questions."

Shifting the aim of his pistol, Charlie broke into a wicked grin. "I like your style, Officer."

Chapter 11

For the past twenty minutes Falcon had been sitting in his darkened hotel room studying the road outside. Satisfied he was not under surveillance, he left the room and began walking into the city. Several hours earlier he'd gone to a nearby pay phone and called the little garage in Hayden, Colorado. True to his word, Bill Jensen had left a phone number where Jake could contact him at 1530 hours, Eastern Standard Time, just thirty minutes from now.

****

Admiral John Bridger stared unseeingly at his empty coffee mug as he absently rotated the cup around and around. He was thinking about Ned Bascomb and the news the former SEAL commander had shared. *Can't believe he's turned to smuggling. I ought to try to get him back into the Navy. But he seems to enjoy what he's doing. That pirate,* he chuckled to himself, *I'll bet he's good at it. He was always good at anything he put his hand to.*

As the commanding officer of Navy Special Warfare Group One (NSWG One), Bridger had the necessary security clearance to look into the incident Ned had shared with him. Since then, he had used every spare moment considering how he might "accidentally discover" something that would allow him to verify Ned's story, but without putting Ned's life at risk, or that of his source.

A little research on accidents involving USAF aircraft had given him an excellent lead. On 10 July of 1986, an F-16 was lost over the Bering Sea during a pilot refresher flight. Bridger knew that anything listed as a "pilot refresher" could be just that, or it could be the secret flight test of an experimental aircraft or aircraft equipment. The aircraft had failed to return to Eielson AFB on schedule. No radio transmissions had been received and no emergency beacon had been detected. The aircraft had not been on radar at the time of the disappearance. A search along the axis of the last known flight path had revealed a small amount of floating detritus that could possibly indicate an aircraft crash. An Air Force major by the name of Jacob Kelly had piloted the lost aircraft. His body was never recovered.

Bridger had examined a copy of the findings of the Accident Investigation Board (AIB) as well as the notes of their primary meetings. The maintenance records on the jet were excellent, and the aircraft had been well maintained. Problems with the aircraft itself were therefore deemed unlikely. There was not any other hard data to provide the Board with a probable cause for the loss of the fighter and its pilot, and so like many inexplicable accidents involving aircraft, this one had been attributed to pilot error. According to the notes, the investigating Board didn't even discuss the curious fact that a debris field had been found, despite the fact that its presence was inconsistent with either a crash or a controlled ditching, in Bridger's experience.

There were several incomplete threads in the accident investigation troubling the admiral. One was an alternate opinion—contained in the meeting notes but not the final report—which had been considered but discarded as unlikely. One of the investigating officers had raised the possibility the aircraft had not in fact crashed, but that the pilot had defected with the airplane. Under this scenario the small floating debris field was disregarded. The minutes indicated that, after discussion, this interpretation of the data was rejected.

Another fact tugging at Bridger's mind was that a search aircraft *had* sighted some floating debris. Very little material in an F-16 floats, and what buoyant material there is, is completely encased in or attached to other parts that *do* sink. Consequently, an in-air explosion that shredded the aircraft—such as a shootdown—was the only scenario that could also account for the debris field.

The third piece of evidence that didn't fit the Board's conclusion of pilot error was the service record of the pilot. Kelly's flight and service record was beyond exemplary. All the additional research Bridger had done on the pilot had convinced him that something mechanical in the aircraft would fail before that particular pilot would make a fatal mistake.

Bridger buzzed Mabel, his secretary. He still couldn't believe that his young, twenty-something secretary was named Mabel. *Who still names their kids Mabel?*

"Yes, Admiral?"

"Is there still coffee in that pot out there?" He could sense her smile over the intercom.

"I'll bring you some, sir."

Bridger grinned at himself. With all this new emphasis on women's liberation and whatnot, he felt guilty about asking his secretary to bring him coffee. So he'd begun to ask if there was coffee in the pot. It never failed. Mabel always volunteered to bring him a cup. It didn't occur to him that she found it a pleasure to serve him because he respected her.

He leaned back in his chair, and put his feet on his desk. He opened the folder containing Kelly's service record. He'd had a devil of a time getting the Air Force to send a copy of the pilot's service record; the unspoken question was, *what business does a Navy admiral have looking at it?*

One piece of information in the record caught his eye. Kelly was serving under General James Franks at Edwards Air Force Base. The major's assignment to Eielson had been temporary duty for some F-16 refresher flights. At the time of the disappearance he'd been under Frank's overall command.

"Here you are, Admiral." The pert woman smiled at the man's relaxed posture.

"Thanks, Mabel. How are Howard's classes going?"

She raised an eyebrow at the question. "You have a good memory, sir! Howie should finish his degree in May." Her husband was finishing up a law degree, with the intent of becoming a military lawyer.

"Just getting my ducks in row if I should need someone to bail me out of trouble," he chuckled, accepting the cup.

When she had shut his door, his thoughts went back to Franks. He remembered that their paths had crossed two years ago in Saudi Arabia. The admiral pressed the intercom again and requested, "Mabel, get me the number for a General James Franks at Edwards Air Force Base, please."

****

Galina Toporova sat on the little bed and looked with wonder at the luxurious surroundings of her small, borrowed bedroom. Even though she'd been in the United States for less than a week, it was long enough to realize that the couple hosting her were not wealthy by US standards. But compared to what she was accustomed to, her surroundings were opulent.

Her request for permanent asylum was being considered by the Immigration and Naturalization Service (INS). In the meantime they had granted her a temporary visa. A telephone call to the Chinese Presbyterian church whose address and phone number she'd been given by her Beijing benefactors had resulted in one of the church's volunteers driving to the airport, picking her up and bringing her back to the church. The storefront building in which the fellowship met was nestled in the old section of Alameda. After a series of interviews, a volunteer family agreed to take her in and provide her with phone and kitchen privileges, and transportation as they were able. It was a community hospitality much as she had experienced in the underground church fellowship in China, and she felt safe and welcome.

Her hosts were a Chinese immigrant family who'd come to the United States about fifteen years prior. Two years ago they had finally become naturalized US citizens. Their youngest child, a daughter, was a PhD candidate in Nuclear Physics at Berkeley, and rarely had time to come home. The couple now had an empty nest and Galina sensed that they were happy to have a young person in the home again.

Her morning had been consumed with interviews at the INS field office in San Francisco. Every aspect of her recent activities in Siberia and her exile into China had been questioned exhaustively. Somehow she knew not to speak of the role that Jake had played in putting her crosswise with the KGB. In fact, she left all mention of Jacob Kelly out of her answers. She portrayed her exile as a case of KGB retribution against her family for the subversive activities of her father. The story was a complete fiction but the interviewer bought it, and at the moment that was all that mattered. Her case officer had told her not unkindly that the interviews would be repeated numerous times over the next several weeks before her request for asylum proceeded to the next stage of consideration. With her fluency in English, her graduate degree in mathematics, her work experience as a teacher, and the fact that she had a host family willing to vouch for her, the case officer assured her that she was a lock for permanent status.

Since returning to her room, the last hour had been spent tracking down the necessary phone numbers to locate information on missing service personnel. She had been given the phone number of the Department of Prisoners of War/Missing Persons in Washington, DC. Galina was proceeding on the assumption that Jake was still somewhere in Siberia.

"You know of a missing serviceman?" Her hosts had been surprised when she asked for help finding the appropriate phone number.

She was not sure how to answer, but knew intuitively that she should say as little as possible on the subject. "It is the friend of a friend of someone I knew in Siberia," she replied evasively. It was true, sort of. Jake was her brother's friend, and her brother was certainly *her* friend, though so much more than that. The answer seemed to satisfy her hosts, so she left it at that.

Thinking of her brother Boris, however, brought tears to the young woman's eyes and she retreated to her bedroom to grieve in private. Boris had been killed in a tragic accident at their logging cooperative the previous November. Kelly had been there to help her through the most painful experience of

her life; Boris was as much a father figure to her as he had
been an older brother. As the girl wept in her room, she
wished desperately to feel Kelly's strong arms around her
again.

****

"Who caught the largest fish on the first trip we made to
Utah together?"

"You did, you braggart, but it wasn't a fair catch because
you were using a spinner in designated fly fishing waters,"
replied Bill Jensen with a hearty laugh.

"Okay, I suppose it is really you, Mr. Jensen. Identity verified. But you know as well as I do that none of us had noticed
the sign in the parking area," Jake said with a mock defensive-
ness.

"Oh, brother! We're not going to have *this* argument again,
are we? You know very well that all fishermen have selective
vision when it comes to fishing regulations and 'no tres-
passing' signs."

"I can't believe you're still fuming over the fact that my
nice fat rainbow was the largest fish caught on that trip. My
dad was as grumpy about this as you are. He never let it die,
and it appears that you won't either."

"Listen, son, if I was to fish with a stick of dynamite and
claim a big catch, you wouldn't find that fair either."

"It wasn't dynamite, it was a beat-up Mepps spinner and I
was within a hundred yards of the boundary!"

"Yes, a hundred yards on the *wrong side* of the boundary,"
Jensen laughed.

Jake neatly segued into the purpose of his phone call,
"Well, Mr. Jensen, I guess I've established a bit of a habit, because I'm on the wrong side of a boundary again and I need
some help to deal with it. I didn't know where else to turn."

The professor sensed the sincerity and the need of the
voice coming through the receiver and replied quietly, "You
are the son of the finest friend I have ever had. I will do anything I can to help you. Now Jacob, why don't you tell me

what's going on?"

Jake took a deep breath and began, "I'll give you the short version. On 10 July of last year I was flying an F-16 over the Bering Sea on a test flight checking out some experimental avionics. I was intercepted and shot down by the Soviets. I ejected. My parachute was immediately snagged by a Russian helicopter. They retrieved me and I was taken to some sort of interrogation center in Siberia. I managed to escape. I've spent the last fourteen months working my way back to the States while avoiding half the Soviet Army, who were trying to re-capture me, dead or alive. That's the short version of where I have been."

Jensen was stunned to silence. The tale he had just heard was so fantastically improbable in every respect that he couldn't have given it a moment's credence were it not for the individual telling it. Bill knew Jake: while the young man might fudge just a little on the size of a trout, he'd never make up a story as serious as the one he just shared.

"Mr. Jensen? Are you still there? Can you hear me?"

Jensen cleared his throat. "I'm still here, Jake. I—I don't know what to say. I don't know where to begin. It's an unbe-lievable tale. In fact, I'm struggling to believe it at all, except for the fact that I view your integrity as beyond question. Are you hospitalized? Is it possible you had an accident and have suffered some delusions or hallucinations? Perhaps a side ef-fect of medications? Were you injured in the accident?"

"It was no accident, sir. It was a shootdown," Jake insisted. "You'll soon be getting information through your intelligence channels—if not the national media—of the rescue of a 'Siberian fisherman,' a Mr. 'John Meeker,' from the Bering Strait. That was me, sir. I gave the name as an alias, because I cannot afford my true identity to become known just yet—al-though I fear it will come out soon anyway."

"Jacob, I'm afraid I don't know what you mean when you say that I will hear something through my 'intelligence chan-nels.' I've told you—I'm just a political science professor. But tell me, why are you afraid of letting your identity out? Why don't you contact your old unit and tell them you've returned?"

"Mr. Jensen, you can keep your secrets. There's no reason to tell me anything about your intelligence work. I know it's true, but we need speak no more about it. The reason that I cannot get in touch with my old unit is simple: I was set up by a Soviet spy, a highly placed mole in the Air Force. If I turn myself in, the Sovs will know where I am and they'll kill me."

"Why would they want to kill you? I don't know much about this sort of thing, but I've heard it's quite rare for an intelligence service to carry out a sanction on a foreign citizen in that citizen's home country. It seems to me that Soviet agents killing an American on American soil would cause more problems than it solves, no matter what you might know."

"Mr. Jensen, I have information about a secret Soviet program that's so explosive they'll do anything to stop me. If they can't assassinate me they're going to discredit me. I've got to establish my credibility before they have a chance to ruin it, and I need to discover exactly who the spy—or spies—are. Sir, whoever it is, they have a great deal of access to classified information." Falcon was becoming frustrated. He sensed he was losing Jensen. There was nothing wrong with the phone connection, but he was picking up all sorts of worrisome signals from his friend's incredulity.

"Jacob, Jacob, now you sound paranoid! What makes you believe you were set up in the first place? On what basis do you think that the Air Force has been compromised?"

"I *know* that I was set up, sir, for a host of reasons. First off, I was shot down by a missile; my aircraft did *not* experience any sort of malfunction. Second, immediately before the missile's impact I detected a Soviet jamming signal that would defeat any distress call I might be able to send. Third, when I ejected I didn't even get wet though I was over a hundred klicks from the nearest land. The Soviet helicopter that snagged my chute was operating at the maximum extent of its range, and so could not have been on station for more than five minutes. Both the chopper and whatever shot me down were waiting for me, right timing, right place. Last of all, I was taken to an interrogation center.

"Now get this part, sir. I was attached to General Jim Franks at Edwards Air Force Base, as part of a top-secret development effort called Project *Hydra*. Forgive me if I can't give you the particulars, as it is highly classified. I'm not even supposed to *name* the project when I'm off the base. Technically, telling you is a violation of an agreement I signed. In any case, my flight—when I was shot down—was actually related to the *Hydra* project even though all records will call it a 're-fresher' flight. Would you like to guess what I was questioned about when I was taken to the Soviet interrogation center, Mr. Jensen?"

"*Hydra?*"

"Precisely. Somehow they knew. I am not delusional. I am not hallucinating. I was not injured in the slightest. Someone—and they have to be in the Air Force—knew my flight path and knew that I was connected with *Hydra*, and communicated that intelligence to the USSR. And the Sovs were waiting for me, sir. You may or may not hear about this part, but my rescue in the Bering Strait was contested by the Soviet Armed Forces, and there's already been one attempt on my life in the few days I have been back on US soil."

For the second time in less than five minutes, Jensen was dumbfounded. In all his years of intelligence work he'd never known a foreign power to commit such a blatant, unprovoked, aggressive act of war in pursuit of an intelligence goal, especially when it was against a non-belligerent nation. The shootdown of Gary Powers' U-2 in 1960 was aggressive, but it was in response to an equally aggressive provocation: the violation of airspace. This, however, was a premeditated attack on a United States aircraft over international waters without the slightest provocation. It had been entirely successful and were it not for Jake's escape, would never have been revealed. It was as ominous as it was shocking.

Jensen now recognized that his young friend was indeed telling the truth, truth with explosive ramifications extending far beyond the recruitment of spies in the Air Force command structure. Someone within the Soviet Union had been *authorized* to commit a risky, high-tech kidnapping of a USAF pilot attached to a highly classified project. This reckless aggression had to be stopped.

Bill cleared his throat again and said, "Jake, I know about *Hydra*, though I didn't know you were involved with it. I've sat in some briefings where it came up. I'm going to level with you. If you have been approved at a security level sufficient to work on that project—which at Langley is beyond top secret, it's 'need-to-know' only—you have a sufficient clearance for me to tell you what my day job involves. My teaching duties at Georgetown are my non-official cover. I actually work for the CIA as a special assistant to the DDO. Have for years, although I have no idea how you could've possibly figured that out."

"Sir, it was relatively simple. Anyone who casts a light fly line into a stiff breeze as neatly as you do has obviously got a lot of time on their hands to practice. That clearly identified you as working for Uncle Sam. Government workers get, what, one hundred twenty-three paid holidays a year?"

"Watch your mouth, boy, or you'll find yourself to be the next lab rat for CIA mind control experiments!" Jensen was silent for a moment. "Jacob, how are you set for resources?"

"I have no identification, but I do have fifteen hundred in cash, and I am—"

"Fifteen hundred dollars! Jake, how did you manage that?"

"Oh, that? I took it off the guy who tried to off me. I don't expect he'll be needing it in the pokey, and he certainly isn't going to tell the arresting officer he's missing the money he was paid to kill me. Technically, he really doesn't know I have it since he was out cold when I relieved him of the burden."

"Anyway, you have enough money to keep your head down for a while?"

"Yes, sir. But by Friday it's going to be crawling with Alaska State Troopers here."

"Okay. Sit tight. I'm going to research this on my end. I won't bring anybody in on it until I can be certain of who we can trust. If we do this right we might be able to bag a major Soviet spy ring and give Ivan a diplomatic black eye at the same time."

"Mr Jensen, there is more."

"More? You're kidding!"

"No, sir. While in the Soviet Union, I learned some other things that will also be a huge diplomatic embarrassment for them, but I'm not going to share what I know at this time. It will be my bargaining chip if the stuff hits the fan and I wind up getting sliced and diced."

"Okay, Jacob, you make the call on that. And look, you make me feel like ancient history with all this 'Mr. Jensen' stuff. You aren't in high school anymore, boy. Call me Bill!"

****

General James T. Franks threw his pen down on his desk in disgust. Project *Hydra* was stalled. The previous summer—at the most crucial point in the program—Major Jacob Kelly's F-16 had disappeared from the sky during a test of the *Hydra* avionics, and the pilot had evaporated along with the aircraft. The disappearance had occurred when the Falcon was out of radar range, so there were no clues as to what actually happened. The AIB had declared it a case of pilot error, a conclusion Franks refused to accept. *Not with this pilot!*

The loss had hit Franks personally. Jake was practically a part of the family. Shandra and the kids had loved the young man. He was constantly in their home on weekends, dueling the general or one of his teenage sons at the chess board, always losing but always coming back for more.

Kelly's disappearance could not have come during a worse time for *Hydra.* They were tweaking the software interfaces and ground equipment and were ready for final testing. Kelly was the only *Hydra* pilot who was cross-trained as a Combat Control Team (CCT) operator, and his knowledge of both ground and air operations was exactly what the *Hydra* team needed to complete the project.

The fact that the Air Force possesses its own branch of special operations is not a matter of common knowledge. CCT operators have a mission range rivaling that of the

SEALs, and the training is no less intense. In addition to the combat, intelligence, and survival training, every CCT member is an FAA-certified air traffic controller. The CCT motto is "first there," because they frequently are. They're tasked with deploying undetected into a variety of hostile environments to provide fire support; forward air traffic control; command and control; and to secure drop zones and airfields, as well as performing other special operations functions.

Project *Hydra* was designed to neutralize the vast Warsaw Pact advantage in armor. It took the precision accuracy of PAVE weapons a step farther, allowing for large cluster releases of PAVE munitions in a target-rich, laser-illuminated environment. In theory, four *Hydra*-equipped F-16s could destroy three companies of Soviet tanks in a single sortie.

Major Kelly had not only brought test-pilot expertise to the project, but Franks had also had him trained as a CCT operator so that Kelly could experience the problems and challenges encountered by the boots on the ground. It was his unique combination of skills that Franks had been counting on to polish off an already successful project. Without Kelly's input, the project would be completed and the munitions deployed but there would be a multi-year cycle of design changes made necessary by the hard realities of the ground combat environment.

General James T. Franks was the Air Force's preeminent expert on the F-16 aircraft. A brilliant man, Franks possessed two Masters: one in Electrical Engineering from Caltech, and another in Mathematics from MIT, earning a 4.0 GPA at both schools. He was a science fiction fan and a Trekkie to boot, with the hull number of the USS *Enterprise*, NC-1701, tattooed on his right forearm.

His driver, personal assistant, and bodyguard, Staff Sergeant Leonard Williams, found out the hard way that there are two things one doesn't say to General Franks. When he'd first joined the general's staff three years prior, he'd made the mistake of sharing with Franks the staff's nickname for him— Captain James T. Kirk. The young man didn't realize that it was a *secret* nickname, held in close confidence. He told the general with a laugh, and was met by frosty silence.

Sergeant Williams' other big mistake was to refer to Franks as an Afro-American. Franks was furious. "I'm not a hyphenated American! I'm an American who is black! There's nothing *African* about me. Don't ever call me an Afro-American, Sergeant!" When Williams asked him wasn't he proud of his heritage, Franks responded, "What heritage? Why? You and I are five, if not ten or more, generations removed from Africa. What do we have to do with anything that ever happened over there? Why would I be proud of an accident of birth? I'm proud of Martin Luther King! I'm proud of America! I'm proud of my momma and my daddy! I'm proud of what I have accomplished. Why would I even care about what happened on another continent three hundred years ago? Listen, son, there are race hustlers out there whose reason for existence will disappear unless they can fan the flames and make us forget that we're just Americans, like everyone else. Don't you buy their hate or their jive!"

Franks had been a weightlifter and boxer in college. While age and a desk job had added a little to his girth, he was still a formidable fighter even though his five foot nine inch frame did not give him much of a reach. He made up for it with a cast iron jaw and a lightning fast right hook that would leave a dent in plate steel.

Although the general had a temper and did not tolerate fools, his streak of pride was kept under control by his faith: Franks was an aggressive evangelical Christian. He came to Christ under the influence of Missions to Military, and presently attended a reformed Presbyterian church.

General Franks looked down at the Gantt chart on his desk, which displayed the projected milestones of *Hydra*, and shook his head. *I've got to land the plane*, he thought to himself. *We've got to wrap this thing up. There's not enough time to give another pilot CCT training and send him out on the requisite five missions. We'll have to go with what we've got. At least we know the system works. I guess the rest of the refinements will have to happen under actual use.*

And just then his phone rang. "General, there's a call for you on line one. Admiral John Bridger, sir."

"Thank you, Susan." *Why is the Navy calling me?* He punched line one and answered gruffly, "Franks here."

"General Franks, this is Admiral John Bridger, CO of Navy Special Warfare Group One. How are you on this fine late September afternoon?"

"Fine, sir, fine indeed. This is the day the Lord has made, we will rejoice and be glad in it."

"Uh-huh. Okay." Bridger was flustered. He'd never heard anyone say such a thing and wasn't quite sure how to respond.

"What can I do for you, Admiral? I know the Navy needs a lot of help, and our Air Force flyboys are real pilots. We can do whatever you need done." General Franks never lost an opportunity to twist the Navy's tail.

This is more like it, thought Bridger. *I know how to handle this sort of thing.* "Thanks, General. I knew we could count on your boys. Listen, could you send four or five of your Falcons over to Pearl, we're running a little short of aircraft for air patrol duties."

Franks caught the mild edge of sarcasm in the voice on the other end of the phone and decided to play along. "Certainly, Admiral. When you want it done right, just call the Air Force. We'll need to call up a little mid-air refueling though, that's a long hop."

Bridger grinned. The good general had just stuck his foot in the loop, and Bridger was ready to spring the trap. "Oh, that won't be necessary, General Franks. I've got a flattop halfway between Edwards and Pearl. The Air Force having such good pilots and everything, your boys can just land there and fill up. No need for a tanker."

Silence for a moment. "That was unfair, Admiral. You know our guys prefer landing strips that don't move around on 'em."

Gotcha, Bridger thought, exulting. "Oh, I *am* sorry, General! I seem to have forgotten that minor detail. *Most* insensitive of me. Do forgive me!" Bridger snickered to himself. It didn't matter what sort of sophisticated toys or training the Air Force got, the Navy was the only service with pilots who could land high-performance fighter aircraft on a pitching carrier deck. It was an eternal sore point with the Air Force.

"Yeah, right," the general grumbled. "Okay, score a point for the Navy. I sure put my foot into that one. Now, Admiral, what's this *really* all about; what can I do for you?"

"General Franks, I'm wondering if you can tell me anything about the disappearance of an F-16 flown by a Major Jacob Kelly on 10 July, 1986?"

Franks stared at the telephone receiver in his hand. *How on God's green earth would a Navy admiral know about that event, and more importantly, why is he interested in it?*

"Admiral—"

"Please, General Franks, call me John."

"Very well, John—tell me what your interest in that event is." Franks did not mean to sound so imperious, but this phone call was getting unsettling.

"General, I know you're working on a secret project involving the F-16 Fighting Falcon. I'd like to know if that aircraft and that pilot were attached to your project." This call was not going the way Bridger hoped it would.

"Admiral—John—I'm afraid I don't know what you're talking about. And I'm not real certain that you do, either." Franks' voice had become icy.

"Actually, General, I do. I know exactly what I'm talking about, and so do you. Two of my SEAL teams provided force protection for a detachment of eight F-16s in Saudi Arabia two years ago. The Falcons were part of Project *Hydra*, which is under your direct command. I also know that you are the leading expert in the Air Force on the F-16, which makes you the world's leading expert on that aircraft. And, I know that Project *Hydra* involves the development of an advanced battle-management avionics package for the F-16." Bridger paused in order to give the obviously surprised general a moment to process what he had just said.

Franks muttered under his breath, "Doesn't anyone keep secrets anymore?"

"I beg your pardon?"

"Just talking to myself, Admiral. Listen, since you want some information from me, perhaps you will return the favor.

How did you come by that information about *Hydra*? Not even the Joint Chiefs know what you just casually told me."

Bridger replied, "General Franks, when a unit of the Navy Special Warfare Group is called upon to provide force protection, we are briefed by both the DIA and the NSA on the reasons why we have been tasked with the mission, and what sort of potential threats to watch for. Your security chief briefed us also, only he didn't tell us anything particularly useful. You need not worry. I don't know a whole lot beyond what I have told you, and everything I know came through appropriate channels."

"What has the NSA to do with this? They're involved with intercepting and decoding communications."

"That is correct, General Franks, that is exactly what they do. And if a foreign power was planning on making mischief against a mission such as *Hydra's* deployment to Saudi Arabia several years back, there would be an increase in communications traffic among that government's intelligence assets in the region. NSA briefs us to tell us whether the bad guys know we are coming, and what they might be planning to do about it."

"You don't say? I had no idea!"

"Well, General, the SEALs are a little bit like your boys, I suppose. We don't like other people knowing too much about what we do."

"Can you tell me why you want to know about the incident on 10 July?" Franks realized uncomfortably that Bridger knew a lot about him, and he knew next to nothing about Bridger, other than knowing he was head of NSWG One.

Now it was Bridger's turn to pause. He knew that he could not tell Franks anything specific yet, not until he was convinced that Franks was not part of the Soviets' surreptitious intelligence network. "General, in the course of my duties I may have come across some intelligence that may have bearing on that event. I'm simply trying to gather the available data from as many sources as possible in order to make sense of this other item. I'm not at liberty to say what I know right now, but I guarantee you that I will personally update you, just as soon as I have it figured out myself. I've studied the AIB report, and I managed to finagle a copy of Kelly's service re-cord. I don't need to know anything more about *Hydra*, but I am interested to know if you have any thoughts on the loss of the aircraft and its pilot."

"I can tell you this, John. In my opinion, there are only two options. Major Kelly either defected with that Falcon, or the bird was shot out of the sky. I knew Jake, and I would suspect *myself* of defecting before I would suspect him. So that leaves the second option as the only viable one."

"What about the floating debris field mentioned in the AIB report, General?"

"Call me Jim. The only thing in the F-16 that floats is insu-lation, and the occasional odd tank or bladder, if empty. But all that stuff would go down with the plane. Unless . . ."

"Unless?"

"Unless an explosion tore up the aircraft. There are two possible sources for such an explosion, generally speaking. Something inside the plane or something outside the plane. The Falcon was carrying no armament at the time of the dis-appearance, so there was no weapon attached to the aircraft that could have cooked off. The next most likely source of an explosion from inside the plane would be the engine. That is a possibility, but I consider it remote due to the maintenance history on that particular jet. John, I am convinced that some-thing *outside* of the aircraft caused an explosion."

"Something outside the aircraft, Jim?"

"Yeah. Outside. Like an anti-aircraft missile. I can't really explain why, but in my gut I am convinced Major Kelly was shot down."

****

Bridger hung up the phone, put his hands behind his head, and looked up at the ceiling, thinking. Franks was trustworthy, he was sure of it. If Franks had been compromised, the Soviets would not have had to go through the planning and risk of a shootdown. If he was a spy, Franks could tell the Russians far, far more than any test pilot.

Bridger was confident that he'd found a trustworthy ally in the Air Force. Franks was clean and he was perfectly positioned to help out. Bridger decided to pay a personal visit on the general, and spill the beans. He'd been wanting to visit Edwards anyway. Besides, the admiral needed more flight hours in the Tomcat to stay current and this would provide him with the perfect excuse. And he figured that those Air Force boys would appreciate seeing a *real* fighter aircraft for a change. Maybe on Friday.

Chapter 12

Friday, October 2, 1987: 0800 local time
Edwards AFB, California

Rear Admiral Bridger's F-14A Tomcat made its signature high-angle-of-attack touchdown on Edwards' main runway, right on the center line. When he was attached to a fighter wing before all the gold braid on his hat and sleeve began to pile up, Bridger had earned an impeccable reputation as an aggressive pilot in the best traditions of the Navy's carrier-rated fliers. With the years and promotions his flying opportunities were fewer and fewer, and then merely to stay current. Soon not even that would be allowed.

It's been a great career and I have enjoyed every moment of it, Bridger thought to himself as the powerful Pratt and Whitney turbofans spun down and he finished the shutdown procedures. *But I'll never be ready to retire—even though most of the flying I do now is behind a desk.*

An Air Force ground crewman was wheeling the stairs up to the side of the plane. In addition to his muffs and goggles, the man was wearing a big grin. The Tomcat tended to have that effect on airplane people—it was one beautiful fighter. Nothing quite like it in the sky. At least, not in a Navy pilot's opinion.

A car pulled up and an Air Force staff sergeant slid out from behind the wheel, snapped off a crisp salute, and announced, "General Franks extends his compliments, sir, and asks that you would kindly join him for breakfast at the Officers' Club." Then, looking a little sheepish he faltered as he said, "He also said to tell you that he was glad your ancient aircraft made it all the way safely, and if you would like we can have our boys check the oil and the tires and make sure it is safe to fly home. Those were his words, sir, not mine," the sergeant added.

"Oh, brother!" Bridger rolled his eyes. "Is your CO always this insulting, Sergeant?"

"Oh, no sir! Usually it's much worse!" the man smiled.

Bridger settled into the back of the car as the sergeant drove to the Officers' Club. "What can you tell me about General Franks, son?"

"Well, sir, he's an outstanding commanding officer. That's not brown-nosing, sir, you will get the same answer from anyone who works under his command. He is something of a religious fanatic, but he cares for his people, sir. He demands excellence, and heaven help the guy who turns in a mediocre performance. He can be a little impatient at times."

"Patient people don't rise to the level of general officers, son. Anyway, that's useful info. But do you have any unusual stuff on him?"

"Unusual, sir?"

"Yeah, unusual. Like, does he cheat on his golf score, or does he hide a bag of candy bars in his desk, or, is he partial to chopped liver? Unusual stuff. See, General Franks and I seem to take great delight in tweaking one another's beaks, and I need some fresh ammunition."

The sergeant looked at Bridger in the rearview mirror and grinned broadly. "Oh, I have some really good stuff on him, sir! I guess I can tell you, since you're an admiral. Please, sir, just don't tell him who you got this from."

"I am the soul of caution, son, have no fear."

"Sir, he is a Trekkie."

"I beg your pardon?"

"He's a Trekkie. General Franks is a *Star Trek* fanatic." The sergeant laughed conspiratorially.

"No kidding?"

"No, sir. In fact, the civilians who work for him call him 'Captain Kirk' behind his back. Nobody—and I mean nobody —calls him that to his face, though. I don't recommend it at all, especially since General Franks boxed when he was a younger man. He's got a mean right hook. I've seen him spar, and he's still lethal.

"Anyway, he has the hull number of the Starship *Enterprise*, NCC-1701, tattooed on his right forearm. But sir, if you tell him I told you this not even the federal witness protection program could save me."

"Captain Kirk, eh," Bridger chuckled to himself, "that is *just* the sort of scuttlebutt I needed."

****

The teletype in the secure communications room of the US Embassy in Moscow woke up, and its printhead began clattering across the page. The Cyrillic characters that appeared in its wake were gibberish to the operator, and not because they were in Russian. He had no difficulty reading Russian. This was gibberish because it was encoded.

The operator had an official State Department cover but he was actually an employee of the NSA. He spent eight hours of his day—every day except Sundays—in this windowless, sound-proofed, electronic-emission controlled room. It was swept for listening devices thrice a day at random times in the hopes that if any data burst devices had been placed by Soviet counterintelligence, they would sooner or later be detected. Implanted in all six flat surfaces of the room—the four walls, floor, and ceiling—were audio frequency-agile, white noise-generating vibrators. Inaudible to the human ear, they played havoc with any listening devices designed to pick up the minute mechanical energy caused by sound waves. It was a completely secure listening post.

The teletype feed was originating from the secure GRU communications network that linked Moscow with East Berlin. An infrared laser signal from the GRU headquarters—the Aquarium—at Khodynka Airfield was beamed to a satellite communications facility about three kilometers away, carrying the encrypted communications traffic on its circuitous route to Berlin. The satellite facility had been built in 1982 and at the time there were no other structures close to it, but in 1985 an apartment building was put up just five blocks away.

During construction, one of the Russian workers had been

paid one thousand dollars in US currency by a CIA handler to trade his lunch box for one that had been prepared by the technology branch of the Agency. Hidden in the false bottom of the box were enough electronics to detect whether any modulated IR signals were being detected. Each week the worker would trade the handler for an identical lunch box, and the box traded in would be examined by NSA operatives at the embassy to see if any signals had been detected.

On the week when the concrete was being poured for the fifth floor of the apartment building, the lunch box recorded a faint modulated IR signal. The intelligence analysts back at Langley correctly guessed that the signal was backscatter, a minute reflection from the satellite transmission facility. At the time they had no idea where the signal originated nor what information it might carry, but it was of sufficient interest to justify the resources it took to plant a device in the apartment building that would capture the errant signal and transmit it to the US Embassy, without the surreptitious transmissions themselves being detected by Soviet counterintelligence.

The result was a gold mine, an intelligence coup on the level of the famous Berlin telephone tap of the 1950's. Much to the delight of the NSA, the signal had proven to be encrypted GRU headquarters intelligence traffic. In May of 1986 the encryption had finally been cracked and NSA voyeurs began sampling the private communications of Soviet military intelligence. The only frustrating part of the scheme was that the backscatter was only available on warmer afternoons. Apparently the minute expansion caused by the heat of the sun deformed the mount of the IR laser transmitter at GRU headquarters just sufficiently that the pattern of the laser beam lapped off the receiver optics ever so slightly, scattering a tiny portion of the signal. When GRU technicians had surveyed the site for the apartment building to ensure that no signal backscatter was occurring, it had been a cloudy, winter day. It was a fortuitous combination of circumstances, with the result that what was whispered secretly between Moscow and East Berlin was heard clearly in Washington, DC. On warm and sunny days, anyway.

The operator tore off the page when the teletype fell silent, and sat down at another communications console. He entered the characters one at a time, then checked, double-checked, and triple-checked the entry before he hit the transmit key. Folding the teletype output, he inserted it into an envelope and set it in the bin for highly classified information. The signal would be re-encrypted, transmitted over the NSA communications network, and interpreted by computers at a secure facility in Maryland within fifteen minutes. The paper copy would wind up at the same facility in about thirty-six hours, just in case he had keyed the message incorrectly.

****

Admiral Bridger had studied General James Franks' service record. The man was a genius: he'd earned multiple advanced degrees from top schools, maintaining a perfect grade-point average throughout his college career. Bridger found himself wondering if the man had ever been academically challenged in his life. *Sure hope he does not look into my background*, he thought, *it would be embarrassing. I graduated 'thank the Laude,' not 'magna cum laude.'*

Franks was waiting for him outside the Officers' Club. "Good morning, Admiral. I see you were able to find the right runway and even managed to keep your aircraft on it long enough to roll to a stop."

"No trouble at all, General. Is there anybody in the Air Force who knows how to cook? I brought my appetite with me this morning." As they walked in the Club, Bridger thought, *I'm going to like this guy. He dishes it up just the way I like it!*

A few moments later both men were hard at work on a batch of steak and eggs, washing it down with good black coffee. Franks had asked a blessing on the meal before they got started. Bridger almost cracked a joke about it, something about Air Force cooks requiring divine assistance, but thought better of it and kept his mouth shut.

When they finally pushed back from the table the general

looked over at Bridger and said, "John, I don't think you flew all the way over here just to get a break from Navy chow. Why don't you tell me how I can help you?"

"Jim, is there any place close by where we can take a walk? I'd rather discuss this where we won't be overheard."

They got up and Franks led the way outside. "There's an officers' family park right over there; let's see if we can find a bench."

As they walked over in the warm, fall sunshine the admiral began, "Jim, I have some information that suggests your gut feeling about Major Jacob Kelly was absolutely one hundred percent correct."

"You don't say?"

"What I'm going to tell you is for your ears only. It cannot be told to anyone else, and I mean *no one*. And by all means, don't make any notes about it and especially don't put it in your computer."

"Okay, John, what's all this cloak and dagger business about?"

"You're good with the restrictions I just named?"

"Scout's honor. Won't tell a soul. Unless of course, you're about to tell me that you're planning to defect with the USS *Nimitz*, or some such. In that case I'll have to kill you right here."

Bridger laughed, "It's nothing like that." He became serious again and added, "But several people's lives *are* at stake, as well as significant national security concerns."

"Fire away, Admiral. I'm all ears."

"How familiar was Jacob Kelly with *Hydra*?"

"Intimately familiar. Specs, design, limitations, projected implementation date, everything. He was my chief test pilot. Losing him set the project back six months. And he was a good man and a good friend."

"Well, General, the major is not dead. He was kidnapped. Shot down by the Sovs over the Bering Sea and then picked up by one of their choppers. I have eyewitness testimony to that fact."

Franks' black face came as close to turning pale as Bridger

had ever seen on a black man. For a moment he was speech-
less, and then insisted, "That's impossible! Even if it were
true, how could you possibly know it? Besides, the Russians
would never do that—it would be an act of war. Impossible!"

Bridger sat down wearily on the bench. "I agree, Jim, I
know. Nevertheless, I have it from a source I trust. And the
witness from whom this information came, via several
mouths, was the pilot who shot him down. That's why we cannot say a word until we can 'discover' this criminal action
through some other means, so that our investigation does not
implicate my sources. The pilot's life and that of his family, his
friend and *his* family, not to mention the American who they
told and his family—well, all those lives will be forfeit if we
don't handle this intelligence properly."

"Are you sure of your source? Are you sure this is not just
a bunch of beer talk?"

"I'm absolutely, positively sure of my source. He was one
of my best SEAL commanders. He is a sober, careful, cautious man. There is no question in my mind that what he has
related to me is absolutely true. And he has the same confidence in his source. Plus, the dates match, the locations match,
and this alone explains the floating debris field mentioned in
the AIB report—which their finding of pilot error does not,
as you well know."

Franks put his head in his hands and muttered, "My word
—I can't believe this. What do they know? How much do they
know? And what about Falcon?"

"Falcon?"

"What? Oh—Major Kelly. Jacob Kelly. We all call him Falcon."

"Ah. I see." Bridger paused for a moment and then said,
"General, I am afraid there is more bad news The helicopter
that snagged his chute was operating at the maximum extent
of its range and could not have been on station long. The Soviet fighter was orbiting in just the right spot. The jamming
signal that came right after the pilot triggered his missile—it
all adds up to one thing: they knew his flight plan, they knew
the timing, and they knew no other US assets would be in de-

tection range. Someone in the Air Force—maybe in your organization—has been turned. Someone who has access to Operations and maybe to classified materials betrayed Kelly."

****

General Patrikeyev looked out of his seventh-story corner office at GRU headquarters and watched air traffic taking off and landing at nearby Khodynka Airfield. Night had fallen, and the runway and taxiway lights glowed in the darkness. Patrikeyev needed a moment to allow his anger to subside and his blood pressure to return to normal. This entire Kelly affair was a never-ending mess. At some point, he realized, it could endanger even his own career.

He abruptly swung around to face the two subordinates standing in front of his desk. "You are telling me that Kelly is not only still alive, but we have *completely lost track of him?*"

"*Da*, Comrade General. And the worst part is we got this information not from our operatives but from yesterday's newspaper out of Anchorage. There's a story of an attempted murder in the hospital at Kotzebue, Alaska, and two suspects have been arrested. They are a pair of assassins that we've used several times for delicate jobs in the US. One of them was trained at the KGB's facility in Beirut six years ago. He recruited and trained a partner and they have worked together for the last three years.

"On Saturday," the man continued, "they were contracted to kill the American in the hospital before he recovered. Evidently they failed and have been picked up by law enforcement."

"Can they be traced back to us?"

"*Nyet*, Comrade. The man we trained was never informed who was doing the training. We don't think he knows who he is working for, which means his partner can't know either. They cannot damage us, but we will have to write them off. It's a pity, as they were good with the wet work."

Patrikeyev nodded. The training at all KGB foreign centers is done by internationals—not by Soviets—and the trainees know better than to ask questions. It was a firewall designed to protect the Soviet intelligence services from just such contingencies. "What about Kelly?"

"At this point, Comrade General, we are reduced to reading the American newspapers, or hoping that one of our assets in the US military or intelligence services will get wind of his whereabouts. We have no one in place to locate him ourselves. Not at the moment, anyway."

"I want to know the instant you hear anything. ANYTHING! Is that clear?" The general was not in the habit of raising his voice, but he could not help it this time. Things were not going well at all.

After the two had left his office, he turned back to the window. Late this afternoon he had met with his other team who were working on the Kelly problem: his disinformation experts. They had transmitted several communiques over three separate GRU communication networks. Patrikeyev knew, or suspected, that one of the three networks had been compromised by US intelligence. He was unable to prove it as yet, or even adduce sufficient evidence to persuade the counterintelligence branch to commit resources to the suspicion, but he felt in his bones that someone was intercepting the traffic.

So they began to release information to implicate Major Kelly as a Soviet plant. Disinformation was a nuanced subterfuge. One could not be too obvious, because that was, well, *too* obvious. It must appear that the damning evidence had been hard won by American counterintelligence, pried surreptitiously out of the most secure Soviet communications. The Americans must not suspect that they were being led by the nose to the conclusion that Jake was a spy. This was an area that Russian intelligence virtually owned. No one else could do it half as well.

Patrikeyev was planning an intelligence coup of his own. The Kelly incident provided the perfect cover for him to ferret out which communication network was compromised. He had released slightly different versions on each network, in hopes that the information flow coming from his people in the USA would later reveal which network the Americans were listening to. With luck they could discredit Kelly and regain the integrity of their communications in a single blow. And he, Patrikeyev, would restore a little glory to his political star, wiping away the tarnish of the Kelly incident.

****

"Gentlemen, if you will be seated we can get started." Jesse Pierce was slightly nervous; all of the men present were older and more experienced than he. Be that as it may, the major players had put him in charge and he intended to take the lead with a strong hand.

He waited while the men poured their coffee and took seats around the conference table. One of the new team members was Bill Ott of Eielson AFB. When Captain Danny Daniels had been helping Pierce assemble his investigative team, he suggested contacting Eielson. Eielson's base commander, General Larry Martin, had already assisted in the recovery effort by sending a flight of Falcons to discourage Soviet aggression. He was happy to lend the help of his intelligence section—especially since it provided a back channel into what in the Sam Hill the Navy was doing.

"Since we don't all know each other, I'll make introductions and then give you a brief rundown of what we know so far about this odd series of incidents." Pierce paused for a swallow of his coffee. "Seated here to my left is Special Agent Jim Stewart of the Seattle office of the FBI. Jim is assigned to the FBI's Foreign Counterintelligence team. His particular responsibility in this case is the analysis of all physical evidence, as well as coordinating the actual physical search for the fugitive. He's cooperating with the Alaska State Troopers, who are represented this morning by Special Investigator Ed Devlin, seated next to Jim. Within the Alaska Troopers organization, Ed is attached to the Alaska Bureau of Investigations, or ABI. The ABI has a special unit that handles foreign intelligence and business espionage: a necessity because of Alaska's proximity to Russia, North Korea, and China. Ed's job is crime scene investigation as well as the attempt to apprehend all other individuals involved in the case, about whom you will be briefed shortly. In addition, the Alaska State Troopers will be providing the boots on the ground for the manhunt for Mr. Meeker, coordinating with the FBI in that effort.

"To my right is Major William Ott, intelligence chief of the 6985th Electronic Security Squadron, stationed at Eielson Air Force Base. The 6985th is part of the Air Force Security Service, known affectionately as the 'Secret Squirrels,' and they're involved in surveillance and SIGINT, eavesdropping on Ivan's conversations. Bill also has many contacts in the intelligence community, throughout the entire Northwest, as well as in Washington, DC. His role will be to assist me with the military intelligence aspects of this investigation. Bill's got to be back at Eielson before noon, so we'll have to keep things moving this morning.

"Seated next to him is Sam Bergman. Sam works for the CIA and is based at Langley. Sam is on loan to us as an additional intelligence resource and also has extensive contacts in the intelligence community.

"I'm Lieutenant Commander Jesse Pierce, the senior intelligence officer at Adak Naval Air Station. My role is the overall coordination of this rather unusual case. You may be wondering why a 'missing persons' investigation is so heavily freighted with intelligence operatives. Once you hear the complete tale, you'll understand."

Jesse turned down the conference room lights, displayed a map of the Bering Strait on the overhead projector, and began the briefing. "On 25 September—last Friday—an Orion EP-3 on patrol over the Strait intercepted a radio call from a Soviet Ilyushin patrol aircraft that had to do with locating an unconscious boater in a kayak, at approximately this position." Jesse pointed to a spot on the map. "What caught the Orion's ear was that the Soviets were sending a small flotilla consisting of a *Nanuchka*-class corvette, two *Osa-1*-class missile boats, and a pair of MIGs to recover the man in the kayak. Considering the Soviet military's distressed economic condition, we thought this was a rather extravagant use of resources."

"You can say that again," responded Bergman, intrigued.

Pierce continued. "Those of us in military intelligence—Bill can confirm this—have been receiving a great deal of SIGINT over the last year pertaining to a massive search that has been slowly moving east and north through eastern Siberia and up into the Chukchi Peninsula, in what we now believe was an effort to locate and capture a fugitive. Several brigades from the Soviet Army were involved in the search. The commitment of all these assets indicates that the target had a very high value.

"Last Friday I gambled that the boater was in fact the same target and decided if the Soviets wanted this guy that badly, we probably wanted him, too. We just didn't know why. We still don't—but subsequent events have vindicated my belief in his value. In military parlance, he was a 'target of opportunity.' After I secured the permission of my commanding officer, the Navy got involved in the rescue.

"We mounted an effort composed of naval, civilian, and air force assets. Due to the professionalism and courageous work of all involved we won the prize. It wasn't a sure thing—the aggressiveness Ivan displayed out in the Strait nearly resulted in a shooting incident. Thankfully no one pulled the trigger and we are not now enmeshed in World War III. As you may imagine, the Soviet Embassy in Washington is registering all sorts of pious protests with the State Department.

"The person in the kayak was suffering from extreme hypothermia and was helicoptered to the hospital in Kotzebue. It was then that things deteriorated from merely strange to really troubling. I detailed a squad of MPs to guard the boater on the remote possibility the Russkies wanted him so badly they would attempt to grab or kill him. It was just a hunch but it paid off in spades, as you will learn in a moment.

"In order to avoid exciting the local populace and generating unwelcome media coverage, the MPs were not dressed in regulation uniforms. They were intentionally outfitted to look like Alaska State Troopers, but without insignias—no shoulder patches, badges or IDs. In order to dodge military regulations prohibiting this sort of thing the men were all 'volunteers' and were granted liberty for the entire term of the assignment. Technically they weren't on duty. We didn't claim to be civilian law enforcement, but we didn't discourage the residents from making that assumption, either. My apologies to Ed Devlin and the troopers."

"No problem, Jesse, just as long as we don't get a bill for your services," Devlin chuckled.

Pierce smiled and continued, "By Saturday the man we rescued had recovered sufficiently to be questioned. He identified himself as an American citizen by the name of 'John Meeker'. His story was that he was paddling inshore and got blown out to sea. It didn't seem credible so we maintained the guard and determined to fly him on Sunday to the hospital at NAS Adak, where we could question him more closely. We never got the chance. On Saturday night an attempt was made on his life. From what we can piece together Meeker was preparing to escape and used his meds to spike the coffee of the MP, putting the guard to sleep. At some point, the alleged assassin entered his room but Meeker managed to cold-cock him and escape.

"When the NCO of the guard detail was called to the scene at the shift change, he found his own man drugged and sleeping in Meeker's hospital bed. On the floor handcuffed to the other bed was another unconscious man. Meeker had also left a note for the nurse, a photocopy of which is in your briefing packet, accusing the man on the floor of trying to kill him and making reference to the alleged weapon, an allegedly poison-tipped pin concealed in the base of a Zippo lighter. Of John Meeker there was no sign, and he remains at large today.

"Ed Devlin is going to fill us in on the progress the ABI has made. When he's done, Jim Stewart will provide the latest update from the FBI."

The lieutenant commander sat down, and the state trooper stood to continue the briefing. Devlin was a barrel-chested, sandy-haired, forty-eight year old. After a six-year hitch in the Marines, Ed had joined the Alaska troopers and was now a twenty-year veteran of the force. His ambition was to eventually head up their Business Crime unit. "Thanks, Jesse. So far, we've been able to establish that on Saturday afternoon, Alaskan Corporate Transport flew two individuals, George Thompson and Carl Stafford, to Kotzebue. The flight was booked and paid for on extremely short notice Saturday morning according to ACT records. The purpose of the trip was supposedly to negotiate a petroleum contract. Thompson and Stafford were instructed by the ACT pilot to be at the airstrip on Sunday morning for the return flight. They never showed. The oil company that booked the trip turned out to be nothing more than a post office box in Dallas, Texas. It has 'front' written all over it. The holding company behind the fake oil company is International Development Corporation, or IDC, and they do their banking in the Cayman Islands. Cayman bank officials are not real good at turning over their records to US law enforcement, subpoena or not."

"Excuse me, Ed?" Sam Bergman was sitting up straight in his seat, fully engaged in the briefing. Bergman was a rising star in the Soviet department of the CIA's Counterintelligence Division. He was held to be one of the most knowledgeable men at the Firm when it came to the affairs of the USSR. Bergman had a weakness for red licorice, and he was clutching a small bag of the stuff at the moment.

"Yes, Sam, what is it?"

"IDC is a front, exactly as you have said. The Firm has a complete file on these people. They're usually mixed up with Soviet intelligence operations, and if there's any wet work—"

Pierce cut him off. "Wet work?"

"*Mokroe delo*, murder, wet work," Bergman clarified. "If there's any murder involved with a Soviet intelligence op somewhere close by you are going to find an IDC goon hanging around. We've known about them for several years but haven't shut them down because they're pretty easy to track. If we make them close up shop it might take years to locate the new thugs. If they're about to wax some innocent we just make sure some sort of 'accident' happens that messes up their job. I don't think that they've caught on to the fact that we are all over them."

"Were you aware of this job?" Stewart asked coldly.

"No, not at all. The CIA had no idea that IDC is active in Alaska. This is news to us."

Stewart followed up, "Well then, I guess there may be some 'innocents' who have gotten hurt without the CIA being aware of it!"

Bergman replied hotly, eyes flashing with anger, "Look, we're not omniscient! We know that! We make the best decisions we can keeping the larger picture of national security in mind!"

The FBI agent rejoined, "The whole point of *national security* is to *protect* the citizens. If the Agency's efforts to protect national security are endangering American lives, it seems to me that you're working against your mandate!"

"Whoa, guys! We are on the same team, remember? None of us in here is at the level to set policy in our respective organizations. Let's try to focus on this case," Pierce soothed.

"Yeah, you're right, Jesse. Sorry, Sam, I was out of line there," the FBI agent admitted reluctantly.

"Forget it," responded Bergman, turning back to Ed Devlin.

"Okay," said Devlin, "that's helpful news about IDC, Sam. I'll get my lead investigator to share with you what he's dug up, just in case it might fill in some cracks for the Agency. It would be great if your people could brief us more completely on IDC. I don't want our work to compromise the CIA's. It wouldn't be helpful for anyone if we sent these creeps underground."

"Done. Glad to work with you," Sam offered.

Devlin resumed his briefing. "The man chained to the hospital bed is a 'Fred Banks,' also known as 'George Thompson.' He runs a small engine repair shop in Anchorage and has a clean civilian record. He was dishonorably discharged from the Army about eight years ago, spending the last part of his enlistment in the slammer for striking an officer. He's not talked at all, other than to a lawyer."

The powerfully built trooper paused and examined his notes before continuing. "On Tuesday we nabbed the second of the two, Jason Devoe, aka Ralph Goodwin, aka Carl Stafford. Until three years ago, Devoe had a burgeoning career as a petty criminal in Anchorage. He's done some time, but never for anything major. His rap sheet is pretty long with burglary and theft—small stuff. Three years ago he straightened up and started to fly right. No offenses since then. He also began working for Fred Banks in the repair shop three years ago."

"That's pretty standard," offered the CIA agent. "Once IDC recruits a goon all the other criminal activity stops. In fact, IDC is so serious about it that if one of their guys steps over the line for a non-IDC job, he's dead within a month. Other than the fact that IDC is fielding trained, professional assassins, their guys make model citizens."

"Well," Devlin replied dryly, "while being apprehended, model-citizen Devoe trashed two of my guys. One of them has a broken jaw, the other pretty nearly bit his tongue in half. Devoe was carrying over one thousand dollars cash—a lot of money for a small-engine mechanic. Anyway, we found fingerprints for both Devoe and Banks on the hospital stairwell door handles. Banks' fingerprints are also on the door leading to Meeker's room and all over the lighter as well. We told Devoe that his fingerprints place him at the scene, and we hinted that Banks was laying the entire operation at his feet. With a little luck Devoe may soften up for us and spill the beans in the next several days. It will probably cost us a plea bargain but he might be induced to provide useful information."

"That will help other aspects of the case," Bergman admitted, "but it won't help on the intelligence side. The IDC hirelings never know who's paying the bills, nor why the contract was issued."

Devlin continued, "We got a subpoena on Wednesday, and searched Banks' business in Anchorage. It turned out to be a gold mine. We confiscated various kinds of weapons and ammunition, disguise paraphernalia, passports, driver's licenses for different aliases, and several different kinds of uniforms—all tailored to fit the suspects. An employee talked and provided seven sets of dates in the last two years in which

Banks and Devoe disappeared for several days at a time. We're already working on matching those dates with any unsolved disappearances, murders, or unusual deaths in Alaska during the same period. Sam and Jim, I'll see that you get everything we have on these two scumbags. It might help solve some other cases, though it's unlikely that any of this will help with the Meeker case itself, unless we can follow the money and find out who is paying the bills and giving the orders."

Devlin wrapped up his comments, "There are four real 'John Meekers' in the state of Alaska. All have been interviewed and none are involved in this case. We are confident that 'John Meeker' is simply an alias that our unidentified fugitive picked out of the air. But we have discovered that the elusive Mr. Meeker is a pilot. We now believe he left Kotzebue in a stolen aircraft. I have agents all over the state looking for the plane, a white Mooney 20J, FAA registration N4148G, serial number 24-0647. It's registered to Dr. Stephen Carrock of Kotzebue. Once we have a little more to go on, the FAA database of pilots may reduce the population of possibilities somewhat. In any case, we have no idea where Mr. Meeker is now. All the relevant info is in your briefing notes. That's all I've got. Jim?"

Jim Stewart got up, and said, "The FBI lab analyzed the lighter. Mr. Meeker was correct in his supposition that the pin was laced with poison. It was a lethal neurotoxin that would have caused rapid death. Unless they knew what they were looking for, most coroners would have overlooked it.

"As far as Meeker's fingerprints go, it appears that he wiped things down before he departed, so the ABI was unable to lift his prints from the room. But we did get several good prints from the note. The bad news is that we didn't get any hits on them from the NCIC database. Our Mr. Meeker's true identity remains unknown." Stewart sat down.

Jesse Pierce got to his feet and summarized. "It appears that the manhunt in Siberia and our Mr. Meeker are related. The presence of two IDC thugs tends to strengthen the connection to the Soviet Union. We know that the USSR wanted him back—badly. We know that Mr. Meeker is a pilot, and his fingerprints are not on the NCIC database. Beyond that, we don't know much.

"Ed has proposed one possible theory. He believes that John Meeker might be an American intelligence agent who was somehow compromised and managed to escape the Soviet Union one step ahead of a manhunt. The fact that he came up east and north across Siberia and the Chukchi Peninsula, finally escaping in a kayak, also leads Ed to suggest that the man is a Native American, trained in Indian woodcraft and survival techniques. In the absence of other theories, that sounds as good as anything we've got so far."

Devlin offered, "That shouldn't be too hard to research, should it? Cross-check the databases for all the spooks of Native American heritage who have a pilot's license and have spent time behind the Iron Curtain. Wouldn't that narrow things down pretty rapidly?"

Bergman responded, "Yes and no, Ed. If there actually existed a single database with all the operatives on it, that should produce a short list of possibilities. But no databases like that do exist. Many of our operatives working in foreign countries don't exist in any database except maybe as a code name. And the various agencies that engage in foreign intelligence don't like to talk to each other. We don't share data. And it's not just simple turfism, either. We can't risk compromising hard-won sources who could wind up dead if the guy in the next agency mishandles the info."

"But why would Meeker remain on the run on American soil? He's had a week—he could have come in from the cold —unless there is some reason he doesn't want to," offered Bill Ott.

"That is the weak part of the theory," admitted Ed. "It *doesn't* make sense. If he's an intelligence agent, he wouldn't be trying to protect his cover because that's already been blown, otherwise the Russians would not be trying to reel him in. I have no answer for that question.

"And consider this, too: he might not even be an American. He could work for one of our allies or even one of our enemies. Coming to our shore may have been nothing more than a handy escape from death or torture in the Soviet Union."

"Maybe he didn't come in from the cold because he's in as much trouble over here as he was over there," mused Bergman.

"Then why did he flee back here? There are other places it would have been easier for him to go. Getting across Siberia, especially during winter, is no small feat for a man with no help or assistance," Major Ott observed, slowly tapping his pencil on his pad as he pondered the question.

"Well, what if he's Russian, or even Siberian? Perhaps he had been spying for the US, was somehow compromised and found out about it before the hammer fell. Obviously he can speak English, whatever his nationality. But maybe the anthropological theory that Ed is floating is off-base. If he is a Siberian, he could conceivably stay one step ahead of a military search. In addition to Russians, Siberia is populated by indigenous tribes who have no love for the Soviets. They might be inclined to help him. And maybe he used a kayak because it was there and his back was against the wall. Or, maybe he had actually trained to use it in case he ever needed a way of escape," Jim Stewart rubbed his chin, and continued, "That's at least as likely, perhaps *more likely*, than an airplane-flying American Indian trained in the ways of the Force who spies for the CIA and manages to get into trouble in the middle of Siberia."

"I never said CIA," grumped Devlin.

"Jim, you got any tea around this place? Coffee does a job on my gut," Ott asked Stewart, who was playing host.

"Sure, I'll get some." He stepped out and returned with a small pot of tea.

As the major stirred in some sugar, he said carefully, "There's another possibility that no one has mentioned yet. Suppose the search and the rescue, the murder attempt, were part of some elaborately staged ruse? Suppose Meeker actually *is* an American intelligence agent—but a *double* agent? Someone that the Soviets are trying to embed in the US intelligence community?"

The room fell silent as the men considered that thought. It seemed bizarre, in some senses. But when *every detail* of the case was surpassingly strange, even the bizarre might have credibility.

The CIA agent was the first to speak. "Why would he run from us, though? He should be running to us, not away," suggested Bergman.

No one responded because no response was possible. Nothing about this entire incident was adding up neatly. Every possible explanation had an equal weight of plausible arguments against it.

Pierce broke the silence. "Sam, can you get a list of CIA operatives that have disappeared in the Soviet Union in the last eighteen months? Perhaps that would give us some actual possibilities to consider."

"Actually Jesse, no, I can't. As I've already said, the identity and disposition of field agents comprise the most closely held secrets of the CIA for the safety of the agents and their handlers. I'm sorry, I'm not trying to be uncooperative but there are lives at stake." Bergman wearily rubbed his eyes.

The remainder of the meeting was spent dividing up additional tasks, trading phone numbers, and establishing the security classification of project *Snowbird*, as they decided to call it. Due to the events surrounding the rescue and the as-yet unknown implications of what might be at work, *Snowbird* was assigned a "Confidential" classification. The five men agreed to meet again on Tuesday, October 6.

Chapter 13

The spy examined the document carefully. It was classified communications traffic destined for the Pentagon detailing the operational status of all the Air Force Special Operations Commands in PACAF, the Air Force command responsible for the Pacific Ocean region. His Soviet handlers would pay handsomely for this one. He got up and poured himself a cup of tea, casually evaluating the position and alertness of the other individuals in the room. Each was absorbed in his own work; none were paying attention to him.

He returned to his seat with his tea and pulled out a cigarette. Taking his Zippo lighter in his hand, he leaned his elbows on his desk and lit up. Through a pinhole in the bottom of the Zippo, a miniature set of precision-ground lenses directed the image of the classified document onto a frame of six millimeter film inside the lighter. A spring mechanism, which had to be rewound when the film was replaced, silently advanced the film to the next frame after every shot.

The camera was a descendant of the KGB-produced Svouk Camera, tailored to fit in a specially modified, working Zippo lighter. The standard Svouk was useful when there was no chance an agent would be observed. However, with this modified version the spy plied his trade in the open, right in his office. In fact it was his very openness that ensured his clandestine activities would go undiscovered. He didn't act suspiciously, and he was handling documents he'd been officially cleared for.

He worked in the Intelligence Office of Eielson Air Force Base. Among his various responsibilities was producing for the entire PACAF security service community a classified daily intelligence briefing culled from the comm traffic that passed through the office. It was the perfect position: he could cherry-pick documents for his case agent from the many pieces of classified information he handled daily. The camera in the lighter allowed him to take snapshots without attracting the slightest glance. His greed had turned him into a chain smoker, but he didn't care since the unnumbered Swiss bank account he had opened several years ago was growing at a rapid clip.

Pocketing the lighter he returned the classified document to its sturdy manila envelope. His four office mates hadn't so much as glanced in his direction. He got up from his desk, cigarette in mouth. "John," he called to the technical sergeant at the desk at the far end of the room, "I'm finished with these documents; take them to the vault and file them with the rest of today's traffic, would you? This stuff is too sensitive to sit around."

"Yes, sir."

After the E-6 had picked up the material and gone to the vault, the spy returned to his seat and logged into his computer. Connecting to DSNET-2, the military communications subnetwork for classified information, he accessed the Defense Prisoner of War/Missing Personnel Office (DPMO) database. Entering the security code that had been supplied to him, he requested the record of Major Jacob Kelly. After skimming swiftly over the account of the AIB, the spy selected the edit screen and added to the summary: "Certain members of the Board suggested that the loss of the F-16 without a trace might have indicated the pilot defected with the aircraft. This possibility was discussed but ultimately dismissed."

Pressing the Enter button on his keyboard, he waited as the command raced through the wires, microwave transmitters, and satellites between Eielson and Washington, DC. After a few seconds "CONFIRM EDIT? (Y/N)" appeared on his monitor. He typed "Y" and waited again. Several seconds later the words "UPDATE FAILED" were blinking rebelliously on his display. Surprised, the spy terminated the connection and with the slightest apprehension looked around the office. All was normal. No one was paying any attention to him.

****

Sheila Turner had half an eye on the clock. In just fifteen minutes she would head for the weekly TGIF celebration at Toadstools, an upscale bar in downtown Alexandria. Unfortunately it might take fifty minutes to get there with DC area traffic on a Friday afternoon. Not for the first time, she seriously considered walking home. *Nah—ten miles would take too long on foot*, she chuckled to herself. Her phone chirped, interrupting her reverie.

"DOD DPMO office. How can I help you?" she said into the telephone handset. The female voice on the other end had a thick accent of some kind. That combined with the local oldies rock station blaring on her radio obscured the response. Sheila reluctantly turned down the rockin' sounds of Creedence Clearwater Revival.

"I'm sorry, ma'am, I missed that. Would you repeat yourself?

"Yes, I can help you locate missing military service personnel. What branch? . . . Air Force? Okay. What was his na-, oh, I *am* sorry, What *IS* his name?

"Kelly? Thank you, and his first name? . . . Jacob. His rank? . . . Major? Okay. Do you have his social security number? . . . No? Without his social security number, ma'am, it will be much more difficult to locate his records, but we'll try.

"Now, I need some information about you. DOD regulations and the United States Code section 1513 require that we establish your right to receive information as to the accounting of your loved one. This means you must be a next of kin, a family member, or a previously designated person. Are you a next of kin to Major Kelly? . . . How about immediate family? . . . Okay, are you a designated person on his file? No?

"I am so sorry, ma'am, but I can't release any information to you—it's department regulations . . . I am sure it *is* important, but I cannot help you unless you've been properly authorized to receive information . . . Ma'am, if he has checked in, he wouldn't be on our file. We only handle *missing* servicemen . . . No, ma'am, I'm not even allowed to tell you if we think he is alive, not unless you are authorized to receive the information. I am terribly sorry."

Sheila replaced the phone in the cradle, oddly moved by the desperation she sensed in the pleas of the woman with whom she had just been speaking. That was the worst part of this job—sometimes it was a girlfriend, a mistress, or an old flame calling, hoping to locate information about a missing lover. Service casualties were so tough on loved ones. There was rarely closure when there was no body: it was as if their loved one evaporated into thin air.

But something about this call struck her as strange, especially the question about whether or not the major had checked in. Perhaps it was the odd accent of the caller. Or maybe the rank of the serviceman—you just don't go around losing many majors during peacetime. Sheila sighed and looked up at the clock. Toadstools could wait just a little longer.

Sheila wiggled the mouse to awaken her dozing computer. Her fingers danced over the keyboard, calling up the Air Force database for the Defense Prisoners of War/Missing Personnel. She entered the name and sat back to wait. The search would not take long; by computer standards the database wasn't that large. As the network handled the request, she idly wondered how many Major Jacob Kellys there might be on file.

A moment later she had her answer. Only one—and what she saw had her reaching for the phone to summon her supervisor. A few moments later Ben Jones sauntered over to her cubicle with an expectant look on his face.

"Ah, Sheil', rethinking my offer I'll bet," he crowed, "it's not too late to get reservations at Toni's. Dinner's on me, and I promise I'll behave myself."

"Sorry Ben, I am not available and not at all interested. You aren't my type and I'm probably not yours."

With a mock downcast look Ben sighed with resignation,

"Okay. Your loss. What's up?"

Sheila explained the phone call and then pointed to the record. "There were several requests for information up to about ten months ago, and nothing since. But look at the data. Major Kelly was last stationed at Edwards. He had an exemplary service record, a real boy scout. He was assigned to an unspecified classified project as a test pilot. At the time of the accident he was on a qualification refresher flight, flying out of Eielson. The details of the incident itself are classified—even we cannot get the information. All we know is that he was lost somewhere in the Bering Sea while flying an F-16. He is missing and presumed dead."

Ben looked bored. "Too bad for him. You called me out on a Friday afternoon to show me this? Why?"

Sheila frowned at the monitor. "Look at the changelog. Earlier *today* there was an attempt made to edit the record. The attempt failed. The failure code here means 'insufficient privileges.' Somebody off-site tried to change the record. And look at the attempted change: someone tried to add information to the AIB report, indicating they had considered pilot defection as a possibility."

Ben mulled over that for a moment in silence. "Okay," he admitted, "that is a bit odd. Anything else?"

"This lady spoke with an accent—some flavor of Russian, I believe. And I got the distinct impression from something she asked that she actually had information—almost like she had seen him. And she wasn't family or PDP."

Ben groaned, "Another one of your hunches, huh? You're not reading Tom Clancy again, are you? Okay, look, why don't you record the attempted access in the record but leave your hunches out. And go home, will ya? It's Friday!" He returned to his cubicle, and began clearing off his desk, preparing to leave for the day.

Unknown outside of the Washington headquarters of the DPMO, a changelog feature had been added to the database. It didn't show up on the user's screen nor was there evidence of it in the data they had access to. It had originated as a "data integrity" feature, providing a before-and-after picture of the

data whenever a record was updated. However, it had morph-
ed into something of a cheap security feature, recording all attempts—successful and unsuccessful—to change the data.
The upshot of this was that whoever attempted to change
Major Kelly's DPMO record would know only that the attempt failed. They would not know that the attempt had been
recorded.

Sheila took another look at the clock and sighed. Now she
was on personal time—the department head never approved
overtime. Never. Another sigh. Sheila pulled up the major's
file on her monitor and made a complete entry, including her
impressions from the phone call. She might be a government
employee but she was committed to doing her job with excellence. Smirking inwardly as her fingers completed their ballet
on the keyboard, she confessed to herself that she was a bit
obsessive. It was just one of her things and had nothing to do
with pay or position. She must have learned it from her dad.
Shutting off her computer and the cubicle lights, her thoughts
were wrapped around the coming weekend before she even
got to the parking lot.

****

It was no secret, really. All DPMO personnel knew that
their work would be constantly reviewed. However, it might
surprise the general public to learn who the reviewers were
and why. Some genius somewhere in one of the intelligence
services had foreseen that the DPMO records were likely targets for terrorists and unfriendly governments. If a foreign intelligence service was able to easily acquire the names and ad-
dresses of family members of US servicemen held in captiv-
ity, they could manipulate that family with threats or promises.
It could also work the other way: interrogations were vastly
more effective if the serviceman realized the animals torturing
him also knew where his wife and children lived. And so to
protect both the serviceman and his family, verification of the
identity of a requester was necessary before the DPMO would
release any information.

All requests for information were dutifully logged along with the DPMO clerk's impressions of the call. The data was salted away in the DPMO database and—in most cases—never looked at again. A record of all accesses of DPMO data was sent to the massive computer bank of the Defense Intelligence Agency (DIA), where it joined with the flood of other daily information, waiting for some pair of eyes to make sense of it. Which rarely happened. There was simply too much, a digital tsunami of data that might have been useful had there been a small army of people employed to review it and connect the dots. No federal budget had ever been proposed that would have made such an evaluation possible—not by the most freewheeling Democratic administrations nor the most defense-happy Republican ones.

Which is why the *Watcher* had been created. The *Watcher* was a sophisticated text-scanning program that examined digital data. The DIA's daily intake of information was filtered by the *Watcher* using a highly classified word and phrase list designed to snag anything of intelligence interest.

DIA analysts and others with a sufficiently potent combination of security clearance and departmental clout could submit their desired word list to the DIA's Office of Data Analysis and receive daily encrypted updates containing a précis of hits. In peacetime intelligence terms, *Watcher* hits on DPMO traffic were generally considered by the big guns at the DIA to be fairly trivial and therefore could be viewed at the requester's location (as opposed to being restricted to a secure location).

And so it came to pass that an encrypted email transmission containing two hits was ghosting through the electronic ether of the secured side of MILNET, landing in the Edwards Air Force Base secured mail server at 2205 hours EDT, addressed to General Jim Franks. One of the hits contained in the email was the unsuccessful attempt to modify Jake's DPMO record, originating from a computer at Eielson AFB. The other was Sheila Turner's access to his record.

General Franks had submitted Major Jacob Kelly's name to the DIA's *Watcher* word list several months after the major disappeared. He had used up a lot of political capital to get his way but in the end he prevailed. Consequently, intel traffic floating around any of the subnets of MILNET containing Jake's name would wind up on Franks' desk. So far it had been a dry well. But then, Jim Franks had never really been sure what he was looking for. He just knew something about this entire deal was not right. His conversation earlier in the day with Admiral Bridger had finally vindicated his longstanding concerns.

The general had never been convinced by the conclusions of the Accident Investigation Board. Jake had been doing low-level slow-flight exercises in an F-16 as part of a test of the *Hydra* avionics: the AIB concluded that he had flown too low and too slow. Since there was no radar operating in the vicinity at the time of the crash, there was no electronic record of the disappearance. With no data available there was virtually nothing to investigate. Even though Jake was the best there was, in the fine Air Force tradition of blaming the pilot rather than the equipment the AIB had ultimately concluded pilot error. Franks didn't buy that conclusion. And so on a hunch he had bargained his way into submitting Kelly's name to the DIA's *Watcher* program. He figured that sooner or later something would turn up. The two accesses on October 2 to the DPMO records were his first hits.

The email would have to wait until Monday morning to complete its electronic journey to the in-basket of his desktop computer. Franks and his wife were already driving north on US 395, headed for the South Fork of the Kern River for a weekend of camping and trout fishing with friends.

Chapter 14

**The weekend of October 3 and 4 (Saturday and Sunday), 1987
South Fork of the Kern River, CA**

Franks' eyes opened and he slowly came to awareness in the still dim, early morning light. He could hear the South Fork of the Kern River busily gurgling as the water ran over the stones on its journey to Lake Isabella. The scent of pine trees filled the little camper. There was a snappy chill in the fresh air. Evidently he had forgotten to light the propane heater before he and Shandra went to bed. The sound of someone pumping up a Coleman stove intruded into the early morning stillness. Roger must have beat him to the task of fixing coffee. He smiled, wondering if his friend would serve it to him in bed. Not likely. But it was worth a try. "I'll take mine with two sugars and a shot of cream," he spoke softly into the brisk morning air.

"Dream on, you sluggard," came the quiet but merciless reply through the thin wall of the pop-up camper. "Get your sorry black butt out of that bed and help me fix breakfast. We came up here to fish, not to sleep."

"Patience, my friend. You know as well as I do that trout keep bankers' hours."

"Get outta bed," was the grumbling reply.

Jim and Shandra Franks had rendezvoused at the Texaco station in Olancha the night before with their dear friends, Roger and Susan Bates. It was well after dark when the two couples met up, each pulling a camper. They took a Forest Service road to the west, driving into the Inyo National Forest. After fifteen miles they turned onto an unmarked, rutted road—little more than a trail—and drove for another mile along the banks of the South Fork of the Kern to their favorite camping spot. With the help of each other's headlights they had maneuvered their little campers into place, leveled them, and turned in.

Several years before Roger had seen the little meadow from the air with the silver thread of the river winding on its eastern edge. After some rummaging around on Forest Service roads with the help of USGS maps, he discovered the camping hideaway, all but unknown to others. Since then the Bates and Franks had been meeting at the spot three or four times a year to recharge and let the tension of military service drain away. Captain Roger Bates, USN, had been a good friend of Jim Franks ever since they had attended the same Presbyterian church in Norfolk, Virginia, years before. Bates had been stationed at Oceana Naval Air Station, and Franks was doing a stint at Langley AFB. Since those days they camped, fished, and hunted together whenever they had the opportunity. Their wives were also close and enjoyed opportunities to get together.

Shivering, Franks reluctantly emerged from his warm blankets and pulled on his jeans.

****

Jake pumped a quarter into the vending machine sitting outside the restaurant and pulled out the morning edition of the *Anchorage Daily News*. He entered the little diner in search of breakfast. After the waitress had taken his order and brought his coffee, he spread the newspaper out on his table and began to examine it. He froze, cup midway to his lips. There staring up at him from the front page below the fold was a sketch of himself, accompanied by an AP story with the headline, *Mystery Man Disappears Without a Trace*. He felt a brief thrill of panic before he realized the sketch was taken from the hospital's description of him, when he still had a heavy beard and long hair. Unconsciously rubbing his clean-shaven chin, he sipped his coffee and began to read the article.

KOTZEBUE, AK (AP) - - Kotzebue is, by

all accounts, not where most people go for thrills. This quiet little town is perched on a narrow finger of land jutting into Kotzebue Sound, some thirty miles north of the Arctic Circle. Fishing and hunting are the major income producers for the local residents. The most excitement citizens have experienced in the last year came when the weekly mail plane hit a flock of geese while on final approach several months back. The pilot and the mail survived, the geese did not. Other than that, things are pretty dull. Until last Friday anyway, when a fisherman suffering from hypothermia was pulled from the Bering Strait and helicoptered to the hospital. A local resident identified the man as John Meeker, address unknown.

Meeker has managed to turn things upside down in the sleepy little community. It seems the fisherman, recovering from a dangerous bout with hypothermia, has disappeared without a trace. He left behind a drugged guard occupying Meeker's own hospital bed, plus an unknown individual who was found handcuffed to the other bed and is now a suspect in a criminal case. These events were followed on Tuesday by a spectacular brawl involving Alaska State Troopers, a gentleman from Anchorage, and Kotzebue's own Charlie Olson, the desk clerk at the local hotel. Add to that the theft of the hospital administrator's aircraft, and the residents of Kotzebue have had enough excitement to last them until next spring. All of these events are somehow connected to Meeker, who is doubtless not welcome to return to the little community even though his presence has produced sufficient mayhem to entertain this northern fishing village for several years.

If piecing together the events is difficult, understanding their significance is next to impossible, as neither hospital officials nor the troopers are talking much about the case. A possible reconstruction of events looks like this: On Friday the 25th, Meeker was brought into the Kotzebue Hospital. A guard consisting of Alaska State Troopers was placed outside his room (no reason has been given for their presence). Shortly after midnight on Sunday morning, Meeker was discovered missing, and one of his guards was found sleeping in Meeker's bed. Handcuffed to the other bed was an unknown individual who was eventually taken into custody by the police. Unconfirmed rumors allege that the man had attempted to murder Meeker.

By late Sunday afternoon, a large team of investigators was scouring the town, interviewing its residents and hunting for Meeker. On Tuesday a second suspect was apprehended in the dining room of the local hotel, but not before two troopers were badly injured in an attempt to arrest him. Hotel clerk Charlie Olson said, "I saw the whole thing. The fellow was a guest in the hotel, registered as 'Ralph Goodwin.' He was eating lunch in the dining room when the trooper walked over to his table. Next thing I know the cop is lying unconscious on the floor. This other policeman ran in and Goodwin dropped him too. So I pulled out my gun and held it on him until the third trooper had him in handcuffs." Olson, the only witness to these events who's willing to talk, reported that the troopers had linked the stolen aircraft to the case.

The Alaska State Troopers refused to comment, but late yesterday afternoon they released a sketch of Meeker, saying only that he is being sought in connection with the felony theft of the hospital administrator's airplane. He is considered armed and dangerous.

Meanwhile, speculation is running rampant in Kotzebue over the whole mysterious affair. Most residents believe that the events are related to a failed drug deal. "Anyway," Olson said, "Meeker left the hospital without paying his bill."

The pretty waitress brought his plate of scrambled eggs and bacon and refilled his coffee cup. Kelly folded the paper and began to eat. The clock was ticking now. The Mooney would soon be discovered, and that would place him in the Anchorage area. The sketch would be re-released, minus the facial hair. Posters would sprout all over the city and some good citizen would spot him. His only hope was that Bill Jensen could uncover something first.

****

"Hold on, sailor! Just where do you think you're going?"

Standing in his waders, fly rod in hand, wearing a fishing vest and a navy blue ball cap emblazoned with *USS Yorktown CG-48*, Roger looked at his wife and said mildly without a trace of sarcasm, "I thought I would walk down to the mall and do some shopping, Sue. Would you like to come?"

She stuck out her tongue at him and replied saucily, "What

about cleaning up the breakfast dishes? Aren't you planning on helping with that?"

"Wait a minute, babe! The guys fixed breakfast this morning, so the girls do the dishes. This evening you two can fix supper, and Jim and I will do the dishes." Roger looked over at Jim and winked, "Besides, Sue, *we* are going out to catch dinner."

Shandra looked at Sue and said dryly, "That probably means we'll have to run down to Olancha for dinner. Last time they promised to catch us dinner I think we wound up going out for steaks."

"O, ye of little faith," rejoined Franks, coming out of the camper in attire similar to that of his buddy. "If the Lord could multiply loaves and fishes in Galilee surely He can give us four nice fat trout in California!"

Shandra rolled her eyes at her husband and said, "We'll see about that. It probably has more to do with whether or not the fish are biting. Anyway, if you two promise to do dishes tonight I suppose you can run along. Try not to get into too much trouble."

****

"Stick him, stick him, STICK HIM! Whatsa matter with you guys? I can't believe it! Where did you guys learn to tackle?" Ed Devlin was screaming at the TV set and pacing around the den, as the speedy Temple running back took a screen pass forty yards into the end zone for a touchdown. Penn State's linebacker corps had blitzed, and the Temple quarterback tossed the ball over their heads to his tailback for the score.

"Boy, I don't know, Dad. The Penn State defense looked a little flat-footed on that play." Devlin's teenage son reached for another Pepsi, shaking his head.

"Tell me about it," grunted Devlin as he finally sat back down. The phone rang, and he went upstairs to take the call.

"Devlin here. What's up?"

"Ed, we found the Mooney!"

"Finally! Where was it?"

"He set it down on a gravel strip northeast of town that belongs to a local flying club. Most of them only go out on weekends. Apparently some of the members went out there today, and noticed a strange aircraft tied down. One of the guys had seen the news reports about Meeker's escape from Kotzebue and called us right away. We lifted numerous prints from the plane, and they match Meeker's. We combed the plane carefully, but found nothing else of value."

"Excellent! Great work, Tom! Listen, I want you to get an artist to redo the sketch of Meeker, only this time shave him and give him a haircut. I want that sketch in every post office, in every diner, and on every telephone pole within thirty miles of the landing strip by tomorrow morning. And make sure the paper prints the revised sketch in its Monday edition."

"Will do. Anything else?"

"Yeah, call Dr. Carrock and let him know we found his airplane. Take photos, search the plane a second time, and then let him come and pick it up."

"Okay. How's the game?"

"We'll win. Temple just took it into the end zone, but Penn State is still ahead. The linebackers have been repeatedly suckered on screen plays, but they'll catch on and shut the Owls down before they do much more damage. At least, I hope they will!"

"Hope so. Well, enjoy the game, Ed. I'll call you back if we learn anything new."

****

Standing midstream, Roger put on his sunglasses and took a second look at the pool formed by the eddy of water around a large rock about thirty feet upstream of him. Though the water was crystal clear there was enough turbulence that, with the shifting patterns of light, he wasn't sure what he was seeing. For a moment he thought he'd seen the shadow of a large fish swimming idly in the eddy. "Likely spot," he murmured to himself.

Bates deftly cast his fly about six feet above the rock, and let the current carry the tiny nymph into the little pool. Immediately he spied a subtle flash, with an accompanying swirl on the surface. He carefully set the hook and wrestled the large trout towards him. He had gotten the fish close when it changed directions and darted downstream. He shifted his footing to turn and face downstream, but stepped on a slick, round boulder underwater. Slipping, he sat down hard in the stream, his waders filling with the icy water. Sputtering and staggering, he went down several more times getting wet from head to toe. At least he was still holding onto his rod. As Roger recovered his footing and turned to continue to play the large trout, he fervently hoped his buddy had not seen the debacle—he'd never live it down.

The fish darted over to a chute where the water was being forced rapidly through a narrow channel. Between the force of the water and the convulsing motions of the fish it was too much for the light leader, which snapped. Just in time for Roger to slip one more time into the water.

Howling laughter erupted from the far side of the stream, and Bates glared over to see Jim Franks sitting on a boulder, doubled up with laughter, enjoying the show. "Wow, aren't you gra—ha ha ha—graceful! Would you, ha ha ha, would you, aha, oh my, would you like me to get your bathing suit? Or maybe you'd like a towel and a bar of soap, ha ha? Oh, my—" Jim wiped the tears out of his eyes and looked up, still grinning and chuckling.

Maintaining as much dignity as possible, Bates sloshed stiffly across the stream and sat down next to Jim without a word. Setting his fly rod down, he pulled his creel around and opened it up. "I have three large trout in mine. What have you got in yours?" he asked indignantly, knowing the answer.

Jim's smile turned to a frown and he said with mock resentment, "Well, you don't have to get nasty about it. You really did look funny out there." He started chuckling again.

"I repeat the question."

"Oh brother! Nothing! I haven't caught a thing all morning!"

"Do you suppose it might have something to do with the fact that you aren't fishing? For crying out loud, Jim, you've been wandering around watching me all morning. I don't even think you've put your line in the water."

"Can't decide which fly to use," Franks said lamely.

"Bull! I know you, buddy! Something is bugging you. What's up? Do you want to talk about it?"

Franks sat silently for a moment pretending to examine the selections in his fly wallet. He closed it without taking one and looked up. "Roger, I can't tell you any details, 'cause it's classified. But, yes, I do have a lot on my mind. One of my men has been missing for the last fifteen months. He was a good friend as well as being a key part of a project I'm working on. I learned yesterday that his disappearance might involve foul play by a foreign government."

Roger responded, "I am sorry to hear that, Jim. Is there anything anyone can do about it?" He unbuttoned the straps on his waders and pulled them off, dumping the water out.

"Yeah, we are taking a second look at it. I have a new friend—he's also in the Navy, by the way—who came up with some new information. We're putting our heads together to quietly re-open the investigation. But there's just not that much to go on right now, and a lot of restrictions on the way we can pursue it. It's a complicated situation with many unpleasant ramifications. We may be on the verge of opening Pandora's proverbial box."

"I'm sorry to hear that, Jim, but you cannot do a single thing about it up here in the mountains. You will be a lot fresher on Monday if you do some fishing today. Here, gimme your fly wallet."

Franks handed it over and Roger unzipped it. He selected a light brown nymph with white hackle and said, "This one. Tie it on and get in the stream. We need at least one more fish for dinner, and frankly, I'd like to have a couple on hand for breakfast in the morning. If we come back without enough fish we'll be hearing about it from our wives from now till Christmas. Get in there and catch some trout!"

"Yes, sir, Cap'n. Right away."

"That's more like it."

****

Roger pumped up the Coleman lantern and then searched through the box of groceries for the kitchen matches. Finding one, he struck it and pushed the match through the lighting hole. Too far! The fragile mantle collapsed into white ash. Turning off the gas, he exclaimed, "NUTS! Susan, did we bring any spare mantles for the lantern?"

Her voice floated through the side of the camper as she pulled on some warmer clothes, "They are in the bottom of the food box, sweetie."

Finally he got it lit and sat down with his wife next to Jim and Shandra as the fading rays of sunlight gradually disappeared from the peak high above them. The two couples sat quietly; the hiss of the lantern and the chuckle of the stream were the only sounds. Overhead a few stars began to push their twinkle into the gathering dusk. On a slope opposite, two deer gingerly walked into the clearing, noses held high, testing the scents on the breeze. Satisfied, they began to graze on the grasses. As the night drew on the temperature dropped, causing tendrils of mist to rise, phantom-like, from the meadow.

After chatting for an hour or so, the girls got too cold and went into one of the campers to play cards. Jim got up and put a fresh pot of coffee on the stove. The lantern cast a small circle of light, just enough to take in their folding table and chairs. All beyond that little circle was darkness. The night was perfectly still, stars glittering overhead like celestial jewelry.

Jim broke the silence. "Where have you been the last year, Rog? Somehow I lost track of your activities after your tour in the Indian Ocean commanding the *Yorktown*."

"Since that tour has been up, I have been working between Alameda and Washington, DC, of all places."

"Washington? What is a swabbie like yourself doing hobnobbing with that crowd?" Jim poured himself a fresh cup and sat back down.

"Well, we have been doing some joint exercises with the Australian Navy, and so I've probably spent as much time with Australian naval attachés in DC as I have spent out here in Alameda. We've been working on coordinated ship maneuvers, ironing out communications frequencies and protocols, and everything else down to examining what spare parts we use in common. The Aussies are good folks and strong allies. I'm glad to see us firming up our relationship with them.

"Last summer we did a joint naval exercise southeast of the Kamchatka Peninsula, far enough from the Soviets where we weren't considered too provocative but close enough to trigger some of their defense networks. We had a couple of Hawkeyes in the air, one near the western boundary of our operation and another further to the east. Both of our airborne early warning setups were able to capture some good data that will be useful in the future. We got to compare our SIGINT with what the Aussies were able to pick up. We also had observers on each major surface combatant in both of our navies observing tactics and procedures. All in all, it was a great exercise. If China ever wakes up we are going to need good allies in the Pacific and Australia is going to figure into that equation." Roger went over and pumped up the Coleman lantern again, as it was beginning to dim.

As he stared into his coffee cup Jim thought about what Roger had just said. Suddenly, a possibility bubbled up in his thinking. "Rog, when were those exercises held?"

"During July of last year."

"Were they going on during 10 July?"

Roger looked at him curiously and replied, "Uh-huh. Why?"

"Roger, what is the passive ELINT range of the electronics in an E-2?"

"Well, it depends on the Hawkeye's altitude and the strength and nature of the signal being emitted, of course. There are atmospheric factors as well. But typically they can detect a strong military emission from five hundred miles, or more."

Franks set his cup on the table, put his hands behind his

head, and gazed up at the stars. "Okay, let's be specific. Would the Hawkeye on the eastern side of your joint exercise have been able to pick up a Soviet jamming signal coming from further north in the Bering Sea?"

"Possibly—that's a really strong signal type. With the interaction of signal bounce from the ionosphere, nighttime would give us a longer range. But we wouldn't be able to peg the position of the source, just the bearing. Why all this sudden curiosity about the E-2?"

"You might be able to solve a puzzle for me. Did you guys save your tapes from that operation?"

"Of course. We always do. There are times when we want to go back and take a second look at the data."

"Roger, consider this an official interservice request from me as an Air Force general to you as a Navy captain. I need you to go back and have your people analyze those tapes for anything—anything—that might have been emitted from air or surface craft north and east of that second Hawkeye on the night of 10 July. I am looking for a Soviet jamming signal intended to jam the communications in an F-16."

Roger looked at his friend in the dim lantern light and knew that he was quite serious. He also guessed that the request was in some way related to their discussion earlier in the day. "Can you tell me anything about this situation, Jim?"

"No, I really can't. It is not a problem of me trusting you. This thing is so sensitive I can't even talk to my own people about it. Do you know Admiral Bridger?"

"Sure, who doesn't? He is a legend in special operations. Probably one of the finest leaders the Navy has produced. In fact, I met him during the work on our joint exercise with the cousins down under. He and the corresponding Australian special ops guy met together in DC last year to get on the same page. I was part of that meeting."

"John Bridger and I are communicating on this situation. Any approval you need can come straight from him. Unfortunately, I can't speak with anyone in Air Force Intelligence. I can't even write this request down on paper. It's that bad."

"Air Force Intelligence. Isn't that what they call an oxymoron, Jim?"

Franks shook his head. "I'm surprised they teach you Navy people words like that. It's kind of like wasting fine wine on a drunk. You learn one four-syllable word and you think that qualifies you to compete with Johnny Carson."

"You need to think of some better insults, Jim, or you won't be as much fun anymore." Roger threw the dregs left in his cup into the dirt, stood up, and stretched. "I'll have those tapes checked for you and let you know what I find. I'll put some guys on it Monday." He picked up the cooler and locked it in the cab of his pickup truck. "I'm going to bed. Don't leave anything sitting around for the bears. I'm not partial to midnight visitors. It's your turn to get up early and make coffee in the morning. By the way, tomorrow's Sunday. Would you mind leading us in a brief time of study and prayer?"

"Be glad to. Did you bring a tie?"

"No, and you didn't either, you old phony. Go to bed."

****

Late Sunday afternoon found Sam Bergman in his office at Langley. Something about the Kotzebue case was nagging him and he could not put his finger on it. He pulled out the briefing materials that Lieutenant Commander Jesse Pierce had prepared and reread everything carefully. He wasn't seeing something that was there, something that was hovering on the fringes of his thoughts.

On a whim he found the sheet with the phone numbers and dialed Jim Stewart's office in Seattle.

"Stewart here."

"This is Sam Bergman, Jim. What are you doing in the office today? Aren't you supposed to be home with your family?"

"Yeah? Ten bucks says you aren't calling from home yourself, Sam."

"Wow, you FBI guys are sharp," Sam replied dryly.

"Somebody's got to keep the Agency in line. What can I do for you, Sam?"

"Just checking to see if you've got anything on Meeker's fingerprints yet."

"Nope. NCIC was no help at all. *Nada.*"

"Hmmm. Too bad. Okay. Thanks anyway. See you Tuesday, Jim."

Bergman hung up the phone, and pulled a piece of red licorice out of the bag in his desk. Chewing on it, he went back over the details of the case, trying to recognize which piece was out of place. He knew something from the data was leading him to yet another conclusion. It just hadn't jelled yet.

Flipping once again through the folder of briefing materials, his eyes landed on the photocopy of the note left by Meeker at the crime scene. He read it and then read it again more carefully.

> *Nurse, this room is a crime scene. Please contact the police. The man in the bed is the guard. He is okay, I just dropped a few sleeping pills in his coffee. The man on the floor was, I believe, intending to kill me. I don't know why. He was carrying $1500 in cash, small bills. I have appropriated that for my use. Make sure the Zippo is analyzed, and don't touch the sharp pin at its base. It's probably got poison on it.*

Bergman studied the note. The penmanship was neat, there were no misspelled words, and the message was thorough and concise. The casual and conversational tone was not what one would expect from someone who had just survived an attempt on his life. His approach to the police was helpful, not adversarial, even to the point of letting them know about the cash the man was carrying.

Putting the pieces together, Bergman figured that Meeker was intelligent, cool under pressure, and observant, and thought of himself as on the same side as the police. The would-be assassin whom Meeker had cold-cocked was a big man, probably a skilled street fighter, and likely trained in martial arts. Which meant, Bergman concluded, that Meeker must be even better. *And he survived Sibera, so he's more likely a military or special ops guy than a spook,* Sam considered.

With a start, the CIA agent sat up straight. He had the missing piece! They were looking for clues—specifically, fingerprints—in the wrong places! Meeker wasn't a criminal—that was clear—he was a trained professional—probably military. No wonder the NCIC database was not helpful in matching Meeker's fingerprints. They were looking for their needle in the wrong haystack.

He dialed Stewart again.

"Stewart here."

"Jim, it's me again. Listen, have you run those prints through the FBI's military database?"

"No, why?"

"I'm working on a hunch. Would you mind submitting them to the military database as well? I took a second look at the note he left in the hospital room and started connecting some dots. I think this guy is military." Bergman explained his ideas.

"Sure. I'll let you know if I get any hits."

Chapter 15

Bill Jensen exited I-495 with its busy, pounding traffic and merged onto the George Washington Parkway. He loved the scenic boulevard contoured to the curves of the Potomac as it meandered past the capitol, especially after the adrenaline-tinged contest on the Capitol Beltway. This time of night the traffic was not bad at all on the Parkway.

As he drove he thought about the AP story that had appeared in the *Washington Post* that morning. Buried several pages inside the front section was an article about the mysterious disappearance of "John Meeker" from a hospital in the quiet little village of Kotzebue, Alaska. He knew that if the story had been printed in DC it must be fairly big news in Anchorage. In any case the DC paper had not carried it for its news value, for it had none, but for the human interest, complete with a vanishing mystery man. Besides which it was a slow weekend for news, anyway.

Pulling into the CIA parking lot, Jensen parked far enough away from the entrance to allow him to enjoy a leisurely stroll to the door under a clear, unseasonably warm night sky. After many years as a case officer with contacts spread across Cambodia, Vietnam, Thailand, and China, he had pulled back from field operations—except for special projects. Presently he was the special assistant to the Deputy Director of Operations (DDO). The nebulous title gave him tremendous leeway to choose his own projects in the Operations Directorate. The DDO had created the position for Jensen out of thin air because he didn't want to lose to retirement a field officer with Jensen's depth of experience. Though Bill was not presently involved in field operations he maintained his non-official cover as a professor at Georgetown. Teaching remained his first love.

At this time of night most of the clerical employees were absent—but Langley never slept. Every division and most departments had a watch officer and a small after-hours duty staff. Most of the professionals were married to their jobs, leaving the office only long enough to sleep—usually at odd hours. Some slept at the office. Divorce was common among Agency employees and was viewed as a sort of collateral damage of the secret war to keep America's enemies at bay. Having kept his marriage a top priority, it was damage Bill Jensen had successfully avoided over many years. He maintained a regular schedule, but tonight was an exception; he'd come in at the late hour to get some uninterrupted time to research Jake's story. Jensen unlocked his office, grabbed his cup, and went in search of fresh coffee.

****

On 4 December, 1984, a Titan 34D had roared off the launchpad at Vandenberg Air Force Base carrying a classified payload. The National Space Science Data Center cataloged the thirteen thousand kilogram orbital satellite as *1984-122A*. Reporters knew that a launch had occurred—it was impossible to hide. But the Air Force remained very tight-lipped about the nature of satellite carried on that particular rocket.

Soon enough, the Soviets knew what it was. It was the sixth in a series of high-resolution, live-video, reconnaissance satellites code-named *Crystal.* The military designation was *KH-11.* Some years later it would be revealed to an amazed public as one of the *Key Hole* spy satellites. The theoretical resolution of the 2.3 meter mirror and the 800x800 pixel Charge-coupled Device (CCD) serving as its optical element would permit this "eye-in-the-sky" to distinguish objects as small as six inches on earth. Due to atmospheric conditions and imperfections in the optics and electronics, theoretical resolution was never attained; nonetheless, the Key Hole was practically like having an agent with camera in place.

At roughly the same time that Jensen was walking into CIA headquarters in northern Virginia, KH-11 number six was passing over the port city of Magadan, USSR, shortly before 1300 hours local time, Monday, October 5. The satellite had been tasked to photograph the harbor facilities and shipping. Among other items of interest, analysts would take a census of the Soviet Pacific Fleet surface ships from the images and ascertain which and how many submarines were in their pens. Magadan served as one of the four major ports of the fleet.

Providentially, the KH-11 satellite had been programmed to begin its reconnaissance three minutes early. At the specified time a stream of images began to be recorded on tape at the NSA satellite receiving facility at Fort Belvoir, Virginia. Included in the data stream were crystal clear images of the new GRU detention facility under construction northwest of Magadan. General Chernikov's project was on candid camera, only no one realized it yet.

****

Jensen had already studied Jake's service records and the AIB report on the loss of the pilot and aircraft on 10 July, 1986. Those documents provided a good baseline of information on the individual and the incident. But they provided no clues as to what sort of mischief might currently be operating below the radar. Some detective work was in order.

But Jensen had to be very careful. If Jake was correct that the Air Force was compromised at one or more levels, then someone might be snooping around to see who *else* was snooping. The professor knew he had to stay under the wire if he was going to be successful. He considered his dilemma carefully and finally decided that it was not quite the Gordian knot that he feared, for two reasons.

First, Bill knew that Jake suspected someone in Air Force Personnel and someone else in Operations. At least on this one point Bill Jensen was quite confident that Kelly was wrong. No one from Personnel would have been required in this particular situation. The Soviets had not wanted to get their hands on Jake because he was Major Jacob Kelly; rather, they wanted him because he was the chief test pilot for *Hydra*. Had John Doe been the chief test pilot they would have gone after John Doe, and not Jake. So they didn't need someone in Personnel shifting officers around—they simply went after whatever man was the *Hydra* test pilot.

The professor allowed himself a chuckle as he imagined what sort of postmortem the GRU would be conducting as a result of Kelly's successful escape from both the detention compound and the USSR itself. He would be willing to bet next year's pay that whoever was in charge was wishing that *Hydra's* chief test pilot had been *any* John Doe *other than* Jacob Kelly. No one else could have escaped as Jake did: of that Jensen was sure.

The second reason that Jensen considered the problem to be a little less intractable than originally feared was that the infiltration of USAF Operations was likely local to PACAF, and most probably, local to the F-16 Wing stationed at Eielson AFB. If his supposition was correct the spy probably wouldn't possess sufficient clearance to discover that Jensen was on the prowl.

As he sipped his coffee and pondered these thoughts, he realized the most likely source for intelligence pertaining to Major Kelly was the DIA's *Watcher* program. It might be interesting reading, he mused, to see who—if anyone—was getting updates based on the name 'Jacob Kelly.'

As the special assistant to the DDO, Jensen had black access to the DIA's sophisticated text-scanning program. He could access the current word list, see who the submitters were, and submit his own word list all without the knowledge of others, unless they also possessed black access privileges.

He pressed his thumb onto the fingerprint scanner attached to his terminal and then entered a password. Using the secured side of MILNET, he logged into the *Watcher* utility interface and queried the word list. In less than sixty seconds he had his answer. Two individuals had submitted Jake's name to the list.

The first was Admiral John Bridger. Jensen raised his eyebrows. Bridger was a heavyweight in the arena of covert operations. He was the CO of Navy Special Warfare Group One, based in San Diego. *Why would Bridger be involved with this?* the professor asked himself. He looked at the data again and was surprised to see that Admiral Bridger's entry to the *Watcher* word list was submitted just two days ago, late Friday evening.

"Whose team are you playing for, Admiral?" Bill wondered out loud. He could not imagine Bridger had been turned. If he had it would be a national security disaster. Something must have prompted the naval officer to start searching for intelligence traffic on Jake. Jensen made a note to investigate the link that connected Admiral Bridger to Kelly.

The second name was General James Franks. Jensen knew that Franks commanded the *Hydra* project. He had placed Jake's name on the watch list about a year ago, shortly after the AIB had presented their finding. Jensen felt sure the general was clean. If Franks had been in the Russian's pocket there would have been no need to kidnap Kelly. "You didn't believe the AIB's conclusion, did you, General?" Bill Jensen muttered. "Were I in your shoes I would not have believed it either."

Looking further down the *Watcher* report, he saw that Franks had gotten two hits on Friday afternoon. The first was an access to Jake's DPMO record. "Strange," he murmured to himself. Someone had tried to add to the record but the attempt had failed. He scribbled down the relevant information and determined to investigate the lead further. The second access was a successful update of the DPMO record by a DPMO employee. Jensen read Sheila Turner's descriptive account of the mysterious phone call and her concerns about the failed access. The professor read and reread Turner's stated impression: she suspected that the caller had actually seen Jake alive at some point since his disappearance. Jensen made a note to bring the item up with Kelly the next time they talked on the phone.

His yellow legal pad had five items on it:

1. *Investigate John Bridger. Why is he checking intelligence traffic on Kelly?*

2. *Interview Jim Franks. Why did he submit Jake's name to Watcher? Does he have information that leads him to doubt the AIB report?*

3. *Get a technician to pull up all the data available on the failed access to the DPMO record.*

4. *Interview Sheila Turner, the DPMO employee.*

5. *Ask Jake for his ideas on Sheila Turner's mysterious phone call.*

Wearily, Bill Jensen looked at the clock. It was a little after midnight. Enough for one day. He locked the legal pad in his office safe, turned off the lights and headed for home. In the morning he had a full day of classes at Georgetown University. Tuesday, he would begin tracking down his leads. It had been a productive night. As he walked back to his car he figured he was going to need his graduate teaching assistants to take his classes for the next several weeks, starting on Wednesday.

****

"Captain, when will this facility be complete?" Chernikov looked at the man with barely veiled contempt. The commander of the GRU engineering detachment was overweight, had a plain, peasant's face, and wore a vacuous look that made Chernikov wonder if he was truly sentient. *He would look perfectly natural wearing a straw hat and sitting on a mule*, the general thought to himself.

"All the footers and concrete pads for the buildings have been poured. Framing is going on in the administrative buildings as we speak, and the plumbers and electricians are roughing in their stuff. The security fencing is going up this week. Next week my men will begin working on interior finishing in the administrative unit, as well as pouring walls and ceilings in the cellblock units. I'd say in another ten days we can begin installing the communications gear and security measures, and you can give it a final inspection within twenty days, end of the month, max. And as you saw a few minutes ago, Comrade General, the helipad just outside the compound is complete."

The man's cool confidence gave Chernikov second thoughts about his first impressions.

"Describe the security arrangements." Chernikov already knew the security arrangements—he had designed them himself—but he wanted to see if the man responsible for construction had bothered to master those details.

"*Da.* Well, Comrade, we are going low-tech for two reasons. First, we believe the security will be more effective by relying on humans than technology. Second, there is no money for the technology.

"As to the specific measures that you requested, Comrade, I'll start from the inside and work out. All the cellblock walls are constructed of reinforced concrete. We are using standard steel prison doors with manual locking mechanisms and a feeding slot. Each cellblock has its own toilet and shower, and a single exit secured by the cellblock guard station and a steel door with a manual lock. None of the doors can be unlocked from the inside, not even with a key. With the exception of the cellblock outermost door, they can only be unlocked and opened from the outside.

"Each cellblock opens onto the compound common area, which is observed by six ten-meter-high guard towers. Each tower has two mounted PK machine guns and two mounted spotlights, one of each facing the compound and one of each facing outwards. Each tower contains a weapons locker with additional small arms. The exterior entrance to every cellblock is in the field of fire of at least two different towers. Mounted three meters above each guard tower is a bank of yard lights, achieving 360-degree illumination without blinding the guards.

"Again, working from the inside: surrounding the entire compound is fencing five meters high. The top two meters are electrified. On top of the fence is razor wire, also electrified. There is an outer perimeter fence, ten meters outside the first, constructed the same as the inner fence. The two fences and the two sets of razor wire are each on different electrical circuits. If one is shorted, the others stay up. Not only that, but if any of the electrified fences are shorted, all of the compound lights automatically come on. Each light bank is on its own circuit, so one failed circuit cannot bring down more than one bank of lights.

"Running between the fences on each side are four dogs, trained to kill. Even the guards will have to be exceedingly careful with the dogs.

"If an escapee was to somehow get past the guards, fences, and dogs there are concentric roads every two hundred meters with sand surfaces that will leave footprints. Hidden trip wires in the forest will trigger air horns powered by small canisters of compressed air. It is low-tech, but if triggered they make a whole lot of noise.

"Returning to the interior of the facility, the interrogation building is inside the cellblock compound and contains a small clinic in case your interrogation techniques require patching up the prisoners. The administrative section is separated from the cellblock compound by electrified and gated inner fencing identical to the perimeter fence."

"And the backup generator?"

"Self-starting, Comrade General. It's already on site, in fact we're using it for power until our electric is connected to the grid. We will test it extensively to ensure it kicks in whenever commercial power is lost. If every single light, searchlight, appliance, and so forth in the facility is drawing power it will consume no more than seventy percent of its capacity."

Chernikov stared in silence at the dull-faced captain. The man had reviewed both the security philosophy and implementation with utter confidence, without missing a beat. Chernikov smiled to himself and made a mental note to never play poker with the captain, as he had seriously underestimated him. "*Molodets*, Comrade Captain, excellent! And you are confident that the facility will be ready for use no later than the end of this month?"

"*Da*, General Chernikov. Barring unexpected weather, I see no reason why my men cannot turn it over to you by then. All our supplies and materials have already arrived and the site prep has been completed. We should have no delays."

****

In her heart of hearts Galina knew that Jake was still alive. She just didn't know where. Though wanting to believe he'd found a way to the United States, she suspected he was still in Siberia. Her call to the DPMO on Friday had been deeply discouraging and she had no idea what to do next. She felt very much alone.

Earlier in the evening her host family took her to their church. The service was in Chinese. If she closed her eyes, she could imagine herself back with her friends in China at their church. Other than the clothing, the worship and study was very much the same. Galya was not a believer but had enjoyed going to the church in China. There was a richness in the relationships that she hadn't felt anywhere else. She could already tell she was going to enjoy this church, too. The people were simple, unpretentious, and gentle. She felt safe. She also felt a strange longing every time she heard the message about a man named Jesus who had forgiven his enemies and given his life for them. She could not understand how the story had survived two thousand years nor yet how it had such power as it evidently did over the people at the church. It made no sense to her, but she was happy to have such people around her.

She was looking forward to next Sunday. The church would be holding a joint service and a fellowship dinner with a sister congregation, an English-speaking Presbyterian church in Alameda. Her hosts had mentioned that the church was near the naval base and had many military families in attendance. Perhaps she would meet someone who could help her locate the tall major whose love had been firmly etched on her heart.

As she lay on her bed she took inventory. She considered herself extremely fortunate. She had managed to escape both Russia and China. She was in the USA. Her application for asylum was being considered. She had a warm and safe place to stay, with people who genuinely seemed to care for her, though they really didn't know her. All things considered, it had turned out much better than she had anticipated. Now if she could just find Jake!

****

General Chernikov climbed into the Kamov Ka-26 helicopter and directed the pilot to fly enlarging concentric circles around the construction site. He wanted to inspect the perimeter roads from the air. After ten minutes he was confident that the captain of the engineering company was as good as his word. The roads had been built and were surfaced with sand.

"Take me back to the airport, Mikhail. I've got to return to Tara," he spoke into his helmet mic. The pilot nodded and pulled back on the collective. The Kamov gained altitude and headed for the Magadan airport.

Several hours later in his office at Prison 87, Chernikov picked up the phone to make his report to the head of the GRU's Ninth Directorate.

"Connect me to General Patrikeyev." Chernikov waited as his secretary completed the connection.

"*Zdravstvuitye*, Nikolai," the general's voice spoke from the telephone handset, genuinely warm even across the distance. "How are things progressing at Magadan?"

"Excellent, Comrade General. We should be able to transfer to our new location soon, next month even. The new security arrangements are excellent. I have complete confidence in the captain who is heading up the construction engineers. He seems to be very much on top of things."

"He better be. I picked him myself, General," Patrikeyev said brusquely. Chernikov felt a slight chill run through him and was thankful he had not mentioned his poor first impressions of the construction commander. It would not have been wise to speak ill of one of his patron's hand-picked men. "And how are the, uh, *special projects* going?" Patrikeyev was referring to the interrogations. Over a non-secure line, he had to be circumspect with his words.

"We had two breakthroughs last week and both men are now answering all of our questions."

"Aha. Good! What specialties are we talking about?"

"One is a chemist, the other a physicist."

"*Molodets!* Have you had any new, ah, deliveries lately, Nikolai?"

"*Nyet*, Comrade General. We have suspended foreign acquisitions until after the move. There are three more, ah, basic research projects in the works, sir, that should provide us with some interesting information on a new technology—the one we discussed." Chernikov was talking about a plan to kidnap the chief design engineer of the F-117 Nighthawk, America's first production stealth aircraft.

"Very well. We have high expectations of you, Nikolai. By the way, I am sorry to say that we have not been able to re-establish contact with your friend, Yakov Sokolov. But we are working on it and have several contingency plans in operation at the moment. I still expect a satisfactory conclusion to the matter." Patrikeyev was speaking of Jacob Kelly, using the alias they had assigned him during their previous attempt to recapture him while he remained in Siberia.

"*Bolshoe spasibo*, Comrade General." Chernikov breathed a sigh of relief. If Patrikeyev's operatives were able to eliminate the American, his kidnapping operation could still prove to be a huge success. It would save the Soviet Union years in weapons research and a great deal of money. Project *Krasnyy Voskhod* had always been a gamble but the payoff was so large that even the unimaginative old men on the Politburo had been able to see the potential benefits. Although they had approved the project several years prior, some were beginning to have second thoughts. If Major Kelly was silenced everything would be back on track. "General Patrikeyev, are you aware that Anatoly Geredin came to see me when I was in Moscow last week?"

"Of course, Nikolai. I didn't get to be head of the Ninth Directorate by not paying attention. What did he have to say to you?" Actually, the general already knew that, too. Chernikov's apartment was bugged by both the KGB and the GRU.

"Well, sir, he was not pleased."

Patrikeyev laughed out loud. "No, I imagine not. Listen, General, just do your job. I will keep Anatoly off your back—

you attend to the task in front of you. Finding your friend is no longer your concern—it is mine. Put all your energy into your, ah, research and I'll take care of the political game."

"*Da*, Comrade General. *Spasibo*."

Chernikov returned the handset to its cradle. So far, his luck was holding out.

Chapter 16

Falcon peered carefully through the gap in his curtains, checking for any signs that he was under surveillance. So far, so good. Satisfied, he tucked the service revolver he'd taken from the guard at Kotzebue into his waistband behind his back, zipped up his coat and stepped out of his hotel room. The weather was changing, and he could feel it right away. The temperature had dropped overnight and the wind had picked up. Putting on his hood, he turned into the wind and went to find breakfast.

As he walked in the brisk wind he considered his situation. It was vital that Bill Jensen stay off everyone's radar while he snooped around, trying to identify the spy. Jake was certain that if the spy suspected someone was onto him, he'd go to ground and they would miss their opportunity forever. *The only way Jensen stays below the horizon*, Falcon thought, *is if I remain free. If I'm captured, I'll have to contact him—Jensen is the only ally I have. But if I contact him while in custody it's a simple matter for the authorities to discover who he is. Once that happens, the spy will get wind of it.*

The clock was ticking. Jake knew it was only a matter of time—days, if not hours—until he was apprehended. If Jensen hadn't discovered the spy by then, Jake's own future looked mighty bleak.

****

"Hello, Admiral Bridger? This is Captain Roger Bates, presently attached to the Seventh Fleet as a liaison to the Royal Australian Navy. Sir, I have been asked to contact you by General James Franks. Thank you for taking the time to speak with me."

"Good morning, Captain. You're quite welcome. I can't give you but a few minutes, I have several meetings coming up this morning. But I am curious, how is it that you know General Franks?"

"He and I are fishing buddies from way back. We get together with our wives and go camping several times a year. This past weekend we were fishing, and he made a request of me that I need proper authorization for. He told me that you and he were working together on a project, and that you could provide whatever authorization I need. That's why I'm calling you, sir."

"Really? Generous of the good general to offer my authorization. What sort of a request did he make?"

"Sir, do you recall RIMPAC, last summer's joint exercise which included the Aussies?"

"Of course, Captain. Now that you mention it, I believe I also remember meeting you in Washington just before that exercise began." Bridger furrowed his brow. He wasn't sure what RIMPAC had to do with General Franks.

"Yes, sir, that's correct. Well, sir, General Franks wants an analysis of the data tapes from our E-2s that were gathering ELINT and SIGINT during the exercise. He specifically wants the tape from the night of 10 July examined. He's looking for any trace of a Soviet jamming signal to the north and east of the operation."

On hearing that the admiral sat straight up in his chair and slammed his palm on his desk in excitement. "Of course," he muttered to himself, "why didn't I think of that? It might be on that tape! That might be exactly what we need to reopen the investigation!"

"Sir?"

"Never mind, Captain. I think I can clear the decks for you on this. Who do you need me to call?" Bridger took a legal pad, and began writing the details of the request.

"Sir, if you could contact Admiral O'Neil, he's in the proper chain of command to authorize this."

"Does the admiral know how to contact you?"

"Yes, sir. We're all operating out of NAS Alameda right now. His office is just a few doors down the hall."

Not an hour later Captain Bates was aboard CVN-70, the USS *Carl Vinson*. The ship was tied up at Alameda taking on stores prior to its next deployment. Bates went down to the OW division of the Combat Direction Center on the huge *Nimitz*-class carrier where electronic intelligence (ELINT) from all over the electromagnetic spectrum was collected, recorded, and analyzed during fleet operations. The tapes from the E-2 could be rapidly analyzed on the division's sophisticated signal-processing equipment.

"Hi, Manuel! How's it going down here in your electronic wonderland?"

"Look who's here, boys! Hello, Cap'n! What brings you out from behind your desk to visit us humble swabbies? I thought that your time in DC had grown on you, thought maybe the next time we saw you you'd be running for mayor or something, sir."

"Mayor? MAYOR? Why, I'm insulted, Manuel! When I run, son, it will be for president!" During the RIMPAC exercises Bates had spent a good deal of time in the CDC spaces and had grown close to the men who ran the OW division. "So what's your latest project, Manny? What are you about to get in trouble over this time?"

Officially, Manny was an Electronic Warfare Technician First Class. But he might as well have been an officer for all the liberty he was given with the advanced electronic equipment on the *Vinson*. Like most technically proficient geeks, Manuel figured that rules were for everybody else and if you could hack it or crack it, it was fair game. While that made him an extraordinarily valuable signals technician, it also meant he was regularly written up for some infraction or another. Thankfully, Manuel's section leader knew when to look the other way.

"Oh, Captain Bates! We hit the jackpot! Turns out the good ol' Vinny's mast is close to the microwave transmission path of one of Oakland's premium cable TV companies. We're just able to pick up the signal. I hacked the encryption and now we can watch whatever's on for free. The skipper is having me patch it in to the ship's television system while we're in port." The young technician looked proudly at a desk sprouting a wire-wrapped breadboard filled with integrated circuits and patch cords. It occurred to Bates that the expression on Manuel's face was akin to that of a new father.

"My tax dollars at work. Great. Listen, Manuel, I have some real work for you. I want you to pull last summer's RIM-PAC tapes from the Hawkeye in the eastern sector of the exercise. I want you to go over the evening of 10 July with a fine-tooth comb. I am looking for any transmission, no matter how weak, that was detected between bearing zero and ninety degrees, true, from 1800 to 0400 the next morning. Catalog everything you find and give me a full report. I want the timestamp for each entry along with the E-2's current position, the bearing of the signal, and your analysis of it."

Manuel looked at him mournfully, "You mean, Captain, after we just got all this wonderful, free TV, you actually want us to *work?*" He looked sadly at the rat's nest of electronics on his desk.

"'Fraid so, Manny. When do you think you can get the results back to me? It's pretty important—critical, actually."

"Well, if my guys can tear themselves away from reruns of *McHale's Navy* we can probably have it on your desk by 0800 tomorrow."

****

Though the biting wind was laden with moisture no precipitation was coming down. Jake looked up at the overcast and wondered if it would be snowing by the end of the morning. The chill followed him into the little diner and he shivered inside his coat.

A few minutes later he was stowing away eggs and ham and washing it down with hot, black coffee. When he finished his breakfast he refilled his coffee cup, stretched his legs out under the table and leaned back, enjoying the thought that he was no longer fleeing Soviet troops and no longer camping out in such cold weather. He had a nice warm hotel room to return to, with a real bed. Even if he was still in a lot of trouble, it was an improvement over the last fifteen months.

An avalanche of cold air blasted through the front door as it opened. An old man walked in carrying the morning newspaper under his arm and took a booth at the other end of the diner. Jake paid no attention to him; the morning customer traffic had been brisk, and the major was lost in his thoughts.

He hoped to stay in the Air Force once this was all behind him. However, there was the small matter of General Chernikov. *You get to know someone up close and personal*, Falcon mused, *when they are burning words into the flesh on your shoulders with a hot soldering pencil*. Jake figured that the general had taken his escape personally and that as long as Chernikov lived, neither he nor Galina Toporova would ever be safe. There were, Jake decided, two ways to handle that—either hide for the rest of your life, or eliminate the threat. Jake decided to take door two. Once this was all sorted out—if ever—Jake would take some vacation time. He'd travel into the USSR under an assumed name with a fake passport, disappear into the woods for a few days—with his training it would not be too hard to throw off his KGB shadows—and then dispatch Chernikov. He'd return to the US with no one the wiser. It would be easy because it would be so unexpected.

With a start, Jake realized the old man was staring at him. The fellow was looking from the newspaper to him in a classic pantomime of surprise. Falcon busied himself stirring his coffee and pretended to be oblivious to the man's stare. Suddenly the old codger appeared to lose all interest and assumed an attitude of nonchalance. It was so exaggerated Jake might have laughed out loud under other circumstances. The elderly fellow got up and ambled toward the little hall in the back of the diner. Jake knew the bathrooms were located back there. And so was a pay phone.

As soon as the man disappeared around the corner the major left enough money on his table for the bill and the tip, and walked calmly to the diner's front door. Zipping up his coat, he slipped out into the cold morning.

Once he was out of sight of the diner he broke into a fast trot, headed for his hotel room. He knew he had been spotted and it wouldn't be long before the area was crawling with police. He wasn't sure what lengths they would go to in a search, whether it would be confined to the streets or go door to door, but he didn't plan on sticking around to find out. He'd grab his gear and leave without checking out. As he ran he began working out a plan to head south, to Juneau first and then to Seattle. He hoped he wouldn't have to steal another airplane.

****

"Hi, John, this is Jim Franks. I've got some news."

"Well, hello, Captain Kirk! What, are the Klingons invading? Starfleet stands ready to help you fight off any aliens. Phasers on stun. Beam me up, Scotty." Bridger grinned, proud of himself although he hadn't the foggiest notion what any of it meant. His teenage son, Jack, had given him a few lines from the television program *Star Trek*, and it sounded good. The silence on the other end of the line told him that he had scored a direct hit. He chuckled again, and waited for the reaction he hoped would come.

"Who told you that?" demanded Franks heatedly.

"What, that the Klingons have landed?" Bridger inquired innocently, toying with him.

"No, not that! That's silly! Who told you about *Star Trek*?"

"Well, my teenage son watches—"

"NO, confound it! That's not what I meant! Who told you that *I* watch it?" Franks was really angry. Bridger smiled again and leaned back in his chair, enjoying his small victory: the torpedo had hit amidships, well below the water line.

"General, no offense or anything, but I *do* think you need to attend more to the security of your staff. You know, 'loose lips sink ships', that sort of thing?"

"It was someone on my staff?"

"Well, General, it was not your wife, with all due respect. But I can keep a secret, and my lips are sealed."

"You better *not* mention this to anyone else!" snapped Franks.

This is a great button, Bridger thought to himself. *Push it and you get a complete show.* "Oh, I was not talking about your love of *Star Wars*, General, I was talking about protecting the identity of my informant on your staff."

"Star *Trek!*" Franks corrected.

"Say again?"

"It is *Star Trek*, not *Star Wars*! Don't you know the difference? What are you, some sort of cultural illiterate?"

"Can't keep 'em separate, General, sorry. You've seen one alien, you've seen 'em all. Now, tell me what your news is." Bridger laughed again to himself, and mentally chalked up a score for the Navy.

"Listen, I submitted Major Kelly's name to the DIA *Watcher* program last summer and on Friday I got two hits. One was a failed attempt to change the major's DPMO record, and the other was a phone call to the DPMO office in Washington from a caller seeking info on Kelly. The clerk indicated that the caller had a Russian accent. She also recorded her impression that she'd seen Major Kelly alive since the accident. If she's right, perhaps he *is* still alive!" The general fervently hoped that was the case. Losing Jake had been a blow not only to *Hydra*, but also to his family. Many Saturday afternoons had been spent grilling hamburgers in his backyard with Kelly and Franks' sons tossing a football.

"Did the DPMO office get the caller's name?"

"No, the conversation must have ended before that point."

"Well, that certainly is interesting, General. On Friday I put the major's name on the *Watcher* word list, too, but I didn't get anything. Must have submitted it too late in the evening. But I have some news for you. I got a call this morning from Roger Bates. I contacted his admiral and asked him to grant authorization for Bates to have the E-2 tapes examined. Jim, that was an outstanding idea you had. It just might provide a means of reopening the investigation without putting my friend or his contacts in danger. If that tape has a jamming signal on it, we're in business."

****

Jake spotted a trio of police cruisers coming from about three blocks away. He decided a running man might look suspicious and slowed to a walk with his collar pulled up and his face toward the ground. The police cars swept past him, headed in the direction of the diner. Breathing a sigh of relief, he quickened his pace. He had not, however, detected the unmarked car that was circling the block.

"All units, all units, suspect is proceeding south on the 700 block of Gambell Street. Make a silent approach, repeat, silent approach. Converge on Fairbanks and West 10th, and proceed on foot. He'll come right to you. Assume the suspect is armed and dangerous."

The three patrol cars had passed Jake, heading north. The first turned off to Hyder, the parallel street east of Gambell, the other two to Fairbanks, on the west. They raced back south to the rally point and with two other cars that had responded, the troopers set up a loose cordon across three blocks.

But Jake had seen them turn off after they had passed him and realized that he had somehow been spotted. He ducked into a parking lot full of cars, raced half a block east, and then began working his way north, between buildings, dumpsters, and parked cars. Somehow he needed to get back to his hotel room, grab his stuff, and hit the road again. He also needed to make a quick call to Jensen's answering machine to let him know that he was dropping out of sight again.

"He's turned north! Suspect is crossing back to the 600 block, between Hyder and Gambell!" Still unnoticed by Kelly, the unmarked car had parked and was watching his every move.

The major crossed 5th and raced west. At this point he needed distance more than he did subtlety. The noose was closing rapidly.

"I've lost him! I've lost him! Suspect last seen turning westbound onto 5th."

The state troopers who were spread out on 10th Street ran back to their cruisers to fan out in the new location. Meanwhile, additional backup units were closing on the area.

Turning north on Denali, Jake reached an alley and worked his way back west again. He spotted a garbage truck emptying a dumpster and waited until the truck moved along, and then jumped into the dumpster to lay low for a couple of hours. He breathed a word of thanks that the dumpster was behind an office supply store and not a fish market.

With a strong, prolonged gust of wind the snow began to fall. The temperature was now down into the teens and the overcast dark and lowering. An early fall storm was moving down from the north, and the wind was laden with moisture. Unless the snow fell really fast, Jake knew that he'd be leaving tracks with every step he took.

From his hideout, he had a good field of view in both directions. But his luck had run out. Two uniformed police officers appeared on Denali, and one took the alley east, the other, west. Jake groaned. They were checking everything carefully: dumpsters, cars, doorways. He had put himself in a box—literally—and he wasn't going to get away. Sinking down into the dumpster, he drew the service revolver and waited for the inevitable.

****

FBI agent Jim Stewart arrived at his office late. Traffic had been awful. He set his coffee and donut down, and logged into his computer. Stewart was a man of routine: he liked to run in his ruts, and he didn't appreciate interruptions. His daily routine when he got to work was to sit at his desk, eat several donuts and drink at least two cups of coffee while working through the various daily reports, counterterrorism briefings, and situation assessments. Next, he would scan his email for anything of importance. Finally, he would get into the particular schedule for the day. The younger agents knew that they should steer clear until they saw him making the third trip to the coffee pot.

There was nothing of particular note in any of the email or briefings. Draining his cup for the second time, he headed for the coffee pot and mulled over his schedule for the day. So far, the search for Meeker had come up empty. Stewart was beginning to wonder if they needed to expand it beyond Anchorage. He made a mental note to call Ed Devlin with the Alaska State Troopers, and suggest it.

"Jim?"

He turned and saw the Seattle office's lone data analyst coming toward him with a sheet of paper in her hand.

"Good morning, Sally."

"Hi. Listen, I have the results of the fingerprint search you requested on the military database. It had one hit. A US Air Force major, by the name of Jacob Kelly."

Stewart took the printout and examined it. Jacob Kelly's home address was listed as a billet at Edwards Air Force Base, followed by the words, "MISSING SINCE JULY 1986. PRESUMED DEAD."

"Huh. Well, I'll be—Sam was right. He's a military guy."

"Was."

"What?"

"*Was* a military guy. Now he's a *dead* military guy, apparently." Sally turned around and headed back to her desk.

Jim thought to himself, *No, actually, he is alive and well and on the run,* but said nothing.

"Thanks, Sal, for running this down. This gives us just the break we needed for a strange case up in Alaska."

"What's it about?" she asked, an inquisitive look on her face.

"Can't talk about it, other than to say it's the strangest collection of people I have ever worked with. Navy, Air Force, FBI, CIA, Alaska State Troopers, all involved. Maybe now that we know he's dead it will close the case." Stewart figured it wouldn't hurt to throw her off the track since the case was classified. Sally had the necessary security clearances, but the best rule of thumb was to keep the circle as small as possible.

Walking back to his desk, slurping his hot coffee, Stewart considered this latest revelation. *An Air Force officer.* That certainly explained why Meeker—or Kelly, rather—was able to make his escape from Kotzebue in an airplane. But it didn't explain what the officer had been doing in the Soviet Union since July, 1986. Or why he had come back.

Well, I guess I better let the other guys know, he thought to himself. He picked up the phone and dialed Lieutenant Commander Jesse Pierce's number.

****

"Sir, you need to see this." The NSA translator's voice was edged with excitement. "We received an encrypted message from the embassy in Moscow on Friday, originating from source *Leaning Tower*. Because of the backlog we were not able to decrypt and translate it until this morning. Now that I see it I wish I had gotten to it on Friday."

"I'll be right down, Miss Stinson."

The duty officer locked his office and went down to the Translation Room to see what the fuss was all about. He was not surprised about the backlog. The small staff of translators who had sufficient clearance to work with the most sensitive intercepts were constantly overwhelmed. In the last week the problem had grown more severe in the Russian section. Signal traffic from their most secret sources had grown dramatically and they were just now beginning to get the translations back. Most of the material from the last seventy-two hours had been intercepted from GRU communications. Much of it was composed of orders recalling to barracks various units that had been deployed on a search mission in eastern Siberia and the Chukchi Peninsula.

The secret, high-security facility was located in Maryland just outside the Beltway. All the sensitive areas were secured with biometric devices. He pressed his thumb on the fingerprint pad and looked steadily into the retina scanner. The door silently opened and he went to the young translator's desk.

Four years ago Evelyn Stinson had been the pick of the

crop from the Masters program in Russian Language at the University of Bristol in Britain. She was an American honors student studying abroad. After graduation she'd returned to the US to enter a doctoral program at Harvard specializing in pre-revolution Russian literature, only to be snagged by an NSA recruiter. Now she was their best and most enthusiastic translator. Stinson had a sense for the nuances of the language that eluded most translators, one that enabled her to read between the lines of even coded messages.

"What did you find, Miss Stinson?"

"The communication is actually three messages, sir, addressed to three different recipients. What's strange is that each message is identical to the others, except that two of the messages have a spelling error—a different error in each message. That was odd, sir, but it's not why I called you.

"As you know, sir, intercepts from *Leaning Tower* are always encrypted *and* encoded. Sir, it appears that these messages are telling of the imminent insertion of a spy into the US military. I am seeing Russian words that are similar to the words that were used several years ago in connection with the Walker spy case. When John Walker recruited his son Michael as a spy in the Navy, the initial communications intercepts from Moscow used very specific words to refer to Walker the son as a new recruit. Those same words are used in this message."

"Are you confident of this?" The duty officer looked somewhat doubtful.

"Yes, sir, I am. I'm asking for permission to work with a skilled analyst from the Soviet section of the CIA for a few hours. I don't have the experience to fully decode this myself and an analyst is not going to know the language well enough to get everything that's here. We'll need to work together. And if possible, I'd like someone who knows more about *Leaning Tower* to take a look at the fact that we have three virtually identical messages here."

The duty officer looked at the woman's face and saw confidence and determination. He sighed, then smiled, "I can see that you're not going to let me off the hook, Miss Stinson, until you get your way. Well, that's why we hired you." He picked up the phone. "Get me Major Shepherd."

Within thirty minutes he had arranged for the NSA's top authority on *Leaning Tower*, and for the CIA's top Soviet counterintelligence analyst, Sam Bergman, to work together with Evelyn Stinson later that evening.

****

Major Kelly huddled down in the corner of the dumpster, gun drawn. He heard footsteps approaching, crunching in the freshly fallen snow. The face of an officer appeared over the edge of the dumpster, and the policeman found himself looking into the muzzle of a .40 caliber Smith and Wesson M&P.

"Don't move, and put your hands on the dumpster. Now!" Jake spoke softly but with authority.

The policeman eyed him with a level, calm gaze and placed his hands on the edge of the dumpster, where the gunman facing him could see them. "Relax, buddy. Don't pull that trigger. No one's going to hurt you," he said soothingly.

"Got that right, officer. Not going to hurt you, either. Just do what I say." Jake stood up. No one else was in sight. Holding the gun on the policeman, he vaulted easily over the side of the dumpster.

He faced the fact that escape was impossible at this point. He wasn't about to shoot anyone and didn't particularly care to complicate matters with an assault on a police officer. But he had to make a call to Jensen, somehow.

"Okay, officer, here's how it's gonna go down. You're gonna knock on the back door of this office supply store. When they come to the door, you're gonna ask if we can use the phone. We want to make a private call from the manager's office. Don't try anything funny. Though my gun will be out of sight in my coat pocket, my finger is on the trigger. Do you understand?"

"What are you going to do in the store? Are you taking hostages?"

"Not planning on it. I just need to use the phone. Got it?"

"Got it."

Jake studied the man carefully. He did not look like someone who would panic or place other people in unnecessary danger. In any case, the major was out of options. "Let's do it. Just stick to the script."

He put his gun hand in his coat pocket where the gun would be out of sight but obvious to the officer, and then tilted his head toward the door. "You first."

The officer walked over and banged on the loading dock door. A young man opened it and looked at the two men standing in the rapidly falling snow.

"We need to use the phone—my radio's dead and I need to call in. Can we use the manager's office to make a private call?"

The teen shrugged, and said, "Sure, dude. He's not here right now, so his office is empty. Just leave a dime on the desk when you're done." Chuckling at his own joke he pointed at the office and sauntered off to serve a customer.

With Jake right behind him the officer walked into the office and the major shut and locked the door.

"Turn around, place your hands on the wall over your head, and don't move so much as a muscle."

Obediently, the officer complied.

Jake needed some information for his phone call. "Who's running this search?"

"Alaska State Troopers."

"Who's the officer in charge? What's his name?"

"Ed Devlin. Do you realize you have not taken my gun yet?"

"Do you realize that if you reach for it, it's the last thing you'll ever do?"

"Touché."

"Now be quiet and stand still." Jake dialed the phone, and waited for Bill Jensen's answering machine to kick in.

"Bill, you can locate me through Ed Devlin, Alaska State Troopers. Look for me using the name, 'John Meeker.' Please do not use my real name. I need to buy as much time as I can. Please contact the state troopers and pull whatever strings you can to get them to keep this under wraps. And Bill, I have broken several laws, including pulling a gun on a trooper and stealing an airplane, so I am going to need help with that, too. Please work as quickly as you can. I will no longer be able to contact you. You will have to contact me." The major hung up the phone.

"What was that all about?" The trooper started to turn his head.

"Don't move and don't talk! Understand?"

The trooper nodded and looked back at the wall.

"Now I'm coming after your handcuffs. Don't try anything." Jake retrieved the trooper's cuffs. Then he quietly laid his gun on the desk and managed to cuff himself with his hands behind his back.

"Okay, you can put your hands down and turn around," he said.

When the trooper turned around he saw Jake's gun lying on the desk, and Jake standing on the other side of the room wearing the handcuffs. The trooper pulled his own gun, barking a crisp order, "ON THE FLOOR! ON YOUR STOMACH!"

When Jake complied he pulled his radio off his utility belt and called in. "I have the suspect in custody in the Anchorage Office Supply Center. Requesting additional assistance." He walked over to the desk, took out his handkerchief and used it to pick up Jake's pistol. Then he unlocked and opened the door. Looking down at the figure on the floor he shook his head and muttered, "Buddy, I sure don't understand you, or what this is all about."

The trooper then crouched down and recited, "You have the right to remain silent. Anything you say can and will be used against you in a court of law. You have the right to an attorney. If you cannot afford an attorney, one will be provided for you at interrogation time and at court. We have no way of giving you a lawyer, but one will be appointed for you if you wish, if and when you go to court."

Jake replied wearily, "I understand my rights. I need you to understand something. This case is going to be different from any other you have been involved with. First of all, please check my gun and tell me what you find."

Curious, the trooper ejected the magazine. It was completely empty. Pulling back the action, he saw that the chamber was empty as well. "It's not loaded," he said.

"Correct. You were never in any danger. Remember that. Second, you *must* get the FBI involved in this case as soon as possible. I don't need a lawyer. But I do need to talk to someone with the FBI or the CIA. Once I can talk to them I will provide my real identity. You aren't going to find my prints in the NCIC system. Third, I need to be kept in isolation and under armed guard for my own protection. Fourth and last, the troopers need to do everything possible to keep my arrest a secret. I would prefer that you didn't even enter it into your system, and I'll waive my right of *habeas corpus* in writing, if necessary, to make this happen."

The officer looked at him, dumbfounded. "Who are you?"

Jake replied, "That's exactly what I can't tell you. Not yet, anyway."

Chapter 17

Monday, October 5, 1987: 1315 local time
Anchorage, Alaska

"Mr. Meeker, the arresting officer informed me that you wanted to talk, and that you had a whole list of conditions. I'm not sure that you understand the trouble you're in. You're not in any position to make demands of us." Devlin paused and evaluated the trim, muscular man sitting across the table from him in the interrogation room. Tall, with blond hair, a strong-boned face and a square chin, John Meeker did not look like anyone's profile of a criminal. His blue eyes were intelligent and cool. The state trooper got the distinct impression that he himself was being evaluated. But he sensed no hostility or aggression, which surprised him. Meeker's attitude seemed to be a mix of self-confidence tempered by respect. There was no sign of physical weakness, nor of his recent bout with hypothermia.

"Officer Devlin, you appear to be a very intelligent man. I'm sure you arrived at your present position by demonstrating skill in investigation and critical thinking. All I'm asking is that you employ those skills right now. You have been fully briefed on how I wound up as a patient at the hospital in Kotzebue, correct?" The man's voice carried an air of authority, but not arrogance. Devlin realized that Meeker was assuming the role of questioner, and for the moment decided to play along.

"That is correct," Ed replied.

"You know that the Soviets were trying to recapture me when I was rescued?"

A skilled interrogator, Ed controlled his expression carefully. His suspect had just inadvertently given away an important bit of data. Apparently Meeker was not only fleeing from the Russians, but he had at some point been incarcerated by them. This was new information. "Yes," he lied.

In fact, Jake Kelly was choosing his words carefully and dribbled that last fact out because he needed an ally, or at the very least, someone who would allow him to talk to an FBI or CIA agent. He needed to convince the trooper without giving away the farm.

"You are aware that an attempt was made to kill me in Kotzebue?"

"That fact has not yet been determined, but for the purposes of this discussion I'll grant it. Yes, I am aware of it."

"Was I right about the pin on the lighter?"

"Mr. Meeker, you need to get to your point. I am not going to answer that question."

"My point is this. I have escaped the Soviet Union and they are trying to kill me. Please put two and two together, Mr. Devlin. What would drive the Russians to attempt to murder a US citizen on US soil? They would not pursue me like this if it was just a criminal matter. But they might come after me if it involved their national security or a significant intelligence issue."

Devlin studied his face. While the suspect had a point, there was too much it did not explain. Devlin played his ace: "Mr. Meeker, you are proposing an interesting, possibly reasonable explanation for about one-quarter of the events associated with this case. But what you are suggesting does not even begin to explain why you would drug a guard, escape from the hospital, steal an aircraft, live underground for a week, and then pull a gun on one of my men."

"But—"

"Yes," Devlin said, cutting him off, "I know the gun was empty. But that one fact does not explain everything else." The trooper wanted to create some anxiety in Meeker by telegraphing with his body language that the interview was over.

"I can't explain my behavior."

"I know. That's what I was just saying."

Jake Kelly looked up at him. "No, that's not what I meant.

The reason I cannot explain to you my obvious desire to disappear once I hit US soil is related to the reason I was in the USSR to begin with. And I will only tell that to someone I trust."

Ah, thought Devlin, *there is a larger explanation involved here. Or Meeker wants me to think there is. But the claim is reasonable.* Because of the discussions with the group associated with the *Snowbird* investigation the trooper already knew that strange forces were at work. And obviously, Meeker was not a common criminal. He might be a very *uncommon* criminal of some sort of international flavor, but he was not your average street thug. That was clear.

Devlin rose and motioned to the guard, who opened the door. As he left the interrogation room he turned and looked at Meeker. "You'll get your FBI agent. He'll be here tomorrow."

"Please, would you at least consider my other requests?"

Devlin nodded, and then strode away.

****

"Take your seats, gentlemen," directed the VF-24 squadron operations officer. "I've asked the base intelligence officer, Lieutenant Commander Pierce, to begin our briefing on this mission. He's going to provide a little of the 'what' and 'why' background info. When he's done we'll get down to the 'how,' and I'll make individual assignments."

"Good afternoon," Pierce offered crisply. "Up until this point, you've been told that you're here for Operation *Coyote*, practicing the rapid forward deployment of a fighter squadron. What you haven't been told is that there's a second mission taking place under the cover of *Coyote*, which is why two additional members of your squadron joined you earlier today. The mission name for this operation is *Screen Pass*."

Pierce displayed a satellite photo of the Kamchatka Peninsula. "The Petropavlovsk-Kamchatskiy military complex is home to large elements of the Soviet Pacific Fleet, including many of their nuclear subs. It also hosts several Soviet Air

Force strategic and tactical units, including squadrons of Tu-95s, Tu-16s, and an assortment of fighters. Needless to say, it is a piece of real estate they are very sensitive about, and they don't like us to get too close. It's also a piece of real estate the US would need to neutralize in any conflict with the Soviet Union."

Pierce switched to a satellite photo of the Olyutorskiy Peninsula. "Three weeks ago one of our Orions picked up a new anti-aircraft radar signal from the tip of the Olyutorskiy Peninsula, south of the Anana River. We didn't know that the installation was even there. So far we don't know if it's a complete SAM site or just a director for other sites. Consequently, we need to update our profile of Soviet defense systems surrounding Petropavlovsk-Kamchatskiy. You, gentlemen, are going to help us do that.

"At 0400 hours tomorrow morning, a *Los Angeles*-class attack sub is going to poke its ESM mast out of the water offshore of the Kamchatka Peninsula. For obvious security reasons, I can't tell you exactly where. In any case it will have some pretty big ears on, listening to Soviet military chatter and mapping the air defense network while you boys are making your moves.

"At 0430, the first pair of Tomcats will approach to within twenty miles of the target on afterburners, at an altitude of one hundred feet. A second pair will follow at 0515, at one thousand feet. The final pair will conclude the parade by coming in at twenty thousand feet at cruise speed, just after 0600. They will approach to within fourteen miles of the target, and loiter for ten minutes. Whatever you do, do not encroach on Soviet airspace. Whoever flies this third sortie will be within two miles of it so be careful and know your position at all times. We are peeking under their skirts, not starting a war.

"Each of you will be carrying an ESM pod so we can gather some very specific location, threat response, and targeting information from their air defenses. None of you will be carrying ordnance. If you get into trouble you'll have to outrun it. Your briefing packets contain all the details, including approach and exit vectors and altitudes. All of you will be flying under strict EMCON conditions beginning at wheels up. A Hawkeye will be orbiting 150 miles off the coast, serving as forward air control if necessary. If he gives the word, you may break EMCON. Are there any questions?"

One pilot raised his hand, "Commander, why is this mission being run out of Adak? Why isn't the Air Force flying this gig out of Shemya? They're a whole lot closer."

Pierce grinned, "Good question. First, we need it done right, which is why we're doing it instead of the Air Force." The aviators chuckled, always happy to twist their competitors' tails. Pierce continued, "And second, Shemya AFB is too close. We'd be unable to achieve surprise, and surprise is critical to the operation. Any other questions?" Pierce waited for a moment while the three fliers looked at each other and shrugged.

"Your operations officer will handle individual assignments and the fine details. Each of you is responsible for briefing your wingman fifteen minutes before takeoff tomorrow morning, but not before. I'll be in my office the rest of the afternoon if anyone has questions." Pierce turned and left the Operations Room, almost running over his secretary as he turned the corner. He was always uncomfortable briefing men who outranked him, and it tended to fluster him. Sometimes the naval chain of command could look like a ball of knotted string.

"Sir, you received two important calls while you were in Flight Ops. Ed Devlin of the Alaska State Troopers called, and Jim Stewart of the Seattle office of the FBI called. They both wanted you to return their calls right away. And Captain Daniels asked you to come to his office before you leave today. No rest for the wicked, sir," she said, smirking. It had gotten out in the intelligence office that he had co-opted a civilian aircraft for an operation last week, something that was not quite by the book, and she had been teasing him about it ever since.

****

In a small, air-conditioned room several hundred feet under the rolling hills of northern Virginia, two NSA employees were about to make a discovery that would ultimately alter the entire nature of the imbroglio in which Falcon was presently ensnared. It was one of those rare but important collisions between providence and the best-laid plans of men in which providence always strolls away with the upper hand.

Surrounded in semi-darkness by flickering monitors and myriads of tiny lights winking on control panels laden with switches and buttons, two technicians loaded the video-taped record of the KH-11's overflight of the port of Magadan. Their job was to take a census of the Soviet Pacific Fleet in the harbor and report anything else that seemed unusual.

It was a boring, routine matter, tasked to the valuable Keyhole satellite only because its orbit placed it on a perfect sweep over the target area. It had not even been necessary to use any of the precious maneuvering fuel, as the satellite was already pointed in right direction—all they had had to do was start the camera and roll the tape. If not for this, the task would have been assigned to a less capable, fixed-image satellite possessing inferior optical resolution.

"Ready?" Al Mercer asked his colleague.

"Wait a sec," Karl Randolph said. He poured himself a fresh cup of coffee, settled into his swivel seat at the console, and said, "Okay, roll it."

The flickering grey images of a thick, pristine, and otherwise boring Siberian wilderness scrolled past in fast forward. The recording operation had begun with several moments of overlap—it was a fudge factor for automated operations to make sure that they missed neither the objective nor its context. They did not expect to see anything of interest until they got to the harbor and could start cataloging the shipping.

"Hmm. Fascinating," Mercer commented to his companion sarcastically. The wilderness they were looking at was unmarked by any evidence of civilization.

"Really," Randolph rejoined dryly. "Too bad we can't use this thing to pick out camping spots and trout streams."

"Actually," Mercer replied," there is a legend that a couple of early operators got reassigned after using the bird to—"

"WAIT! Freeze that frame!" Randolph interrupted.

Mercer pressed a button to stop the scrolling display and they found themselves looking at a construction site with a finished helipad. On the pad was sitting a Kamov Ka-26 helicopter.

"Let's see . . . that looks like a Hoodlum, doesn't it," Karl mused, using the NATO designation for the Ka-26.

"Uh-huh, it does. There's a civilian version of it but this baby has a military paint job, and if I am not mistaken that is the Soviet Army General Staff insignia on it."

"Yep, I agree. Zoom in, Al, and center on that chopper."

They stared at the picture in silence for several seconds, as the computer responded to Al's instructions and redrew the image.

"Let's try to read the number on the fuselage."

Again the technician's fingers worked lightly over the controls. The image was now at the edge of the Keyhole's resolution. Using a mouse, Al drew a box around the numbers and instructed the computer to enhance the pixilated image.

"Who are you, chopper?" muttered Karl as he entered the identification numbers into a database that held all the known serial numbers of Soviet aircraft along with the units or individuals to whom the equipment was attached. Instantly the computer came back with the name and picture of the last known general staff officer to whom the Hoodlum had been assigned. "Gotcha!" he crowed. "That chopper is assigned to a general in the GRU by the name of Nikolai Chernikov," Karl said.

"Bring the good general up on the DIA and CIA notifications databases. Let's see if anyone is looking for this guy."

Karl accessed the notifications database, which was a low-security application that had only "notify-me-if-someone-hears-about-this-guy" sort of information in it. In seconds, he had his answer. "Oooo—we got an 'Immediate Notification' status on the general! We haven't had this much excitement since the coffee pot shorted out last week."

Their sarcastic humor belied the fact that the two technicians were actually quite excited. These kinds of breaks in the intelligence community were not real common. It was satisfying to be able to chalk up a score against the other team every once in a while.

"Who are we supposed to call, and who gets the honor?"

"Somebody by the name of Jensen, special assistant to the DDO over at the Agency. I think it's *my* turn to make the call," Karl affirmed confidently. This argument was replayed everytime they had a significant find.

"Well, you *did* kill the coffee pot last week, and we *did* have to go through three whole days with nothing but water. I think *I* deserve it."

"Look at it this way, Al," Karl said as he picked up the phone and started to dial, "if it was not for me, we wouldn't have a new coffee pot, now, would we?"

****

"Hi, I understand you are Evelyn Stinson? My name is Sam Bergman. The Agency sent me over, said that you had a communication intercept you wanted to translate with the help of an analyst. Not sure how I can help you, but I'll be glad to try. My Russian is actually quite poor."

"Can I call you Sam? Thanks! Call me Evelyn. My supervisor is so formal, he calls me 'Miss Stinson,' makes me feel like an old maid."

Sam simply smiled and nodded, but thought to himself, *Anyone who looks at this lovely young lady and associates her with an old maid needs a new pair of glasses. Wow!*

"Okay, what are we working on?" Sam needed to keep the day moving as he was flying to Alaska tomorrow for the next meeting of the Project *Snowbird* group, and he had some thinking to do on that case before he called it quits today.

"This message came from a highly placed source in the USSR, code-named *Leaning Tower*."

"I'm familiar with *Leaning Tower*, and the quality of the intelligence we get from him." Only a small handful of people were aware that *Leaning Tower* was a sophisticated communications line tap, and not a human agent. Bergman and Stinson were not among those people.

"This message came in on Friday. It arrived in triplicate—I don't understand why, although each copy does have a different addressee. All three copies were sent by the same individual. There's a spelling error in two of the messages, although it occurs in a different place in each message. I've never translated an intercept from *Leaning Tower* with this characteristic. I've asked to meet with someone who has more technical background on the source; he should be here anytime, but we don't need to wait for him. Is there anything in your experience that would explain why this message is in triplicate with slight, seemingly innocuous differences between each one?"

Bergman thought for a moment and then responded, "There is a technique in counterespionage work that could normally explain this sort of thing. When you suspect your communications are compromised somewhere among a group of people, one way to ferret the leak is to give a slightly different version of the same confidential message to different individuals. If the message shows up in the enemy's hands, all you need to do to identify the leaker is find out which version the enemy has. So, normally, this sort of thing can be explained by proposing that the sender, let's see . . . " he said, examining her decoded version, ". . . the sender—Valeriy Patrikeyev—is trying to identify a leaker in his organization."

"You stressed 'normally,' as though you don't believe that's what's going on here," she observed.

"Correct."

"Why not?" she asked.

"Because the three messages were sent together, apparently bundled. Consequently each recipient will see all three copies. A spy would notice the differences and be alerted to sanitize the message before sending it to his handlers, so that he can not be identified. Either Patrikeyev is very clumsy, or there is some other, better explanation. I've studied Patrikeyev for several years now—he's the head of the GRU's Ninth Directorate. The man is one cunning old bear and would never make an amateur mistake like this.

"Other than that, I have no explanation for the spelling errors. Maybe they are innocent typos." Sam shrugged.

Stinson looked at him, nodding. "Could be, I suppose. I guess it will remain a mystery for now. But there's something even more pressing about this intercept, which is why I asked for your help. What concerned me in particular was that this message, if I am translating and decoding it correctly, seems to indicate that a Soviet agent is being successfully inserted into our military."

They worked through the message several times and, between Bergman's knowledge of the Soviet Union and Stinson's intimate knowledge of the language, were able to come up with what they both considered to be an accurate translation and decoding. It confirmed Stinson's initial concerns. The message stated that there was an imminent penetration of the US military by a highly placed agent, an officer who had been turned.

"There's still one thing that bothers me." She looked at the original, shaking her head.

"And that would be . . . what?"

"This word." She pointed at a word on the page, *begat'*. "The code word for 'insertion,' used in the context of inserting an agent, is the Russian verb 'run.' Russian verbs have a quality that English ones don't, which is referred to as 'aspect.' The aspect of a verb changes subtly the action of the verb. For example, *bezhat'* means to run, but more than that, to run with direction and purpose." She looked at Sam, hoping to find comprehension.

Instead, he looked at her with a blank expression and said, "Uh-huh. Okay."

She continued, "This verb in the message is in the wrong aspect for the code. It is *begat'* rather than *bezhat'*."

"I can hear the difference when you say it. But is it still the same lexical word as the code word for 'insertion,' just a different aspect?" Sam queried, puzzled.

"Yes, that's right. But in every translation I have ever made, especially when we later learned through other means that a message had to do with an agent insertion, the word was *bezhat'*. For example, it was used when John Walker recruited his son Michael. Moscow notified a few field officers in their consulates in San Francisco and New York, and they used *bezhat'*."

"Hmm. That is strange." He thought for a few moments, shutting his eyes to concentrate. He weighed the Russians' proclivity toward the obvious in most aspects of the culture, as opposed to their cunning and paranoia when it came to the intersection of their culture with the wider world around them.

She thought he had actually dozed off when he finally opened his eyes and advised, "Evelyn, I would encourage you to release the message as translated, with a footnote stating that the code word for 'insertion' appears in a previously un-used form, but belongs to the proper lexical word. I think if we err it needs to be on the side of caution. Somewhere, today, it might be that some United States military officer is returning home from an overseas trip or deployment, and he is bringing back with him a malicious intent. I think the word should get out immediately despite this anomaly."

At that moment the NSA's top technical analyst entered the room. If Bergman was a button-down sort of guy, Clifton Edwards was a throwback to the flower children of the early seventies. He walked up wearing a tie-dyed tee shirt, bell-bot-toms with rips in appropriate places, and sandals. His hair was a frizzy golden mane that would have gone below his shoulders if it had been laying flat. Which it wasn't.

Bergman viewed the apparition with some bemusement and murmured, "Yo. Dude."

"Dude," the apparition acknowledged, "I understand you've got this, like, really spaced-out message you need some help with. CE at your service."

"CE?" Evelyn asked doubtfully.

"My name. Clifton Edwards. CE. Everybody calls me CE."

In a few moments Evelyn had explained her concerns about the triplicate form of the message, and CE was nodding with understanding. He ignored the subtle misspellings and in-stead focused on a seemingly random set of numbers that apparently comprised some sort of prologue to each message. After muttering some incomprehensible technobabble about packet headers, he zoned in again and announced, "I'll need to contact the embassy in Moscow and get them to send me a byte-for-byte hex dump of the message. I think I know what's going on, but I want to look at the low-level transport protocol on the original, unparsed, digital message envelope before I say."

Evelyn looked at Sam and murmured softly, "Did you understand any of that?"

"Not a word," he whispered back.

They both looked at CE and said in unison, "Okay."

****

"Hi, Ed, this is Jesse. What's up? I understand you called earlier."

"Well, hello, Jesse! This is your lucky day. Would you like some good news?" Devlin was savoring the successful capture of Meeker.

"Lay it on me, man. It's been a good day but it could always get better. Tell me you've got some news on Meeker's location." Pierce had been feeling like Project *Snowbird* was beginning to languish.

"Happy to oblige; I have some news on Meeker's location," Ed parroted coyly.

"And . . . and . . . well, where do you think he is?" Jesse did not have time to play this game all day.

"His location is right in a holding cell downstairs! How's that for good news?" Devlin crowed.

"GREAT! When did you snag him, and where?"

"We picked him up about 90 minutes ago, in Anchorage. A patron in a diner recognized him from the description in the newspaper and called in the tip."

"Did he give you any trouble?"

"Nobody got hurt, if that's what you mean. But, Jesse, there are some mighty weird things about this guy. For instance, he got the drop on one of my officers and pulled a gun on him. Managed to use my guy to get to a telephone and make a phone call to someone named Bill. He must have been talking to an answering machine because the officer said it sounded like a one-way conversation. He told Bill that he could be found in the custody of the Alaska State Troopers and gave him my name. Indicated that he would need help beating several of the charges that will be filed against him."

"Sounds like this Bill must be a lawyer," Jesse observed.

"Could be, but I don't think so. The officer said it sounded more like Bill might be someone high up in government, somebody who could make the problems go away. Then the whole scenario got really strange. Meeker makes my guy turn around and put his hands on the wall, like he's about to frisk him. Instead he takes his cuffs, and after a moment Meeker tells the officer to turn back around, and guess what? He had put his gun out of reach and handcuffed himself!"

Jesse chewed on that, then acknowledged, "Okay, that is unusual—you're saying he basically turned himself in."

"Exactly. And it turns out that his gun was empty the whole time. And he insists that he be allowed to talk not to a lawyer but to an FBI or CIA agent. He asked us to keep him under armed guard, and to keep his arrest secret. He intimated to me that it had to do with national security." Devlin had spilled his piece and now the weariness of the past week was catching up to him.

"Guess I'm not surprised, Ed, about the national security thing. When you consider the assets that Ivan devoted to reeling him in, I figured he had to have some sort of intelligence value to us. And the assassination attempt tells me they want to make sure we can't have him. 'Meeker' is a pretty transparent alias; did he give us his real name?"

"Nope. Insists that he won't give that to anyone but an FBI or CIA agent."

"Okay, Ed. Great job! Go ahead and put a guard on his cell. Can't hurt. And let's keep the arrest under wraps for the time being. You can tell us the whole story tomorrow when we get together. We'll send Jim and Sam in to talk to him."

"You got it, sailor. See you tomorrow."

Jesse hung up the phone and sat at his desk, thinking. He was pleased with himself. His original instincts back on Friday the 25th had been confirmed. *Meeker, or whatever his name is, really is of intelligence value. The gamble I took on the 'rescue' is going to pay off.* He picked up the phone, and dialed Jim Stewart's Seattle number.

"Stewart here."

"Hey, Jim. It's Jesse. Sorry I missed your call."

"No problem. Listen, our Mr. John Meeker is actually a Major Jacob Kelly of the United States Air Force. He's been missing and presumed dead since July of last year. We got a hit when we submitted his prints to the military database."

Jesse was surprised. A 'missing and presumed dead' military officer was not one of the scenarios he had imagined when he thought about who Meeker might be.

"You still there, Jesse?"

"Yeah, I'm here. I'm just thinking that this case is getting stranger by the minute. Have you talked to Ed yet?"

"No, I was just about to call him. Why?"

"Oh, I'll let him tell you. Don't want to spoil his fun. I'll call Bill Ott and tell him our man is an Air Force officer. Maybe he can bring a complete copy of the Air Force dossier on Kelly to our meeting tomorrow."

"Sounds good. See you tomorrow, Jesse."

****

It was past 2000 hours and Bill Jensen had not even been home yet. His pager had gone off at the university and the message was one of the best he'd had in a long time. The sender had used a code from the Notifications database indicating that General Nikolai Chernikov had been located.

Jensen downshifted his Porsche 944 Turbo and zipped around a slow-moving truck. Chernikov was a rising star in the GRU: ruthless, efficient, honest to a fault, and apparently incorruptible. Bill knew that General Valeriy Patrikeyev had taken Chernikov under his patronage as a protégé. But about three years ago Chernikov dropped from sight completely.

Now a couple of NSA techs claimed to have the man on camera.

Thirty moments later an escort shepherded him through security and into the darkened room where Al Mercer and Karl Randolph were finishing their count of Soviet Pacific Fleet shipping. He took a seat and waited until they were done.

Finally, Al turned around in his swivel chair. "You must be Dr. William Jensen. I'm Al, and this is Karl. You're here to take a look at Nikolai Chernikov, correct?"

"That's right. Understand you boys got a bead on him. How did all this come to pass?"

"We're taking a census of the Soviet Pac Fleet at Magadan. The best bird to shoot the pictures just happened to be a KH-11. Lucky for you, because none of the other birds have the resolution that enabled us to pick the serial number off the Hoodlum we spotted.

"Anyway, we set the bird to start sending the feed a little early. At first we were looking at the trackless wastes of the Siberian forest, but then the satellite passed over some new construction. We noticed a military helicopter at the site and were able to identify it as one assigned to the good general."

"Could I see it?"

"Sure. We figured you'd want to get a look, so we've got it queued up and ready to go. Have a seat right there," Karl said, motioning to one of the swivel chairs at the console.

The image of the wilderness flickered by for several seconds, then Jensen saw a road float by and then a second. Then a construction site scrolled onto the monitor. Karl froze the view once the site filled the whole monitor. Jensen studied the grey image, and then directed Karl to zoom in and enhance various parts of it. He studied the image for several seconds, and then nodded, "Okay, go to the chopper."

Karl advanced the tape a several dozen frames, and the helicopter scrolled into view as well as several men standing around the edge of the helipad.

Al spoke up again. "We digitally enhanced the numbers on the fuselage of that Ka-26, and the database identified it as

Chernikov's personal whirlybird."

"Have you boys had a chance to study this construction site?"

"Yes, sir. Back up, Karl, then zoom out to wide angle . . . good, freeze and enhance. That's good right there." Al turned back to Bill Jensen and began to point out features in the picture. "We spent about two hours examining the site this afternoon and I think we can give you a best guess. You'll notice that the whole site is in the middle of a cleared area and is surrounded by what appear to be preparations for fencing—double fencing, in fact. These here," he pointed to several large circles on the screen, perhaps three feet in diameter, "appear to be coils of wire. We're guessing that it is razor wire. The fencing also goes through the midst of the site, right here, sir. Six concrete pads appear at the edge of the fencing, spaced around the perimeter. They're just the right dimensions to be the footers for guard towers. Now if you'll notice, these four buildings are all identical in size. This one here has no roof yet, but the walls have been poured, and you can make out the floor plan because of the angle of the sun and the shadows. I'd say that's a prison cellblock."

"So what's your initial conclusion, boys?"

Karl offered, "Based on what we can see, Dr. Jensen, and filling in with a few guesses, I'd be willing to bet a steak dinner that we are looking at a high-security GRU prison compound."

Jensen nodded. Their analysis appeared to be right on target. There was just one problem, Jensen thought. *Nikolai Chernikov is far too valuable a player to be a common jailer. But there he is. Hmm. What if his prisoners were people like Jake Kelly, who had simply vanished from sight by hook or by crook, and were being held at facilities like this one for interrogation? Yes, that would be a project worthy of Chernikov's rank and status.*

"Men, you've done outstanding work," Bill affirmed. "What you have discovered here fills in a lot of blanks for questions I've been asking lately, and several that I've been asking for three years. For obvious reasons I'm not allowed to tell you the significance of this intelligence, but I *can* tell you that you struck pay dirt. I promise you this: if the case I'm working on ever goes public I'll send you a note and tell you as much as I am permitted."

"Thank you, sir." Both men had big grins, and looked quite pleased.

"Can you send a complete set of enhanced stills, with co-ordinates, and a report of your conclusions to my office at the Agency?" Jensen asked, giving them his card.

"You bet! They'll be on your desk in the morning."

****

Jesse knocked on Captain Daniel's partially opened door. His CO looked up and waved him in.

"Come in Jesse, thanks for stopping by. Got a couple of things I want to check on. First, how did your intel briefing go with the airdales?"

Daniels knew that his young intel officer had done a good job because he'd already asked the squadron operations officer. But he was subtly teaching Jesse accountability and the value of communication by debriefing him. One of the things that made Dan Daniels good at developing first-quality leaders was that he did not run up a flag and say something like, "Now I'm going to teach you accountability and the value of communication, so listen up." Instead, he simply modeled it. He knew that over time Jesse would absorb the influence unconsciously.

"Fine, sir. It's going to be a good, short operation and I expect we will capture some valuable data from it. But are you sure you want the third sortie to close to within two miles of their airspace? That's mighty provocative." In mission planning Daniels himself had directed that the third flight get so close to Soviet airspace.

"Um-hm, I know. That's exactly *why* we're getting so close. We need a strong reaction from their air defenses, including targeting radar data. I'm hoping the Soviets will paint them up, especially whatever's on Olyutorskiy."

"What if the Russians shoot them down, sir?"

"They won't, Jesse, and here's why: each sortie is composed of only two aircraft. Ivan is a big thinker. He knows we aren't going to mount an attack with just two airplanes, because he wouldn't attack with just two—he knows we're just causing mischief. He'll probably return the favor in a week or so, and approach our coastline with a couple of fighters.

"On the other hand, if the Sovs thought we were too close to sensitive parts of the Petropavlovsk-Kamchatskiy complex, yes, they would shoot our boys down. But the mission planning we did provides the pilots with strict approach and exit vectors that won't take them within recon range of those sensitive areas. Don't worry, son, we should be all right."

"Yes, sir." Pierce did not like that phrase, "*should be*," but he let it go knowing that Daniels was willing to assume the risks. His entire perspective of his captain had changed significantly in the last ten days.

"What about Project *Snowbird*? Do you have any developments yet?"

"We do, sir. The FBI has identified 'John Meeker' as Major Jacob Kelly of the USAF. According to what we know so far, he has been missing and presumed dead since July of last year. This afternoon the Alaska State Troopers bagged him in Anchorage.

"Tomorrow I will be meeting with the whole group. Besides comparing notes, we'll begin interrogating Kelly. There continues to be a great deal about this whole affair that is curious, sir. Kelly has not requested a lawyer but is demanding to speak to the FBI or CIA. He's implied that this shindig is a national security affair and not only has he requested protection in the prison, he's also asked that we keep his arrest a secret."

Daniels frowned, "And what have you done about his requests, Commander?"

"At the moment we are doing as he asked because it is no trouble to do so and it can't possibly advantage him with respect to our investigation. This whole convoluted episode begins to make sense if he's telling the truth, except for one point brought out by Ed Devlin. Devlin's sticking point is this: if Kelly is a good guy working for us, why did he flee from

Kotzebue and go underground?"

"Have you got any theories about that, Jesse?"

"No, but in my opinion his actions weigh heavily in some other direction."

"Perhaps. But one thing to remember in intelligence work, Jesse, is that the obvious explanation is rarely the right explanation. Especially when it is the Soviets who are lining up on the other side of the ball: they are masters at misdirection."

Chapter 18

The snow was falling steadily as the spy turned his GMC Jimmy south on Highway 2, towards Delta Junction. He wasn't concerned about the weather: people who worried about weather needed to find somewhere else to live. He didn't like the snow but it presented no great problem. The forecast was for steady snowfall through Tuesday noon. Because of the Air Force Base, Highway 2 was kept clear from Fairbanks all the way to Delta Junction, seventy-five miles south, which was where he was headed at the moment.

The man needed to make a phone call—an untraceable phone call. Rarely did he communicate with his Soviet field officer this way. The sort of intelligence he normally sold to the USSR was not immediately actionable stuff. It tended to have a longer shelf life, such as reports and assessments, and consequently he was usually able to set up a standard dead drop. But what he had to tell them now could not wait, not for a week, not even until tomorrow. The "Siberian fisherman" had been recaptured. The spy's handlers would want to know immediately.

When he had been installed in his present position, his field officer, operating out of the Soviet diplomatic mission in Seattle, had set up a protocol for urgent communications. It was that protocol he was now following. He was to drive to either Delta Junction or alternately, Anderson on Highway 3, and place a call to a number he had memorized. He would give the voice on the other end an encoded message. An hour later he would place a second call from a different telephone to a second number. If there were any additional instructions they would be relayed to him at that time. The first number had a San Francisco area code; the second connected him with somewhere in Phoenix.

The nice thing about being a spy in the Alaskan backcountry—as long as you didn't mind the weather—was that it was virtually impossible for someone to put a tail on you. The little red-line roads running on glacial moraines had sight distances of multiple miles and very little traffic—a tail would be immediately obvious. He had been checking his rear view mirror whenever the snow let up since leaving the base housing area. No one was following him.

****

It was after midnight when Jensen got home. His wife Susan was in Texas celebrating her sister's forty-fifth birthday so the house was dark and empty. He armed the security system and walked back into his study. After he set his briefcase down he fired up the computer to check his email. As the professor turned back to the doorway, he noticed the light blinking on his answering machine: two messages. Ignoring them for the moment Jensen walked into the kitchen, piled a bowl high with chocolate ice cream and returned to his study.

Settling in at his desk he played with his ice cream for a moment, thinking. The NSA's video record of Chernikov and the construction project was a providential find. It confirmed virtually every aspect of Jake Kelly's story. A high-security, isolated compound would be perfect for interrogations, especially ones that were kept secret even from members of your own government. The fact of Jake Kelly's escape would necessitate that the Sovs build a new facility and Jensen was confident that it was the new facility they were seeing on the video. The Russians would know that the major could identify the location of the original facility where he'd been held, and would anticipate that the Americans would have it under satellite surveillance in a matter of hours. But they could not have known that by a fluke coincidence—providence, as far as Bill Jensen was concerned—the new camp would be discovered even before the concrete had set. That one video at the NSA, if one connected the dots, sealed and certified Jake Kelly's account.

Before leaving the NSA facility he had called in a few favors and managed to obtain authorization to bury the entire discovery of Nikolai Chernikov and the construction site for two weeks. He didn't want to raise the visibility of any issues surrounding Jake Kelly's abduction. If there were Soviet agents whose fingers were in the US military or intelligence apparatus, he did not want them to get any sense of the existence or progress of his investigation. For now, the new intelligence concerning Chernikov would be limited to his eyes only, or those of the DDO.

Coming out of his reverie, he remembered the answering machine and the two messages on it. He picked up the notepad and a pencil and pushed "PLAY."

> *Hi Bill, just wanted you to know that I got in safely. Sally picked me up at the airport. The flight was smooth and even my luggage made it all the way. I'll be back next Tuesday, honey. I love you. Bye.*

He deleted the message and went on to the next one.

> *Bill, you can locate me through Ed Devlin, Alaska State Troopers. Look for me using the name "John Meeker." Please do not use my real name. I need to buy as much time as I can. Please contact the state troopers and pull whatever strings you can to get them to keep this under wraps. And Bill, I have broken several laws, including pulling a gun on a trooper and stealing an airplane, so I am going to need help with that, too. Please work as quickly as you can. I will no longer be able to contact you. You will have to contact me.*

Jensen made some rapidly scribbled notes and then deleted the message. Rewinding the tape, he pressed "MEMO" and let the machine record for about two minutes. Then, confident that he had thoroughly overwritten Jake Kelly's message with the bogus memo message, he pressed "DELETE."

He sank back into his desk chair with his rapidly diminishing bowl of chocolate ice cream. *So . . . the game is on. Now it will be a race to see who can accomplish their objectives first*, he thought. Jake Kelly's life and career hung in the balance. But Jensen knew that there was more at stake than just matters concerning his friend. The trouble was, he had no idea of what that "more" might demand from all of them.

Dr. William Jensen had a tough decision to make. On the one hand, he wanted to swoop in with the power of the federal government to protect Jacob Kelly. On the other hand, there was a highly placed malefactor on the loose in the Air Force, undoubtedly jeopardizing the security of the country. What to do? He needed time to identify and capture the spy. If Jensen came to Kelly's assistance before the traitor was identified, the spy would go to ground and they'd never catch him. On the other hand, if he delayed coming forward with the video footage of what the NSA techs had discovered—which would clear Kelly of any suspicion of treason—Kelly would remain in jail, a sitting duck for anyone who was targeting him. The son of his best friend could wind up coming home in a body bag, the victim of an assassination.

The decision was all the more difficult in that ever since the deaths of Clancy and Galina Kelly, he and Susan had virtually adopted Jacob. He'd become like a son to them. How could Jensen even think of putting one he loved like a son at risk?

In the end it was Kelly's oath that settled the question. As a commissioned officer of the US military, Jacob Kelly had sworn to protect and defend the Constitution of the United States. Every member of the military knows that when they sign up it could cost them everything, including their life.

Jensen put his face in his hands. The decision was clear. It had been made years ago when Jake had taken his commission as an officer. Jensen ground his teeth as he realized the implications. He would have to use Jake as bait. And he couldn't step in to help him, not until he'd bagged the spy. He bowed his head and prayed for wisdom—and success.

****

Other than a few streetlights creating eerie halos in the falling snow, Delta Junction was dark and silent by the time the spy had arrived. The little town had rolled up the sidewalks and gone to bed, hunkering down in the early October blizzard. The ninety-minute drive had taken four hours. For most of the trip he'd been stuck behind a snow plow. He could tell it was going to be a long night. Since everything was closed in the little town he was not going to be able to find a bathroom or refill his thermos of coffee. He cursed the plow and he cursed the snow and he cursed the "Siberian fisherman." Retirement to a beach in the Bahamas sounded really good at the moment. If he could keep selling the secrets of the United States to his paymasters in the Soviet Union just a little longer, that wonderful retirement would come soon enough and would be all that he'd hoped for. He sighed: it was going to be hard to stay awake tomorrow.

Delta Junction was just barely big enough to merit three pay phones. The spy would only need two. He pulled up to the first, and leaving the car and heater running, got out and waded through the snow to the phone booth. No dial tone! Cursing again, he waded back to the Jimmy, and went in search of another phone. He had better luck with the next one. He dialed the number, and waited for an answer.

"Bay Area Security Service, please hold." The spy waited, thinking that whoever set up this particular cover did an excellent job. BASS was a real monitoring service for home security and consequently had a 24/7 answering service. BASS was also a front operation doubling as an emergency information collection point for Soviet spies in the US.

"This is Jill. How may I help you?" The voice was cheery and pleasant and disgustingly awake.

"I am unable to activate my security system, I seem to have forgotten my password."

"I can help you with that, sir," Jill chirped. "First, for security purposes can you give me your home phone number?"

He provided an actual Bay Area home phone number, but the number identified the call to Jill as an intelligence information exchange. She did not miss a beat and continued with the standard BASS protocol.

"Can you give me your name?"

"Joseph Wilson."

"And, Mr. Wilson, your mother's maiden name?"

"Stockbridge."

"Very good, Mr. Wilson. Now, there is a ten-digit code on the front panel of your alarm system. Can you read me that code?"

The spy looked at the telephone number of the pay phone, and read it back to her with the area code digits reversed and a dash in the middle of the ten numbers, "70989-54657."

"Please wait while I look that one up . . . ah, here it is. Your password is 09347. Why don't you try that while I stay on the line . . . ."

He put the receiver down, counted to thirty silently, and picked the phone back up. "That did it! Thank you so much!"

"Is there anything else I can help you with, Mr. Wilson?"

"No, that's it. Thank you!" He hung up the phone and waited. While he was waiting he pulled two pages of four digit numbers out of his shirt pocket and unfolded them. Within five minutes the phone rang and he answered it.

"09347," said the spy, repeating the code number given to him by the BASS operator.

"Go," said the voice at the other end.

"Zero-niner-five-two."

"Zero-niner-five-two," the voice repeated.

"Six-one-six-five," he continued, reading from his encoded message.

"Six-one-six-five," the voice confirmed.

This went on until both pages of numbers had been given and verified. When he got to the end of the list, he simply said, "Stop."

"Stop," the voice repeated, and then the connection was terminated.

The spy pulled out his lighter, cracked the door of the phone booth, and burned his papers. He stamped on the ashes and then went back to his warm, waiting vehicle. He checked his watch. It was twenty minutes after midnight. He would make the second call at 0120 hours. He figured he'd better go ahead and locate the other pay phone.

After ten minutes he found it. He turned off the car, fearing that a running automobile would attract attention. The warmth of the heater slowly escaped, and the inside of the vehicle grew cold. Outside the car, the snow let up momentarily, then resumed with fresh intensity. He shook his head in anger, poured his last cup of coffee from the thermos and cursed the snow plow again. An hour in these conditions was going to be a long wait.

****

The message was immediately relayed to the Soviet Consulate in New York, from where it was transmitted directly to Moscow Center. It was decoded by a cryptologist a little over twenty minutes after the spy had hung up the phone.

> *SOURCE FLOWER-BLUE. ROUTE GRU NINTH-DIRECTORATE. PRIORITYONE. EYES ONLY.*
> *BEGIN.*
> *TARGET APPREHENDED. CUSTODY AK STATE TROOPERS ANCHORAGE. OIC SPEC AGNT EDWARD DEVLIN. BREAK.*
> *INVESTIGATION DESIGNATED SNOWBIRD, CLASSIFIED. OIC LCDR JESSE PIERCE USN, ADAK NAS. BREAK.*
> *SNOWBIRD MEETING 6OCT 1000 LOCAL, ANCHORAGE FBI OFFICE. PARTICIPANTS JESSE PIERCE, EDWARD DEVLIN, CIA SPEC AGNT SAMUEL BERGMAN, FBI SPEC AGNT JAMES STEWART, MAJ WILLIAM OTT USAF. BREAK.*
> *WILL ATTEMPT TO HAVE TARGET TRANSFERRED TO EIELSON AFB BY AIR, 8OCT. BREAK.*

> *REQUEST   IMMEDIATE   INSTRUC-*
> *TIONS. BREAK.*
> *END.*

****

Five minutes before noon on Tuesday, General Patrikeyev's aide knocked on his boss's door in the gleaming office tower near Khodynka Airfield, Moscow, that served as the home of the GRU.

"Enter," said the general without looking up.

"Comrade General, I have priority traffic for you, eyes only. It came from *Flower-Blue* less than an hour ago and was just decoded. *Flower-Blue* is waiting on an immediate response."

At the mention of the source the general's head snapped up out of his work. This communication, he knew, must have something to do with Major Jacob Kelly. "Bring it in," he commanded.

The message was the best possible news: Kelly was in custody! He barked for his aide and the harried man popped into his office again. "Take this message, have it encoded, and send it as a response: 'Good work. Make every effort to move transfer up to 7 October. Stay clear of target during transfer.' Send it right away!"

As his aide hurried out and shut his office door, he picked up his phone, and dialed a secure number in the Cayman Islands.

"Hello, Victor? Scrambler algorithm forty three." The general adjusted a dial on the scrambler attached to his phone, and then resumed his conversation. Half a world away at Sugar Grove, West Virginia, the NSA's *ECHELON* software that was monitoring all international calls routed to the Caymans automatically dropped the real-time surveillance on the call when the scrambler kicked in. However, the squeaks and squawks of the scrambled call were recorded for later attempts at unscrambling.

"I have a job for you. I need two teams, one in Anchorage,

one in Fairbanks, and I need them there right now. The target is a USAF major, who is being held in custody by the state police in Anchorage, Alaska. His name is Jacob Kelly, aka John Meeker. He will be transferred to Fairbanks tomorrow or Thursday, probably by air. Kill him, and make it look like an accident. Collateral damage is permissible. Understand? . . . Good! I am counting on you." He hung up the phone and switched the setting back to unscrambled.

Patrikeyev got up from his desk and paced over to the windows of his fifth-floor office. Watching an Ilyushin IL-62 lumbering down one of nearby Khodynka's taxiways, he considered his next steps carefully. He had a plan in place to eliminate Kelly, but decided as insurance to continue his disinformation campaign. He sat down at his desk and composed another deceptive message to be placed on the GRU secure communications network. He also decided to use the same strategy as before, triple messages with subtle differences, in hopes of discovering the point of leakage. The general summoned his aide and dictated the message. He gave careful instructions for selective misspellings, and then left it to the aide to attach the necessary routing and destination information.

> *AGENT IN PLACE, CODENAME LA-*
> *FAYETTE. BREAK*
> *COVER STORY SUMMARY: SHOT*
> *DOWN, CAPTURED, INTERROGATED,*
> *ESCAPED, RETURNED. BREAK.*
> *PERSON RESPONSIBLE: GENERAL*
> *NIKOLAI CHERNIKOV, GRU. BREAK.*
> *DESTROY MESSAGE UPON RECEIPT.*
> *BREAK*
> *STOP.*

****

There were now three sets of Americans focusing on USAF Major Jacob Kelly, most of whom were unaware of the efforts of the others. Admiral John Bridger and General

James Franks, using information originally gained from smuggler and former SEAL Ned Bascomb, were investigating the disappearance of Kelly and hoping that data tapes from the RIMPAC exercises fourteen months earlier would reveal the Soviet jamming signal on the night when Kelly's F-16 was lost. Neither Franks nor Bridger knew that Kelly was in custody in the United States, and they were likewise unaware of either the *Snowbird* investigation or Bill Jensen's work on the case.

The *Snowbird* group led by Lieutenant Commander Jesse Pierce had Kelly in custody but knew only that the Soviets wanted him dead. They did not know the larger story, nor were they aware of Bridger's and Franks' efforts. They also were unaware that Sam Bergman wasn't the only CIA employee looking into the matter. The DDO *was* aware of it but was keeping the information compartmentalized at Jensen's request.

Professor William Jensen was the one man who was aware of both groups. He knew where Jake was and that his tale was true. Aside from Jacob Kelly, Jensen was the only one with an inkling of the much larger issues surrounding the shootdown. And he'd just decided to keep his mouth shut.

****

Three hours later, as the bleary-eyed spy was returning to Fairbanks in a raging blizzard—once again following a snow plow—a group of three white males in their late twenties boarded an early morning flight from Chicago to Fairbanks. The tickets were charged to the travel account of the Dallas office of the International Development Corporation. A similar group boarded a commercial flight in LA bound for Anchorage. Both groups checked sealed luggage containing an assortment of disassembled weapons and equipment. Neither of the two IDC hit squads were aware of the other.

Instantaneously, the ticket transaction was picked up by a federally authorized tap on the airline reservations database, and a notification was sent to the duty officer at Langley. Due to a routing error, the message was assigned low priority and wound up submerged in the avalanche of daily information. It would not be seen by human eyes until much later in the week. Meanwhile, another intercept from source *Leaning Tower* landed in NSA translator Evelyn Stinson's in-box.

Tuesday would be a busy day when it finally dawned over the east coast of the United States.

Exciting sneak preview of book three of the Falcon Trilogy:

Falcon Strike

Tuesday, October 6, 1987: 0730 local time
Washington, DC

William Jensen, special assistant to the DDO-CIA, was getting an early start on his day. He had arranged for teaching assistants to take his classes at Georgetown University for the next several weeks, and he had gotten clearance from the DDO to pursue an intelligence "research project," which is how he was designating the Kelly affair. This gave him official sanction without requiring him to specify the nature of the research. It would open all the necessary doors.

Before going to his office at CIA Headquarters, he made a visit to the DOD's Defense Prisoner of War / Missing Persons Office (DPMO) at the Pentagon. Each branch of the service maintained its own Service Casualty Office. But the DOD's central office at the Pentagon housed the master database, ensured uniform access and security policies, and handled escalated issues with families and loved ones. It took Jensen several minutes to penetrate the bureaucracy to the point where he was actually able to speak face to face with Ben Jones, Sheila Turner's supervisor.

"Hello, Mr. Jones. I'm Bill Jensen, special assistant to the Deputy Director of Operations over at the CIA. I understand you have a Sheila Turner working for you. I would like a few moments to speak with her. Could you arrange that for me?" As he spoke Jensen pulled out his badge and showed it to Ben.

Surprised, Ben wondered what Sheila had done to warrant a visit from one of the spooks at the Agency. "Certainly, Mr. Jensen. I'll send for her. May I ask what this is about?"

"I'm not at liberty to say, other than to assure you that it has nothing to do with Sheila herself. I'd really rather speak to her at her desk, if that's permissible."

"Of course."

Several minutes later the professor was pulling a chair into Sheila's cubicle. "Miss Turner, my name is Bill Jensen. I'm with the CIA, and your supervisor has been kind enough to allow me a few moments of your time. How are you today?" Jensen attempted to put the surprised young woman at ease.

"I'm fine, Mr. Jensen," she said cheerfully, "please call me Sheila. What brings the Agency to my desk this morning?"

"Sheila, on Friday you handled a telephone inquiry about an Air Force major by the name of Jacob Kelly. I'd like to ask you a few questions about that call."

"Sure. Fire away, Mr. Jensen."

"Bill—please call me Bill. First, can you bring the record up on your screen?"

She swiveled around to her computer and quickly brought Kelly's record up on her display. Jensen scooted his chair a little closer. "May I?" he asked, reaching for the mouse.

"Be my guest," she replied. "In fact, let's switch chairs, so you can drive."

After trading places, Jensen silently scrolled through the entire record, reading it carefully. Turning to the young woman, he queried, "I've read your entry, but I want you to tell me in your words every thought, suspicion, or intuition that caused you to flag this access, no matter how unfounded you feel your concerns may be."

She stared at the monitor for a moment before beginning: "I think . . . I think the biggest reason was that on the same day as the phone call, someone else attempted to modify the record. As you can see, down at the bottom of his record, there was an effort on Friday to color the conclusions of the AIB." She reached across him and tapped a few keys and the transaction audit log appeared. She pointed at the first line and said, "There! See? On Friday morning—same day I got the call. Someone tried to change the record. Why would someone want to add a statement about the AIB discussions a full year after the fact, when the investigation has been closed?"

"I don't know," the professor admitted. "But that's directly related to what I'm investigating. If this unknown person had been successful, what would the record have looked like?

Would it be obvious that it had been modified?" Jensen asked.

"No, not at all. The text would have been added seamlessly to the comments field, there." She pointed to it on the screen. "You would not know that the record had been edited unless you checked the transaction audit log, and this office is the only one that has access to the audit log. None of the Casualty Service Offices even know the transaction audit log exists. It's a security feature."

The professor looked at the monitor and felt a chill go down his spine. Jake Kelly had been correct in his suspicions about the spy and that the Soviet Union would attack his credibility. On the monitor right in front of him was the evidence. Someone was trying to plant a hint of treason on Jake's record but the attempt had backfired, big time. *Everybody makes mistakes,* Jensen thought. *Everybody gets careless now and then. But this guy has just left me his calling card, and he doesn't even know it!* Jensen smiled to himself. *I am going to nail this guy!*

There was not much additional information that Sheila was able to tell the professor. He thanked her, and then admonished, "Sheila, my inquires about this record are not to be logged, under any circumstances. Here's my card. I want to know of any further activity pertaining to Major Kelly immediately. You are not to speak of this meeting or enter anything into your computer about my visit today. Do you understand?" He raised his eyebrows and did his best to look stern.

"What you are saying, Bill, is that your access to this information is *black* access. I understand. This sort of thing is unusual, but it does come up from time to time and we've been trained to honor requests such as yours."

His last stop before leaving the DPMO was to the database administrator. After exchanging pleasantries and demonstrating his security clearances, Jensen got down to business. "There was a transaction on Friday—an attempt to modify this record." He showed the attractive black woman a hard copy of Kelly's DPMO record. "I would like a dump of every last byte of raw data in the transaction record from that transaction including the security audit fields. Is that available?"

"No problem, sir. I can bring it up right now." Her fingers stroked the keyboard and in a matter of seconds the line printer behind her burped out a green bar page with the raw information. She tore it off and handed it to him.

"Help me interpret this, will you? I am looking for the workstation address and login credentials used by the person who attempted to change this record." He handed the printout back to the administrator. She opened a binder and turned to the record layout in the database definition. Then she ran down the column of data with her index finger.

"Let's see . . . oh, here it is. The request came from IP address 11.107.6.15."

"Where would that terminal be located?"

"Let me check." She brought up a search utility that accessed the Network Information Center's host table for MIL-NET and scanned for the IP address. "Okay, here it is, Mr. Jensen. That IP belongs to a computer somewhere at Eielson Air Force Base, in Alaska. Eielson has a whole block of IPs. Their network technicians could tell you exactly which computer it was."

"Excellent. What are the login credentials that were used to access MILNET and the database?"

"Military standards, sir, specify that the user's first initial and last name shall compose the login name by which they authenticate." She examined the data dump again and pointed to a line near the bottom of the sheet. "There. WOT-T@EIELSENAFB. Must be someone with the last name of Ott. Evidently he didn't have sufficient clearance to modify the record. The database rejected the transaction."

"Is this thing time-stamped?"

"Yes, sir, right here, see? 2337 hours. That time, by the way, is GMT—not local. So at Eielson it would have been, um . . . 1537 hours," the database administrator said, doing a quick calculation in her head.

"Excellent," Jensen said again, "you've been most helpful! Thank you!" After cautioning her to not log his visit or his questions, he retrieved the printout and locked it his briefcase.

As he returned to his car, the CIA agent mentally checked off two of the five tasks he had set for himself today: interviewing Sheila Turner and getting the data dump of the failed DPMO transaction. His morning had been very productive already. He pulled out of the parking lot, and headed west to

Langley.

****

In Washington, DC it was now 0815; at NAS Adak it was 0315. Under a clear, cold, black sky two F-14 Tomcats roared off Adak's Runway 18, banked right, and headed north for their rendezvous with a KC-130 Hercules tanker orbiting five hundred miles north-northwest of Adak. The other two pairs of fighters would take off with ten-minute spacing between them.

Each fighter would refuel, both going and coming. The flying gas station was their insurance policy. Other than the ECM (Electronic Counter Measures) pods slung under their fuselages and the super-secret ESM (Electronic Surveillance Module) pods, which were not in the official Tomcat inventory, all six aircraft were outfitted in a ferry configuration in order to give them maximum range. None of the jets carried any ordnance, which didn't make the pilots happy. And it did not help that they were prohibited from activating the ECM pods unless specifically directed to by the Forward Air Controller (FAC) located in the E-2 Hawkeye orbiting several hundred miles offshore of the target area.

****

Just after 0530 hours Adak time (0330 hours the next day on the Kamchatskiy Peninsula), the USS *Honolulu* SSN 718 silently ascended from the frigid depths of the black water some twenty-four miles southeast of the Petropavlovsk-Kamchatskiy port area. It surfaced to ESM mast depth, all systems and personnel on full quiet.

The *Honolulu* was a silent black shadow in the water, one of the quietest submarines in the United States Naval inventory. A *Los Angeles*-class attack sub, she was capable of wreaking destruction on multiple land- and sea-based targets with her horizontally launched Tomahawk cruise missiles. But land and surface targets were not her real forte. Subs in this class were intended to shadow and, in the event of war, eliminate the large Soviet "boomers" before they could launch their nuclear missiles. Capable of a submerged speed in excess of twenty-five knots, the *Honolulu* was designed to be a huntress.

The keel of the boat had been laid in the Newport News Naval Shipyard in 1981. The mission at Petropavlovsk-Kamchatskiy was her first covert operation. New as she was, submarine technology had advanced so rapidly that just one year after commissioning, the SSN 718 was already an old boat. Numerous design changes were implemented in the hull that followed the *Honolulu*. The USS *Providence*, SSN 719, received an upgraded S6G nuclear reactor which raised its power output by eleven percent, even while making it quieter. The launch system for its cruise missiles had been improved from the horizontally launched system, to the newer vertical launch systems (VLS).

Nevertheless, as the *Honolulu* loitered just off the coast it was a formidable and dangerous opponent. If it was discovered the Soviets' response would be unpredictable. Which meant that its crew was well motivated to remain undetected.

Within fifteen minutes of arriving on station the ambient level of electronic emissions from the nearby Soviet military installations had been established and all active radar emitters had been identified, classified, and plotted. Meanwhile, passive sonar was tracking commercial shipping in the area. It did not appear that the *Honolulu* was being shadowed.

"Skipper, aside from numerous surface contacts identified as local shipping, sonar reports an intermittent contact far to the south. Rusty's not able to get a solid bearing on it, much less a course or distance. But the acoustic signature pegs it as a *Kilo*. Probably on patrol." The executive officer was practically whispering.

"A *Kilo*? How the devil did we hear him first?" The newer Soviet *Kilo*-class of submarine was one of the quietest diesel boats in service. Having a run-in with one of them could be lethal.

"Well, sir, we don't know that we heard him first. But Rusty says Ivan is snorkeling and making about as much racket as a *Kilo* will ever make. He's not behaving as though he hears us. If he wasn't snorkeling we probably couldn't have picked him up at all."

"Okay. Spread the word. We need to make like a hole in

the water. Anybody drops a wrench on the deck, I'll launch him out of one of the forward tubes myself!"

The *Honolulu* had spent eight hours creeping into position. While getting this close to a major Soviet military port was a real coup, it was also very dangerous. The Russians were to be forgiven if upon detecting the American attack sub less than thirty miles from some of their most sensitive military installations, they interpreted the *Honolulu's* intentions as somewhat less than benevolent. It could get real dicey.

Watching his young crew, the captain decided that if the *Kilo* came closer they would abort. The *Honolulu* would hitch a ride with the noisiest merchant freighter leaving the port. They would simply shadow the freighter out of the area, several meters under its keel, until back in blue water. The noise level of the ship would mask their own acoustical signature. At least, that was the hope.

"How are our guests, Bubba?" The captain looked at his short, lean XO and wondered for the thousandth time how such a scrawny sample of humanity had earned the handle "Bubba."

"Happy as clams, Roscoe. They have their stuff all set up and are just waiting for the show to begin. I think they're listening to early morning Soviet talk radio while they wait."

The "guests" were a small contingent of civilians that had boarded at Pearl ten days ago, whose baggage included a great deal of electronic equipment now connected to the receiving end of the *Honolulu's* ESM antenna circuitry. The J2 at Pearl (the Director of Naval Intelligence) had said they were "civilian contractors" who were to be "afforded every courtesy and given every assistance" in carrying out their "testing." That bit of bureaucratic blah-blah was intended for public consumption. Captain Roscoe Raines truly hoped his crew were not so dull of wit that they couldn't see through the charade. The admiral had gone through the entire mission and its purposes with him. The "civilians" were on the NSA payroll and were assisting the Navy with Operation *Screen Pass*.

"Good, Bubba. See that they have whatever they need. Let's get this thing over with and get those spooks off my boat."

"Will do, Cap'n."

****

Cup of steaming coffee in hand, Jensen opened the sealed manila envelope. It had just been delivered to his office by a secure courier coming from the NSA's facility, and contained the photographs and analysis of the construction site identified by Al Mercer and Karl Randolph the day before. He pulled out the material, and spread it on the desk. After studying the photographs with a magnifying glass for twenty minutes, he began to read the report. Several pages described the various features seen in the photographs and an analysis wrapped it up:

> *The entire site footprint, plus the individual building foundations—especially those where the roofing has not been installed—support our original conclusions. This appears to be a highly secure prison facility. We estimate that the final construction will include six cellblocks, six guard towers, and seven other buildings. Rolls of what are assumed to be chain-link fencing and razor wire can be seen in the photographs. The fencing will apparently be doubled, with an interior space that might be policed by dogs. Small huts within the double-fenced area support this conclusion.*
>
> *The ground plan appears to have a maximum security area containing the cellblocks plus an additional building of unknown purpose, all surrounded by the fencing and guard towers. A second area, which appears to have the same sort of security arrangements (minus the towers) connects to the main compound gate. We believe this second area to be an administrative section of the compound. It contains six buildings, one of which is probably administrative, three appear to be barracks, and another can be identified as the physical plant containing a standard Soviet centralized steam heating system. The purpose of the remaining building in the administrative compound is unknown.*
>
> *Based on an observed history of Soviet*

construction speed, we estimate this site to be two months, possibly more, from completion. An absolute minimum time-to-completion we estimate to be forty-five days.

From what we can determine the maximum census for this facility is thirty-six prisoners if each prisoner is kept in isolation. With four prisoners per cell the maximum census would increase to 144 prisoners. In order to adequately staff and secure three shifts, we estimate this facility will require slightly over one hundred personnel. There is adequate barracks capacity to accommodate a staff of this size.

Although we believe we can with certainty identify this site as a prison facility, there are three unusual aspects that may call for a revision of our conclusions. First, on the scale of other known Soviet prison facilities, including criminal/political, KGB, and GRU facilities, this site is very small. This fact is admittedly contrary to all previously identified trends in Soviet construction which tend toward the large or even massive. Second, its location and remoteness could argue for a different or at least unusual use. And third, the presence of General Chernikov seems to be highly irregular: it is unusual to have a man of his rank inspecting a prison this small.

Jensen tossed the report on his desk and leaned back in his chair, thinking. *The writers of this analysis captured the anomalies perfectly: the construction site is unusually small, unusually remote; and Chernikov is too distinguished an officer to be cruising around inspecting prison construction. Unless . . . unless you are running an operation so politically explosive that it needs to be kept way, way below the public radar, to the point of even isolating the staff from the public. An operation that could involve interrogating foreigners whom you have acquired illegally. Such as Jake Kelly.*

He took a sip of his coffee and considered a question that nagged at him. *Why would they be building this facility now, after Jake Kelly got away from them? Hmm. Answer? Because they have other detainees. Because the program is still going on. They need to move the location of the operation lest Jake is able to compromise it. In fact, their desire to eliminate or discredit Jacob probably has to do with keeping this program secret. Jake mentioned that he has even more to tell me. I bet I know what it is.*

Little by little the pieces were falling into place, confirming every statement and suspicion Major Kelly had shared with him. *If I keep getting so many good leads, I'm going to need some help running them all down. This whole affair is unfolding very rapidly,* he reflected.

He looked at his to-do list that he had made on Sunday night. He still needed to interview Bridger and Franks, and call Jake Kelly. He added two more items to the end of his list:

> *1. Investigate John Bridger. Why is he checking intelligence traffic on Kelly?*
> *2. Interview Jim Franks. Why did he submit Jake Kelly's name to Watcher? Does he have information that leads him to doubt the AIB report?*
> *3. ~~Get a technician to pull up all the data available on the failed access to the DPMO record.~~*
> *4. ~~Interview Sheila Turner, the DPMO employee.~~*
> *5. Ask Jake Kelly for his ideas on Sheila Turner's mysterious phone call.*
> *6. Contact Eielson AFB network people, and find out whose computer has IP address 11.107.6.15.*
> *7. Nose around Eielson, and find out who W. Ott is.*

It was too early to make his phone calls: folks on the West Coast were just getting out of bed. He stared at his list. Everyone he needed to talk to was in California or Alaska. It was time to head west. Jensen began throwing stuff he might need into his briefcase. He picked up his short-notice travel bag, locked his office, and headed for Washington National Airport.

****

The first two Tomcats swept in at 0430 hours local at the prescribed altitude of one hundred feet. The leading jet broke left, his wingman broke right, and they both executed a tight 180-degree climbing turn, leveling off at four hundred feet.

The Soviet air defense system was caught completely off guard. Because of the low altitude approach the ground-based Soviet radar had been unable to pick the F-14s out of the ground clutter, and the bogeys popped up right under their noses.

The ESM pods carried by the F-14s were recording both the aircraft maneuvers as well as all ELINT emissions. Later analysis showed that there was a full forty-five-second window between the pop-up maneuver and initial acquisition by Soviet targeting radar. The FAC in the E2-C Hawkeye speculated that the officer responsible for the air defenses surrounding Petropavlovsk-Kamchatskiy would be losing his job this afternoon.

What none of the Americans could know is that an enraged Soviet commander was just seconds from issuing orders to fire on the aircraft. He stood down only because there were but two invaders and they were in full retreat, rocketing out to sea at Mach 1.7.

Phase One of Operation *Screen Pass* was complete with a successful penetration of Soviet air defenses operating on a peacetime mode. But now the situation resembled something closer to a wartime scenario, with all the air search and SAM site radar lit up. The next two Tomcats would be making their approach with the opposition at full alert. Phase Two was about to begin.

Meanwhile, in the black waters just off the coast the technicians in the attack sub were quietly recording and plotting the locations of each newly activated Soviet radar site. Other than the NSA workers recording the data and a few of the *Honolulu's* officers, the crew of the submarine was unaware of the action going on overhead, as all three flights of fighters were flying under EMCON conditions, not emitting any signals that could be detected by the submarine's passive sensors.

At 0505 hours the second pair of F-14s approached at one thousand feet, inbound at supersonic speed. Soviet radar picked them up while they were still 160 miles out. By the time a flight of four MiG-31 Foxhounds was scrambled the Tomcats had reached the turn-around point.

"Diamond Flight, Diamond Flight, this is Lone Wolf. Four bogeys inbound at niner three zero knots, range four zero miles, bearing two one zero, altitude five angels. Request you drop to the deck and light the burners, zone 5."

"Roger, Lone Wolf, inbound bogeys. Dropping to the deck and going to full afterburner. Request we go active."

"Negative, Diamond Flight, maintain lights out."

The Foxhounds gave chase and overtook the American bandits, but were unable to match the low-altitude agility of the F-14s. After about one hundred miles of harassment the MiGs gave up the chase.

Phase two of *Screen Pass* had come off with resounding success for the Americans, although the pilots' flying suits were drenched in sweat as well as other bodily fluids by the time they made it back to the Hercules tanker.

Rather than returning immediately to base, the four Foxhounds set up an ad hoc CAP, going active with their powerful Zaslon RP-31 phased-array radars. More data was captured by the sophisticated instruments in the Hawkeye and the snoops in the submarine.

The final pair of inbound Tomcats was detected at the maximum range of Petropavlovsk-Kamchatskiy's ground-based radar systems, 230 miles out, and the Soviet fighters were vectored to intercept the inbound sortie. They closed to within one hundred miles of the F-14s before they had reached the margin of safety on their fuel reserves and had to return to base, leaving the inbound fighters uncontested.

Twelve minutes later the sensitive receivers on the submarine and in the Hawkeye picked up the signature emission of a TIN SHIELD, the NATO designation for a Russian 36D6 surveillance radar, belonging to a mobile SA-10 surface-to-air missile defense system. Seconds later a second signature appeared: a 30N6 command guidance radar, known to NATO pilots as FLAP-LID. The firing system radar probed the airspace indicated by the surveillance radar, and soon achieved target lock on the inbound US fighters. By this time the Tomcats had closed to within fifty miles.

"Gold Flight, Gold Flight, this is Lone Wolf. You are being painted by a SAM site. Break off, and exit on vector xray alpha. Maintain EMCON." The FAC on the E2-C was taking no chances. Seconds later, four new contacts appeared on the Hawkeye's threat display.

"Missiles launched! Missiles launched! Four Grumbles in-coming, repeat, four Grumbles incoming, locking on you, Gold Flight! Break off, break off, break off. You are go for ECM!" The FAC was beginning to sweat; he could feel per-spiration trickling down between his shoulder blades.

Gold Flight pulled a tight turn, lighting their afterburners and climbing while they accelerated on their new vector: they were now just forty miles from the port. The SAM site was using the improved 5V55R Grumble surface-to-air missile, with a powered flight range of about fifty-six miles. The Grumble's guidance system was the semi-active radar homing (SARH) type. With SARH, the FLAP-LID fire-control radar would simply bounce a signal off the target and the Grumble would fly the reflection right to the target. It was remarkably accurate with a disheartening kill-ratio.

The top speed of the missile was thirty-eight hundred miles per hour. The Tomcats of Gold Flight were accelerating past thirteen hundred miles per hour, a mere one third the speed of the missiles. Holding his breath, the FAC on the Hawkeye watched his screen as the blips drew close. The mis-siles closed to within one thousand feet of the aircraft, before they fell, fuel spent, into the sea.

"Gold Flight, you are in the clear." The controller hesitated for a second, and then added, "Mission accomplished. Good job." His voice was clear, but his hands were shaking. It had been a close thing.

An hour later, the *Honolulu* retracted its ESM mast and si-lently returned to the depths. Gliding under a departing mer-chant ship they crept away, shielded from the listening ears of the *Kilo* by the loud machinery noises of a tramp freighter.

****

The aftershocks of *Screen Pass* would continue for days. After all the local finger-pointing was complete, the old men of the Politburo were convinced by Anatoly Geredin that it had something to do with the escape of Major Jacob Kelly from Chernikov's interrogation facility. They assumed that the probe was a prelude to an in-kind covert response from the United States. Though assured repeatedly by General Valeriy

Patrikeyev that the major had not yet given the US intelligence community any important information, the council was nonetheless suspicious. Unknown to the GRU or even many in the Politburo itself, Geredin began to forge plans to shut Chernikov down and to eliminate the embarrassment he had caused to Mother Russia. The old bear of the KGB still had many useful contacts with people who knew how to *do things*. The Russian way.

A PRAYER OF MOSES

A DEVOTIONAL STUDY OF PSALM 90

C.H. COBB

The Church has rendered God *safe*.
His wrath is a matter relegated to days of antiquity. It seems rare that we connect the brevity and frailty of this existence with His overflowing anger at sin. Unfortunately, having dispensed with His wrath we've also diminished His holiness and His majesty, and made the cross less necessary.

This study invites the reader to take a second look at God and His wrath—and His Christ—through the eyes of Moses. Suitable for individuals or groups.

Chris Cobb's exegesis of Psalm 90 is solid and sobering. In a world that takes sin lightly, Christianity needs to hear the message of this Psalm which Chris Cobb has brought to life.
Dr. Brent Aucoin
President, Faith Bible Seminary, Lafayette, Indiana

Pastor Cobb's exposition of Psalm 90 combines two sets of ingredients that make it a joy to read: on the one hand, exegetical precision together with the sweep of redemptive history; on the other, technical mastery with warm, personal application. There are Scriptural studies in which the author maintains a safe distance from the reader. Pastor Cobb allows us to get to know him along with the text he is expounding. This, in my opinion, is the best way to do pastoral theology.
John L. Marshall, Ph.D.
Christian Studies/History Department, Eastern University

Please help independent authors

Independent authors usually don't have someone managing their books' publicity plan or marketing. We don't have the support of an organization getting our novels in front of retailers who will carry them in their stores. Other than what marketing efforts we can cobble together on our own, we have only one source of publicity that can encourage others to buy our books, and that's you, our readers.

Your word-of-mouth recommendation, your Facebook comment, your tweet, your Amazon or Goodreads review is likely the only way an unknown author will get the word out about his or her books.

Let me hasten to admit that the reader is certainly under no obligation. If you don't like the tale, or if the editing was sloppy, or the cover or packaging amateurish then by all means don't encourage someone else to read it. The last thing the independent publishing movement needs are products that fall short of genuine quality.

Even if you think the product is the best work since Bunyan's *Pilgrim's Progress* or Tolkien's *Lord of the Rings*, you still aren't obligated. Art doesn't create a debt or obligation on the part of the viewer. You're free to enjoy it and walk away. Artists take that risk when we create our work.

But if you find a tale you like and you'd like to read more by that author, give him or her a hand by letting your friends and loved ones know where they can get a good story. Post a review, mention it on Facebook, send a few emails, tell a few friends. Once the word gets out, a good story will sell itself; but getting the word out is the challenge. Thanks for your help!

About the Author

Chris Cobb's resume reads like a patchwork quilt. He's driven a forklift, worked as a technician doing component-level repair on digital circuitry, been a programmer-analyst, a data-center shift operator, taught high school science and mathematics, and been an Information Technology Director at a graduate school. Most of his career he's been a pastor.

He lives with his wife, Doris, in western Ohio, and is presently the teaching pastor at Bible Fellowship Church in Greenville, OH. They have three adult children, two fine sons-in-law and a wonderful daughter-in-law, all of whom are actively engaged serving Christ in the arts at some level.

Chris received Jesus Christ as his Savior in 1974, and seeks to incorporate a biblically faithful worldview into everything he does, including his writing.

You can find Chris on Facebook, or find additional works by him at chcobb.com.